TEXARKANA

TEXARKANA

A PERLEY GATES WESTERN

WILLIAM W. JOHNSTONE

AND J.A. JOHNSTONE

PINNACLE BOOKS

Kensington Publishing Corp.

www.kensingtonbooks.com

PINNACLE BOOKS are published by

Kensington Publishing Corp.
119 West 40th Street
New York, NY 10018

Copyright © 2021 by J. A. Johnstone

PUBLISHER'S NOTE
Following the death of William W. Johnstone, the Johnstone family is working with a carefully selected writer to organize and complete Mr. Johnstone's outlines and many unfinished manuscripts to create additional novels in all of his series like The Last Gunfighter, Mountain Man, and Eagles, among others. This novel was inspired by Mr. Johnstone's superb storytelling.

All Kensington titles, imprints, and distributed lines are available at special quantity discounts for bulk purchases for sales promotion, premiums, fund-raising, educational, or institutional use.

Special book excerpts or customized printings can also be created to fit specific needs. For details, write or phone the office of the Kensington Sales Manager: Attn.: Sales Department. Kensington Publishing Corp., 119 West 40th Street, New York, NY 10018. Phone: 1-800-221-2647.

First Printing: December 2021
ISBN-13: 978-0-7860-4906-6
ISBN-13: 978-0-7860-4907-3 (eBook)

10 9 8 7 6 5 4 3 2 1

Printed in the United States of America

Chapter 1

"You charge a helluva lot for a shot of this rotgut whiskey you're sellin'," Dan Short complained to Marvin Davis. "You oughta be payin' us to drink this stuff."

"Two bits a shot ain't bad when you think about where you're headin'," Marvin replied. "You said you was headin' across the Red River to Injun Territory, and there ain't supposed to be no whiskey sold there a-tall. You'd be smart to buy a couple of bottles to take with you."

"Hell, I heard there was a lotta places to buy likker in Injun Territory," Tiny Wilson spoke out. "Ain't that right, Dan?"

"Yep, lots of places."

Dan and Tiny were really heading for Arkansas to join up with Duke Thacker's gang, holed up near the little railroad crossing called Texarkana. They'd told Marvin they were heading to The Nations in Oklahoma Territory, in case any Texas Rangers might show up at the saloon asking about them.

Ned Bates was standing at the front door, looking out across the prairie. "Hey, Dan. Lookee here."

"What is it?" Dan asked, not inclined to bother. When Ned called him again, he walked over to the door. "What is it?" he repeated.

"Lookee yonder," Ned replied, and pointed out across a wide grassy plain. That's a nice little herd of horses. I don't see but three fellers tendin' 'em, and one of 'em is headin' this way."

Dan squinted as he took a hard look at the rider approaching the trading post. "Young feller. Not much more 'n a boy."

Overhearing their remarks, Marvin said, "Most likely some of the boys from the Triple-G. Their range starts about five miles west of here. They're a pretty big outfit. Some of their hands stop in here from time to time."

After a few minutes, Sonny Rice pulled his horse up at the hitching rail and dismounted. Dan and Ned, still standing in the door, stood aside to let him enter.

"Howdy," Sonny said with a nod as he passed them. "Howdy, Mr. Davis," he greeted Marvin and nodded to Tiny, who was staring openly at him. "I need to get some bacon and some flour, and some coffee, too, if you've got some roasted."

"I've got some roasted and I can grind it for you, if you want," Marvin said. "Ain't seen you in a while. Where you headin' with those horses?"

"We're drivin' 'em to the Double-D ranch, just over the Arkansas line. We're just short a couple of things," Sonny replied.

"Well, I can fix you up with those," Marvin said. "You need a bottle or two of whiskey? Sounds like you boys are gonna be on the trail for a few days."

"No, sir, I reckon not," Sonny replied. "It's just me and

Perley and Possum. Neither me nor Perley are much for drinkin', and if Possum wanted any, he'd a-told me."

Over by the front door, Dan and Ned exchanged wide-eyed glances.

Dan whispered low, "You know, sometimes ol' Lady Luck just walks up and lays it down right in front of you."

"She sure does," Ned agreed and walked out onto the porch to get a better look. "Those are some pretty good-looking horses. Ain't no nags in that bunch." They were still on the porch calculating the worth of the herd when Sonny walked out of the store with his packages.

"Need a hand, there?" Ned offered politely, thinking he would most likely want Sonny's purchases as well.

"No, sir. Thank you just the same," Sonny replied. He tied his sacks to his saddle, then climbed up.

"Reckon you boys will be driving that herd till dark," Dan commented. "It's a ways yet before you strike the Arkansas line."

"We ain't in no hurry to get there," Sonny said. "We want those horses to be in good shape when we get 'em to the Double-D. Perley might be plannin' to make camp right there by that creek tonight."

"Well, that's always smart thinkin' when you're sellin' horses," Dan declared, "especially if you're sellin' off your old horses."

"Oh, there ain't no old horses in that herd," Sonny was quick to inform him. "There ain't a horse there that's over five years old."

It just gets better and better, Dan couldn't help thinking. He couldn't resist asking, "How much are you sellin' 'em for?"

"I don't know what the price was," Sonny answered. "Perley knows, if you wanna come ask him."

"Oh, that's all right," Dan said. "I was just curious."

"Well, good day to ya." Sonny wheeled his horse and started back to the herd.

"You know what I'm thinkin', don't you?" Dan said as they continued to watch Sonny ride away.

"You're thinkin' we could take that herd without no trouble a-tall," Ned answered.

"That's what I'm thinkin'," Dan confirmed. "And I'm also thinkin' there ain't no sense in cuttin' Duke and the others in on it. We'll just be a little late gettin' out to Arkansas to join Duke's gang."

"Where you reckon we can sell 'em in a hurry?" Ned wondered.

"We'll worry about that after we get the horses," Dan said. "It don't matter how long it takes. It'll be more money in our pockets than any splits we're fixin' to get riding with Duke Thacker.

Sonny reined his horse up beside the campfire and dismounted. He untied his purchases, then pulled his saddle off the paint gelding he called Lucky, then turned the horse loose to join the others by the creek. "I took a little look up ahead, then circled back around the creek. Everything looks peaceful. I hope you two ain't drank up all the coffee," he said as he pulled his coffee cup out of his war bag.

"I was fixin' to drain that pot," Possum Smith japed,

"but Perley said I had to save some for you. So I poured a couple of swallows back in the pot."

"Pay him no mind, Sonny," Perley said, "that pot's still half-full."

Possum chuckled in response to Perley's remark then asked Sonny, "Why did you name that roan Lucky?"

"'Cause he was lucky *I* picked him out to be my horse," Sonny replied, "instead of somebody like you that's hard on a horse."

Perley shook his head as if impatient with their juvenile behavior. Sonny had recently celebrated his eighteenth birthday while Possum, with his gray ponytail, was considerably up there in years. No one knew how old Possum really was. He was not willing to confess his age. In fact, he wouldn't even divulge the date of his birthday, as if refusing to have any more birthdays, and consequently, staying the same age forever.

Perley suspected that Possum was afraid if Rubin knew how old he was, he might fire him. The thought brought a smile to Perley's lips. Possum should know by now that Perley's brother, Rubin, would have to go through Perley to fire him.

When Rubin had asked Perley who he wanted to take with him to move a small herd of horses to Arkansas, he'd picked Sonny and Possum. Perley figured the two of them would entertain each other. All three of them could enjoy a few days away from the chores at the Triple-G, a trip that would actually take about a week to go to Texarkana and back.

The herd they were moving to the Double-D was only thirty-five horses. And they were taking it nice and easy, pushing the horses about thirty miles a day, so as to deliver fresh stock to Donald Donovan. The Double-D Ranch was about 115 miles east of the Triple-G, just across the Arkansas border, southeast of Texarkana.

Sonny poured his cup of coffee and sat down to join them.

"I reckon ol' Marvin Davis is still kickin'," Possum commented.

"Yep," Sonny said. "He wanted to sell me some whiskey, but I told him didn't none of us drink the stuff. I told him especially Possum didn't have no use for it."

"Huh," Possum snorted. "You might think you're japin', but I ain't got much use for that rotgut he sells. One of the boys gave me a drink of some he bought from Davis and it like to peeled my throat skin off."

"There was three fellers at the store," Sonny said. "They were drinkin' it. They were mighty interested in this herd of horses. Asked me how far we were gonna drive 'em tonight, if there was any old horses in the bunch, and I don't remember what else." He didn't notice the look Perley and Possum exchanged in reaction to his comments, but he didn't miss the fact that both of them got up and came to stand over him.

"You say they asked you a lot of questions about the horses, huh?" Perley prodded. "Did they wanna know anything about how many we were? Anything like that?"

"Well, they know there's three of us," Sonny answered, at last realizing why Perley was anxious to know. He didn't confess that he'd volunteered the information about their number before any of the three fellows had a chance to ask.

"I expect it'd be a good idea to keep watch over the horses tonight," Perley said. "I sure wasn't expectin' any trouble between here and Texarkana. But this time of year is when a lotta drifters are riding the grub line. If some rustlers got their hands on the thirty-five horses we're herdin', they could sell 'em for a pretty good price."

"How much you reckon they'd be worth?" Sonny asked.

"They could sell 'em for a better price than what Donald Donovan's payin' for 'em," Perley answered. "Rubin is makin' him a special price of sixty dollars a horse. Even that'd be a pretty good payday if they were to sell 'em at that price."

"I reckon." Sonny thought about it. "How much would that be?"

"Figure it out," Perley said. "Just like they taught you in school, you got thirty-five horses at sixty dollars apiece. Didn't Miss Bessie Sanford teach you multiplication?"

"I must notta been there that day," Sonny said. "Can you figure it out?"

"Not in my head," Perley replied. "I'll show you how to do it, then maybe you'll remember some of your schoolin'." He found a bare spot of ground, took a stick and scratched out the numbers. Then he went through the numbers as he did the multiplication to come up with the answer. "I expect they'd try to get more money than that for 'em. A good ridin' horse, like Buck or Possum's dun, would cost a hundred and fifty."

When Sonny heard the total Perley came up with, he was duly impressed.

Possum, on the other hand, was not fascinated with the arithmetic lesson. He was more in tune with the present-day world. "That's mighty interestin', Perley," he began sarcastically. "Now, if those three jaspers Sonny met at the store get it in their heads to take this herd of horses off our hands, why, then, we can tell 'em how much money they're gonna make. And if any of us make it back to the Triple-G, we can tell your brothers what happened to the horses."

Perley nodded in response to Possum's comments. "You're right, Possum. We need to be thinkin' about whether we need to get the horses movin', or if we're better off sittin' right here."

"I say we oughta set right here and let 'em come after us," Possum said right away. "We'd be able to handle 'em easier if we're hunkered down on each side of the herd and knock 'em outta the saddle. Especially if they come whoopin' and hollerin' in here."

"I expect you're right," Perley allowed. "'Course we ain't got any idea if those three men are outlaws or not. I hope we're wrong about 'em." He looked at Sonny and asked, "What did you make of those fellows?"

"I don't know," Sonny replied and tried to think back on his conversation at the store. "They just looked like every other drifter that rides through town."

When Possum asked if they were young or old, Sonny said, "Oh, they was older. Not as old as you, but older than Perley." He paused, then asked, "How old are you, Possum?"

Perley couldn't stifle his chuckle when Possum responded. "None of your damn business. You don't go around askin' people how old they are. I didn't ask you how old you are, did I?"

"I'm eighteen," Sonny said, baffled by Possum's reaction. He looked at Perley for help in his confusion over Possum's sudden fit of temper.

Smiling, Perley, said, "Possum ain't comfortable tellin' anybody his age. He's afraid if folks find out how old he is, they'll wanna ask him questions about how it was around here back in Biblical times. Ain't that right, Possum?"

"I reckon we'd best decide what we're gonna do with these horses," Possum responded unemotionally, signaling the end of the horseplay.

Taking charge then, Perley made the decision. "We'll stay here tonight, make camp right where we are. The horses are in a good spot. They've got grass and water by this little creek and we weren't gonna push 'em much farther today, anyway. In case we have visitors, we'd all best take night watch tonight, one of us on the other side of the creek."

"Don't look like we're gonna have to wait till dark," Possum said. "Those three friends of Sonny's just left Marvin's store and they're headin' this way right now." That caused Perley and Sonny to set their cups down by the fire.

"Might be a good idea to spread out a little," Perley suggested. It wasn't necessary to advise them to make sure their weapons were handy. "Is that the same three," he asked Sonny.

"Looks like 'em," Sonny said as the riders continued a path directly toward them.

"Looks like they ain't takin' no chances," Dan Short commented as the three men approached the camp by the creek. "They're spreadin' out and holdin' on to their rifles, so don't make no sudden moves."

Tiny and Ned grunted in response.

"Howdy," Dan called out when they were about twenty yards short of the campfire. "Mind if we come in?"

"Not at all," Perley called back. "What can we do for you?"

Dan didn't answer until they pulled up before the fire. "We was talkin' to that young feller there over at the store." He nodded toward Sonny. "He said you boys was drivin' a herd of horses over to Arkansas. Me and my partners are in the horse breedin' business. We're on our way right now to an army post up in Injun Territory to work with the soldiers breedin' mares with some of them wild range horses."

"Is that a fact?" Perley replied. "Breedin' horses for the army. What fort's doin' that?" He waited for an answer.

But Dan couldn't think of an army fort in The Nations. He looked quickly from Tiny to Ned, but both wore the same blank expressions.

"Fort Grover?" Perley asked.

"Right," Dan quickly answered. "That's the one." Tiny and Ned both echoed the name while nodding vigorously. "Well, your young man there—"

"Sonny," Perley interrupted.

"Right, Sonny," Dan repeated. "He was tellin' us what fine stock you boys were drivin', so we just thought we'd take a look at 'em. They look like pretty decent horses at that and I'm thinkin' this might be your lucky day when you bumped into us. I expect we can get you a helluva lot better price for them horses at Fort Grover. Not only that, we'll help you drive 'em up there to Fort Grover. It must be a lotta work with just the three of you. You could most likely use the help."

"It ain't but thirty-five horses," Perley said. "They ain't much trouble for us."

"Fort Grover's a lot closer than Arkansas," Dan insisted. "You'd have your money and be on your way to the saloon before you got close to Arkansas."

"I'll say this for you, mister," Perley responded. "You made a right temptin' proposition. The truth of the matter is, these horses ain't ours to sell. They've already been paid for. We're just deliverin' 'em. And there ain't no place in The Nations named Fort Grover. Somebody's been pullin' your leg about breedin' horses for the army. I'm sorry we're the ones who had to tell you."

Dan didn't say anything for a long moment, feeling the full effect of having stuck his foot in his mouth.

Ned and Tiny were speechless as well, until Tiny made an effort to salvage their scheme. "Maybe you ain't been up in Injun Territory in a while. Fort Grover ain't been built very long."

Dan's anger for having been exposed so easily at first caused him to become tense with thoughts of reaching for the army single-action .45 he wore. He was stopped short of that by the sight of the three men facing him, trying to appear casual as they held cocked rifles at the ready. Gradually, his anger began to dissipate, and a wry smile formed on his lips. "Well, friend, I reckon you saw right through that one. You can't blame some of us who've had some hard times, from tryin'. No harm done. We'll be on our way."

Unable to remain silent any longer, Possum asked, "Just what were you plannin' to do after you turned our horses toward Injun Territory? What were you gonna do with us on the way to this new fort you claim?"

Dan had no answer for him. He wheeled his horse and said, "Come on, boys. We're wastin' our time here. We got places to go."

Neither Ned nor Tiny objected and they filed out behind him, leaving the three Triple-G men scratching their heads.

"I reckon they shoulda worked on their plan a little longer before they came ridin' up to ask us to turn the herd north," Possum commented. "They musta thought the Triple-G didn't hire nobody but idiots." He turned toward Perley. "You reckon they really thought we might just turn the herd and go with 'em?" Back to Sonny, he said, "You musta made a right smart impression on them fellers."

"I don't think there's any question about who the idiots are," Perley said. "They'd decided they were gonna take this herd away from us. I expect they were plannin' to just shoot us down and take the horses. When they saw us ready for 'em with our rifles in hand, the one that did all the talkin' decided to make up that little story about the soldiers wantin' to buy horses. If we bought it, then it would be less risky to shoot us in the back while we were driving our horses toward The Nations. Ain't that how you see it, Possum?"

Possum and Sonny nodded in response.

"That don't mean they've given up the idea," Perley continued. "They're still comin' after these horses. They're just gonna wait to jump us after dark."

"I think you're right," Possum said. "We need to be ready for 'em." His concern at that point was for Sonny, who had never shot a man before. Possum asked him, "You gonna be able to set your sight on one of those fellers and pull the trigger?"

"I guess so," Sonny answered, not really sure.

"Make no mistake about it," Possum said, "when they come ridin' back in here tonight, they'll be hopin' to put a bullet into all three of us. Men like that don't think twice about killin' a man to make that big a payday. Ain't that right, Perley?"

"He's right, Sonny. They'll kill for a lot less than these horses will bring. It might make it a little easier on you, if you remember the law usually hangs a man for stealing a horse."

"That's right," Possum spoke again. "If you was to nail one of 'em, you'd be doin' the law's work for 'em."

Sonny didn't say anything for a few moments while he looked back and forth from one to the other. Finally, he spoke his peace. "You're both wastin' your time, tryin' to talk me into shootin' some feller who's tryin' to shoot me. I'm eighteen years old. Perley, I don't reckon I have to be told to do whatever it takes to save my behind. If I was you or Possum, I'd be more worried about what Rubin would do if we lost these horses."

He'd most likely think Perley stepped in another cow pie, Possum said to himself, recalling Perley's brothers' favorite saying, "If there wasn't but one cow pie between the Triple-G and the Red River, Perley would step in it."

Chapter 2

Dan Short held his horse to a lope for almost two miles before he reined him to a stop and waited for Ned and Tiny to catch up with him. Out of sight of the camp by the creek, he wheeled his horse around to meet them as they rode up.

"Well, that went just about like we wanted it to, didn't it?" Ned Bates asked sarcastically. "I thought for a minute, there, they was gonna turn them horses right around and head for the Red River with us."

"You go to hell," Dan responded. "I had to think of somethin' to tell 'em, when we rode up there and found the three of 'em standing apart with their rifles ready to shoot at the first move we made. It damn sure changed my plans to shoot 'em down before they knew what hit 'em. I noticed you and Tiny didn't make any moves to get the party started either."

"Hell, we thought you was callin' the shots, didn't we, Tiny?" Ned responded.

"That's right," Tiny answered him. "Leastways, we got a good look at them three fellers. Ain't nobody but that young boy, an old man, and that other jasper that did most of the talkin'. Didn't none of 'em look like they'd give us much trouble. We might shoulda gone ahead and drew on 'em. Most likely woulda gunned 'em down before they got them rifles up to shoot."

"Whaddaya think, Dan?" Ned asked. "Wanna ride back and go in blazin' while all three of them are right there together?"

"Why take a chance on one of those jaspers gettin' off a lucky shot and hittin' one of us?" Dan replied. "Might as well wait till dark and shoot 'em in their blankets. We'll keep an eye on 'em to make sure they're still plannin' to camp right there tonight. It ain't too long now before it'll be gettin' dark."

"That suits me just fine," Ned commented. "We might as well get us a fire goin' and fix somethin' to eat while we got the time." He looked at Tiny and winked. "I never like to rustle horses on an empty stomach."

Using some of the fresh coffee that Marvin Davis had ground up for Sonny, Possum set up a new pot. They wanted to make sure they stayed awake that night.

"I don't think I'd be able to go to sleep, if I drank a lotta coffee or if I didn't," Sonny confessed.

"Well, don't think you're the only one that ain't a little edgy," Perley assured him. "I don't know what direction they'll come at us from. Whaddayou think, Possum?"

"I expect they'd try to sweep through our camp on this side of the creek. 'Cause it'd be easier to stampede the horses outta the trees and into that flat east of us," Possum speculated. "'Course, that 'ud be the smartest way to flush 'em outta there, and they could shoot us when they rode through the camp after the horses. But after our little meetin' with those three, I ain't too sure what they'll do."

"I think you're right," Perley said. "So, I reckon we'd best have two of us on this side of the creek. The other one can watch our backs from the other side, and we'll use the creek bank for cover. Might as well go ahead and pick us a spot, maybe take your shovel and dig you out a little hole to make you a smaller target. It'd be a good idea to saddle your horse, in case we have to go after the herd real quick."

They made their defensive preparations, hoping they were wrong and the three drifters weren't willing to risk a raid on the horses. Perley decided to station Sonny on the other side of the creek, telling him his young eyes were better than Possum's. The truth of the matter was Perley figured Possum a better shot and wanted him on the nearside with him.

As darkness approached, they built up the fire, saddled their horses, and led them back into the trees, hoping to tie them out of the line of fire. As the last touch, they rolled up some cottonwood branches in three blankets on the off chance the rustlers were dumb enough to think they were three sleeping bodies.

As the night crept over the creek and the darkness deepened, there were no sounds to be heard other than the steady chirping of the crickets and an occasional snort from the horses standing in the cottonwood trees.

The hours dragged by with no sign of the anticipated rustlers until Possum, some five yards down the creek bank, whispered loudly. "I don't know. Maybe we figured these jaspers wrong. I'm about ready to fry up some of that bacon Sonny picked up today."

"I can't say as I'm disappointed they didn't come to the party," Perley whispered back to him. "I'll cross over the creek and see if Sonny's awake." He got up from the hole he had dug out of the bank and started down to the water when pandemonium broke out in the form of gunfire and yelling. Perley, his reactions always lightning fast, spun around to see the three rustlers charging into the camp, firing at the bundles of cottonwood branches.

Without consciously realizing he had drawn his six-gun, he pulled the trigger, and Tiny bolted straight upright, then slid out of the saddle. Aware then of the trap they had ridden into, Dan and Ned veered away from the camp, but not before Possum put a .44 rifle slug into Dan's back. He fell forward to lie on his horse's neck but remained in the saddle as his horse galloped away from the creek after Ned's horse.

"Reckon that was enough to run 'em off for good?" Possum asked when Perley ran back from the creek bank.

"I don't know. Maybe," Perley answered as they hustled over to check Tiny's body.

"Don't have to worry about this one," Possum declared. "You nailed him plum center of his chest." He bent down to get a closer look. "He's a big 'un, ain't he?"

Sonny hurried up from the creek to join them. "I swear," he exclaimed excitedly, "that's the one called Tiny! Who shot him?"

"Perley got him," Possum answered him. "I shot one of the other two, but I don't know how bad. They was runnin' flat out. The feller was layin' on his horse's neck. Dead or not, I don't know."

"I swear," Sonny repeated. "You reckon they'll come back?"

"Not unless they want some more of what they just got," Possum said. "Ain't that what you say, Perley?"

"It would surprise me if the other two tried it again," Perley answered, "since there ain't but one of 'em that ain't been shot. I expect we'd best stay awake for the rest of the night anyway, in case that one comes sneakin' back just to get a shot at one of us. I figure they ain't in any shape to drive a herd of horses, even one this small, but they might want some payback for this 'un." He tapped the bottom of Tiny's boot with his toe.

Possum turned and looked back toward the trees by the creek. "It was over so fast, there weren't enough time to stir up the horses much. That volley of gunfire wasn't enough to cause them to panic. I reckon we were lucky we was rustled by some greenhorn outlaws." He took a look at the holes in the blankets they had wrapped around the tree branches. "Ain't no doubt what they had in mind for us."

Approximately one and a quarter mile from the camp by the creek, Ned Bates reined his horse back to a walking gait and guided the sorrel through a little patch of pines to a stream beyond them. Dan's horse followed, the wounded man still lying on his horse's neck. Tagging along behind them, Tiny Wilson's dun gelding with an empty saddle walked down to the stream where the two packhorses were tied and waiting.

Ned dismounted and went immediately to help Dan

off his horse. "How bad is it?" he asked, attempting to brace himself to catch him.

"I don't know how bad." Dan groaned painfully, the back of his shirt soaked with blood. "It hurts like hell. My back feels like it's on fire." He let go of the horse's neck and slid cautiously over to the side.

Holding onto him and set to take the load of his body, Ned staggered when he caught the full weight of Dan's body but managed to lay him gently on the ground. Dan moaned as Ned tried to examine the wound.

"They was waitin' for us, " Dan said. "I saw Tiny get hit, just before we tried to run. Did he make it?"

"No, he didn't," Ned answered.

Dan's question brought back the image of the shooter and the lightning-like move when he'd turned and fired. There was enough light from the fire to see him when he got up from the creek bank and started to walk down the bank. Ned was sure it wasn't the old man or the kid. It was the one who'd done all the talking when they were there earlier.

"I saw who shot Tiny. He turned and fired so fast Tiny never had a chance." Ned paused a few moments while he tried to get Dan's shirt off him, but every way he tried was met with difficulty and pain. He took his knife and cut a hole in the back of the shirt, then ripped it apart, so he could see the wound. "You need a doctor," he announced after studying the angry-looking wound for a few minutes.

"That slug is in your back pretty deep. It's too dark for me to see real good, but it looks bad. You want me to try to dig it outta there? There ain't no doctor around here,"

Ned told him. "Maybe that woman at Marvin's store can do some doctorin'. We could go see her in the mornin'."

Dan didn't like that idea.

"I don't know what else to do for you, Dan. We ain't got no money to pay Marvin's wife to take care of you, anyway."

"Well, I need some help now. I'm bleedin' like a gutted hog," Dan complained. "I can't do it on my own."

Ned was aware of Dan's complaints, but his mind was on something he considered more important than the bullet hole in Dan's back. "What the hell am I gonna tell Mavis?" he mumbled over and over. When Dan asked him what he was saying, Ned repeated, "What am I gonna tell Mavis?" He'd promised his younger sister he would take care of her husband and bring him home safely. Mavis had tried to talk Tiny out of going with Dan and Ned, but he wanted to go.

Ned spoke to Dan. "I promised her we weren't gonna do nothin' dangerous. Now I gotta tell her I got him killed on his first job with me."

With no interest in Mavis Wilson's loss, Dan recalled something Ned had said. "You said Tiny's horse followed us back here. We could give Marvin Davis that horse for his wife's doctorin'."

"I've gotta pay that gunslinger his due for killin' Tiny. That'll help make it right with Mavis," Ned said.

"You ain't listenin' to me," Dan blurted. "I might be dying here. It ain't your damn sister layin' here with a bullet in her."

Ned got to his feet and stood looking down at the suffering man for a few long moments before saying, "There ain't nothin' I can do to ease your pain. You just lay there and try to be still, so you don't aggravate that bleedin' any worse than it is. I'll get a blanket to spread over you. You just lay still, and in the mornin', we'll go back to Marvin's store." He walked over to the packhorse Dan used to carry his possibles and pulled out a blanket, then went back and spread it over his wounded partner.

"I 'preciate it, Ned. Tough luck about Tiny, but he shoulda known the chances you take in this business. I 'preciate you takin' care of me."

"You oughta know I ain't gonna leave you out here sufferin'," Ned said. "You just lay still now." He took a couple of steps toward the horses again, then stopped. Turning back toward Dan, he held his pistol in his hand and paused briefly to look at the wounded man, now seeming to be quiet. His mind made up, he took a step closer and aimed the .44 at the back of Dan's head.

The last sound Dan Short heard on this earth was the clicking sound of a hammer being cocked.

"There weren't nothin' I coulda done for ya, Dan, but I weren't gonna leave you to lay out here and bleed to death. It was nothin' but bad luck with them fellers. I've gotta go after that gunslinger and I couldn't take you with me, so I did the next best thing I could think of." He holstered his weapon, unbuckled Dan's cartridge belt, and pulled it out from under his body. Then he checked Dan's pockets for any cash he might have. "You wasn't always real truthful about whether or not you had any money left, but I reckon this time you weren't lyin'. Maybe I can sell your horse and saddle. That oughta help out a little."

Finished talking to Dan's corpse, Ned decided he owed it to him to dig a hole to keep the scavengers away from him. He got the short-handled shovel from the packs and found a spot where the ground didn't look too hard. When he had a shallow hole that looked big enough, he dragged the body over and rolled it into the grave. By the time he finished filling in the grave with the loose dirt, the first light of morning had begun to break over the little stream. It occurred to him that he was hungry and was in desperate need of a cup of coffee.

In the light of a new day, he was still committed to his vow to avenge Tiny Wilson's death. It occurred to him that he would be avenging Dan's death as well. If it hadn't been for one of those men shooting Dan, he would still be alive today.

Ned knew he needed food and a little rest after the night just past. His plan was to follow the herd of horses and wait for a chance to ambush the gunslinger. He couldn't just ride into their camp and call out the man. All three would most likely shoot him on sight. So he gathered enough wood for a fire, made some coffee, and cooked some bacon.

He awoke with a start, not sure for a moment where he was. Feeling the sun on his face, he sat up and realized he had fallen asleep after eating some breakfast. He looked across the ashes of his fire to focus on Dan Short's grave and reminded himself once again that it had been the best thing to do for his old partner. He thought then of the three men driving the herd of horses. No doubt they were well on their way again. He could catch up to them in plenty of time, and took his time getting his horses ready to go. He had five to take care of now, so he rigged up a lead rope for four of them and started back to the camp he had fled the night before.

He felt confident the herd would be gone but thought it a good idea to look over their campsite and find the trail they left on.

Entering the deserted camp from downstream the creek, just as he and Dan and Tiny had done the night before, Ned remembered approximately where he'd been when he saw the man turn and fire. That was the end of Tiny. He was knocked off his horse, and had it not been for his own immediate turn away from the creek, Ned might have been the next one to get shot. With that in mind, he walked his horses into the clearing, looking right and left, until he was stopped suddenly by the sight of Tiny Wilson, laid out flat on the ground.

Ned dismounted, walked over to stand by the body, and muttered, "I swear, Mavis, I'm sorry for what they done to him. And they just left him for the buzzards to feed on. Well, I reckon I can dig a grave for my sister's husband." He wanted to be able to look his sister in the face and tell her he took proper care of her dead husband. Already suffering sore muscles from one grave digging, Ned soon found that the interment of Tiny was going to be an altogether harder job than Dan Short's. For Tiny was a huge man. In bulk alone, he would make two of Dan.

Ned was committed to do the proper thing, so he got his shovel out again and picked a spot to dig. He labored away to dig a hole that he thought adequate for one of Tiny's bulk. When it was ready, he dragged the huge body to the grave then dragged it into the shallow grave by holding a boot under each arm and walking the corpse into it like a horse pulling a wagon. He pulled Tiny into the grave until his head dropped in, then he released the boots and let them drop. To his great relief, head and boots fell within the grave.

Ned took a few moments to rest before beginning to fill in the grave. He soon encountered another minor problem. With Tiny lying on his back, Ned had not dug the grave deep enough, for the toes of Tiny's boots were just even with the top of the hole.

"Dadgum it." Ned snorted as he considered the problem. *I could haul him outta there and dig a little hole at that end for his boots to fit into. Then I can turn him facedown and his toes could go in the hole.* He really didn't want to remove the huge body and dig the grave deeper, so he continued to think about it. The toes of Tiny's boots were really just level with the top of the grave. *If I pulled his boots off, his toes ought not to stick up that high.*

That seemed to be the simplest solution, and there would be a little mound of dirt to cover the grave, anyway. Removing Tiny's boots was not the simple task he anticipated. He didn't know if the big man's feet had swollen overnight, or if the boots were just too small for his feet. Ned had to strain with all the strength he could muster before one, then finally the other one, came off.

While pausing to catch his breath, he noticed the boots were better looking than the old pair he wore, and they didn't look that much bigger than his own. He pulled off his boots and tried on Tiny's. They were too big, but not by a lot. He decided to keep them, hesitating for only a moment when he wondered if Mavis would notice. "Nah, she ain't gonna notice, and I deserve somethin' for killin' that coyote that shot Tiny." For want of a better idea for what to do with his old boots, he put them in the grave with Tiny. There wasn't much room in the hole he'd dug, but they fit nicely with one boot under each of Tiny's arms. All done, he filled in the grave, feeling he could honestly tell his sister he had given her husband a decent burial.

With a trail easy to follow, Ned Bates set out to track the herd of thirty-five horses.

"You sure you know how to find this place?" Possum asked when they struck the Sulphur River. "You ain't never been this far east in your life."

"I'm just tellin' you what Rubin told me," Perley replied. "He said if we kept drivin' 'em straight east, we'd eventually strike the Red River where it swings down a little farther south, and to just follow it till we get to Texarkana. He said we leave the river where it loops around north of the town and head south for about twelve miles." Possum looked unsure, so Perley added, "He said, if we get to the Louisiana border, to turn around and come back. We'd gone too far."

Ignoring Perley's japing, Possum said, "Might save a lotta time if we park this herd somewhere outside Texarkana and go into town and ask somebody how to get to the Double-D."

"Maybe," Perley allowed, "but we'd just be drivin' the horses a few miles more to get close to Texarkana. Rubin says the Double-D ain't as big as the Triple-G, so if we go like he told me, we'll most likely be on Double-D range right after we cross into Arkansas. Even if we don't find the headquarters, we'd at least be on their range. We've struck the Red about where he said we would, so let's follow it and see if he knew what he was talkin' about."

So, that's what they did, driving the horses on an old trail that started out to the east. After traveling a distance they figured to be at least eighteen or twenty miles, they decided to stop and rest the horses. They picked a spot with a wide grassy gap in the short oak trees that lined the banks of a creek. As soon as their horses were taken care of, Perley got a fire going and charged up the coffee-pot, while Possum attempted to make some pan biscuits.

Not one of the three men mentioned the possibility of a lone rider, who had been following them all morning.

Chapter 3

"I ain't sayin' these are the best biscuits I ever made," Possum declared when he offered the pan to Perley, "but they'll be somethin' to go with that bacon."

Perley speared one of the biscuits out of the pan and Possum then offered the pan to Sonny, who speared one as well.

Perley took a bite out of his biscuit and smacked his lips after he swallowed it. "You're bein' a little too modest. Some of them widows around this part of Texas taste one of these biscuits and you'll have a list of marriage proposals to consider."

Possum just grunted in response to Perley's japing, instead of a customary comeback of his own.

That prompted Perley to study his friend for a few minutes. He had ridden with Possum long enough to know the man's mannerisms and moods and decided something was bothering him. "Something is eatin' at you." He asked outright, "What is it?"

Possum shrugged, then replied, "Oh, it ain't nothin'. I just got a feelin'. I was thinkin' about those three that jumped us back there, figured we were done with them, but I don't know. We killed the one, but you reckon the other two ain't give up yet?"

"I think we have seen the last of those fellows," Perley said. "We killed the big one, and that one you shot looked like he was hurt pretty bad. I doubt he's in any shape to come after us again. The other one surely ain't foolish enough to come after us by himself."

"Maybe he knows he can't take the horses," Sonny offered his thoughts, "but wants to pop one of us when we ain't lookin', just to get even for shootin' his partner."

Perley and Possum looked at Sonny and shrugged.

"I don't know," Possum said. "I just had a feelin' all mornin' like somebody was tailin' us. I stopped and looked behind us a couple of times. Don't know why, I just had a feelin'."

Perley nodded while he considered what Possum was saying. "Tell you what. It ain't ever a bad idea to check your back trail, just to make sure ain't nobody tailin' ya. Buck ain't nowhere near tired yet. I'll throw my saddle back on him and take a little ride a mile or two back to make sure we ain't got somebody else eyein' our horses."

"Well, I'll tell ya, that ain't a bad idea," Possum said. "One of us can ride along with you, if you want. I know I'd hate to be surprised by more horse thieves."

"No, thanks," Perley replied. "I'd rather go by myself. I'll cross the river and go back on the other side—be less chance of bein' seen. If somebody is followin' us I'll get back here, so we can get ready for 'em." He called Buck up from the water's edge and the big bay gelding came to him at once to stand patiently while Perley threw his saddle back on. "Shouldn't be for too long, boy," he cooed to the horse as he tightened the cinch.

"Don't be takin' no wild chances," Possum lectured as Perley climbed up into the saddle. "You see anybody, get back here quick as you can, so we can get ready for 'em."

"I will," Perley replied and guided Buck back down to the river and crossed over to the other side. He rode through the trees that framed the creek and was gone from Possum and Sonny's sight immediately.

"He's right," Possum commented. "It'd be mighty hard for somebody on this side of the creek to see him riding up the other side."

"If anybody's followin' us on this side of the creek, won't it be just as hard for Perley to see them?" Sonny wondered.

The question stumped Possum for a moment. That possibility hadn't occurred to him. If so, he reckoned Perley would handle it. "Perley will be lookin' through the trees, searchin' for anybody on the other side. Anybody followin' us will be lookin' straight ahead, so they don't run up on us too soon."

Possum and Sonny nodded to each other, accepting that as the way it would happen.

"Might as well have another biscuit," Possum said. "Perley will know what to do."

In fact, Perley was troubled to some degree by the very obstacle Sonny and Possum had discussed. For the most part, he was able to see the trail they had followed on the other side of the creek. But where the trees were growing in bigger clumps, they impaired his vision of the trail. He had no intention of riding back any farther than a mile and a half or so, figuring anyone following would most likely stay at least that close and probably not much farther behind.

When he got as far as he intended, he turned Buck around and started back. He had ridden no farther than the last thick clump of trees he had passed when Buck whinnied and was answered by a couple of whinnies from the other side of the creek. Perley immediately pulled the big horse into the cover of the trees and dismounted. With his rifle in hand, he made his way cautiously through the bushes, inching up to a position where he could see the creek and the bank on the far side. Down at the water's edge on the far side, he saw five horses watering. His first thought was five men, then he figured it more likely two or three men with a couple of packhorses. Either way, it looked like more trouble.

Better confirm it, he thought, so he would know exactly how many they had to be ready for. He started to move to a closer position when he was suddenly stopped by the sight of a man walking down to the creek to check on the horses. Perley recognized him! He was one of the three men who had attempted to steal their horses, the only one who had not been shot. No doubt, he was the same man. Close to Possum's age, he figured, judging by the gray mustache and sideburns. He had not spoken much—maybe not at all—when the three outlaws had come to their camp in the afternoon.

Perley had questions. What was he doing following them? Where was the wounded one? Were they still determined to steal the herd of horses? Perley found that he had to have answers to all those questions, because it didn't make sense. Then he remembered Sonny's speculation that revenge might be their objective.

Perley knew what Possum would advise him to do. It was an easy shot with his rifle. The man was standing at the water's edge. He could cut him down and be done with it. But Perley had never been able to take the role of an assassin and commit outright murder. He fired only when he was under attack and in many of those cases had been given no time to think about his actions.

To give himself another excuse not to commit murder, he reminded himself he had to worry about a second man. It would be better to have them together, so he watched the man turn and walk back into the trees. Making a mental note of the path he took, Perley moved back from the position he had taken and went to get his horse.

Ned walked back to his little campfire and cut some strips of beef jerky to roast over the flame. He was not concerned about the smoke, for his fire was small and the little bit of smoke it produced was dissipated in the branches of the trees overhead. As he had figured, it had not taken him long to catch up to the herd of horses. In fact, he had to drop back for fear he was following too close and might be discovered.

When the riders had stopped and made camp, it was obvious they planned to stay a while to let their horses rest and graze. He had sneaked through the trees on foot and gotten close enough to see they were preparing food for themselves. He'd decided to take the opportunity to do the same. The thought had entered his mind he might get a shot at the young man who'd killed Tiny, but he was afraid he could not have gotten away fast enough to escape a bullet from one of the other two.

As he'd continued to follow along behind the three

men and the horses, his mind had been in turmoil the entire day. Not at all sure he should even try to get a shot at the man he figured to be a professional gunslinger, Ned stared into the fire. It was difficult to pin the total blame on a man who fired back when someone fired at him. But it was his sister's husband the man killed, and he knew what Mavis would tell him he should do. He thought about how he was going to explain Tiny's death to her as he reached over and twisted the limb so the strip of jerky would cook on the other side.

"I didn't expect to see you again."

The sudden statement shut down Ned's whole nervous system and he found he could not move.

"Looks like you dropped your dinner in the fire."

Trembling and not caring if the piece of jerky fell into the ashes, Ned turned to face the voice behind him. The .44 he wore felt as if it weighed a hundred pounds in his holster as he identified the voice as the lightning-fast machine who had knocked Tiny out of his saddle.

"Looks like it's just you," Perley said then. "The other fellow didn't make it?"

Finding his voice, Ned answered, "No, he's dead."

"That's too bad. It was a damn-fool thing you fellows tried to do. It was a terrible waste of two lives. Where are you headed?"

Ned was just about to come to pieces, certain that he was about to be assassinated at any minute, yet afraid to try to prevent it, thinking that would only speed it up. "I don't know," he answered Perley's question. "I mean, I was just headin' to Arkansas, I reckon." His mind was in a complete state of confusion and he wished he and Dan had gone on to Texarkana instead of rustling horses.

The man talking so calmly looked to be a harmless young fellow. If Ned had not witnessed the speed with which he turned and shot Tiny dead, he would have never thought to fear him.

"Where did you come from?" Perley asked.

"What?" Ned responded.

"Before you and your friends came here, where did you come here from," Perley asked patiently.

Still confused, Ned was certain the man was just leading him on, hoping to make him go for his gun. He was convinced that would mean sudden death. "Waco," he finally answered.

"Why don't you go back to Waco, then?"

"I don't know," Ned pleaded.

"I don't think it's a good idea for you to keep taggin' along behind us," Perley said. "You've got some things mixed up in your mind. You've lost two partners, but it ain't my and my partners' fault. It was your idea to steal our horses. You came in the middle of the night, blazin' away with your guns, shootin' at what you thought was me and my friends. You played a foolish game and you lost. So pack up your horses and head on back to Waco before you pay the ultimate price. And if you'll take my advice, you need to find yourself another line of work."

Ned was not sure he was not being played with. Still in a state of shock, he finally mustered up enough spit to ask, "You mean you ain't gonna shoot me?"

"Not if you get your stuff together and head back to where you came from, or anywhere else as long as it ain't where we are."

Without consciously aware that he was holding his breath, Ned exhaled a long sigh of relief. Still afraid the man might simply be amusing himself by keeping him guessing, Ned declared, "I reckon there ain't no reason I can't turn around. I ain't never been to Texarkana, anyway. I can just as easy go back to Waco."

"Good idea," Perley said. "You might wanna get started right away. Go ahead and fetch your horses. I'll take care of your fire. There's plenty of daylight left, so you oughta be able to get a good start toward home."

"Right," Ned responded, convinced finally that Perley really meant to let him go unharmed, but he still couldn't understand why. "I'll go bring the horses up and saddle up again. Won't take me no time a-tall."

Perley nodded but followed him down to the creek and watched while Ned put the packs back on the two pack-horses, then saddled the other three. As he tightened the cinch on his own saddle, a thought entered his head. With his back toward Perley, it would be easy to let his hand drop down to rest on the handle of his .44. He could pull it as he turned back around before the man knew what he was doing. His chance for vengeance might still be possible.

While he made up his mind, he stole a sideways glance only to see the man's unblinking gaze zeroed on his every move and the slowly shaking of his head a deadly warning.

"Right," Ned responded again. "I'll be goin' now." He stepped up into the saddle.

"Have a good trip home," Perley wished him soberly.

"Obliged." Ned turned his horse back toward the west, aware only then that his shirt was soaked with sweat but thankful to be alive. He still didn't take a deep breath until he had ridden out of pistol range.

Perley watched him until he had ridden out of sight before he went back in the trees to get his horse. "Now, I wonder how I'm gonna explain this to Possum and Sonny," he said to Buck. He knew he would have to come up with some reason why Ned had withdrawn and would not likely try again. With no way he could guarantee that, he decided not to ever mention the incident to anyone.

Almost a quarter of a mile back up the trail, Ned Bates asked aloud, "How am I gonna explain this to anybody?" He decided it best not to ever mention this day's activity to anyone.

"We was just about to decide for one of us to go back and see what happened to you," Possum greeted Perley. "Only reason we didn't was because we didn't hear no gunfire."

"I rode a little farther back than I planned to," Perley lied. "There ain't nobody on our trail."

"I figured you musta rode farther," Possum said. "That's what I told Sonny."

"Any coffee left in that pot?" Perley asked. When told there might be a cup, he poured it into his cup and sat down by the fire to drink it. "What you think we oughta do? Stay here tonight, or ride on a little farther? We've got a lotta daylight left and we've got time to rest the horses a little longer if we want to. I'm just thinkin' we can't be but six or seven miles from the point where we strike the river right at the Arkansas line. We might wanna go on and make camp there.

"Then tomorrow we wouldn't have but a short trip to the Double-D. We could get there a little before dinner time. Give us a chance to see if their cook is as good as Ollie, back at the Triple-G." Perley was still thinking about the outlaw. Had he read the man wrong? What were the odds that he might pay them another visit? And might they feel a little more comfortable if they put a bit of distance between the creek and the horse thief?

If Perley had known the image of him Ned had built in his mind, he would have found it difficult to believe.

"I don't care, one way or the other," Possum said. "It's your decision to make. Whatever you wanna do is all right with me and Sonny, ain't it, Sonny?" Sonny didn't answer, but Possum knew he couldn't care less. "That ain't a bad idea, though, to hit the Double-D in time for dinner."

"All right, then that's what we'll do," Perley said. "That oughta make it two short rides and we're done. Let's give the horses about another half hour or so." He took his cup of coffee and moved away from the fire to lean against a tree, positioning himself so he could look in the direction of their back trail.

Underway again, with no visit from Ned Bates, they continued to drive the herd along the river. As it turned out, Perley's estimate of the distance proved to be not very far off. It was late afternoon, but still daylight, when they reached the point where the river took a turn to the north, and according to Rubin's instructions, made a loop up and around Texarkana. They went into camp there.

After a peaceful night with no unexpected visitors,

they packed up the next morning, left the river, and continued east into Arkansas. They traveled only a half dozen miles before crossing a creek, where they saw a few cows bunched up at the edge of the water. Figuring they were on Double-D range, Sonny commented that somebody needed to be checking the strays.

Almost as soon as he said it, they spotted a rider approaching from the south, angling to intercept them. Perley and Possum rode out to meet him.

"Howdy," the rider called out when they met. "You boys from the Triple-G?"

"That's right," Perley answered. "We've got thirty-five horses that belong to the Double-D and we're lookin' for the place to leave 'em."

"Well, I can show you the place. My name's Billy Dean and you fellers just earned me ten dollars."

"How's that?" Perley asked.

"Me and some of the other boys threw a little money in the pot and the one who found these horses gets the pot. This is a big range and somebody that ain't never been here before can get lost."

"Well, I'm proud we made you some money, Billy." Possum was tempted to remind the young man that they were from Texas and knew a little something about big ranges. Instead, he said, "My name's Possum Smith and this here's Perley Gates. The young feller back there with your horses is Sonny Rice. You just show us the way and we'll get these horses home so you can inspect 'em to make sure you got what you paid for."

"Well, you boys didn't miss it by much," Billy said, assuming Possum was the man in charge. "The headquarters ain't but half a mile south of here. Let's just head 'em down that little draw right yonder and that'll take you to the ranch house pasture. I expect that's where Shelton wants 'em."

"Who's Shelton?" Possum asked.

"Price Shelton," Billy answered. "He's the foreman of the Double-D. He'll most likely look the horses over. Mr. Donovan might come look at 'em, but it'll be up to Shelton to okay 'em."

"I don't think he'll find anything wrong with this bunch of horses," Possum said. "So let's get 'em headed down that draw."

Billy led the way and they drove the horses down to a pasture bordering a wide creek. The Triple-G men herded the horses close to the creek, then waited while Billy rode up to the back of the ranch house, a large, two-story building, to inform Donald Donovan that his horses had arrived. From the steps, he gave the message to a woman then hurried back to the horses. Price Shelton had seen the herd arrive and was already walking toward the pasture.

After a quick introduction of Possum by Billy Dean, Shelton nodded to each one of the men but wasted no time on conversation. He was a serious-looking man, wide-shouldered with a quiet strength that seemed to convey an image of a big ranch foreman. He walked into the middle of the herd of horses and began a close inspection.

Donald Donovan came out the front door of the main house to look at the horses. Billy did another quick introduction and Donovan nodded to the three Triple-G riders and flashed a warm smile. "So you found our little cow ranch, did you?" he asked good-naturedly.

Perley decided he liked the man immediately.

"They were within half a mile when I found 'em," Billy answered for them.

Shelton came back from his inspection of the horses then, so Donovan called out to him. "Whaddaya think, Price? They look like a pretty good lot of horses."

"Yes, sir, Mr. Donovan," Shelton replied. "They're not bad, I reckon. They ain't the best I've ever seen, but I reckon they'll work."

That prompted Perley to speak up. "I'm sure your foreman knows horses, Mr. Donovan, else he probably wouldn't be your foreman. But I'm afraid I'm gonna have to challenge his opinion of the horses you've already bought. I'd be willin' to bet that you ain't workin' any horses on this ranch that are in better shape than the thirty-five we just delivered. They're all of good breed, they're healthy, and there ain't a one over five years old. My guess is that Mr. Shelton doesn't know you've already paid for the horses at a pretty low price, so there ain't no bargainin' left to do."

Perley's outburst was met with surprise by Donovan and Shelton.

"Who'd you say you are?" Donovan asked, having paid little attention during the initial introductions.

"Perley Gates, sir," he answered.

"Like the Pearly Gates in Heaven?" Donovan asked.

"Yes, sir. Sounds the same, but it's spelled different."

"It sure ain't hard to remember a name like that," Donovan said. "I apologize for not recognizing it. You're one of the three brothers, right?"

"Yes, sir, the youngest," Perley answered.

Donovan stepped forward and extended his hand.

"Well, I'm mighty glad to meet you, Perley. I wired the money to your brother, Rubin, and asked him to send me a bill of sale."

"Yes, sir," Perley said. "I've got it right here." He reached into his saddlebags, pulled out an envelope, and promptly handed it to Donovan. He waited while Donovan looked over the bill of sale, then said, "Now, if you ain't satisfied with the condition of the stock, we'll turn 'em around and drive 'em right back to the Triple-G. And I'll have Rubin wire your money right back to ya."

Donovan smiled as he stuffed the bill of sale back into the envelope. "How 'bout it, Price? Are we satisfied with the horses?"

Shelton grinned back at him. "Yes, sir, they're a fine-lookin' bunch of horses."

"Then I reckon we'll keep 'em, Mr. Gates. Now, I expect you and your men could use a little something to eat. It oughta be just about time to eat. The bunkhouse cook's name is Poison Pearson, but don't let that scare you. Ol' Poison's a pretty good cook. Matter of fact, I'll join you there."

"We 'preciate the invitation," Perley responded. "We've been broke in by Ollie Dinkler back home. After you eat Ollie's food for a while, it's hard to find anybody's cookin' that doesn't go down smooth."

Shelton went with them to unsaddle and water their horses, then escorted them to the cook shack at one end of the bunkhouse. The chuck was good and after they were given a general introduction as three visitors from the Triple-G over in Texas, they concentrated on consuming it. Before they were far along, Donovan arrived and shoved in between two of his men across from Perley, so he could visit with him. While Perley worked on his plate of beans and steak, accompanied by biscuits and coffee, he was subjected to a lengthy account of when Donovan had met Rubin at a North Texas Cattleman's Association meeting in Fort Worth.

"That was a long way to go to that meetin'," Possum inserted.

"Yes, it was. I went as a guest, " Donovan replied. "There ain't nothin' around these parts like that, and I wanted to see if there was anything I could learn." He looked back at Perley again. "I'm sure your brother told you I pretty-much talked his ears off."

Perley just smiled in response. He knew Rubin had gone to Fort Worth for over a week to go to some kind of meetings. At least, now he knew how Rubin managed to sell some horses to a ranch in Arkansas. He had wondered. It occurred to him that he really didn't involve himself in the overall running of the ranch, having been more than happy to let Rubin and John worry about that. He was more content in the saddle.

Another thought struck him at that moment. Now that a general understanding had been reached between him and Becky Morris, was he going to be expected to take on a more active role in the management of the Triple-G? *Damn*, he thought, *I ain't ready for that*.

"What?" he blurted, just then aware that someone had asked him a question.

"I said, are you gonna turn around and go right back today?" Shelton asked.

"Oh," Perley responded. "No, I think we're gonna go back by way of Texarkana, just so we can say we've been there, I reckon. But I promised to buy 'em a drink of likker when we delivered those horses safe and sound."

"Well, Texarkana ain't much of a town, but it looks like it's a start of one and it will be lively tonight, since it's Saturday," Shelton said. "I'm sure some of our men will be up there, too. It's a pretty long ride for a drink of whiskey, but there is a saloon and it's the closest thing around here for our boys and some of the small ranches to let off a little steam. If you decide you don't wanna start back west after you've had a few drinks, just come on back here and bunk down with us. Four or five bunks in the bunkhouse are empty. You can take your pick of any bunk with the mattress rolled up. Then to-morrow mornin', you can eat breakfast before you start for home."

"Well, thank you, sir," Perley said. "That's mighty neighborly of you. We'll see how things go in town. You're right, we might not feel like findin' a campin' spot and makin' camp, if we get started too late. We'll take our packhorses to town in case we decide to make a quick stop and go ahead and start for home."

Chapter 4

They thanked Donald Donovan and Price Shelton for their hospitality and left the Double-D on a trail to Texarkana, pointed out to them by Billy Dean. "Me and a couple of the other boys are goin' into town in a little while. It's a twelve-mile ride, and the ride back is twice as long." He laughed at the thought. "Maybe we'll see you at the Last Chance Saloon. Right now, that's the only place to get likker and anything else you might have a hankerin' for."

"We'll most likely just settle for a drink of likker," Possum said with a chuckle, "and leave the other stuff to you and the Double-D."

"Twelve miles," Sonny remarked. "It'll be almost suppertime by the time we get there. What are we gonna do, Perley? Make camp somewhere close and stay there tonight?"

"I don't know," Perley replied. "Let's just wait and see when we get there."

* * *

The little town was just as Shelton had described it, including a feed store, a stable, a blacksmith, a small railroad depot, and a post office. A little building proclaimed itself to be the Last Chance before leaving Arkansas. The hitching rail in front of the saloon was crowded with horses, so much so, that it was necessary to tie their horses on the side of the building.

Inside, it appeared there was already a fanny for almost every chair at a table, so the Triple-G men had no choice other than to belly up to the bar.

"Howdy, strangers," Shag Felton greeted them. "What's your poison?"

"What kinda whiskey you pourin'?" Possum asked. When the bartender said he had corn and rye, Possum said, "I'll take a shot of corn."

Perley and Sonny said that would do for them as well, so Shag turned three shot glasses off a stack and filled them.

"Any chance we could get some supper here?" Possum asked after he tossed his whiskey back.

"Yes, sir, there's a good chance," Shag said, "long as you're satisfied with beef stew and beans. We got a cook, but she don't fix no fancy meals."

"Can we get some coffee to go with it?" Perley asked, as he always did.

"Sure can," Shag answered. "You want me to tell her to fix three plates?"

"Yep," Perley answered him then pointed toward the corner. "You can bring 'em right over yonder to that back corner table." While they'd been talking, he had been watching the table where one of the occupants was struggling to get his friend on his feet. "We'll take the bottle with us. Come on, Possum."

Much to Possum's surprise, Perley picked up the bottle and made his way through the crowd of drinkers before someone else saw the opportunity to sit down at the table.

Reaching the table, Possum saw what was happening and said to the younger man, "Here, lemme give you a hand. Looks like your pa is havin' a little trouble." He took hold of the older man's elbow and helped lift him up on his feet.

"He ain't my pa," the younger man replied impatiently. "He's my boss, and it's my job to make sure he gets home all right. There's some fellers down at the other end of the bar that want this table. I told 'em we'd be out of their way in a few minutes."

"Yeah, we talked to 'em," Possum said. "They said they changed their minds and for us to set down and eat our supper."

Sonny looked at Perley and they slowly shook their heads. Perley looked back toward the other end of the bar to see if anybody was watching to see what was happening at the table. As far as he could tell, no one seemed to show any interest in that particular table. He glanced back at Sonny again and shrugged.

Possum looked around then said, "That looks like a back door over there. It might be easier to take your boss out that way, in case some of his friends might see him comin' outta the saloon in the shape he's in." He also figured the fellows waiting for the table might not notice they'd left.

"I reckon that would be a good idea," the young man

said. "It don't look too dignified for the town marshal to be seen like this."

Possum looked at Perley and grinned. "No, I reckon not. You got him all right?"

The young man said he thought he could make it. They watched him slowly walking the lawman through the back door then sat down at the table.

"Now," Possum declared, "I wanna know why you bought that whole bottle of whiskey. I ain't never knowed you to buy a whole bottle of whiskey. You don't ever take more 'n two drinks. What's goin' on with you?"

"I'm sorry I got you all excited," Perley answered. "I figured I'd most likely have one more tonight, and you and Sonny can have however many you feel like. Then you might have a little left to have a drink or two on the way home."

Possum looked at him as if he still didn't believe him.

Perley said, "We might have to offer a drink to those fellows that young man promised to hold this table for." He had hurried back to the table simply because he could see the young man was trying to get the drunken marshal to his feet. When he found out someone was already waiting for the table, he would have honored the first party's right to take the table. But Possum went a step farther. Perley hoped no one would notice the change of parties at the table.

Fascinated by the whole incident, Sonny felt inclined to ask, "Is this the kinda stuff that goes on all the time when you and Possum are on one of those trips you're always takin'?"

"No, I don't know what's got into him," Perley replied facetiously.

Further discussion was interrupted by the arrival of a woman twice the size of Perley or Possum. She was carrying three large plates of food, one in each hand, and one on her forearm. Perley couldn't help noticing a long string of gray hair on the plate she placed before him. It was a perfect match for the gray hair hanging around her face. Attempting to make it look like he was being polite, he quickly slid the plate over before Sonny and took the one that was riding on her arm.

"You want cornbread?" the huge woman asked.

"Yes, ma'am," Perley answered. "And coffee."

"It's comin'," she said. "There ain't two of me."

Possum was just about to insist she was wrong about that, but Perley sensed it in time to stop him.

When she left to fetch the cornbread, Possum remarked. "I can tell you right now this food is delicious, and I ain't even tasted it yet. I just ain't man enough to tell her if it tastes a whole lot like it looks."

"It's a wise man who knows his limitations," Perley pronounced. "You can learn a lot travelin' with this man, Sonny."

"Shoot," Sonny said, "you're both crazy. This stuff don't look a whole lot different from what Ollie feeds us on the trail." He picked up his fork and attacked the stew. After a couple of bites, he remarked, "It ain't bad."

So Perley and Possum joined him.

They weren't halfway finished with the supper when the somber-faced woman brought a plate with three pieces of cornbread on it and placed it on the table. She stood, silently watching them for a brief moment. Then, satisfied that they were eating her supper, she turned around and went back into the kitchen. She had no sooner left them when they were confronted by two men who walked over from the bar.

"What the hell?" One of them, a sizable man, held a drink in his hand. "Where the hell did you fellows come from?"

Perley formed as friendly a smile as he could and answered, "About a hundred and fifteen miles west of here, a little town called Paris."

"I ain't askin' you where you come from," the man snapped. "I'm askin' you what you're doin' settin' at this table. Where's them two fellers that was settin' here?"

"You mean the marshal and his deputy?" Perley replied. "They went out the back door. We thought they were never gonna leave." He glanced over at Possum and gave him a little shake of his head. "We were sittin' here, waitin' for our supper, but we got up and let the marshal and his deputy sit down long enough to get the marshal's head straight, so he could make it out the door. Took longer than we thought, didn't it, Possum?"

"Well, I'll be—" the larger of the two started, obviously unhappy. "That lowdown drunk of a marshal never said a word about somebody else already settin' here."

"I bet that's really the reason he went out the back door," Perley said. "I feel bad about you fellows havin' to wait so long just to set down. The best we can do is finish up our supper and you boys can have the table. How's that?"

"It ain't good, but I reckon it'll have to do, if we don't find another one before you finish up your supper. Can't hardly blame you fellers for it. Come on, Slim." The large man turned about and returned to the far end of the bar, grumbling as he left. "That damn drunken fool." Had it been any other town than the one he was trying to maintain a peaceful existence with, he would have simply cleared the table under threat of violence.

"You know, that coulda turned out a whole lot different," Possum commented as he watched the two men walk away. He noticed the little group of drinking men standing at that end of the bar was gradually getting bigger and they all seemed to know each other.

"You're right," Perley said. "I got caught up in the middle of that story you made up and had to come up with some reason to give him." He looked at the group of regular customers at the end of the bar just as they were joined by a couple more. One of the new arrivals had a familiar face.

"There you go." Perley pointed toward the door. "That's Billy Dean who just came in. He'll tell 'em who we are, if anybody wants to know." That seemed to lighten their concern at the moment. Another familiar face joined the drinkers a few minutes later. Unfortunately, he went unnoticed by all three Triple-G men.

"Well, I'll be." Duke Thacker started when he saw Ned Bates. "I was wonderin' when you boys were gonna show up. Where's Dan?"

"We run into some bad luck on the way here," Ned answered. "Dan's dead. My brother-in-law, Tiny Wilson, is dead, too. I was just lucky to get away."

Duke asked what happened.

Ned admitted the three of them had tried to steal a small herd of horses and they walked into a trap. "We was hopin' to bring somethin' to the party besides just the three of us. We thought we coulda sold those horses and paid our way into the gang."

"Where were they goin' with the horses?" Duke asked. "Maybe it ain't too late."

"They were takin 'em to the Double-D," Ned replied. "I expect they're already there by now."

"Young feller over there works for the Double-D," one of the group of drinkers said and pointed to Billy Dean. "Hey, Billy, did ol' Donald Donovan just get some new horses?"

Surprised by the question, Billy stood up and answered. "Yeah, we did. It was just a small herd of thirty-five good cow ponies." About to sit down again, his eye happened to catch the three Triple-G men at the table in the corner. "Matter of fact, yonder's the fellers that brought 'em in." He pointed them out. "If you're interested in horses, you could ask them about 'em."

Duke was stunned for a moment as his eyes fixed on the three men eating supper at the back corner table. He had made it a policy not to rile the people in any town he was holed up near in order to avail himself and his gang of the supplies and services they needed. That was the only reason he had patiently waited for the marshal to sober up enough to leave his preferred table. He figured it the least he could do, since he was the source of the marshal's whiskey.

"Them's the fellers settin' at your table," someone said.

"Yeah, they were settin' there before the marshal and his deputy needed a place to sober up a little, so they let 'em set there till he was ready to go," Duke said.

Ned's sudden siege of panic went unnoticed by Thacker and the others.

An interested listener to the discussion, bartender

Shag Felton, made a simple statement that served to light Duke's fuse. "Them three fellers weren't here before Marshal Creech came in tonight. They came in after he did."

Realizing the full meaning of the bartender's statement, Duke was immediately furious. He didn't appreciate being made a fool of, and his natural impulse was to strangle each one of the three with his bare hands. His sense of reasoning was fighting for its life in an effort to remind him of his peaceful policy in regard to Texarkana. They would pay for their mistake, but it might be necessary to have it done so as not to implicate himself, a fact that irritated him even further.

He glanced at Ned standing at his elbow, and something occurred to him. "Those are the three fellers that ambushed you, right?"

Ned nodded.

"And they killed Dan Short and Tiny Wilson, right?"

Again, Ned nodded.

That put a different coat of paint on the whole picture. Straining to remain calm, Thacker turned to ask Billy Dean, "Who's the man in charge of the three?"

"That would be Perley Gates."

"Say what?" Thacker was not sure he had heard correctly.

"Sounds like those gates up in Heaven, but it ain't spelt the same," Billy explained. "Perley Gates, just like the way it sounds."

"Ha." Thacker got to his feet and snorted. "Ned!" he called loudly. "Are those the three men who ambushed you and Dan, and killed him and your brother-in-law?"

When Ned said that they were indeed the men who'd

ambushed them, Thacker nodded, then motioned for one of his men to come to him.

"You want me, Boss?" Spade Devlin asked.

"Yeah, maybe," Thacker replied. "You ready for some work?"

Not certain what Thacker had in mind but knowing it would call for his quickness with a six-gun, Devlin grinned. "I'm always ready."

Thacker motioned for Devlin to follow, then pushed his way through the crowd of drinkers, all of whom were aware something was about to happen. He stopped before the back corner table.

Possum looked at Perley and asked, "You reckon he's got something he's wantin' to tell us?"

"Wouldn't surprise me none a-tall," Perley answered. "I don't know if you noticed or not, but that's one of the jaspers that tried to steal our horses back there."

"Kinda disappointin', ain't it, when you need a friend and one of the only two you know in the whole room is a feller who's already tried to kill you once," Possum remarked.

Sonny looked back and forth between Perley and Possum, thoroughly confused by their light exchange of conversation in a situation that didn't have a chance of turning out positive.

While Duke Thacker indulged himself in a long moment of silent intimidation, Perley broke the ice. "I know what you're wonderin' and I'm happy to tell you we've finished our supper and we're willin' to turn this table over to you. And thank you kindly for your patience. You're a real gentleman."

Ignoring Perley's blatant sarcasm, Thacker demanded, "Which one of you is Perley Gates?"

A bit of snickering sounded in the crowd at the pronunciation of the name.

"Why, that would be me," Perley confessed. "What do your friends call you, sir?"

"Everything's funny to you, ain't it?" Thacker asked, scowling menacingly. "Let me tell you what ain't funny to anybody in this town—saddle tramps like you three who ambush honest cowhands like the two you murdered." He paused and looked around the crowded room to make sure he had everyone's attention. "Hangin' is what we do to scum like you in this town."

A couple of his gang members spoke out loud at the mention of that, calling for somebody to get a rope.

"Since you've turned this saloon into a courtroom, I think it's only fair to hear what the accused has to say." When the spectators went silent, anxious to hear what he could say to prove his innocence, Perley continued. "First of all, I'm the only one who shot anybody. My two friends here weren't in camp at the time, so I'm the scum you're tryin'." He frowned for Possum to keep quiet when he started to object. "And I'm confessin'. I rolled up three blankets to look like we were sleepin', then hid in the creek. A little past midnight, those three horse thieves came ridin' into our camp with guns a-blazin'. I recognize one of 'em standin' back there by the bar." Perley pointed to Ned Bates. "Well, what man in here wouldn't shoot back at three robbers shootin' up his camp and tryin' to stampede horses he was drivin' to the Double-D? So naturally, I plead not guilty of anything but trying to protect myself and the horses I was deliverin'. Havin' said that, I guess as a common courtesy, we oughta get up and give the man his table now, and we'll be on our way." He got to his feet and looking at Possum and Sonny, he asked, "You fellows finished eatin'? We'll pay the bartender for this fine supper and get goin'."

"Not so fast, Perley," Thacker said and held up his hand. "There's somebody else here who's got a grief with you. You mighta heard of him, Spade Devlin."

"That so?" Perley said and paused to stroke his chin as if tryin' to remember. "Can't say as I have." He looked over at Possum. "You ever hear of Spade Devlin, Possum?" When Possum said that he had no recollection of anyone by that name, Perley looked back at Thacker. "I expect, if we were from around these parts, we might have. Is he famous for somethin'?"

"I'll let him tell you, smart-ass," Thacker said and stepped aside so Devlin could step forward to confront Perley.

"Perley Gates," Devlin slurred. "What kinda name is that? Sounds likc you oughta be wearin' a skirt, instead of a pair of pants."

"I reckon it strikes different folks in different ways," Perley replied. "Is that the grief he said you had with me?"

"That's just one of 'em. I don't like your looks."

"I don't especially care for 'em, myself," Perley responded. "That kinda gives us somethin' in common, doesn't it?"

"And I damn sure don't like your smart mouth," Devlin said before his outright challenge. "I'm takin' satisfaction outta you for killin' my friend"—he paused to quickly whisper a question in Thacker's direction—

"what was his name?" Thacker whispered back, and Devlin repeated it, "Dan Short. You murdered my friend, Dan Short. Now, I'm callin' you out, Perley Gates. We'll settle this trial with six-guns, since I notice you're wearin' one. You want it right here, or you wanna take it outside?"

"Oh, I don't want it at all, Spade. 'Preciate the offer to draw with you, but my friends and I were just havin' a drink or two and an early supper, so we could get started back tonight. Next time I'm in town, if nobody ain't gunned you down, maybe I'll look you up." Perley looked back at Possum and Sonny and said, "Let's go, boys. We owe the man some money for our supper."

Certain that Perley didn't have the guts to face him, Devlin fixed an amused sneer upon him and declared, "You ain't leavin' this town without facin' me, you dumb turkey." He stepped in front of Perley to prevent his leaving.

With almost all eyes on the two men involved in what would appear to be a public execution, no one noticed Ned Bates pull Thacker aside. "I don't know if that's a good idea or not, Duke. I saw that man when he turned and shot Tiny outta the saddle. I ain't seen anybody that fast before."

"That's because you ain't ever seen Spade Devlin in a face-off," Thacker assured him. "There ain't anybody faster and it don't look like Mr. Perley Gates has got the stomach to face him, anyway. We might end up hangin' him after all, but it'd be a whole lot less trouble if Spade could just shoot him."

When Devlin stepped up to look Perley right in the eye, Perley took a step backward. "No offense, Spade, but whatever you've been eatin' ain't doin' your breath much good a-tall. I'm tryin' to make you understand that I ain't got any notion to have a duel with you over what amounts to your boss gettin' snookered out of his table for twenty minutes. I'll apologize to him if that'll satisfy you, but I ain't gonna participate in a gunfight over something that unimportant."

"Oh, you ain't gonna *participate* in it, are you?" Devlin mocked. "Well, let me set you straight. You're gonna be in the middle of one. If you don't get your cowardly butt out in the middle of the floor, I'm gonna shoot you down like the skunk you are."

"As obnoxious as you are," Perley remarked, "I don't choose to shoot you. So I'm goin' now, and you can crow about how you ran me off. All right?" He told Possum to go ahead and untie the horses, then turned and went to the kitchen door, leaving Devlin to stand there confused by the word *obnoxious* but positive that it was another reason to shoot somebody. The scowling woman who had cooked the stew and beans looked up in surprise to see Perley standing in the doorway.

"Here's the money for the three suppers. There's a little extra for you. We thought we'd let you pay the bartender and keep the rest. I just wanted to let you know we enjoyed it." He turned and started for the front door without the benefit of seeing the almost permanent scowl move upside down to form a smile on the woman's face.

Back in the barroom, the crowd of spectators were still parted to form an empty lane in the middle for the gunfight. Spade Devlin was still standing at one end of the floor, waiting for Perley. But Perley never looked at him and continued walking toward the door. Devlin looked at Duke Thacker and Thacker nodded his okay to kill him.

"Turn around, coward!" Devlin warned, but Perley ignored him.

Devlin glanced at Thacker again. Thacker nodded strongly, so Devlin reached for his six-gun. Perley whirled around and fired, having heard the sound of Devlin's hand slapping the handle of his pistol seconds before he heard Possum yell "Perley!"

Stunned as much as the spectators watching the duel, Devlin doubled over and staggered backward, still holding his pistol, the muzzle never having cleared his holster. Then he released the pistol to let it slip back into the holster and slapped both hands over the rapidly growing bloodstain just beneath his breastbone. The usual smug, cocksure face of the gunfighter had faded to one of dismay and disbelief.

Standing at the door where he had remained after sending Sonny to bring the horses around, Possum watched the patrons of the Last Chance Saloon. His weapon was drawn, ready to prevent any retaliation for Devlin's death. He noted a definite look of disgust on the face of Duke Thacker. Possum would enjoy telling about it later when sure they were not being followed.

Watching the still stunned witnesses, he and Perley waited in the doorway until Sonny came around from the side of the building with the horses. They backed across the porch, keeping an eye on the front door and expecting the town marshal to show up. To no one's surprise, he failed to show, and they didn't think it wise to wait any longer. Wasting no time after deciding that, they jumped into the saddles and galloped away into the night.

Once they were a good distance from town and saw no sign of anyone chasing them, they pulled up to consider their options. It was awfully late to be starting out for home as they had originally intended, so they decided to ride back to the Double-D, as Price Shelton had suggested.

"Makes scnse," Possum concluded. "We can get us another good breakfast before we start back."

Chapter 5

All three were glad they'd decided to return to the Double-D for the night. After they took care of their horses, they carried their saddlebags and war bags into the bunkhouse where they said another howdy to a couple of the men who had not turned in yet. Perley offered them a drink from the bottle he brought back from the Last Chance Saloon. The offer was gratefully accepted, and the bottle was passed around while Perley, Possum, and Sonny selected bunks with the mattress rolled up. The bottle of whiskey was soon empty, and all hands decided it was time for bed.

Everyone was asleep by the time Billy Dean, Hank Martin, and Wilbur Cash returned from town. Billy found it difficult not to wake the sleeping bunkhouse with the news from town, but Price Shelton had a strict policy regarding men who wanted to ride into town for a few drinks of whiskey—he would not tolerate the interruption of other men's sleep upon the drinkers' return to the bunkhouse. The second part of his policy was a full day's work would be expected the day after their visit to the saloon. Those who broke the rules were fired. So news of the unimaginable death of Spade Devlin had to wait until morning.

As usual, Price Shelton was the first body stirring in the bunkhouse the next morning, beaten only by Poison Pearson in the cook shack by half an hour. Practicing a procedure he had made customary, Shelton paid a visit to the outhouse before returning to check the bunks in the bunkhouse to make sure he had a full crew to work that day. Discovering he had three extra bodies this morning, he went out to the cook shack to tell Poison he would have three extra mouths to fill. He knew it was unnecessary—Poison always cooked more than was needed. It was one of the reasons the Double-D raised a fine lot of fat hogs for hams and side meat.

When he returned to the bunkhouse, Shelton saw that Papa McCoy had awakened and was sitting on the side of his bunk, rolling himself a smoke. He would light it and inhale a few deep breaths before pulling on his boots and heading to the outhouse, or halfway to the outhouse, depending on how much business had to be attended to. If Shelton had ever known McCoy's given first name, he had long since forgotten it. The old man had been called *Papa* for so long, probably because he was the oldest hand on the ranch. He'd already been working at the Double-D when Shelton was hired. To the younger boys, he was much like a papa, and his prematurely gray hair and mustache seemed to fit the picture.

"Mornin', Price," Papa mumbled. He was the only one of the crew who called the foreman by his first name, instead of *Boss* like the rest of the men.

"Mornin', Papa," Shelton returned. "I see we got some visitors durin' the night."

"Is that a fact?" Papa asked and turned to look toward the back of the bunkhouse. "Well, damned if we didn't. I didn't even hear 'em when they came in. Triple-G?"

"I reckon they are," Shelton answered. "Don't know who else it could be. I told Perley last night to come on back here if they changed their minds about startin' back to Texas from Texarkana."

"They was awful quiet about comin' in," Papa said. "I never heard a peep outta any of 'em."

"Shoot," Shelton japed, "you wouldn'ta woke up if they'd fired off their guns."

"Maybe not," Papa said, chuckling over the thought. He was about to complain that it was getting to where he thought he might be needing some eyeglasses as well as an ear trumpet, when one of the bodies in question stirred and set up.

Seeing them talking, he pulled on his boots and went to join them.

"Possum, ain't it?" Papa asked.

"That's right," Possum answered. "Good mornin' to ya."

Shelton and Papa returned the greeting, then Papa said, "See there, Price. I might be gettin' where I can't hear or see, but I ain't lost my memory."

"I reckon so," Shelton replied, then asked Possum. "You boys find everything you went lookin' for last night?"

"Yes, sir," Possum answered, "I expect so. That little saloon was as busy as you said it would be on a Saturday night. We had us a couple of drinks and ate some supper that weren't near as bad as it looked. We decided we'd accept your invitation to come on back here afterward, instead of settin' out for home, though."

By that time, Perley was awakened by their talking, and he pulled on his boots and joined them. "Mornin'," he greeted them, nodding to Shelton and Papa in turn.

"Sleep all right?" Shelton asked.

"I sure did," Perley answered. "That bunk was right comfortable. The only thing is I woke up with a bad cravin' for a cup of coffee."

"I expect you can get a cup by now," Shelton said. "You might even be able to get some breakfast. Poison oughta be ringin' that bell any minute now. I'll check with him and see."

"I'm gonna have to make some room for it before I drink any coffee," Perley said.

"Me, too," Possum said.

"Me, too," Papa echoed. "The outhouse is a single seater," Papa informed them. "But if you ain't gotta do nothin' but sprinkle a little, we can just go around back of the bunkhouse where nobody that might be up at the main house could see us."

"I'll go check with Poison," Shelton said while Perley, Possum, and Papa filed out the door behind him and turned to go around behind the building to submit to nature's insistence.

When they were finished, they returned to find Shelton waiting to go with them into the cook shack for breakfast. The cook told them to grab a plate and he'd fill it for them.

"I'll pour 'em some coffee," Shelton volunteered. Then he paused to consider the line. "Poison, Perley, Possum, and Papa," he recited, then chuckled his amusement. Since he was not known for any particular sense of humor, they all stared at him in wonder. Before he had a chance to explain, they heard a shout from the bunkhouse.

"Hoo-boy! Perley Gates!"

Shelton recognized the voice as that of Billy Dean. It was followed by the sound of everybody in the bunkhouse getting up, a sound unusual for a Sunday morning.

"Perley Gates!" Billy blurted out again.

"That's Billy yellin' in there," Shelton said. "That young pup musta got drunk as a skunk last night."

In only a few minutes' time, Billy came rushing in the doorway of the cook shack.

"Billy, what the hell's the matter with you? Are you drunk? Knock off that yellin'. It's Sunday mornin', for Pete's sake, they'll hear you up at the main house."

Billy stopped immediately and stood staring at Shelton in amazement for a few seconds before asking, "Ain't they told you?" Not waiting for Shelton's answer, he stated, "They ain't told you!"

"Ain't told me what?" Shelton demanded. "How much did you drink?"

Billy chortled his delight when he realized why Shelton didn't understand. "Boss, you're settin' with the fastest gun in the county! Last night in the Last Chance Saloon, Spade Devlin drew on Perley and Perley cut him down before Spade could get his gun outta the holster." He grinned, tickled by the stunned expression on Shelton's face. "And he ain't said the first word about it, just like it was somethin' to do on Saturday night, if you can't think of nothin' else to do."

Shelton knew there must be a catch to the story and Billy was having a good laugh over it. Finding it hard to believe, the foreman turned to Perley. "What is he talkin' about?"

"I'm afraid what Billy said is true," Perley said. "Possum can tell you. We tried to avoid any trouble with that fellow, Devlin, but he didn't give me any choice."

"Was that fellow, Thacker, there?" Shelton asked.

"Yep," Perley answered. "He was the one who brought Devlin into it." Perley went on to explain the setup they were planning for his death, a penalty he thought a little severe for stepping ahead of him to get a table. "We did our best to leave, but Devlin gave me no choice. We didn't tell anybody we were headin' back here to the Double-D. We didn't wanna bring any trouble down on you folks."

Billy was impatient to make sure Shelton appreciated the whole picture. He couldn't hold it any longer, so he proceeded to set the scene. "He ain't tellin' you everything, Boss," he inserted. "Perley was walkin' to the door, had his back to Spade when Spade went for his gun, Possum yelled, and Perley spun around and cut Spade down like a stalk of corn."

Billy would have been even more amazed if he could have known Perley had heard Devlin's hand even before Possum's warning. Had he not, Perley might not have made it in time.

Billy stood grinning, certain now that Shelton understood the magnitude of what Perley had done. Shelton looked for a few moments at the seemingly unassuming young man. Then, afraid that Perley was too modest to give an honest answer, he asked Possum, "Is he really that fast with a six-gun?"

Shelton had asked seriously, so Possum answered

equally serious. "Yes, sir. He's the fastest hand with a gun since God invented lightnin'."

Shelton looked back at Perley, who seemed extremely uncomfortable. Still talking to Possum, he said, "I'm surprised we haven't heard of him before this if he's that fast."

"That's because he ain't lookin' to be famous for killin' people," Possum replied. "Perley will do anything he can to avoid a shootout with somebody. He ain't suicidal. He'll pull his gun to keep from gettin' shot, but he ain't wantin' no reputation."

Feeling extremely uncomfortable and thinking his peculiarity had been discussed far more than necessary, Perley felt compelled to apologize. It seemed to him he was always apologizing for having been caught in a tight situation where his natural ability with a gun was the only way out. "I'm sorry this had to happen in your little town." He then repeated, "We didn't tell anybody we were coming back here to the Double-D. So I'm hopin' you folks don't hear anything more about it."

"I appreciate that, Perley," Shelton told him. "We ain't exactly on friendly terms with that bunch of outlaws ridin' with Duke Thacker. We've had some trouble with his men. They killed one of our men in a fight in that damn saloon and I ain't ever been able to replace him so far. We've tried talkin' to the town marshal about it, but that drunken fool gets his whiskey outta Duke Thacker's pocket. Thacker helps himself to our cattle to feed that gang of gunslingers. The men who work for the Double-D are good men, but they're cowhands, not much of a match for Thacker's outlaws. We try to keep our cattle a good ways south of Texarkana, so it won't be so convenient for

Thacker's men to rustle 'em. His answer for that seems to be to send some rustlers down here in the middle of the night and cut out ten or fifteen head, so they don't have to come so often."

"That sure don't sound good a-tall," Possum commented. "I'm glad we didn't say nothin' to make him think we had any ties to the Double-D. Else that mighta give him an excuse to raid your stock." He looked at Perley. "Reckon we need to get started back home?"

"I reckon," Perley answered. "Soon as Sonny gets through eatin' his breakfast and I have one more cup of this coffee."

"I'm through, Perley," Sonny sang out. "I'll go bring up the horses while you drink your coffee."

"I'll give you a hand," Billy Dean said, still feeling a high from the show Perley had put on in the Last Chance. "Don't worry, Boss. I'll make sure they just take their horses," Billy japed. The two young men headed down to the creek to cut out the Triple-G horses.

"You gonna check the brands on these horses?" Sonny joked as he started separating them.

"I might," Billy laughed. "You ever see Perley shoot like last night before?"

"I've seen him shoot in a couple of different situations," Sonny said. "It's always like you saw last night. Somebody makes him draw, then when he does, it's so fast it's hard to see it."

"He must have to practice a lot to keep up that kinda speed." Billy commented. "I still can't believe how fast he cut Spade down. It was like you say, so fast it was hard to see it."

"That's the strange part," Sonny said. "Perley don't

practice a-tall. He don't know why he's as fast as he is. It just comes natural to him."

"Dang!" Billy exclaimed. "That's really somethin', ain't it?" They picked out the horses Sonny identified and started leading them back to the bunkhouse where their saddles were.

"Which one of these horses is Perley's?" Billy asked.

"That bay you're leadin'," Sonny answered and nodded toward the horse. "He's Perley's favorite horse. His name is Buck."

Billy turned halfway around to look at the horse. "So that's ol' Perley's horse, is it? He's a fine-lookin' horse. Why does he call him Buck?"

"'Cause he does," Sonny said with a grin, answering the question with the same answer Perley always used.

Misunderstanding, Billy asked, "'Cause he does what?"

"Bucks," Sonny answered.

"He bucks?"

Sonny nodded, so Billy asked, "Ain't he been saddle-broke?"

Sonny nodded again. "Well, I reckon you'd have to say he has, but not for anybody but Perley."

"You sayin' can't *nobody* stay on him but Perley?"

Sonny nodded.

Billy thought about that for a moment before stopping and turning to look at Sonny. "I bet I can stay on him. He wouldn't be the first wild one I've stayed on." Still impressed with the lightning-like reactions that cut Spade Devlin down, Billy was inspired to be the only other person who could ride Perley's horse. "Here." He held out the reins to the other horse he was leading.

Sonny didn't take them right away. "You gonna try to ride Buck?"

"I ain't gonna try," Billy said. "I'm gonna ride him."

Sonny still didn't accept the other horse's reins. "I don't think you wanna try that. Shoot, he ain't even got his saddle on him yet. You'd better wait and ask Perley if you can ride Buck, but he's gonna tell you no. He's gonna tell you the same thing I just told you."

"I don't need no saddle," Billy insisted. "I'll ride him bareback. I'm just gonna ride him around the bunkhouse a couple of times. It ain't gonna hurt him. Have you ever rode him?"

"No, I told you, ain't nobody but Perley ever rode him. I ain't ever tried."

That's all Billy wanted to know. He dropped the reins of the other horse to the ground and pulled Buck's reins back over his head. Grabbing a handful of the bay's mane, he jumped on his back. With a flip of the reins and a nudge of his heels, he said, "Come on, Buck. Let's go!"

Buck stood like a statue, his eyes rolling back to look at Sonny, standing shocked at the sight of Billy on the horse's back flailing his arms and kicking his feet.

"Billy," Sonny said calmly, "get down off that horse while you still can."

The cowboy just grinned at him but only for a few moments more. For Buck suddenly reared up on his front legs with his hindquarters almost straight up, throwing Billy over his head to land hard on his side. Unfortunately, due to his flailing arms grabbing for anything in midair, he landed with one arm under him, breaking it cleanly above the wrist. Beating Sonny to the victim, Buck walked to stand over him and calmly sniffed Billy's injured arm before turning his head toward Sonny to see what he was going to do about it. Sonny's reaction was to yell for Perley.

Startled by what certainly sounded like a cry of alarm, half of the crew eating their Sunday breakfast came out of the cook shack in response, Perley and Possum among the leaders.

Seeing Billy lying on the ground, Perley exclaimed, "What happened?"

"Billy tried to ride Buck," Sonny answered.

"Didn't you tell him . . . ?" Perley started as he walked toward Billy.

"I told him not to," Sonny insisted as he walked along beside him. "He just jumped on him. I couldn'ta stopped him if I'd tried."

Shelton, already kneeling beside the injured man, ordered everybody back and sent a man back to the cook shack to get the cook, who also served as the doctor. "Tell him Billy's arm is broken," he called after him. "Just try to lay easy," he told Billy. "That arm don't look too good, but the bone ain't stickin' outta the skin. It is broke. There's a lump stickin' up in your arm. We oughta be able to pull it back in place." He shook his head as he looked at the broken arm, thinking he was now another man short at a time when they were going to have to move all the cattle to the south range, all the way to the river. "How the hell did you break your arm?"

"I got throwed off a horse," Billy gasped between sharp pains running up his wrist to his shoulder.

Shelton didn't understand. He looked around him for a saddled horse, and seeing no horses but those standing quiet and peaceful with Sonny holding them, he asked, "What were you doin' on a horse? Where is it?"

"It's this bay here, Mr. Shelton," Sonny spoke up. "He tried to ride Buck and Buck won't tote nobody but Perley."

"It ain't no fault of his," Billy groaned. "He told me not to get on the blamed horse, but I jumped on him anyway. I thought I could stay on him."

"I swear, I oughta shoot you for bein' so dumb," Shelton said. "We're short of men already and you go and do a fool thing like this." He moved back out of the way when Poison Pearson came out with his little satchel of medical instruments. "See if you can fix it, Poison. If you don't think you can set it, I reckon we'll have to put him down, like we would a horse."

He was joking, but to Perley, it sounded as if he really meant it. He thought back to the foreman's complaint about being shorthanded.

Concerned that Shelton would blame him for Buck's belligerent behavior, Perley stepped up beside Shelton. "I'm just as sorry as I can be about this, Mr. Shelton. Buck's always been like that. I raised him from a colt and he never would let anybody stay on him but me. And believe me, a lot of people have tried. There's only one I know of and that didn't make no sense a-tall. He just decided he'd let a lady friend of mine sit on him, and even she ain't tried it since. He might not let her now. Other than that little flaw, he's the best darn horse I've ever rode. And to tell you the truth that little habit of his has come in handy a time or two when somebody tried to steal him. I'm just sorry, your man, Billy, didn't listen to Sonny when he warned him about Buck."

"It ain't no fault of yours or Sonny's," Shelton assured him. "Billy said Sonny warned him not to get on that horse. He was just too damn hardheaded to listen. "It's just a bad time for me to lose another man." They were interrupted then by a call from Poison.

"I think we oughta be able to put that bone back in place," Poison said. "I'm gonna need some help, though." Everyone gathered around Billy, anxious to help out. No one was needed but Shelton, however. Following Poison's instructions, he took a firm hold of Billy's injured arm, just above the elbow. Then Poison took a firm grip on Billy's wrist and looked at Billy. "You ready?"

Billy said that he was, but he was not too convincing.

Poison asked, "You want a shot or two of whiskey first? I keep some for medicinal purposes."

Billy said he didn't need anything, whereupon several of the onlookers immediately complained of feeling faint and needing a little help.

"A little glass of sausage gravy is best for them kind of faintin' spells," Poison told them. "Soon as I get done here, I'll fix you up with a shot."

"Never mind," Papa McCoy declared. "I'm already feelin' better." His remark brought forth a round of chuckling from the rest of the gallery.

While everyone was still laughing, Poison looked at Shelton and nodded. With no further warning, Poison clamped down with both hands and pulled as hard as he could on Billy's wrist. Billy clenched his teeth and turned white as a sheet, but he didn't utter a sound as Poison continued to pull until the bone slowly came back to what appeared to be its original position.

Letting up on the pressure, Poison felt Billy's arm to

determine if the two ends of the broken bone had fit back properly. "Near as I can tell, that bone's gone back the way it was. I'll put a splint on it and wrap it real good. You ain't gonna be able to use it a-tall for six or eight weeks. It'll swell up pretty much for a few days, and when the swellin' goes down, I'll tighten that splint up real tight."

"What if it gets to bleedin' real bad in there where it broke?" Billy asked. "Can I get blood poisonin' or somethin' serious like that?"

"Ain't no problem," Poison answered casually. "If that happens, I'll just have to cut your arm off." He paused for Billy's reaction, then continued. "Right below your chin. . . . Nah, yours ain't the first arm I ever set. It'll do just fine. One of you boys cut me some slats for a splint."

Billy looked up at Shelton. "I'm awful sorry, Boss. I reckon I done an awful dumb thing. I know how short-handed we are right now, but I never thought somethin' like this would happen to me. I ain't gonna be no good for you till this arm heals up, so I don't expect to get paid till I can work again. I've got a little money left. Maybe I could pay you for my grub and my bunk."

The chatter died out a little when the other hands understood what Billy was saying to Shelton, and they realized the desperate position he had put himself in. Perley heard it as well and felt sorry that his horse had played the major part.

Shelton looked at Billy and slowly shook his head. "You still ride for the Double-D. Don't worry about nothin' but lettin' that arm heal up. I ain't got no rule about firin' hands who do dumb things, although I might start thinkin' about makin' one."

The meaningless chatter immediately resumed.

Properly impressed by the foreman's sense of compassion, Perley walked over to the horses Sonny and Billy had brought up. He motioned for Possum and Sonny to follow him. "See all the trouble you made?" he asked his indifferent horse while scratching its face and ears.

When Possum and Sonny joined him, Possum commented, "We're gettin' a late start, ain't we? But I don't reckon we're in a big hurry to get back."

"Yeah, I was just thinkin' about that," Perley replied. "They ain't in no big hurry to have us back home, either. I was thinkin' about Shelton's problem a little bit, too, him being short of men and all. I figure he could use some help now, so I might stay on here a while, at least till he can get most of his cattle down to the lower part of his range where the river cuts across it, like he was plannin' to do. I ain't said anything to him about it yet 'cause I wanted to tell you about it first. If you two want to stay and help out, it's entirely up to you. I'm just sayin' that I'm gonna stay."

Possum was the first to respond. "Seems to me that's a right neighborly thing to do. I don't reckon your brothers are holdin' their breath till I get back. So count me in. I'll stay, too."

Sonny laughed to himself upon hearing Possum's decision. It was no surprise. Anybody on the Triple-G could tell you that wherever Perley goes, Possum goes there, too.

"Well," Sonny said after pretending to give it a lot of thought, "that's a long lonesome ride all the way back, so I reckon I might as well stay with you two."

"All right," Perley said, "I'll tell Shelton we're stayin'

a while if we're welcome. Might as well leave our saddles here till we find out, the packhorses and packs, too." He waited until Poison walked Billy back inside the cook shack and the rest of the men dispersed.

Some went back in the cook shack to finish a breakfast interrupted by Billy's accident, others to the barn. It was Sunday, but the animals didn't know it, so they still had to be taken care of.

Turning to see Perley and his men waiting for him, Shelton walked over. "Sorry we ain't showin' you fellows much of a polite send-off, are we?"

"The three of us have been talkin' this over and we figure you might need a little help to move your cattle." Shelton's eyes widened immediately, so Perley continued. "Well, we figured we might stay and give you a hand."

"There ain't no doubt we're gonna have a job to do," Shelton said. "What kinda deal are you proposin'?"

The question surprised Perley. "No deal. We'll just work with your men till we get your cattle where you want 'em. Just feed us is about all we ask and a bunk in the bunkhouse when we ain't on the range." He paused then to think. "And all the coffee we want."

"That's a mighty fine thing you're offerin', Perley," Shelton replied, hardly able to believe it. "I'd accept it in less than a second, but you deserve to know that things are a little rougher than I told you about before. It's a while yet before it's time to get 'em ready for the fall roundup and brandin'. My real problem is to keep from losin' cattle all over the northern part of our range. What I told you before wasn't exactly true. We ain't losin' a few cows now and then to feed Duke Thacker's gang.

He's rustlin' our cows all over the north range and sellin' 'em. By the end of the summer, we ain't gonna have enough left to round up. I lost three men because Thacker told 'em it was gonna be bad for their health if they stayed here. That's the real story. Still wanna stay and help out?"

"'Reckon so," Perley said.

"You're hired," Shelton said. "And I don't feel comfortable with you callin' me Mr. Shelton all the time."

Before he could suggest a first name, Perley was quick to say, "We'll just call you Boss, like everybody else."

"Except Papa," Sonny reminded him.

"Except Papa," Perley repeated.

Chapter 6

"Who the hell is that jasper?" Duke Thacker demanded. "And where'd he come from?" He had not cooled down from the incident in the saloon the night before that cost the life of Spade Devlin. He looked around the table at the blank expressions that greeted him.

Wylie Parker finally spoke up. "Don't nobody know where he came from. They said his name was Perley Gates." He pointed up toward the ceiling. "Sounds like them gates up there but ain't spelt the same, they said."

"That's a bunch of chicken litter," Thacker roared back at him. "Who told you that was his name?"

"That young feller with them boys from the Double-D," Wylie answered, "Billy Somethin'."

"That's some name Donald Donovan made up, just to suck Spade into a face-off." He glared at the men sitting around his breakfast table, his anger spilling from his eyes as he shifted his glare to Ned Bates then. "I don't suppose he gave you a name when he shot Dan Short and Tiny Wilson down, did he?"

"Doggone it, Duke," Ned replied. "I told you how that happened. There weren't much time to introduce ourselves to each other when we rode into that ambush. And I tried to warn you. I told you that man was fast as greased lightnin'."

"A man that fast has got a name, a name Spade Devlin woulda known, and might notta been willin' to face in a fair fight, if he had known who he was really facin'."

"Well, he did tell Spade he wasn't gonna fight him," Lem Pickens choked up the nerve to remind him. "It was Spade that kept after him."

"The hell you say!" Thacker roared. "That was as fine a little piece of bait as I've ever seen. That gunslinger had his partner standin' in the doorway to give him the signal when Spade went for his gun! That whole show was to let us know how fast he was, and I expect it's supposed to be a message to me to leave Double-D cattle alone. But I think it's about time to cut out a couple hundred head and drive 'em across the Red. You boys have been settin' around too long, gettin' fat and lazy.

"Mutt," he yelled at Mutt Thomas. "Take a couple of the boys and go find out where Double-D is grazin' the range north of their headquarters. If you can find enough of 'em bunched together, we'll slip down there tomorrow night or the next and drive 'em across the Red and on up into Indian Territory."

When Ned looked at him, puzzled, unable to guess his intention, Thacker explained what he had in mind. "This year, I'm plannin' to join the big ranch owners. I'm downright weary of rustlin' twenty or thirty cows at a time. I'm plannin' on drivin' my own herd to the railroad to ship east. And the way I'm fixin' to build that herd is by cuttin' out a big part of the ranches in this territory. That's the reason I moved my home base over here, north of this little town. We're gonna hit two or three ranches between here and the Mississippi. There ain't no real cattle ranches up that way, but there's some farms with a hundred head or more. Where I'm plannin' to get most of my herd is from the Double-D. They're workin' more cattle than they can handle, and I'm gonna make their job a lot easier for 'em."

"You think you can really get away with that?" Ned asked. "What about all them different brands?"

"Who's gonna stop me?" Thacker responded. "Double-D has been losin' men every month since last spring's cattle drive. I'll take their cattle while they're grazin' 'em this summer, and by the time summer's over, I'll have a nice size herd to round up this fall, do some brand changin', and get 'em ready for winter. The Double-D brand is easy as hell to change. And when we take those cows to market, every man ridin' with me gets a share of the sale."

Telling Ned about his plans to become a major rancher the easy way served to cool Thacker's anger over the killing of Spade Devlin but only for a few moments. He soon re-kindled the fire he had started. "The rest of you boys keep your eyes sharp. I wanna know if that damn hired gun is still in town." He nodded toward the end of the table at a sinister-looking man, dressed in all black, with a thin black mustache to match. "And that don't mean to call him out if you do see him, Slick."

His remark was met with a smirk from Slick Bostic. "I told you you was wastin' your money when you hired Spade Devlin. He's been around so long he was startin' to rust. I coulda took him left-handed, and I coulda took care of that little problem for you last night. And you wouldn'ta been out no extra money."

"Right now, I need you men to drive cattle. I ain't lookin' to help you build yourselves a reputation as fast guns," Thacker said. "Besides, you musta not been lookin' when that jasper turned and shot Spade. You'd best stick to back shootin'."

"Damned if that ain't the truth, Boss," Lem Pickens blurted. "If that feller hadda been standin' in a tub of sweet cream, he spun around so fast, it 'da turned to butter when he shot Spade."

Thacker got back to business. "Like I said, if Perley Gates, or whoever the hell he is, is still hangin' around, I wanna know about it. If he is, we'll plan a little party for him. But first, Mutt, you and a couple of the boys ride on down there and see where their cattle are bunchin' up."

"You mean today, Boss? On Sunday?" Mutt replied. Sunday was normally a day when they didn't do much of anything.

"Yeah, today," Thacker responded sharply. "Why, was you plannin' on goin' to church or something?"

Most of the others at the table immediately started looking in every direction except that which would give them eye contact with Mutt.

Seeing their reaction, Thacker made the decision for him. "Wylie, you and Lem go with him."

After breakfast at the Double-D cook shack, Price Shelton went to the kitchen door at the main house. Donovan's cook, Annie Hagen, opened the door when he rapped.

"Good mornin, Price," she greeted him pleasantly.

"Mornin', Annie," Shelton returned. "If Mr. Donovan has finished his breakfast, I thought I'd give him a little news he might be glad to hear."

"Yes, he's finished eating. Come on inside and I'll go see if he's finished his shaving. He always shaves after Sunday morning breakfast. You want a cup of coffee while you wait for him?"

"No, thank you just the same," Shelton replied. "I've drank enough already this mornin'. I'll just wait here by the door."

She went into the hall and reappeared within a few moments. "Mr. Donovan said to come on back to the washroom." She led him to the washroom door then left him to go on by himself.

Inside, he found Donovan standing before a high table with a basin of water on it, a razor in his hand, and looking into a mirror hanging on the wall. "Good mornin', Price," he greeted him. "What's on your mind?"

"Mornin', sir. Well, I figured you'd like to know what happened in town last night, but I didn't wanna bother you too early."

Set for some bad news, Donovan resumed his shaving. "Before you tell me how it happened, tell me how many of our men did we lose?" He wished he could prevent his men from ever going to the Last Chance, but he knew it was impossible to keep them away from the nearest saloon.

"Well, sir," Shelton began, "that's what I came to tell you. We didn't lose anybody last night. Thacker lost one. That big-time gunslinger he brought in here to scare the hell out of us, Spade Devlin. He lost him." Shelton couldn't help grinning when he said it.

Donovan's attention was immediately captured. He turned to face Shelton and asked, "How did it happen? Was he shot? Does Thacker know who did it?"

"Oh, he knows, all right. Everybody in town knows. It happened in the Last Chance, just the place Devlin likes for all his killin's. Only, this time, he went down." Shelton was prolonging the mystery of it for as long as he could. He was set to enjoy Donovan's reaction when he told him who shot Devlin.

"Well, who shot him?" Donovan asked impatiently.

"Perley Gates."

"Perley Gates?" Donovan exclaimed. Something more unlikely, he couldn't imagine. He knew the three Triple-G men had successfully protected the herd of horses he had bought from some would-be horse thieves, but he'd assumed it was a result of all three of them in ambush for the outlaws. "How'd it happen?"

"Devlin drew on him and Perley cut him down before he cleared his holster." It had the effect on Donovan that Shelton expected—total disbelief—so he re-created the whole scene for him, as Billy Dean had told the foreman. When he finished, he put the icing on the cake with the news that Perley, Possum, and Sonny had volunteered to stay on to help move the cattle to the south range. "At no pay," Shelton added. "Just bein' neighborly."

For once, Donovan was at a loss for words. He formed a picture of Perley in his mind but could not imagine him as a gunfighter. "That's a helluva thing," he blurted gratefully. "I'm gonna owe the Triple-G more than I can repay.

I still can't figure that young man as a gunfighter. He just doesn't fit the image."

"That's the strange part," Shelton remarked. "He's about the furthest thing from a gunfighter you can find." He went on to explain the person, Perley Gates. "From what I've learned from Possum Smith, Perley is kind of a mystery to his family and everybody else who knows him. Hasn't got a mean bone in his body, has a sharp mind, and lends a helping hand, just like he's offered us. What nobody can explain is his natural reflexes. He was born with defensive reactions like a mountain lion. He reacts before he has time to think about it. In other words, he's a good man to have on your side."

"That's quite a story, if only half of it's the truth," Donovan said. "I'm sorry I'm so late in expressin' my appreciation for his help. I need to thank him personally. When you go back to the bunkhouse, tell him that Matilda and I would like to invite him to have Sunday dinner with us today. You can invite the other two to come with him. Let 'em all know how much we appreciate their help. I'll tell the women we're gonna have company for dinner. You tell him dinner's at one o'clock on Sundays and we're lookin' forward to havin' him."

"Yes, sir, I'll tell him. By the way, Billy Dean broke his arm this mornin'. If you heard a little ruckus outside the cook shack, that's what it was about."

"What kind of ruckus?" Donovan asked, at once suspecting a fight between some of the men.

"It was between Billy and Perley's horse, Buck. Billy tried to ride him, and the horse threw him," Shelton said. "He landed wrong and broke his arm." He left Donovan shaking his head as he turned back to finish his shaving.

Outside the door, Shelton found Annie standing in the hallway, a few feet from the door. "I reckon you heard," he said, guessing why she happened to be standing there. "You better cook a little bit more food than usual."

"I reckon so," Annie replied. "Ain't nothing like finding out a long time ahead about extra mouths to feed."

Shelton chuckled. "Better 'n findin' out right when he comes knockin' on the door." He got serious for a few moments. "This is a good man, Annie, treat him kindly."

"Oh, I'll take care of 'em," she assured him. "Mrs. Matilda will make 'em feel welcome. It'll just be Frances who sits there like they ain't even in the house."

When he returned to the bunkhouse and found Perley and the others still there, talking about Billy's accident, Shelton wasted no time in forwarding the dinner invitation.

Perley's reaction was predictable. "There ain't no cause for those folks to go to all that trouble for us," he replied, clearly not enthusiastic about the prospect. "You tell them that we surely appreciate the invitation, but we'd best eat with the rest of the crew."

"I think it would really please Mr. Donovan if you were to visit with 'em," Shelton urged. "He'd like to do something to show his appreciation. I'd appreciate it if you went."

"It would be awful impolite if you didn't go," Possum added.

Perley thought about it for a minute. "I reckon you're right. We oughta go. Wouldn't hurt us to sit at a dinin' room table like civilized adults."

"*You* oughta go," Possum corrected him. "Not us. Me and Sonny ain't got no business there."

"That's a fact," Sonny seconded. "Me and Possum ain't got no business at the main house for dinner. I'd most likely turn somethin' over in the middle of the table."

"I'll tell Annie you're comin' alone," Shelton said before Perley could come up with any argument. "One o'clock. You'll enjoy it. Annie's a good cook and Mrs. Donovan is a fine lady."

One o'clock sharp, Perley was knocking on the front door of the big two-story house that served as the head-quarters for the Double-D Ranch. He had cleaned up as best he could and put on his extra shirt that he congrat-ulated himself for bringing. He started to rap on the door again but heard the sound of footsteps approaching from the other side, Mr. Donovan he assumed by the sound of a heavy tread. A few seconds later, the door opened.

And Donald Donovan held it wide as he invited Perley to enter. "Welcome, Perley," he said and extended his hand. "Come on in."

"Thank you, sir," Perley replied and removed his hat.

"Come on. We'll just go on back to the dinin' room," Donovan said. "Annie's already puttin' the food on the table. Just follow me." He led the way through the parlor and down the hall.

In the dining room, they found Matilda Donovan and her daughter, Frances, seated at the table.

"Good afternoon, Perley," Matilda greeted. "We're so glad you could join us for dinner today."

Perley had a sinking feeling that told him he was out

of place here. "I hope I ain't late," he managed, afraid that he was, since they were already seated and waiting.

"Not at all," Matilda was quick to reply. "We just came in a minute ago."

"More like fifteen minutes ago," Frances saw fit to remark.

Perley could feel her eyes appraising their dinner guest, and her expression conveyed a sign of rejection. He found himself wishing he had made Possum come with him to share this ordeal. If he had to guess, he would say Frances was close to his age and appeared to be bored with life. He was glad when her mother asked him a question and he could concentrate his gaze on her.

"Donald tells me that your ranch in Texas is about a hundred and twenty miles from here," Matilda remarked. "And that you and just two men drove that herd of horses all the way over here."

Perley didn't know how to answer beyond confirming it. Then she started in with questions about the Triple-G and his family.

Frances interrupted. "I heard you gunned Spade Devlin down in the Last Chance Saloon last night," she stated bluntly.

Perley, as well as her parents, all seemed stunned by the remark. She looked back and forth between them as if puzzled by their reaction. Focusing her gaze on Perley again, she insisted, "Well, didja?"

"That's hardly a subject for dinner table conversation," Matilda Donovan corrected her daughter. "Mr. Gates, I'll bet you don't have a chance to eat meatloaf very often, do you? Meatloaf is one of Annie's specialties. I hope you enjoy it."

"Well, didja?" Frances repeated, her gaze zeroed in on Perley's eyes. "Did he draw first, and you spun around and cut him down before he could clear his holster?"

"Frances! That's enough!" Donald Donovan ordered. "Where do you hear talk like that? Let the man eat his dinner." He looked at Perley and said, "I apologize for my daughter's lack of manners. I hope you ain't offended."

"Not at all," Perley replied. Directing his comments to Mrs. Donovan, he said, "And to answer your question, I ain't ever had meatloaf before. It sure is good. I know I'll be wishin' I had some more of it when I get back home." He glanced back at Frances to find the mischievous young woman directing an impish grin at him.

"I hope I didn't offend you, Perley." She dragged his name out slowly, so it sounded more like *Purely*.

He wondered how she could possibly have some grievance with him. He had never met her before that moment.

"But did it really happen like I just described it?" she asked.

"I don't know, Miss Frances," he answered. "I was kinda busy at the time, so I didn't get to see it myself."

"There, you got your answer," Donovan said. "Well said. Now, will you let the man eat?"

"Yes, Papa," she said, displaying the same impish grin. "Enjoy your dinner, Mr. Gates." She didn't make another comment during the rest of the meal, but the grin seemed to stay in place for the entire time until she excused herself. "I'll be back to help Annie clean up," she told her mother. "Nice to meet you, Perley."

After Frances left, there were more questions about the Triple-G—the ranch itself, Perley's brothers and their families, and what they saw in the future for the ranch. Most of the questions about the family came from Matilda. Her husband talked some about what the plan was for safeguarding his cattle and expressed his thanks again for Perley and his men's help.

As soon as he thought it proper, Perley thanked them for the dinner and took his leave.

As he walked back toward the bunkhouse, a thought occurred to him, and he immediately rejected it. But it did seem like he had just been interviewed as a possible candidate for a husband for their daughter. He thought of all their questions that pertained to his future and it made even more sense. The prospect sent a shiver down his spine. Frances was a comely woman, that was certainly true, but she was a bona fide piece of work for the man who ended up with her. Perley shook his head in an effort to clear such thoughts.

Halfway to the bunkhouse, he changed his mind and decided to go check on Buck. Preferring to start out with him, Perley wanted him ready to go first thing in the morning. Depending on how the day turned out, he would be working with horses out of the remuda, so he wanted to look the herd over to see which ones fit his eye. Walking toward the barn, he decided to look in the tack room to see if Sonny put his saddle in there like he said he would. Just as he approached the barn door, he got a glimpse of Frances Donovan slipping out the back door of the tack room.

What, he wondered, *is she doing in the barn?* It was a common practice for chickens to nest in the barn. Maybe she was looking for eggs. If she was, she had had no luck, for she was not carrying any. In the next couple of seconds, the mystery was solved, for he almost bumped into Billy Dean coming out of the barn, his left arm wrapped in a splint and supported by a sling.

"Perley!" Billy exclaimed. "You surprised me."

"I see I did," Perley said "What were you doin' out here in the barn? You oughta be sittin' in the bunkhouse, restin' that arm."

"Well, I was goin' to, but I needed to check some things in the tack room first,"

Perley grinned. "Frances givin' you a lotta help?"

"Frances?" Billy replied, trying to play dumb. "Whaddaya mean?"

"I just saw her slippin' out the back door to the tack room. Don't see how you coulda missed bumpin' into her."

Billy became immediately flustered, trying to come up with something to say that might be believable, confirming Perley's suspicions more with each attempt.

"Billy," Perley stopped him. "You've got something goin' on with Donovan's daughter. That ain't no business of mine, and I ain't gonna say anything about it to anybody."

"I swear, Perley, I appreciate it. If Shelton found out, he'd fire me today. If her papa found out, he'd shoot me. Him and the missus are hopin' to marry Frances off to somebody with some future, and there ain't nobody like that in these parts."

Perley almost laughed when he thought of the interview they'd conducted with him at the dinner table, but he made no mention of it to Billy.

"Hell, Perley, Frances is a fine-lookin' woman. What was I gonna do when she took a shine to me? Tell her to go away? It's hard to keep her from doin' anything she wants to do, anyway, so I figure I might as well enjoy it." He shook his head as if exasperated. "Right now, she's put out with me because I broke my arm and I'm feelin' kinda puny today. I told her I'd be all right in a day or two, just wouldn't be able to use my left arm."

"Well, your secret's safe with me. You don't have to worry about that. She'd probably like to take it out on Buck for your broken arm, so don't tell her which one he is." He had to grin when he thought about how puzzled he had been over her acid attitude toward him at dinner. She was angry with Buck and angry with him for owning Buck.

"You might be japin' when you say that, but when she was in here a few minutes ago, she was cussin' your horse. And she asked me which one it was. I didn't want her takin' out her anger on a horse, so I told her that horse was somewhere with the horse herd down in the pasture." Billy gave Perley a plaintive look. "I told her it was my fault. Sonny told me not to get on that horse, but she said she didn't care. Said to show her the horse, and she would beat him to death."

"'Hell hath no fury like a woman scorned,'" Perley recited. "I heard that somewhere."

Chapter 7

"Mutt and them are back, Duke," Ned Bates called out from the front porch of the house. "They're pullin' up to the porch now."

"Well, tell 'em to come on back here," Thacker yelled back. "I'm still eatin'."

Within a few minutes, Mutt, Wylie, and Lem entered the kitchen where Thacker was sitting at the table, finishing up a steak. "Cora, throw three more of them good Double-D steaks on the stove. I reckon you boys are hungry."

"You can say that again," Mutt replied and went to the coffeepot to help himself to a cup of coffee while he waited for his steak. Wylie and Lem followed suit.

"You're gonna need another pot," Mutt told Cora Cross. "We done emptied this 'un."

The mournful-looking little gray-haired woman said nothing but took the pot from him and took it to the pump to refill with water. She paused a moment to flip the steaks over before putting new coffee in the pot and placing it back on the stove. "You want beans?" she asked as she placed three empty plates on the sideboard.

Everybody did.

"Well?" Thacker blurted.

"Just like you thought," Mutt said. "They must have two-hundred-fifty or three hundred cows north of that ranch house. Most of 'em are huddled up together over by the river. Ought not be no trouble a-tall to round up the whole bunch and drive 'em off their range in two hours and be halfway to Indian Territory by mornin'."

"You see any sign of anybody watchin' those cows?" Thacker asked. "It bein' Sunday and all, was anybody checkin' on 'em?"

"Not nobody watchin' 'em, and we rode all the way to the river on the east side of their range," Wylie answered him. "We saw a couple of fellers ride past the cattle on the other side of the herd. They wasn't payin' much attention to the cows. Looked more like they was headed to the Double-D. One of 'em was that feller that shot Spade, but they was the only riders we saw all day."

His casual remark about seeing Perley Gates caused a sense of alarm in Thacker's mind. It was not good news that he was still around. It didn't necessarily mean he was going to stay around, just that he hadn't left yet, he told himself. Donovan was not likely to hire a gunslinger.

"I reckon they're all good Christians," Thacker said. "They figure the Good Lord is watchin' their cattle for 'em on Sundays." The fact of the matter was that Donovan's crew was too small to tend all the cattle he had. Thacker took pride in knowing he was responsible for a great part of Donovan's shortage of men.

"When we goin' to get 'em, Boss?" Mutt asked.

"Tomorrow night," Thacker answered. "No use waiting till the damn cows wander back down deeper in his range. We'll head out from here right after sunset."

The others nodded their acknowledgment.

"If you've got your mind set on drinkin', do it tonight. I ain't plannin' to take any drunks on our little party tomorrow night."

"Fair enough," Lem commented. "The rest of the boys has got a head start on us, so we'd best get at it as soon as we finish this supper."

"I mean what I say about that drinkin' tomorrow," Thacker sought to emphasize. "I'm thinkin' any man that looks too drunk to ride, I'll leave behind. Just to make sure, I'll leave him with a bullet in his head."

"I swear," Wylie japed. "I believe he's serious about not wantin' us to drink too much."

"There's always one way to find out for sure," Lem said, "if you feel like testin' him." All three laughed at that remark, knowing Thacker as well as they did.

Papa McCoy had volunteered to act as a guide for Perley Sunday afternoon after the dinner with the Donovan family. Perley was interested in riding the northern boundary of the Double-D range. Since he already knew how far the town was from the ranch headquarters. Perley was interested in riding the northern boundary of the Double-D range. He'd wanted to get an idea of how far it was from the northern range boundary to town.

He had been somewhat surprised when they rode up the river and discovered a small herd of perhaps three hundred cows grazing in a pocket at the foot of a line of low hills. "Did you know this herd of cows was up here?" he asked Papa.

"Yeah, we knew there was a bunch of 'em up here," Papa replied. "Tell you the truth, though, I didn't know there was this many of 'em. We've been so short of men, we couldn't get around to workin' this part of the range. Price talked about it, but we had our hands full movin' the main herd to the southern part of the range."

"I reckon it wouldn't matter that much if you were this close to most towns, but your town has the likes of Duke Thacker and his gang. You know he's a cattle rustler and you've stuck a good supply of cows right under his nose. He oughta be embarrassed because he ain't stole 'em before now. When we get back to the ranch, I'll tell Shelton that Possum, Sonny, and I'll ride up here first thing in the mornin' and move these cows down below the ranch. It'd be good if he could let one of his men ride with us. Four of us could move 'em with no trouble a-tall. If he can't spare one man, the three of us will do it. I wouldn't leave these cattle here another day."

"I expect Price will be glad to lend you a man," Papa said. "Is it all right with you if I ask him to let me go with you?"

"Yes, indeed," Perley replied. "We'd be glad to have you."

When they returned to the ranch for supper, Shelton was the first to ask how their ride went. Perley told him it gave him a better idea of how the northern boundary ran in relation to the town. Then he said he wanted to rustle about three hundred head of his cattle. "Me and Possum and Sonny will be the main rustlers, but I wanna know if I can borrow Papa from you to help us."

Shelton was not at all sure what Perley was talking about until Papa explained that the strays they knew had been drifting too far north had grown to a full-sized herd.

"If it's all right with you," Perley continued, "we'll fetch those cows back to the main herd tomorrow mornin'."

It was unnecessary to point out what an inviting temptation it was to graze that many cattle so close to known cattle thieves. He turned toward Papa and asked, "That many?"

Papa nodded his confirmation.

Shelton wore an expression like that of a man having just been stabbed between his eyes with a knife. "Then you sure have my blessin'. We slipped up on that corner of the range. It's a good thing you two went up there before we fooled around and lost half the herd up there. You need more than Papa to go with you?"

"No, sir," Perley replied. "Four of us can handle it. You're gonna need all the men you've got south of here, if your herd is as scattered as you say." He paused a moment when another thought entered his mind. "What about the main house here? Do you need to leave somebody here with Mr. Donovan to look after him and the women while we're drivin' the cattle downrange?"

"We never have before," Shelton replied. "I don't think Thacker would chance actually threatenin' Mr. Donovan's family, especially since he's been tryin' to paint a picture of himself as a rancher. So far, he ain't made no sign of goin' after Donovan personally. We'll have Billy here to kinda look after things. Billy can do that one-handed. All the rest of us shouldn't be gone for more than a week. They oughta be all right till most of us are back here."

Perley nodded his understanding. He figured Shelton knew the situation far better than he. "You say Thacker is tryin' to make folks think he's a rancher, just like Donovan? Where is Thacker's ranch?"

"He ain't got no ranch," Shelton answered. "Least none that anybody's been able to find. Oh, he's holed up in an old farmhouse north of Texarkana across the Red River. Spends as much time at the Last Chance Saloon as he does on his so-called ranch. He ain't nothin' but a pure and simple outlaw. The only cattle you might find on his ranch will sure as hell be wearin' somebody else's brand. I don't know what he's got in mind to do, but it ain't gonna be any good for the town. I know Mr. Donovan figured Thacker and his gang wouldn't hang around Texarkana long 'cause there ain't anything here to hold him and his gang of outlaws. But he's still here, and he don't show any sign of leavin'. One thing for sure, he's doin' his best to thin out Double-D's crew. I swear, it looks to me like he's thinkin' about a damn range war. I think he's set on takin' over Double-D, land, cattle, everything. And he's got soldiers while we've got boys and old men." Shelton paused abruptly and exhaled a deep breath. "Sorry, I get myself worked up over that sorry piece of crap when I think of the hard work that built this ranch to the state it's in now. To have him come along and decide he'll just take it for himself, well, it kinda makes my blood boil."

"I believe I've got a lot bigger picture of your situation here now," Perley said. "Possum and Sonny and I will help all we can. We'll start by ridin' up the river and movin' those three hundred cows down here to go with the main herd. Then I reckon we'll just do whatever you need us to do after that."

"You're a good man, Perley. We never had any idea we were gettin' such a good deal when we bought those horses from the Triple-G."

Just as Thacker had ordered, the Duke Thacker gang assembled in front of the barn shortly after sundown Monday evening. When everyone was accounted for, they filed out of the barnyard with Mutt leading the way. Riding around Texarkana, he led them to the east, heading toward the river. They followed it south for about eight miles until reaching a low line of hills running east and west.

Mutt signaled a halt then waited for Thacker to ride up beside him.

"About three hundred head on the other side of those hills, all bunched up near the river, and waitin' for us to come get 'em." Mutt turned and pointed back toward the west. "It's hard to make out in the dark, but maybe you can see a cut through those hills about a quarter of a mile back that way. Me and Wylie and Lem figured the easiest thing to do is drive 'em back that way and turn 'em through that cut. We wouldn't have to chase 'em up over the hills and collect 'em again on this side. Whaddaya think?"

"Sounds like the thing to do." Thacker looked up at the sky. "There's gonna be a moon tonight, but we oughta be halfway around Texarkana before it gets high enough to see us. And by that time it'll be high enough to throw some light that'll help us move the cattle." Pleased with the way their plan was working, he said, "Let's go get 'em." He turned to the men behind him. "Nice and quiet," he reminded them. "Let's not spook 'em."

They started up the hill and when they reached the top, Thacker signaled them to halt so he could look the situation over and decide how best to split his men. He wasn't concerned with assigning flank, swing, and drag for the short distance they would be going. And there was not going to be a stampede as they often employed.

He'd paused for only a short time before he asked, "Where are the cows?" For there were no cows in sight in any direction. He turned in the saddle to look at Mutt and repeated, "Where are the cows?"

As baffled as Thacker, Mutt insisted, "They was right here yesterday. Wylie and Lem can tell you that. About three hundred of 'em, all bunched up here with good grass and plenty of water. They wouldn'ta gone anywhere on their own. Double-D musta moved 'em today."

"While we was layin' around waitin' for dark," Lem saw fit to add.

The remark didn't help Thacker's disposition at all, and the first thing that came to his mind was Wylie's report that he had seen Perley Gates riding on the Double-D range. Maybe Donovan had hired him after all, and it was on Perley's order they'd moved the cattle right away.

The more he thought about it, the more it bedeviled Thacker. He figured Perley Gates hadn't been hired to help tend Donovan's cattle, the other two men with him maybe, but not Gates. It was his gun Donovan had hired. And it was for the same reason Thacker had hired Spade Devlin, to methodically thin out his men and eventually put him out of business. "Well, there's one big difference in this war."

"How's that, Boss?" Mutt asked.

Thacker realized he had blurted that last thought out loud. "Nothin'. I was just thinkin' to myself."

The big difference between him and Donald Donovan was that the rancher was an honest businessman who employed honest ranch hands to work his cattle. While he, on the other hand, had no conscience and hired outlaws who would shoot a man for the pleasure of it. With those thoughts still in his mind, Thacker remarked, "Too bad you didn't pull your rifle out and put a bullet in Mr. Perley Gates' back."

"I never even thought about it," Mutt said, surprised. "We was just layin' low to keep anybody from seein' us. You think I shoulda took a shot at him?"

"Yeah, it'da been worth a little money for ya."

"Is that so? How much?"

"A clean shot and nobody sees you, that's worth fifty dollars to me," Thacker answered. "That's my goin' rate for any of you boys who takes that jasper out. Fifty bucks."

"I ain't heard nothin' about this," Mutt said. "How long has that deal been goin' on?"

"Just started today. You're the first one I've told about it."

"Don't tell the other boys about it till I have a chance to run up on him again," Mutt requested anxiously.

"Don't tell the other boys about what?" Slick Bostic asked, having overheard Mutt's request as he pulled up beside them.

"Fifty bucks to the man who kills Perley Gates and gets away with it clean. No witnesses," Thacker told him.

"Fifty bucks for just shootin' him?" Slick asked, already assuming he would be the one to collect it. "It still counts if I call him out and kill him in a fair fight, don't it? There'll most likely be witnesses that see me do it, so there ain't no way anybody can say he was dry-gulched."

"Yeah, that's worth fifty, but I don't advise you to try it that way. He's faster than you." Thacker had to smile to himself and wonder why he had not thought of it before, instead of just encouraging his men to pick fights with the Double-D hands. *I could have saved the money I spent hiring Spade Devlin,* he thought.

"You ain't seen me shoot lately, Boss. I'm a lot faster than I was," Slick insisted.

"Maybe so, but you ain't faster than that gunslinger," Thacker told him, still thinking of the fight in the Last Chance. "Take the easy way. Hide somewhere and shoot him in the back. That feller's got a name we've most likely heard of, and it sure as hell ain't Perley Gates."

Thacker spat the name out on the ground, as if he had tasted something rancid, then got back to business. "Let's ride on down this river a ways, just in case those damn cows drifted that way on their own. They wouldn't hardly have moved away from the water unless somebody made 'em go."

They continued on down the river for about two miles before giving up and turning back toward Texarkana. There were no cows to be seen. It was a bitter pill to swallow for Duke Thacker, knowing he had dawdled too long before deciding it time to pounce on that herd. For one day too many, a nice little chunk of Donovan's herd had been left sitting there just begging to be stolen. He still had it in mind that the cattle would have still been right there had not Perley Gates told Donovan or Shelton, to move them farther away from their northern boundary.

I propose to make you pay for that, Mr. Gates.

While Duke Thacker's gang of would-be cattle rustlers rode home empty-handed, most of them dropping out to visit the saloon they had avoided all day, the Double-D crew was in camp. After a full day rounding up all the strays that had been allowed to wander from the herd for the biggest part of the summer, they were ready to retreat to their bedrolls.

Poison Pearson announced he was preparing to empty the coffeepot so he could rinse it out. Perley and Price Shelton both stepped forward with empty cups.

"I didn't think nobody drank as much coffee as Boss," Poison commented as he drained the pot equally in their cups, "till I met you, Perley."

"I've heard tell that the more coffee you drink, the smarter you are," Shelton commented as they walked back to join Possum.

"I reckon I can't disagree with that," Perley declared and they both laughed.

Shelton sat down cross-legged, Indian style, and sipped away gingerly at the hot coffee. It heated his tin cup hot enough to blister his lip, if he was not careful. Perley judged him to be contented with the results of the day.

Shelton confirmed it when he said, "We had a better day than I expected. By the end of the day tomorrow, we oughta have almost all of 'em grazin' on that range formed right there where the Sulphur River joins the Red. And that's where we wanna keep 'em for the rest of the summer." He tested his cup again and took a bigger gulp of the strong coffee. "You Triple-G boys moved those three hundred cows right along in good fashion. By the end of the day, you were right behind the rest of us, and you had farther to drive those cows. I might wanna hire the three of you full time."

"Better not tell him Rubin has been tryin' to get rid of us for a long time," Possum joked to Perley. "Rubin says it costs him too much for coffee, compared to the amount of work he gets out of us."

During the next couple of days, Shelton would be deciding how many of his men to leave in a line camp on the south range. He also planned to scout the Sulphur River for a few miles from the confluence with the Red, in case he had strays wandering along its banks. Perley assured him that the Triple-G men would stay a while longer until he was satisfied that everything was under control.

Meanwhile, those at the Double-D range headquarters were getting along just fine. As Shelton had predicted, Billy Dean, with only one arm, was managing to look after the small chores. Ordinarily an older man, Clyde Humphrey, took care of those little jobs, but on this occasion, all hands were drafted to help move the cattle. To her parents' surprise, Frances Donovan had volunteered to help Billy with some of the other chores, like slopping the hogs, feeding the chickens, and milking the cow.

Her cooperative spirit had caused her mother to remark to her husband, "Maybe she's finally beginning to grow into a proper lady."

Billy was still sleeping in the bunkhouse as usual, but he had his meals at the main house—not at the dining room table, but at the kitchen table with Annie Hagan. As he'd told Frances when they were "feeding the chickens," he thought he could get used to that life in a hurry. "I ain't gonna be worth a nickel by the time the other boys get back."

Chapter 8

He rode into town a little after noontime. A slender man, his dark features were shaded under a flat-crowned, wide-brim hat. Riding a large Palouse gelding and leading a sorrel packhorse, he walked the horses slowly along the short street of Texarkana until reaching the Last Chance Saloon, where he stopped to dismount and tie his horses to the hitching rail. He took another moment then to look around him at the empty street. He saw no sign of life anywhere in the little town except at the saloon, where three other horses were tied. Although a warm summer day, he wore a black vest over his white shirt, and a Colt .45 six-gun rode high on his left side, the pearl handle facing forward.

Walking across the short porch, he paused at the batwing doors to look the room over before entering, a practice he had long before found to be wise. In the back corner of the room, a couple of men were seated at a table, drinking. Near the center of the room, a three-handed card game was underway. He looked toward the bar to find one man talking to the bartender. He pushed through the batwings and walked over to the bar.

"Howdy, stranger," Shag Felton greeted him. "What's your pleasure?"

"Rye whiskey," the stranger answered.

"Rye it is," Shag replied, took a shot glass from a stack on the bar, and proceeded to pour a shot. He and Lem Pickens, who he had been talking to, watched the stranger toss the whiskey back, then tap the empty glass on the bar.

Shag promptly filled it again. The stranger tossed that one back as well but held on to the glass.

"So," Shag asked, "what brings you to Texarkana? I don't recollect ever seein' you in town before."

The sinister-looking stranger paused to take a thorough look at Lem, then said to Shag, "I'm lookin' for a man, goes by the name of Spade Devlin." He kept his eyes on Lem, as if watching for any unusual reaction when he heard the name.

Lem snorted, his reaction unusual. "Huh. You got here too late to catch Spade."

That was not the kind of reaction the stranger was prepared to act upon. "I was told he came to this town. Has he already gone somewhere else?"

Lem and Shag looked at each other and grinned.

"Yes, sir. Spade's passed through already. I'd tell you where he went, but I ain't sure what part of Hell Spade was shipped to, Shag answered. "I hope he weren't no kin of yours," he quickly thought to say, in case he was. "He was gunned down right here in this saloon. Weren't he, Lem?"

"That's a fact, mister," Lem confirmed. "Right here in the Last Chance."

A definite look of disappointment entered the stranger's

otherwise expressionless face. It was difficult to determine if it was sorrowful, or just a look of inconvenience. "Who shot him? Was it a face-off, or a shot in the back?"

"It's kinda hard to say, ain't it, Lem? You couldn't say it was a fair fight 'cause Spade drew on the other feller when his back was turned."

"That's right," Lem remembered. "He was walkin' out the door when Spade drew on him."

"Who?" the stranger exclaimed impatiently. "Who shot him?"

"Perley Gates." They said it almost in harmony, both watching for the expected reaction from the stranger.

He did not disappoint. "Who?" he asked. When Shag repeated it, the stranger frowned as if he suspected he was being japed.

"Perley Gates," Shag repeated again. "That's the feller's name. Sounds like them gates you hear about up in Heaven, but it ain't spelt the same. Anyway, Spade went for his gun when Perley was walkin' out the door, but Perley turned and shot him down."

When the stranger stood there looking perplexed, Shag asked, "Was Spade Devlin a friend of yours?"

The stranger frowned. "Hell, no. I came here to kill him. He's been runnin' his mouth all over Missouri and Arkansas about how he's the fastest gun in the territory, and I'm tired of hearin' about him. I came to see just how fast he is. I reckon I got my answer. He wasn't fast enough to kill some local gunslinger. I went to a lot of trouble to pick up that blowhard's trail. I'd rather had the chance to show him what fast is with a gun. What was he doin' in this little town, anyway? Did he come here lookin' for this Perley Gates jasper?"

"No, didn't nobody know about Perley Gates when Spade came here," Lem answered. "Duke Thacker hired Spade to come work for him here."

"To do what?" The stranger asked.

Lem hesitated, not sure he should talk about the purpose for bringing in Spade Devlin.

"Just whatever needed to be done," Lem finally said. "You know, one thing and then another." It was pretty obvious he was only confusing the stranger, so he suggested something else. "Look here. I work for Duke Thacker. That's him back there at that table. He's the big feller facin' this way. Why don't you come on back and talk with Duke? He might be better at tellin' you what Spade was supposed to do."

The stranger eyed Lem for a few moments as if trying to determine if he was up to something fishy. Then he turned and looked at the two men at the back corner table. "All right. Let's go talk to your boss." He tossed some coins on the bar for his whiskey and followed Lem to the back of the room.

Having taken notice of the stranger at the bar, Thacker and Ned Bates were openly appraising him as he and Lem approached them.

"Duke," Lem stated, "this feller just came to town, lookin' for Spade." He was about to introduce the stranger then something occurred to him. "I didn't catch your name."

"Kane," he answered, looking straight at Thacker. "What's yours?"

"My name's Duke Thacker. What can I do for you, Kane?"

Lem answered for him. "Kane's just passin' through

town. He came here lookin' for Spade Devlin. I told him Spade's dead. So he's wantin' to find Perley Gates now."

"Is that so?" Thacker replied, already with a good idea why. He asked, anyway. "Whaddaya wanna find Perley for? Was Spade a friend of yours?"

"Never met the man," Kane answered, his somber expression never changing. "Your man said Devlin worked for you. Maybe the man who shot him works for you now. Maybe that's the reason you don't want to tell me where he is right now."

"Perley Gates is fast. What makes you think you can beat that man in a showdown?"

"The same thing that makes me know the sun will set in the evenin' but will rise again in the mornin'," Kane said. "I've seen it happen too many times not to believe it won't always happen. And that's the way it always happens when I face a man. He will go down. It's nature's way. The viper is faster than the toad."

Thacker was impressed. The man talked with the quiet confidence of a holy man. Now that he thought about it, the man reminded him of a viper, with his neat, slender body, his dark features and neatly trimmed mustache.

"No," he said, "Perley Gates doesn't work for me. Spade Devlin did and Perley Gates killed him, but Lem already told you that. Perley Gates is a threat to my business plans, so he has to be dealt with. That's what Spade was hired to do. I've offered any of my men a bonus of fifty dollars if they kill Perley Gates. I'd be happy to make you the same offer if you kill him."

Kane continued to stare somberly into Thacker's eyes without responding to his offer for several long moments, long enough for Thacker to begin to feel annoyed.

Just before he was about to tell Kane so, the viperlike assassin spoke. "So, you want someone to kill the man who killed your hired assassin, right?"

"That's what I said," Thacker answered, irritated by the viper's attitude of superiority.

"I wouldn't kill a mangy dog for fifty dollars," Kane stated flatly. "If that's what his life is worth to you, maybe one of your men will get a chance to shoot him in the back. This Perley Gates person is worth more than that to me. I will seek him out and give him the kind of death he deserves." Kane backed gracefully away, resembling an actor playing a part in an opera.

They might not be able to appreciate the fact that Perley was worth more to him because he'd out-dueled Spade Devlin. And he was not inclined to explain it to them.

"Well, ain't he somethin'?" Ned Bates felt inspired to comment. "I'd pay to see that feller shoot. If he's anywhere near as good as he makes out, it'd be somethin' to see between him and Perley Gates. I wonder how long he's gonna hang around. Nobody knows if Perley Gates is still out at the Double-D or not."

"That's somethin' I need to know," Thacker said. "I'm gonna send some of you boys down there to see what they're doin' if some of their hands don't show up here in town in the next couple of days."

They continued to watch Kane as he paused by the bar. He, in turn, kept a wary eye on the three still at the back corner table. "I didn't see anything resembling a hotel when I rode in," Kane said to Shag. "Is there any place to get a room?"

"Nope, no hotel," Shag answered. "We've got a couple

of rooms upstairs that Mr. Powell, he's the owner, rents out. Duke Thacker keeps one of 'em rented all the time. Sorta his headquarters here in town."

"Thanks just the same. I'll be back for supper and a drink later." Kane walked out of the saloon.

Since it was still early afternoon, he decided to take a look at the stable at the end of the street. If it was reasonably clean, he would sleep with his horse. He didn't care for the prospect of taking one of the two rooms over the saloon, with Thacker and who knew who else in the room next to his. That would be giving a gang of saddle trash too great an advantage over him.

He climbed up on the Palouse gelding and turned his head back toward the end of the street. He passed a small building bearing a sign that proclaimed it to be the jail. It didn't look big enough to house a real jail. *Perhaps there's a cell room in the back*, he thought. It did indicate, however, that there might be a law officer in the town. A little farther up the street, he came to the stable. Pulling the Palouse up in front of it, he was met by Chester Rivenbark, the owner.

"How do?" Chester greeted him. "Need to stable them horses?"

"Yes, I do," Kane replied. "Thought I'd take a look at your accommodations for myself as well."

"Well, step down and come on in," Chester invited. He was proud of the way he ran his stable. "How long you fixin' to stay here in town?"

Satisfied to see that it was well maintained, Kane answered honestly. "That depends on whether or not I find some reason to wanna stay."

Chester nodded as if he understood. "Tell you the

truth, there ain't a helluva lot to interest you in this town, unless you're lookin' for drinkin' and gamblin'. Some of us folks that have a business interest in the town hope it's gonna grow up before very much longer. We've got a railroad, so we oughta attract hotels and other businesses."

He saw in the bored expression on Kane's face that the stranger wasn't really interested in the development of their town, so he changed the subject. "That's a mighty fine-lookin' horse you're ridin' there. You leave him here and I'll take real good care of him. It's been awhile since I've seen one of those horses the Nez Perce bred. I've got three empty stalls. I'll let you pick the one you want, and I'll make sure it's clean and put in some fresh hay."

Not waiting to be escorted, Kane walked back into the stable to have a look for himself. Chester walked along behind him, ready to answer questions, but Kane had none after he was shown the empty stalls. "Put me and the Palouse in this one," he said when he came to the last stall. "Put the packhorse in that one next to it."

"Yes, sir, Mister"—he paused and waited until Kane responded then repeated—"Kane." My name's Chester Rivenbark and you can find me here most any time, except when I go to pick up feed or somethin', and that's right across the street at Johnson's." He pointed in the direction of a feed store, even though they could not see it, since they were standing inside the stable. They quickly agreed on a price with not much hassle, leaving Chester to scold himself for not asking a higher price, but he was glad to get the business at any price.

"I'm gonna take a little ride to look around town," Kane said. "I won't be long. Then I'll leave my horse while I go to supper. What time do you lock up?" Told

Chester usually locked the doors at seven, Kane nodded and said, "Maybe you can let me take a key to that back door, in case I decide to do some drinkin' tonight after supper. I'll pay you in advance for tonight and tomorrow night, if you're worried about lettin' me take a key."

"I reckon I trust you," Chester said, although he wasn't really comfortable with the idea. He was a little uneasy about refusing the request, but didn't want to admit it as something seemed sinister about the man. Chester took a key to the small door in the back of the stable off a large ring of keys and handed it to Kane.

"Obliged," Kane said and slipped it in his pocket. He turned to leave after paying Chester but paused to ask, "Do you know where I'm likely to find Perley Gates?"

Chester was surprised by the question. "Perley Gates. He's the feller that shot Duke Thacker's gunslinger. No, sir, I wouldn't know where you could find him. He ain't been to town but just that one night. If he's still around here, I expect he'll be at the Double-D. That's who he came to town with. There's been some talk that Donald Donovan, he's the owner of the Double-D, finally got fed up with Thacker and his gunmen and bought him a gunslinger of his own. Like I said, that's just some talk. Ain't nobody asked Donovan, as far as I know." He studied Kane's emotionless face. seeing no indication that what the man had just been told had any effect upon him at all.

Chester's gaze fell from that stone-cold face to light upon the shiny pearl handle of the weapon cradled close up on Kane's left side. The weapon seemed as impersonal as the somber man who wore it. That was evidence enough to tell Chester he was standing face-to face-with a deadly killer. He felt how it must feel to stand face-to-face in a showdown with a real gunman.

"How do I get to the Double-D Ranch?" Kane asked.

"That's easy enough," Chester replied. "Ride out past the train depot. You'll see a wagon trail that crosses the tracks a few yards past the depot. It'll lead off to the south and take you right to the Double-D. It's about a twelve-mile ride out there."

Kane changed the subject suddenly again. "I'll bring my horse back before I go to supper." He left the stable to complete his tour of the little town.

As he had said, Kane was not gone very long before returning to release the Palouse gelding into Chester's corral with instructions to feed the horse a portion of grain when he put him in his stall, and a portion for his packhorse as well. He went from there to the Last Chance Saloon, since that was the only place in town where meals were served. He recognized none of the handful of customers as any he had seen when he was there earlier. It was his guess they were the regular customers who came in almost every day for a drink of whiskey and maybe a few hands of cards. Not one of them resisted the urge to stare openly at the stranger.

Shag Felton greeted him at once. "Howdy, Kane. I was wonderin' if you'd be back to see us."

"Is that so? Why is that?" Kane replied.

Thrown a little off balance by Kane's somber reply to his greeting, Shag answered, "Why, I don't know. I mean, I was just wonderin' if you mighta passed on through town. You know, 'cause you missed Spade Devlin and Perley Gates, too."

"I'm not in a hurry," Kane said, "and decided to come buy some supper. I was told I could buy something to eat here."

"Right, you sure can. I'll tell Bertha she's got a customer for supper. You want me to pour you a drink before I go tell her?"

"No, I'll have a couple of drinks after I eat supper," Kane told him, then walked over and sat down at a table next to the wall.

Shag relayed the supper order, and in a few minutes, the huge woman came out of the kitchen carrying a plate of food. Sweating profusely from standing over a hot stove, she paused at the end of the bar and shot an impatient look in Shag's direction. He immediately pointed to Kane across the room. She walked the plate over to his table and asked if he wanted coffee. He said he did, and she did an about-face to go get it. While she was gone, he poked around on the plate with his fork but did not sample it.

When she returned with his coffee, he asked, "What is this?"

"Hash," she answered.

"What did it start out as?"

"A goat," she snarled.

"I don't eat goats," he said.

"Then you don't eat here," she informed him and picked up the plate.

"Leave the coffee," he ordered when she started to

pick up his cup. "What do you serve with this goat crap? Biscuits or cornbread?"

"Cornbread."

"Bring me some of that," he said.

She curled one side of her mouth up in its customary sneer and returned to the kitchen where she dumped his plate of hash back into the pot. Pulling a pan of cornbread off the edge of the stove, she cut a couple of square pieces, put them on the plate that had held the hash, and started out of the kitchen but stopped to think some . . . then picked up each one of the cornbread squares, patted it gently under her sweating armpits before putting it back on the plate, and carried the plate of cornbread back to him.

"Enjoy."

Chapter 9

"I brought you some more coffee," Bertha announced when she arrived at his table again. "I see you ate the cornbread." That was the real purpose of her return with the coffeepot. She was curious to see if he ate it and how he liked it. "Was it all right? I tried to pick out two good pieces for you, since that was all you was gonna eat."

Wearing his usual sober expression, he pushed his coffee cup over toward her. "It was too salty, but I had to eat something or starve."

"I reckon you can't please everybody," she commented as she refilled his cup. "I'll most likely cook somethin' you'll like better tomorrow, if you're still in town." She returned to her kitchen just as Duke Thacker and a couple of his men walked into the saloon.

"Lookee yonder, Duke." Ned Bates nodded toward the wall opposite the bar. "The Undertaker is still in town." *Undertaker* was the name some of the gang had given Kane, due to his grim persona and confident nature.

"How long has he been here?" Duke asked Shag when they walked past the bar.

"Almost an hour," Shag answered. "He asked for some supper, but he sent it back when Bertha brought him a plate. Didn't suit his fancy, I reckon."

Thacker chuckled at the thought. "He's lucky Bertha didn't yank his skinny butt outta that chair and jerk a knot in his backbone."

"Even Bertha knows better than to rile that killin' machine," Ned Bates commented.

"Hell," Slick Bostic spat out. "You shoulda let me take care of that cocky little rooster the first time he stepped in here. Talkin' like he's gonna cut down every fast-draw in the whole country. Wonder if he's gonna take care of Mexico and Canada after he finishes here."

Thacker ignored the comments and started walking toward the back of the room.

"You'd best be satisfied to leave that viper be," Ned told Slick as they walked behind Thacker to his favorite table. "He's fast. Faster than Spade was, I expect."

"Hell, I was faster than Spade was," Slick complained.

The subject of their conversation seemed to take no notice of their arrival, concentrating on his coffee instead.

"I tried to tell Duke that," Slick continued. "I coulda saved him the money he spent gettin' Spade to come out here."

"Bring us a bottle, Shag," Thacker called out and turned to face Slick. "I'm tired of hearin' your constant complaining and cryin' about how fast you are. Now, you might beat me or Nate, here, or some of the other boys, but you ain't grazin' in the same pasture as killers like that feller over there. If you wanna prove me wrong, maybe you can get the Undertaker to face you in a shootout. I'll wish you luck, but I'll put my money on Kane."

Thacker remained standing with his gaze fixed on Slick, awaiting his reaction.

Quite accustomed to never having his claims taken seriously, Slick hesitated to respond at first, not convinced that Thacker really meant what he'd just said. "You sayin' it's all right with you if I call this jasper out?" He felt certain Thacker had forbidden him before because he didn't want to chance losing him. Maybe now, he had changed his mind, and that thought tended to arouse Slick's anger.

"Yeah, it's all right with me," Thacker responded. "I ain't your Lord and Master. If you wanna stick a gun to your head and blow your brains out, I ain't gonna stop you. Callin' this feller out amounts to the same thing as suicide, so if you're at peace with the world, go ahead and do it."

Ned stepped up close to Thacker and whispered, "You sure you wanna let the fool do that? We'll be short another man."

"We'll be short a pain in the ass," Thacker replied. "I can do without that." Back to Slick then, he asked, "So, what are you gonna do?"

"I'm gonna show you I wasn't blowin' smoke when I kept tellin' you how much faster I am now. When I put an extra airhole in this jasper's head, I'll expect to be worth a lot more money to ride with this gang."

"Well, if you're sure that's what you want," Thacker said, and nodded in Kane's direction. "Yonder he sets. What are you waitin' for?"

"You think I'm bluffin'," Slick said, and started across the room toward the one man seated at a table against the wall.

With no change of expression on his stone-cold face, Kane's eyes shifted up to watch the man approaching his table. Making mental notes of what he saw, he formed a picture of a half-fast gunslinger hoping to make a name for himself. He shifted his gaze beyond Slick's heavy-footed approach to the table in the corner behind him and the two men watching from there. *A setup?* he wondered but decided not. *Just a stupid decision by an ignorant clod*, he concluded. He shifted a little in his chair, just enough to give his right arm free movement and waited.

"It's time you was leavin'," Slick declared as he marched up to the table.

"I haven't finished my coffee yet," Kane responded calmly. "It'll be a little while."

"You've finished it when I say so, and I say *now*," Slick came back. "So get your sorry behind outta that chair and get outta here."

Still speaking calm and unhurried, Kane asked, "Did your boss send you over here to tell me that?"

"Hell, no!" Slick blared. "*I'm* tellin' you that! So, get yourself outta that chair and drag your butt outta this saloon. If you don't, I'm gonna shoot you down right here."

"All right." Kane slid his chair back and got to his feet. To Slick's surprise, he walked past him toward Thacker's table, leaving him confused and with no choice but to turn around and follow him. He reached the astonished two men at the back corner table and asked Thacker a question. "Did you send this fool over to my table to tell me to get out of here?" When Thacker failed to answer at once, Kane asked, "Have you got some kind of problem with me?"

Recovering from Kane's unexpected reaction, Thacker smiled at him. "I've got no problem with you. If I did, I wouldn't have said anything to you. I'da just shot you where you were settin'." He pointed to Slick. "He's got the problem with you. He's pretty sure he's faster with his gun than you are with that pearl-handled one, settin' backward in the holster."

Thacker glanced at Slick. "You still wanna call him out, Slick?"

"You're damn right I do," Slick said, his anger fanned by having been made to look foolish. "I'm callin' you a lowdown yeller dog and you ain't fit to sit in here where men drink."

Kane did not respond to the insults, his calm manner never changing. "I should warn you," he said, talking directly to Thacker, "I don't indulge in playin' games with every fool who thinks he's fast enough to earn a name for himself by killing other fools. If I draw my weapon, I intend to shoot it. And if I shoot it, I aim to kill." He looked back at Slick. "Is that understood?"

"Yeah, that's understood," Slick blurted. "Now, enough talkin'. You ain't talkin' your way outta this one." He walked into the middle of the large room where there were no tables and took his stance. "Come on, big shot," he said and eased his six-gun up and down a couple of times to make sure it was riding free and easy. "I ain't got all day."

"You're right," Kane told him, "you've already used up all your day." He walked out into the middle of the room and turned to face the grinning outlaw. "Whenever you're ready."

It was a small affair as far as gunfights go—a total of nine spectators to watch the face-off, including Shag behind the bar, and Bertha standing in the kitchen door.

After a few seconds passed, Kane repeated, "Whenever you're ready."

Slick made his move.

As soon as his hand dropped onto the handle of his pistol, Kane's pistol was drawn and leveled at Slick's chest before Slick's gun cleared his holster. Kane's move was like a well-oiled machine, but he didn't fire. "I'll wait," he said calmly.

In complete shock, Slick panicked and cleared his six-gun from his holster. Before he could raise it, Kane shot him through the heart. Slick spun around, dropped to his knees, then fell, crashing to the floor.

Kane turned toward Thacker and calmly stated, "I warned him." He stood ready to react to any further attack.

"That's right, you did," Thacker said. "You ain't got nothin' to worry about from me. This was all his doin'."

Seconds later, Wylie Parker and Mutt Thomas burst through the front door, looking right and left, their guns drawn. Seeing Thacker and Ned standing with Kane, and under no threat, they calmed down enough for Mutt to ask, "What was that shot?"

Lem Pickens appeared in the doorway. "Who got

shot?" he asked when he saw the body in the middle of the floor.

"That's Slick," Thacker said. "He decided he'd try Kane out and found out he wasn't as fast as he thought. Couple of you boys drag him on outta here and lay him across his saddle. We'll take him back to the ranch with us and dig him a hole somewhere."

With each new arrival at the saloon, Kane saw the odds increasing against him and could not be sure if Slick had any close friends in the gang. Had he known what an irritation Slick had been with his constant boasting, he might have thought he had done the gang a favor. He had been given no choice in the face-off with Slick Bostic, and he had realized no gain from the shooting, in fame or fortune.

Kane soon realized, however, that his little display of swiftness had duly impressed Duke Thacker, for he was eager to tell those who had not witnessed the duel about the smooth speed of Kane's draw. Thacker was convinced he had been witness to the two fastest gunmen in the country. After the pitifully simple killing of Slick, who was faster than the average gun hand, and the lightning-like reactions of Perley Gates when Spade drew on him, Thacker could not predict who would be the faster. But he knew it would be a duel he would really like to witness.

"So, Slick finally got to show everybody how fast he was," Wylie Parker commented, "and he turned out to be about as fast as we figured." His assessment brought forth a few chuckles from the others standing around the body.

Kane was surprised by their attitude but decided it

wise to take his leave before they drank enough to fondly remember 'good ol' Slick'.

He was stopped before he reached the door by Thacker's booming voice. "Hold on, there, Kane. I believe I owe you a drink of likker."

"Is that so?" Kane replied, his gaze bouncing back and forth across the room, prepared to react. "How do you figure that?" He knew there was a good chance he was going down, even though he would take two, maybe three, of them with him. He preferred to quietly walk away.

"For gettin' rid of one big pain in the butt for the rest of us," Thacker answered him. Addressing the rest of his men in the saloon, he announced, "Boys, ol' Slick is dead, all on account of him wantin' to shoot it out with Kane. Kane never had no part in baitin' him to fight, and I told Slick that Kane was faster, but he thought he knew better." He paused when Kane stopped halfway to the door, then pressed, "What's your hurry?"

Kane hesitated, but he could read nothing in their faces that indicated the baiting of a trap. "No hurry," he replied. "I can take time for a drink." He nodded to Thacker. "I'm obliged." All was said with no change in the stone-cold expressionless face. He turned, walked to the bar, and picked up a clean shot glass before going back to Thacker's table.

"Have a seat," Thacker invited and picked up the bottle, ready to pour Kane's drink.

Kane placed his glass on the table, pulled a chair back and angled it so there would be no one behind him and far enough away from the table so it would not interfere with his right arm.

Watching the whole procedure with interest approaching amusement, Thacker asked, "You don't trust anybody, do ya?"

"No," Kane answered frankly. "In my business, it doesn't pay."

"What is your business, Mr. Kane?" he paused, then asked, "Is it Kane Somethin', or Somethin' Kane?"

"It's just Kane," he replied coldly.

"Fair enough," Thacker allowed. "What exactly is your business, Kane?" he asked again, although he was pretty sure he already knew. "I wouldn't expect a man could make much of a livin' just ridin' all over the country to see who's fastest with a gun."

Kane almost smiled. "Well, that's certainly true. I'll put it this way. You're offering fifty dollars to have Perley Gates killed. My services come much higher than that."

Curious, Thacker had to ask. "What would your price be to eliminate Perley Gates?"

"Perley Gates is an unusual project," Kane answered. "I don't know who he is, so I don't know what it would be worth to me to take care of him. I suspect Perley Gates is not his real name, but if it is, he's a nobody and you'd be just wasting your money. Go ahead and let one of your men shoot him in the back, if he's as fast as you say he is. I intend to find him, just on the chance I might know who he really is. A few gunmen with known names have made it a policy to avoid me. I suspect one of them might have taken the name Perley Gates as a precaution against my findin' out he's operating in this territory." He paused to toss his drink back, then concluded. "So you see, Mr. Thacker, I won't charge you anything for killing Perley Gates. Because I'm going to kill him, anyway."

"Fine!" Thacker responded. "In that case, I'm gonna wish you the best of luck. I'm gonna warn you, just like I warned ol' Slick, he's more dangerous than he looks."

"Thanks for the warnin'," Kane said with more than a hint of sarcasm in his tone.

"You know, I reckon I'm forgettin' my manners," Thacker said, realizing that he was really enjoying the plot for eliminating Perley Gates. "There ain't no hotel in this town. Where are you sleepin'? With your horse in the stable? You're welcome to bunk in with my boys out at my ranch. Or if you rather stay here in town, there's a room upstairs that's empty."

"Thanks just the same," Kane replied, well aware of Thacker's tendencies to take control. "I'm just fine where I am." He got up from the table. "Thanks for the drink." With that he left the saloon.

Watching Kane walk out the door, Thacker had a solid feeling that Perley Gates was no longer a problem for him. The more he thought about it, the more he was convinced that it was the time to strike the Double-D, while most of their crew were probably on the south range, rounding up their cattle. No reason to wait. He and his men could hit the ranch headquarters tonight. And if Perley Gates happened to be there, so much the better. Maybe he would just capture him and lock him up like a caged rooster, throw him in to face Kane and they could put on a show for him to determine who really was the fastest gun.

That's a helluva idea, he thought.

In the next moment Duke Thacker realized he had arrived at his date with destiny, for he suddenly knew his path to power and riches had been laid open for him. Like the great armies of the past, his army of cutthroats was primed to conquer weaker kingdoms. It could not be clearer to him. The stage had been set for him to virtually walk in, unopposed, and take control of the Double-D while their entire crew was south of there rounding up the cattle that would eventually be his. Donovan was too old to fight for his kingdom, and his pathetic army of old men and young boys, none of whom were trained to kill, would be of little use when thrown against Thacker's hardened raiders. They would sweep into Donovan's unprotected headquarters and take complete control of it so quickly his crew would not even be aware of the takeover for days after it was complete. Most of the Double-D hands would choose not to attempt a counterattack, leaving the foolish few who did to sacrifice their lives uselessly.

And what of the law? None in that remote part of Arkansas. And even if there were, what would the issue be ultimately classified? A range war, which most often settled itself when the shooting stopped, and peace returned. In the years that follow, when it became the biggest cattle empire in Arkansas, no one will care about its violent past.

Thacker smiled. The time to begin all of that is tonight!

Ned Bates sat watching his boss staring seemingly at nothing. Eyes never blinking, Thacker appeared to have released his mind to some far-off place, saying nothing for long minutes. Ned wondered what could be going through that scheming mind that cut him off from the outside world. Wherever Thacker was, Ned was afraid to awaken him. While sitting quietly waiting for his boss to return to the real world, he couldn't help thinking about an earlier conversation with Mutt Thomas—concern about Thacker sometimes talking like he was not thinking straight.

Ned decided to put that out of his mind right away.

Chapter 10

His mind made up, Thacker suddenly grabbed the bottle off his table, then snatched the bottles off other tables where his men were sitting. "No more drinkin' tonight till after we're done!" he commanded. He gave the bottles to Shag. "Stick these under the counter and we'll get 'em when we come back." Turning back to his dumbfounded men, he said, "We're workin' tonight, boys, only we ain't goin' after cattle. We're goin' after a whole damn cattle *ranch.*"

"What the hell are you talkin' about?" Ned Bates reacted.

"I'm talkin' about what we've been lollygaggin' around here for . . . for the past year. *Now's* the time to start this range war! *Right now*—when Double-D's got their hands full and half their crew out chasin' down all their strays. I don't know what the hell we've been waitin' for. It couldn't be a better time to go after 'em."

The reaction of his gang was one of amazement and confusion.

Thacker didn't let them think about it. "Get yourselves

up from there. We're headin' back to the house to get armed and ready."

Long used to obeying his every order, they got up from the tables and started toward the door.

Urging them to hurry, he continued. "We've got a long ride tonight. We need to get packed up with everything we need."

It was surely chaotic, but they all managed to get outside, climb into the saddles, and head for the farmhouse Thacker referred to as his ranch. Some might even cite it as an example of efficiency, the instant mobilization of his 'troop'. Whatever your opinion, the gang was back in the saddle and on the trail to the Double-D Ranch before seven o'clock that night.

Some time after nine o'clock, Thacker held up his hand to signal a halt when lights in the main house of the Double-D could be seen from the ridge short of the barnyard. He sent Lem and Wylie to ride in close to scout the layout. No lights shone in the bunkhouse or the barn, which would indicate the crew was still with the cattle. Wanting to make sure, Thacker waited for his scouts' report before riding in.

The two scouts were not gone twenty minutes before they returned with their report. "There ain't nobody there a-tall," Wylie told Thacker. "Nobody in the bunkhouse. Ain't no sign of anybody."

"I checked the barn," Lem said. "Ain't none of the crew there. There's lights on in the house. Looks like the parlor or dinin' room and the kitchen. I don't believe anybody's here but Donovan and his wife and daughter, and maybe a cook."

"Well, then I reckon we'll just ride on down and pay

'em a visit. Looks like we'll have plenty of time to get ready to welcome their crew of old men and boys when they come back." Thacker gave his horse a kick and led his party of raiders down into the yard. "Ned," he ordered, "take a couple of men and go around to the back to make sure nobody runs out the back door."

He waited to give Ned a little time to circle around the house, then rode his horse up to the front steps and dismounted. With three of his men behind him, Thacker tried the door and found it locked, so he started pounding on the door.

"Who is it?" Donald Donovan called out from inside.

"Open up!" Thacker ordered, "or we'll break the damn door down."

"Who are you? What is your business here?" Donovan demanded.

Thacker stepped aside and motioned for Shorty, a wide bull of a man, to open the door. Shorty lowered his shoulder and ran into the door, splitting the knob and lock from the frame, flinging the door wide open. He was met with a blast of a shotgun in the hands of Donald Donovan.

Donovan was immediately shot down in a hail of return fire and the outlaw gang charged into the house. Screams from the back of the house told the intruders where the women were, so they ran into the dining room where they found Matilda Donovan and her cook, Annie Hagen. The two women stood hugging each other, terrified. Annie held a butcher knife in her hand.

"Whatcha fixin' to do with that knife, honey?" Mutt Thomas scolded.

"Get out of this house," Annie replied, holding the knife in a threatening manner before her.

"Who else is in the house?" Thacker demanded.

"Nobody," Annie answered, thinking Frances was upstairs in her room. "What do you want here?" she demanded. "They don't keep any money in the house."

"Where is my husband?" Matilda was finally able to get up the courage to speak.

"He's back yonder layin' on the parlor floor," Thacker answered her. When he saw her knees buckle and she strained to hold herself up with help from Annie, he said, "He shot Shorty. Didn't give us no choice."

Unable to hold her grief, she cried out her husband's name and sobbed outright. Unable to support her, Annie had to place her knife on the table, so she could use both hands to settle her in a chair.

"Mutt," Thacker said, "pick that knife up before she cuts herself with it."

Mutt stepped forward and picked the knife up, made a few playful slashes through the air with it before stepping back again.

"Lem," Thacker ordered while some of his men rummaged through the rest of the main floor, "go upstairs and see if anybody's up there."

"There ain't nobody upstairs," Annie insisted. "I told you that."

"That you did," Thacker said. "And I believe you, but Lem, here, don't believe everything he hears. Ain't that right, Lem?"

Lem grinned at her before turning and heading for the stairs in the hall.

"And look out you don't walk into another shotgun."

The deep look of concern on the women's faces, told him that Lem just might do that. Distraught and knowing Frances was in her room, the women could only sit there clutching each other's hands, and hope she could somehow escape before they found her. Matilda sobbed anew when she thought of what they might do to her innocent young daughter.

There might have been some relief for Matilda, had she known that her daughter was not in her room as she supposed. Fast asleep in the swing in the arbor next to the creek behind the house, her head resting on Billy Dean's good shoulder, Frances was startled awake by the sound of a shotgun blast. It was followed immediately by a barrage of pistol shots. "What was that?" she exclaimed and came out from under Billy's arm. "That sounded like it came from the house!"

"It did!" Billy blurted, now fully awake. He ran out of the arbor but immediately dropped to one knee when he saw the horses in front and back of the house, some fifty yards away. "They're in the house! It's that Thacker gang! Can't be nobody else!"

In a near panic, he wasn't sure what he should do, but he knew he had to do something. When he thought about the sound of the gunfire they had heard, it was easy to picture Donovan answering the door with his shotgun and getting cut down by the return fire. He didn't share his feeling with Frances. "I ain't even got my gun. It's in the bunkhouse."

"What should we do?" Frances cried. "We can't help them." She had genuine concern for her parents and Annie but knew she and Billy were helpless against the whole gang of outlaws. "We better run before they start searching the whole place and catch us."

"We have to find Shelton and the rest of the men," Billy said as he continued to stare in the direction of the house. "They haven't started searchin' the barn or the stable or the bunkhouse yet. We've got to get to the stable and get my horse saddled. Come on!" He grabbed her by the hand and started running along the creek.

She didn't protest and soon dropped his hand so she could run freely along the dark creek bank.

"You're gonna have to help me with the saddle. I can't do a damn thing with my left arm," he told her. "If we're lucky, maybe we can get a good piece away from here before they start searching the whole place."

They stopped directly behind the stable and looked back toward the house to make sure all the outlaws were still inside. That appeared to be the case, so he took her hand again and they ran across the open space between the stable and the creek. Once safely inside the back door, Billy paused only a moment to see if anyone came out of the house. There was no sign of anyone, so they went directly to the tack room to get the saddles.

"We'll saddle Spunky first, then we'll cut that little mare you like to ride outta the corral after Spunky's ready to go," Billy said.

Dragging their saddles behind them, they hurried between the stalls until reaching the one where Billy had put the buckskin gelding he had given the name, Spunky. Doing the best he could with only one good arm to work with, and with help from Frances, he managed to saddle the horse. "Now, let's get you a horse. Then I'd best run over to the bunkhouse to get my six-gun."

"Your rifle's in your saddle sling," she reminded him.

"Yeah, but with just one good arm, it'll be a whole lot easier to use a handgun," he replied.

"I'll use the rifle then," she declared. "Let's get my horse."

They ran to the corral where the mare was with eight other horses. Unable to use a rope, Billy started to open the gate to walk in and get the horse.

Frances stopped him. "Billy! They're coming!"

He turned to look toward the house and saw what had alarmed her. Four of the outlaws had come out the kitchen door and were already walking toward the stables.

"Ohhh, hell," Billy muttered. "We've got to get outta here!" He put the latch back down, grabbed her hand again, and they ran back inside the stable. He took a quick second to throw her saddle on a side rail so it wouldn't be found in the middle of the alley, then grabbed the saddle horn with his good hand and climbed up into the saddle.

She stood ready, and when he was seated, she put a foot in the stirrup. He took her hand and pulled her up behind him. As soon as she was settled, he rode the buckskin out the back door, keeping the stables between them and anyone coming from the house.

Clear of the stable and barn, they rode away in a straight line, the ranch buildings blocking the view of anyone behind them. Asking for a fast lope from the buckskin, they continued on across the prairie on that same line for about a mile before Billy reined the horse back to a brisk walk. Free to turn in any direction then, he set Spunky on a track that would take them straight to the confluence of the Red and Sulphur rivers. He was pretty sure he would find most of the cattle there, and consequently, most of the men. The only problem was that it was a distance of about fifteen miles.

Once they had ridden far enough to feel sure their escape hadn't been discovered, Billy let Spunky drop into a comfortable walk, and both riders relaxed the tension they had been traveling under.

It was when she no longer felt under immediate danger that she began to lament the fate of her parents. "What could we have done to help them?" she kept asking Billy. "I feel so guilty for going to sleep."

"If we hadn't gone to sleep, I expect I'd most likely be dead and you'd be wishin' you were," Billy said.

"Do you think Papa's dead?"

"Might as well tell you what I think is true," Billy answered. "I expect Mr. Donovan was killed right after we heard that shotgun go off. I hope I'm wrong, but I don't think I am. A whole lotta pistol shots went off right after that."

"What do you suppose they'll do with Mama and Annie?" she asked then.

"I ain't got no idea," Billy declared, "but they ain't gonna want any witnesses to what they're doin' at the Double-D tonight. They might just keep 'em prisoner to cook and do for 'em. I reckon we'll have to see what Boss Shelton has to say about it and see what we're gonna do."

They continued on through the night at the same steady pace. Billy knew the buckskin could make the whole distance with no trouble, but they stopped for a short rest at a wide stream because of Frances' earnest need to visit the bushes. Billy let Spunky drink.

When they started again, Billy walked a few miles, since Spunky was carrying double.

They had been gone from the Double-D about two and a half hours when Billy spotted a tiny red dot in the distant darkness. He could feel Frances' head against his back, her arms around his waist as they continued toward the small campfire and knew she had gone to sleep.

They reached the fire, but no one was there. Billy stopped his horse near the fire and waited.

In a few moments, he heard, "Billy?"

Papa McCoy stepped out of the darkness, his rifle ready to fire.

A moment later, Wilbur Cash stepped into the light from the other side of the fire, also with his rifle. "Billy, what in the world. . . . ?"

Papa and Wilbur stepped up closer to be sure before Papa exclaimed, "Miss Frances?"

Frances woke up with a start when she heard her name called.

"Man, I'm glad to see you boys," Billy declared. "I was hopin' we'd be lucky enough to find somebody quick. I've gotta find Shelton. We got hit hard back at the ranch. Me and Frances just made it outta there by the skin of our teeth." He went on to tell them about the raid on the main house and that he feared Mr. Donovan was dead. "We're gonna have to ride back to take the ranch back. Where's Shelton?"

"He's at the main camp where Poison set up the chuck

wagon. Right by the river, yonder way"—Papa pointed the direction—"about a mile and a half."

"We better get goin'," Billy said. "There ain't no tellin' what those killers will do before we get back there."

"How did you and Frances get away from there?" Wilbur asked after hearing what a surprise raid it had been.

"Just plain lucky, I reckon," Billy answered, trying to think fast. "Thacker's murderers, I know that's who they are, all went into the house. 'Course, I sleep in the bunkhouse, but I heard the shootin' and went to see what it was. That's when I saw Frances. Come to find out, it bein' kinda hot early this evenin', she had gone out to that swing under the arbor. Well, she went to sleep and didn't wake up till she heard the gunshots." He looked at her. "Ain't that about the way it was?"

"Exactly," she answered.

"Well, you was mighty lucky you bumped into each other," Papa said. "Ride on in. Me and Wilbur will stay right here till somebody tells us what we're gonna do. I don't know if Price will leave anybody with the cattle or not."

"Right," Billy said as he nudged Spunky to get moving. "I'll tell him you're waitin' for orders."

They found the main camp right where Papa said it was, with all hands rolled up in their bedrolls close to Poison's chuck wagon.

"Boss! Boss Shelton!" Billy shouted when he pulled the buckskin up near the center of the camp. He was loud enough to roll all hands out of their sleeping bags. Surprised to be awakened in the middle of night, the men were further amazed to find Frances Donovan in their midst. Soon several of the men stepped up to help Frances off the horse and Poison Pearson got his chair out of the wagon and set it by the fire for her to sit in while Billy repeated the report he had made to Papa and Wilbur. All hands were in a state of total shock, for none believed that even Duke Thacker had the gall to pull a sneak attack on a cattle ranch the size of the Double-D.

Range wars were not a new thing, but attacks upon a man's family, his women and children, was akin to barbaric.

"Are you sure about Mr. Donovan?" Shelton asked.

"I didn't see it happen," Billy said. "But what else could it have been? Frances will tell you the same thing. This gang of murderers bangin' on the door, a shotgun blast, then six or eight pistol shots. Then the whole gang charges in the house. What I ain't got no idea about is what happened to Mrs. Donovan and Annie Hagen. I thought I heard one of 'em scream after the shootin' stopped." He looked around him at those gathered close to hear what happened as if to apologize. "I didn't even have my gun with me. I didn't know what I could do against their whole gang, but I figured I could at least get Miss Frances away from there before they saw her."

"Sounds to me like it woulda been plum foolish for you to try anything else," Shelton told him. "You did the right thing gettin' the word to us as soon as you could. We've been talkin' about the possibility of a range war with Thacker, but I've got to admit, I thought it was all just talk. And if it did come to war, I thought it would be fought out on the range to keep the thief from stealin' our cattle. I never thought the man was crazy enough and evil enough to do what you just told me."

He looked around at his men gathered there. "I'm goin' back tonight, men. How many of you can I count on to fight? To save those two women and save the Double-D from that band of outlaws?" Every man answered his call.

He looked at Perley then, standing with Possum and Sonny by his side. "You are volunteerin' your men to help, too?"

"No," Perley said, at once generating a few sounds of grumbling. "I can't volunteer for Possum and Sonny. I'm just volunteerin' myself. What they do is up to them."

"Shoot," Sonny said. "Everybody at the Triple-G knows that wherever Perley goes, Possum goes with him. And I'm gonna stick close to Possum. So, I reckon you've got the Triple-G in this party with you." His statement was met by a series of guffaws and slaps on the back for the three Triple-G riders.

Price Shelton was visibly relieved. He needed their support and especially their firepower. Even so, he was not yet sure what his plan should be. The very concept of Duke Thacker capturing the Double-D ranch house was so outrageous the U.S. marshal in Fort Smith should be contacted. With no time to wait for the law to send in a troop of lawmen to arrest Thacker and his men, Shelton knew he should have left some of the men to protect the family. He hadn't realized the rustler was such a madman and decided to talk the problem over with Perley and Possum.

Both men could definitely appreciate Shelton's problem. Thacker's raid on the ranch house was comparable to an attack on the house by Indians, but in this case, all the Indians were well armed and well supplied with ammunition.

"Just takin' over the house says he's crazy in the first place," Possum stressed. "So there ain't no tellin' what he's gonna do with those women." He looked around to make sure Frances was still sitting in Poison's chair by the fire before stating, "They might already be dead. It'd make a difference, if we knew that for sure."

"Yes, it would," Shelton said. "'Cause, if I knew that, I wouldn't hesitate to set the house on fire and shoot the varmints when they came runnin' out. We can build a new house."

"I reckon you're right," Perley agreed. "We need to know if those women are alive, and if they are, where they're keepin' 'em. I think we need to get into that house without Thacker knowin' it and I think we oughta get Billy and Frances in on this plannin'."

Shelton looked surprised, but after hearing Billy's accounting of how he and Frances happened to be outside the house in the middle of the night, Perley had some reservations about the story. His one brief exposure to Frances Donovan tended to strengthen his suspicions as he thought about that day he caught the two of them in the barn.

"I don't know," Shelton replied. "I can't see how they'd have any idea what to do. Besides, Frances is most likely too upset to be able to talk about it right now."

"I'll guarantee you that Frances knows a way to sneak in and out of that house without anybody knowin' about it. And Billy might know a way to sneak in, himself," Perley insisted.

"Ohhh . . ." Shelton dragged out the thought and

turned to look at Billy standing beside Frances by the fire. "You think . . . ?" he started again while he considered the possibility.

"Come on." He led Perley and Possum over by the fire to talk to them.

"I think you and Billy might be able to help us find out if your mama and Annie are all right," he said to Frances. "We need to know if there's a way to sneak in and out of that house without gettin' caught."

"How would I know that?" Frances replied at once.

"In case you wanted to slip outside in the middle of the night without your folks knowin' it," Perley answered her question.

"You son of a—" she started, then quickly bit her lip. "If I wanted to go outside in the middle of the night, I'd walk out the front door."

"I'm sure you would," Perley said, "but I'm talkin' about when you were a little girl. You musta found a way to slip outta the house when you were supposed to be takin' a nap or something. Right now, we need to know if there's a way to get to your mama without bein' seen."

"Oh," she reacted. "When I was a little girl. I forgot about that. There was a way, but I don't know if a grown man could get into the house that way or not."

Perley glanced over at Billy, and he nodded slowly, letting Perley know he could get detailed instructions from Billy later. They waited while Frances gave a brief trail to follow to get to the upstairs rooms in the house.

Perley went with Billy to cut out a fresh horse for the return trip to the house. While he saddled Buck for himself, Perley got more detailed information on how to get to the bedrooms and which one was the Donovans' room.

When they returned to the chuck wagon, Shelton had his men ready to ride.

"I'm leavin' Poison, Wilbur, and Papa here with the cattle," Shelton told Perley. "I reckon there ain't no reason to worry about the cattle since all the rustlers are holed up in the ranch house." He had an idea why Perley went with Billy to get their horses. "Did you get some more details on the way to get in that house?" At Perley's acknowledgment that he did, Shelton said, "Well, tell me what you found out. You ain't volunteerin' to try it, are you?"

"Well, yeah, I thought that I would," Perley answered. "Would you rather I didn't?"

"No, hell no," Shelton replied immediately. "Just surprised, that's all." He looked at Possum.

Possum just shook his head as if impatient with him.

Shelton hesitated, then turned back to Perley. "I can't think of anybody better to take it on than you. And thanks for helpin' us out." With that, he gave the order to mount up and they started back to the ranch.

Chapter 11

The column of Double-D riders reached the ridge just short of the barnyard with about two hours of darkness left before sunrise would lift their cover.

Inside the house, the atmosphere was pretty much laid back since the escape of Billy and Frances had never been discovered. Thacker, feeling much like a conquering general, was enjoying a drink of Donald Donovan's scotch whisky while he ate the food he had ordered Annie Hagen to cook. She had done his bidding only after he informed her that performing cooking services was the only reason for keeping her alive. He had not really made up his mind to kill the two women since he enjoyed the advantage of having a cook. He told Ned that he would most likely go ahead and kill Matilda because she seemed to be useless for anything but blubbering over her husband's death. For the time being, he had ordered her upstairs to sit in her bedroom.

As far as her husband was concerned, Thacker had ordered a couple of the men to drag his body out onto the porch. Just for entertainment purposes, they sat the corpse in one of the rocking chairs on the porch, tying a shoelace around his neck to keep him from slumping away from the back of the chair.

"He looks like he could say 'howdy' to anybody comin' up on the porch," Lem Pickens commented.

One thing that troubled Thacker was the missing daughter. He knew for a fact Donovan had only one offspring—about nineteen or twenty is what he had been told—yet there was no sign of her. He'd asked Annie Hagen where was the daughter, and was told she had gone home the day before with some friends of the family who had a daughter her age. He was not sure she wasn't hiding somewhere on the property, but a thorough search of the outbuildings turned up no sign of her. A sobbing Matilda Donovan swore what Annie had told him was true.

He decided they were telling the truth. It was too bad the daughter had gone visiting, however. She might have provided some extra entertainment for his men.

Confident he had successfully captured the Double-D headquarters, Thacker was not prone to be careless in his conquest. Donovan's foreman, Price Shelton, would be back with some of his men at any time, probably tomorrow morning. Thacker was determined to let Shelton ride into a surprise ambush and find the former ranch house was occupied by a band of gunmen. He pictured the cowhands Donovan had employed, and could easily imagine the whole crew turning tail and running. Although he didn't expect Shelton before midmorning—*if* he returned tomorrow—Thacker would still post some guards at night to make sure there were no surprises.

His thoughts were interrupted when Annie came in from the kitchen. "There's plenty of coffee in that pot on the stove, and I pulled that last pan of biscuits out of the oven. I'm goin' upstairs now and try to sleep. I'm gonna need it if I'm gonna cook breakfast for that bunch of hogs you brought with you."

He turned in his chair to give her a wide smile. "Yeah, Miss Annie, you do that 'cause I'm gonna expect a good day's work outta you tomorrow. One of my men is gonna be settin' in a chair at the bottom of the stairs in case you have to go somewhere tonight."

"That's mighty thoughtful of you, General Thacker," she replied sarcastically. "Maybe I'll tell him to go saddle a horse for me."

He forced a chuckle for her sarcasm. "You know, you're lucky you ain't a good-lookin' woman, else I mighta had some more little chores for you before breakfast."

"Oh, dear," she japed, "to think what I missed." She folded her apron over the back of a chair and went out the door.

Ned Bates, sitting through the sarcastic exchange between the two, got up and walked to the hallway to make sure she went upstairs.

"She's makin' it awful temptin' to go ahead and cut her throat," Thacker remarked. "I'd take great pleasure in doin' the job."

Ned chuckled. "Don't let her get to you, Duke. I guarantee you ain't gonna like my cookin' a-tall." He sat back down at the table. "I oughta try to lay down and go to sleep, myself. It ain't but a couple of hours before daybreak. I'm gonna feel it tomorrow."

* * *

With their horses tied behind the ridge, the Double-D cowhands knelt on the top and watched the buildings some fifty yards beyond them.

Hank Martin broke the silence. "Yonder's one"—he pointed—"Comin' around the corner of the barn."

"I see him," Shelton said. "That makes two. I ain't sure that first one is a guard. Walking between the front of the house and the outhouse in back he mighta just had to go to the outhouse."

"They ain't walkin' no regular routes," Possum remarked. "They're just wanderin' all over the place." After another moment, he said, "There's somebody settin' on the porch."

"Where?" Shelton asked.

"In that rockin' chair back by the door," Possum said. "Don't that look like somebody settin' there?" He turned to ask Perley, "You sure it's a good idea, you trying to sneak in there?"

"Probably not," Perley said frankly. "Ask my brothers. They say I don't ever have good ideas."

They watched the guards a few minutes longer, till Perley grew impatient. "We're burnin' what darkness we got left. I'm gonna take that extra horse we brought for the women. I'll ride Buck in a wide circle around to the north of the house just in case that is a lookout sittin' on the front porch, and then I'll sneak back to the house from that direction. That okay with you, Shelton?"

"Hell, it's all right with me," he answered. "You know what you're doin' better 'n me."

Sonny spoke up then. "I'll go with you, Perley, and hold the horses."

"Good. That'll help," Perley said. "Let's go."

"You boys be careful," Possum said, "and don't step in no cow pie."

Shelton looked at him, thinking that an odd thing to say.

Perley and Sonny raced around in a wide circle, until coming back to the creek that ran behind the house and stables. They dismounted and walked to a point about thirty yards from the back of the house and Perley told Sonny to wait for him there. They hesitated, waiting to spot a guard.

Just before Perley gave up and made a dash for the house, one of Thacker's men ambled lazily around the front corner of the house. They watched until he walked along the side of the house and finally disappeared around the back porch. Perley took off across the thirty yards of open, moonlit prairie, heading for the back porch. While he ran, he called up every detail of the house he had learned from Billy. It took only seconds to cross the open space, but he could see his shadow in the moonlight. It was with great relief that he gained the safety of the porch and dived under it. One man walking between the front of the house and the outhouse in back had already been spotted.

The main house was two stories. The back part of the house that held the kitchen and behind it, the washroom, was only a single story with a high-pitched roof. The attic over the kitchen served as a storage space for the upper floor of the main house. Following Billy's instructions, Perley scrambled under the porch floor until he found the pipe from the pump in the washroom above him. He felt around the pipe until he found the outline of a trapdoor next to the pump that provided access to the pipe.

It was the first critical test he faced, for if the latch was locked, he couldn't open the trapdoor. At that hour no one should be in the washroom, but he waited a minute or two, listening for any sound above him.

Hearing none, Perley pushed on the door, and it didn't give at all. He tried again, pushing harder. Still no give. *Damn!* It should have been unlatched, if Frances was the last to go through. He thought, what to do? He didn't want to alert everyone in the house by breaking through the trapdoor. For a long moment, he stared up into the darkness of the floor above him, thinking. Quickly, he felt across the trapdoor to the opposite side, pushed up, and the door lifted easily. He had been pushing on the side with the hinges. *If I get out of this alive, I'll never tell anybody about trying to open the wrong side of this damn door.*

Very slowly, he lifted the door just enough to see into the empty washroom. Satisfied no one was in the room, he pushed the door open and crawled up into the room. Remembering Billy's instructions again, he found the small lantern on the table by the door to the kitchen and patted his pocket to make sure he had matches. Next, he moved carefully through the doorway and into the kitchen. He stopped and dropped his hand on his Colt .44, for he heard voices in the dining room beyond the kitchen. Knowing he had to get to the pantry door before anyone walked in, he hurried as best he could without making any noise.

Inside the pantry, he closed the door tight. A wooden box on the floor proved handy to an access door in the ceiling. Standing on the box, Perley pushed the attic access door aside and put the lantern up in the attic before grabbing a rafter knee brace and pulling himself up into the attic. While there was still enough light up through the access hole, he lit the lantern, replaced the access door, sat on the ceiling joists for the pantry below him, and looked around. Boards were scattered randomly to provide walkways over the joists. He got to his feet and held the lantern up, seeing that only part of the attic over the kitchen and washroom had been floored with rough-cut lumber to provide a platform for several trunks, some broken furniture, and odds and ends of various keep-sakes. In the flickering light, he saw what he was looking for—the door to the upstairs hallway. Moving carefully to make sure he didn't accidentally step between the joists and stick his boot through the ceiling below, he walked the random boards to the floored part of the attic.

At the door, he stopped and listened. The voices he heard sounded far away. *Probably from downstairs,* he thought. Turning the wick down in the lantern, he placed it by the door, then carefully turned the knob and eased the door open very slowly. If a guard stood by the bedroom door, Perley's whole rescue plan was likely to explode in a hail of gunfire. He opened the door a little wider until he could see no guard appeared to be in the upstairs hallway.

Wasting no more time, he quickly stepped out of the attic and went directly to the first door on his right. Billy had told him it was Donald and Matilda's bedroom. Perley turned the knob, found the door locked, and felt a moment of minor anxiety. He didn't want to chance knocking on the door and possibly causing a loud response of panic from Matilda Donovan. He realized, however, that he had no choice, so he tapped lightly on the door. Receiving no response right away, he kept on tapping. Suddenly he heard a voice on the other side of the door.

"Go away! If you want breakfast in the morning, you've got to let us rest."

He realized at once it was not Matilda's voice. "Annie!" he whispered. "It's me, Perley Gates. Can you unlock the door?"

"Perley?" she replied, astonished. "What are you doing here?"

"Tryin' to find you," he whispered back. "Can you unlock the door?" A second later, he heard the key in the lock and the door opened. He stepped inside and quickly closed the door behind him to face a confused Annie Hagen.

Behind her on the bed was an equally astonished Matilda Donovan. They were fully dressed, which would save some precious time.

"I've come to sneak you outta here," he whispered, "the same way I sneaked in. It's risky. Are you up to it?"

"Hell, yes!" Annie exclaimed, forgetting to whisper and immediately grimacing afterward. "Sorry," she whispered. "We're up to it, aren't we Matilda?"

"Any risk is better than staying here with these animals," Matilda answered. "Just let me put my shoes back on." She went around to the other side of the bed to retrieve her shoes.

Perley whispered softly to Annie, "Mr. Donovan?"

"They killed him," Annie answered, whispering softly just as he had.

He nodded. "That's what we figured."

In a minute, both women were ready to flee, so he told

them what they had to do to escape without alerting their captors. "It sounds harder than it is," he assured them, thinking how many times Frances had probably left the house that way. "You ready?"

They said they were, so he opened the door quietly to make sure none of the men had come upstairs since his arrival. Perley stepped out into the hallway, held the door for them, and pointed toward the attic door. Matilda went immediately to the attic, but Annie waited until he closed the bedroom door, then inserted her key and locked it before she followed Matilda to the open attic door.

"There's a lantern right beside the door," Perley whispered. Annie picked it up, then he pointed to the access over the pantry.

As he had told them, the escape procedure was not unduly difficult. They wrapped their skirts tightly around their legs before they lowered themselves into Perley's arms, waiting below in the pantry to catch them. Once they successfully made that passage, the rest was a matter of sneaking through the kitchen into the washroom. Perley opened the trapdoor beside the pump and told them they would have to crawl out from under the porch. Annie asked why they didn't just go out the back door. He almost said, no reason, then remembered guards were walking around the house, which meant the escapees would be too easily seen on the porch or walking down the porch steps.

They dropped through the trapdoor to the ground under the washroom as he directed, justifying his reasoning as they crouched under the back porch and waited while one of Thacker's men walked past them on guard duty.

They made the final dash to freedom across the open space between the house and the creek.

"Lord A'mighty!" Sonny Rice exclaimed when he saw Perley and the two women running toward him by the creek. "He did it!" He brought the horses up from the edge of the water to meet them. "I'm mighty glad to see you ladies safe," he greeted them. "I knew if it could be done, Perley could do it."

"We just brought one horse for you," Perley told Annie, "figured you might wanna hold on to each other." He held his hands for Matilda to step in while he lifted her up on the horse. "It's just a short ride." He performed the same service for Annie and lifted her up behind Matilda, so she could hold the older woman. When she was settled on the horse's back, he was prompted to ask, "Why'd you lock that bedroom door when we left?"

"Thacker locked us in that room and put the key in his pocket," Annie answered. "But Matilda had a key and that's the one I used. Shoot, if I had the key to my room with me, I coulda used it. All the bedroom locks use the same key."

"But why did you bother to lock it after we left?" Perley asked again.

"Like I said, Thacker locked us in, and every once in a while, I'd hear somebody go by the door and try the knob to make sure it was still locked. I figured if they tried it again and it was still locked, they wouldn't start looking for us." She shrugged. "Besides, it'll give him something to figure out when he finds out we're gone and the door is still locked."

* * *

"Riders comin'!" Billy Dean called out, and everybody in the Double-D posse became alert. A minute later, Billy called out again. "It's them! It's Perley and Sonny, and they've got the women!"

The men of the Double-D crowded around the horse bearing the two rescued women with many willing hands to help them dismount, then parted to make a path for Frances to go to her mother.

As mother and daughter embraced, Matilda began to cry again as she told her daughter that her father was dead. "They shot him down," Matilda sobbed. "He died trying to protect us and he killed one of them, but there were too many."

Frances began crying even though she had reconciled herself to her father's death already.

Matilda looked in the eyes of Shelton and asked, "What are we going to do, Price? They've taken over our home and everything we have."

"I know, ma'am," Shelton told her. "We ain't gonna let 'em get away with it. We're goin' to war is what we're gonna do and take back your home. We've got to decide how we're gonna do it, even if we have to burn 'em out."

His statement caused Matilda to inhale suddenly, gasping at the thought of seeing everything they owned go up in flames.

Seeing her reaction, Shelton quickly said, "That would be the last thing we'd do. You and Annie go with Frances and find you a place to set comfortably."

As Frances took them to sit under a tree and await the

coming dawn, Shelton gathered his men around him. "We need to decide how we're gonna attack that bunch. Anybody got any good ideas other than just start shootin' 'em down—at least the ones we can see outside the house? We're runnin' outta time."

"That'll take care of the ones we can see outside the house," Perley commented. "The rest of 'em will just hole up inside, and it'll be pretty tough tryin' to root 'em out. Seems to me it'd be a good idea to have some of us fightin' 'em from inside. I don't see why some of us can't get inside the same way I did. We could do a lot of damage before they even know we're in there."

"That's a helluva idea," Shelton responded. "Do you think we could really slip some of us in there without them catchin' us? You, by yourself, can move pretty good, but I don't know 'bout the rest of us fumble-footed cow pushers. How many do you think we could sneak in?"

"If it was up to me," Perley answered, "I'd send three men inside. Three men that are good shots can take out most of the gang that's in there."

"Are you volunteerin'?" Shelton asked.

"I reckon I have to, since I'm the one who knows how to get in there," Perley answered.

"Then I'll go with you," Shelton said. "I'm a pretty good shot with a handgun."

Possum spoke up. "I don't know if that's a good idea. That's a dangerous thing, tryin' to sneak in there like that. You're the boss of this outfit, and if somethin' happens to you, there ain't nobody to run the show."

"He's right, Boss," Perley said. "Anybody volunteerin'

to go with me is takin' a pretty big risk. So who are the best at handlin' a six-gun?"

"Hank," Shelton answered right away. "Then Johnny and maybe George. But they have to volunteer to do it. Ain't nothin' gonna be held against 'em if they don't wanna risk it."

"I'll go," Hank Martin spoke up.

"Me, too," Johnny Sawyer was quick to follow.

"I'll go, too," George Stone volunteered almost as an afterthought. He was definitely lacking the enthusiasm of the other two.

"All right," Shelton said to Perley. "I reckon it's you, Hank, and Johnny. How soon do you wanna get in there? You ain't got much time before first light. You'll have to get under that house before it's light enough to see the three of you runnin' from the creek."

"I expect we'd best get on over to that creek right away," Perley said. "I wanna be up in that attic by the time they start thinkin' about gettin' breakfast and takin' care of their horses."

The three volunteers went to their horses. Perley found himself accompanied by Possum and Sonny.

"You know, I'm pretty good at handlin' my .44," Sonny said.

"I know you are," Perley told him, "but I couldn't afford to risk any more of the Triple-G's top hands."

"He's right, Sonny," Possum said. "We don't wanna send more 'n one damn fool on these suicide missions." He looked at Perley and shook his head as if disgusted. "I swear, Perley," was all he said.

"You worry too much, Possum. I've got two young

sharpshooters to take care of me. If you ain't careful, you're gonna get some more gray hairs in that horse tail hangin' down your back." Perley climbed up into the saddle, gave Buck a nudge, and headed for the creek around back of the house, his two volunteers following close behind.

Chapter 12

They left their horses in the same spot Perley had left Buck before. As he had done the time before, the three of them knelt at the edge of the bushes by the creek and watched for the guard to pass the side of the house and disappear around the back. Then, with Perley leading, they scurried across the open space to dive under the porch, crawled to the pipe feeding the pump, and had to wait there when they heard the sound of heavy boots walking across the washroom floor above them. The boots continued across the length of the washroom to the back door and went out onto the porch. It was just beginning to get light outside.

Lying flat on his stomach, Perley watched through the pilasters that supported the porch until he saw the boots step off the bottom tread of the porch steps and head in a straight line toward the outhouse. "Let's go, and we'd best hurry. Ain't no tellin' how long he'll be in that outhouse." Perley pushed the trapdoor up far enough to see no one was in the room, then crawled up into the washroom. Johnny and Hank followed his lead and Perley closed the trapdoor, anxious then to get the three of them through the kitchen without being seen.

As they passed through the kitchen, they could hear a chorus of snoring seeming to come from every part of the house. Perley ascertained, however, that the majority of it came from the parlor where the men were lying on any surface available, including the dining room table in the room next to the parlor. He remembered to pick up the lantern from the small table beside the door, and they crowded into the pantry and closed the door behind them.

The climb into the attic was completed without a hitch and they waited in place for the signal the battle was on. That was to come from the sound of the first gunshot outside that hopefully would mean the first sentinel was dead. It could not be much longer until dawn, so Shelton should have the rest of his men in firing positions around the edge of the yard. The volunteers checked their weapons and waited in the darkness of the attic, the lantern having been extinguished once they made their way to the solid flooring.

After what seemed a long time, they heard the sound of footsteps coming up the stairs from the main floor. Almost as one sound, all three hammers were cocked at once, but Perley signaled his two partners to hold still and listen. They held and they listened, and they heard the footsteps go to the master bedroom door.

Whoever was wearing the boots must have tried the doorknob.

After a few seconds of silence, they heard an obviously irritated voice yell, "Wake up in there! Get your lazy behinds downstairs and get some breakfast started! It's damn-nigh daylight and there ain't even no coffee made yet." The owner of the voice waited but a few seconds before threatening, "You better get outta that bed and open this door, or I'm gonna break the damn door down!" As before, his threats were met with silence.

The next sound the three raiders in the attic heard was that of the impatient caller's shoulder against the door of the bedroom, and finally, that of the door giving way.

Hank and Johnny started for the door, but Perley stopped them. "Wait. There'll be more comin'." Even in the darkness of the attic, he could feel their tension. "Just hold real still and listen."

In a matter of sixty seconds, during which time he found the room empty, the dumbfounded outlaw was completely confused. After looking in the bed, under the bed, and behind the dresser, he burst back out of the room to yell out the news to his friends below. "They're gone! They ain't in the room!"

"Search them other rooms!' Wylie Parker yelled as he and three others ran up the stairs. "Check the attic!"

"Now!" Perley opened the door to meet a startled outlaw who raised his pistol too late to beat the .44 slug that slammed into his chest.

Right behind him, Johnny Sawyer stepped to the side and fired point blank at one of the outlaws coming up the steps. He and Hank fired at the other two outlaws who were running up the steps behind Wylie. Wylie roared in pain when he caught a bullet in his shoulder. He aimed a shot at Hank but failed to get it off before Perley cut him down. As suddenly as the gunfire had started, it was over.

But there was general confusion by the remaining outlaws, for the volunteers could hear the sound of rifle fire outside and knew Shelton's men had started sniping at any targets they saw. That, in turn, drove any outlaws caught outside scurrying inside for protection from the snipers.

"Where's Duke?" Red Bowden blurted when he ran across the porch and burst in the front door. "There's a damn war goin' on out there. We're surrounded! They're shootin' from all around us."

"Well, watch your butt," Lem Pickens told him. "You ain't safe in here."

"Whaddaya mean?" Red responded.

"I mean they're in the house, too," Lem said.

Red immediately looked all around him, ready to pull his weapon again. "Are you loco? What are you talkin' about? Where's Duke?"

"If you think I'm loco, you can stick your head in that doorway to the hall and take a look at Wylie and four others layin' on the steps," Lem said. "But I wouldn't advise it. And I don't know where Duke is. He mighta got shot, for all I know. He went to the outhouse a little while ago, and he ain't come back."

"I swear," Red said. "Whadda we gonna do? How many of 'em is upstairs?"

"I don't know," Lem answered. "Can't tell how many, but it's more than one. I can tell you that."

"How many of us are left?"

"I ain't sure," Lem replied. "Ned and Mutt went to the barn before all this hell broke loose. And, like I said, Duke went to the outhouse. He might still be in there. Farmer's in the kitchen, watchin' the back door, although we still don't know how those shooters got upstairs without nobody seein' 'em."

"Sounds to me like they've got us pretty-much treed," Red declared. "I reckon we could hole up in here and hold 'em off, but I don't know about them fellers upstairs. I don't much like the thought of that. If they got ways to slip in this house without us knowin' they're even here, they might have some more secret ways to get at us down here."

"I don't think holin' up in here is a good idea," Lem said. "We ain't got enough of us left in the house to cover all the windows and doors. They could storm right over either one of us, if they was to rush us." He held his hand up then, callin' for Red's attention. "I ain't heard another shot outside since you came in. I'm thinkin' that means they're all dead or run off and left us to make out any way we can."

"Well, that don't sound too good," Red replied. "Whaddaya gonna do?"

"Give the hell up!" Lem exclaimed, as if Red was mentally unsound for thinking anything else. "There ain't nothin' else we can do, unless you'd rather end up on the floor like Wylie and them layin' on the stairs."

"How do we know they won't shoot us, anyway, if we give up?" Red asked. "They might wanna hang us, maybe."

"Maybe," Lem answered him, more convinced that surrendering was their best bet. "But maybe not. They might just turn us over to the law." He was thinking about the law as it was represented in town, and the better than even chance they could walk right out of Marshal Jonah Creech's jail. "Anything's better than just tryin' to hold out here till we all get shot down."

"Better listen to what he's tryin' to tell you." Startled

by the sudden suggestion from behind them, Lem and Red turned to see Jim Farmer coming from the kitchen.

Behind him, walked Perley, his six-gun aimed at Farmer's back. Lem froze, but Red reached for his .44. He howled in pain when Perley's shot struck his hand, causing him to drop the pistol on the floor.

"Kick it away from you," Perley said and Red did as he was told, his face twisted in pain. "Now, you with the fancy gun belt, unbuckle it and let it drop to the floor."

Without hesitation, Lem unbuckled his belt and let it fall. He had been a witness to Perley's contest with Spade Devlin.

"Now, if you would all step over there by the front door and just stand quiet, I won't make you wait long." Perley yelled out, "Hank! You and Johnny come on downstairs now! It's clear!"

Descending the stairs by avoiding the sprawled bodies, they went down with guns drawn and eyed the three outlaws standing against the front wall, one seeming in pain with a bloody hand.

"I knew there was more than one up there," Lem murmured. "Where was the one that jumped you?" he asked Farmer.

"He was in the pantry," Farmer answered. "I ain't got no idea how he got in there. He had to come right through the kitchen to get to the pantry."

"Keep your eye on these three," Perley told Hank and Johnny when they joined him in the parlor. I think all the shootin's done outside, but I wanna be sure. I figure Shelton and the rest of 'em oughta be closin' in on the house if they can't see anybody else to shoot at. I don't want him to take a notion to attack us now." He went to the front door and opened it wide but stood back inside. Then he yelled out, "Shelton! Can you hear me?"

"I hear you," Shelton came back. "Is that you, Perley?"

"Yeah, it's me," Perley yelled again. "It's over inside the house, and we've got three prisoners!"

"Good, but what are you yellin' for? We're right under the porch."

Perley recognized that last voice as Possum's.

Surprised, Perley walked out the door to see Possum's and several other heads sticking up over the porch floor near the corner of the house. Possum and Shelton were the first to crawl out from under it to greet Perley.

"What were you doin' under the porch?" Perley asked when they came up the steps to join him.

"We was fixin' to attack the house," Possum replied, "to see if you three lunatics were still alive."

Shelton spoke up. "I'd say we won the battle for the Double-D. We didn't lose a soul and we killed most of the ones outside. One or two in the barn slipped away from us, and I reckon they're still runnin'. We knew there was shootin' goin' on inside the house, but we didn't know who was doin' most of it." He nodded toward Possum and chuckled. "We had to come to attack the house 'cause, if we didn't, Possum was gonna attack it by himself. I think he was a little worried about you."

"It was just time to take the house back," Possum said. "Wasn't no use in waitin' any longer."

"You say you have three prisoners?" Shelton asked. "I hope one of 'em is Duke Thacker."

"'Fraid not," Perley replied. "Thacker wasn't in the house." He saw the immediate disappointment in Shelton's face and concluded, "So he was one of the few who got away, right?"

"Dammit," Shelton swore. "It looks that way. We killed the body of the snake, but the head is still alive and it's liable to grow a new body." Frustrated, he walked inside the parlor to look at the three prisoners. He didn't recognize Jim Farmer or Red Bowden, but he knew Lem Pickens as one of Thacker's old troublemakers. "Lem Pickens," he pronounced. "You and your gang of saddle trash couldn't be satisfied with stealin' cattle, could you? You had to attack a man's family, take his home and his livelihood. This time you didn't stop there. You had to add murder to your dirty tricks."

"I don't blame you for bein' sore about it, Shelton," Lem attempted to say in his defense. "But I didn't murder nobody. Like these two fellers with me, I was in it to rustle cattle, and that's all. We didn't have no intention of killin' anybody."

"And yet, we found the body of Donald Donovan tied to a rockin' chair not ten feet from the front door, shot full of holes, murdered," Shelton said.

"That weren't no murder," Lem protested. "He killed Shorty James and a couple of the boys behind Shorty had to shoot back to keep from bein' killed, theirselves." He paused and thought about what he said, then concluded. "So it weren't murder. It was self-defense. They didn't have no choice." He paused again and looked from Shelton to Perley. "Anyway, it wasn't none of us three. We didn't have nothin' to do with it."

Shelton shook his head in disbelief that Lem thought to argue such ridiculous claims. "You dumb horse thief, what did you think you were bangin' on this front door for? What did you think was gonna come of you and the trash you ride with when you broke into a man's home? You're all, every one of you, guilty of murder, and a judge would hang every last one of you." Shelton was working himself up into a need for justice that was beginning to infect his men standing around him.

Perley thought he should remind Shelton it wasn't their place to do the court's job for them. "I gave these three men a choice of comin' peacefully. I was thinkin' we would turn them over to the law to try 'em."

"What law?" Shelton responded. "Are you talkin' about Marshal Jonah Creech and his two-room jailhouse? Might as well send 'em to the Last Chance Saloon 'cause most likely that's where Creech will be."

One of the men gathered around sang out, "Hang 'em. That's what the court will do."

Another one said, "That's right. Might as well save the time and trouble."

In no time at all, the whole crew was yelling for their execution and Shelton was all for it. "Somebody get some rope," he ordered. "We need three ropes for three guilty murderers."

Several of the men ran at once to their horses for the rope. The only suitable tree was a large oak near the creek where the swing that served as Billy Dean and Frances Donovan's secret tryst was hung. In short order, three horses were brought up while the three outlaws' hands were tied behind their backs.

Perley was the only one opposed to the hanging. His feeling was based solely on the fact that they had volunteered to surrender and face their charges before a judge. Possum pulled him aside and told him what the

Double-D men were doing wasn't right, but it wasn't wrong, either. The three men were just as guilty of breaking into a man's home, killing him, and holding his womenfolk prisoners as the ones they had shot down that day. They deserved hanging and more than likely they would get away scot-free if turned over to the marshal.

"I reckon you're right," Perley finally said. "I shoulda shot 'em, instead of capturin' 'em. At the time, I thought I was doin' the right thing."

"If it's hurtin' you to think about it, look at it from the side these boys that ride for the Double-D see it," Possum told him. "That gang of murderin' cattle thieves came ridin' into their home like a band of wild Injuns set to take everything they had to make a livin'. They waited till there weren't nobody to defend the family and killed the owner. These boys feel like justice oughta be done."

"I reckon you're right when you put it that way," Perley said. "While they're stringin' up those three, I think I'll go to the barn and get a pick and shovel." When Possum asked for what purpose, thinking he was going to dig graves for the three hanging victims, Perley said, "To put Mr. Donovan in the ground before his wife and daughter see him like he is now."

"Oh, good idea," Possum replied. "How you know where to bury him? You reckon Shelton knows where they wanna be buried?"

"There's a little plot of ground over yonder near the willows that's been lined in a square with little rocks," Perley told him. "That looks like a good place. I expect they mighta been planning to put a little fence around it, but didn't seem to be that much of a hurry. Didn't know they'd need it this soon, I reckon."

"Hell, I'll give you a hand," Possum decided. "If we plant him in the wrong place, they can move him to wherever the missus wants him. It'll be better 'n the women seein' him."

They started toward the barn, while the hanging was going on behind them.

In the back of the hayloft, one more person was interested in the hanging underway at the creek. Desperately waiting for an opportunity to leave the loft, as well as the whole ranch, Duke Thacker had lay hidden, completely covered with hay while the Double-D men had made a quick search through the stables and the barn. With no horse, the rapid onset of daylight had prevented him from making a run for it. He had been sitting comfortably in the outhouse when the first shots rang out. Thinking at first that some of his men were shooting at a pig or some other animal to eat, he was not overly concerned. But minutes later, shooting broke out all around and he hustled out of the outhouse, only to dive flat on the ground to keep from being spotted by the riflemen closing in around the house. The sentries he had posted were all being hit with rifle shots. And those who could, ran toward the barn and the few horses there.

Thinking the best place to withstand the attack was the house, he sought to return there. But the backyard he had walked across on his way to the outhouse was a shooting gallery. He hadn't seen himself as having much of a chance to make it across without taking a couple of hits, so he took the next best option. Staying close to the ground, he had crawled behind the outhouse, then ran to the creek. Charging through the bushes along the bank, he ran to a point directly behind the barn. He had started running toward the rear barn door when it suddenly opened and Ned and Mutt rode out, the two of them on one horse.

Seeing him running toward them, Ned had shouted, "Duke, find you a horse. You can't stay here!" And they kept on riding, whipping the horse for all the speed they could get.

Caught with no options, his only choice was to keep running to the barn in hopes of finding a horse to go after Ned and Mutt. With his six-gun in hand, he ran into the barn, looking frantically from right to left, looking for anything with four legs to ride out of there. Nothing. He'd started to cross over to look in the stables but saw a group of four men coming toward the barn. Although armed, he knew he might kill one or two but would eventually be smoked out of the barn. His best chance was to hide. He'd climbed the ladder to the hayloft, made his way to the back of it, and tunneled into the hay bales.

He had no way of knowing how long he had been lying there under the hay. It seemed like a long time. Finally, the shooting stopped, and he could hear men shouting back and forth. He heard voices under him as some of the men brought their horses to the corral. They seemed to be in a hurry, and they were talking about lynching some men captured inside the house. It struck him then. He might have been one of those to be hanged if he had not gone to the outhouse. His whole raid on the ranch had gone to hell, and although he had no proof of it, he suspected Perley Gates was the influence behind the Double-D's defiance. He could feel his hatred of the harmless-looking man burning in his veins, but he told himself to concentrate on escaping first.

As Thacker lay there listening, there finally came a point when he realized he had heard no more voices in the barn or stable since someone had brought a few more horses to the corral. That must have been fifteen or twenty minutes ago. The voices he could hear were faint and hard to make out, and it occurred to him that they must be coming from the hanging.

More than likely, he figured, everybody on the ranch was at the hanging. It was his chance! He crawled out from under the hay and went as quietly as he could to the hayloft door. Looking out toward the creek on the far side of the house, he saw the hanging party. Three ropes were hanging from a single limb of a big oak. At that distance, it was hard to tell who the victims were, but one looked as if it might be Lem Pickens. *That was tough luck*, he thought, *but good luck for me*. Lem and the other two were giving him a chance to escape.

Thacker dropped his six-gun back into his holster and hurried to the ladder to go down from the loft. Climbing onto the ladder, he placed one foot on the next rung down then froze when he heard the voices below him.

"I got a shovel," the first voice said. "I don't see a pickaxe."

"I found one," the second voice replied.

Unaware of how hard he was gripping the ladder, even when his hands began to ache, Thacker was only aware of how vulnerable he was. He clung to the top of the ladder, afraid to make a move, lest he give himself away.

In a few seconds, he heard the voices leaving the barn and his relief was so immediate that he almost dropped off the ladder. He collected his senses and went at once to the stable where he picked the best of the saddles. Moving as rapidly as he could, he took the bridle, walked into the corral, and picked out the best horse he saw, a spirited buckskin gelding. The buckskin made no effort to resist so Thacker slipped the bridle on him and led him into the stable where he saddled him.

Feeling back in control again, even in the face of total disaster as far as his plans for becoming an immediate cattle baron were concerned, he boldly took the time to look toward the hanging site again. The spectators were still gathered around the three swinging bodies. He grunted half a chuckle and thought, *but you didn't get the big gun, did you?*

The image of seeing Ned and Mutt on one horse returned to prompt him to pick up another bridle and saddle. He went back to the corral to pick out another horse. As it came natural to him, he rode out the back of the barn, leading an extra horse, and feeling he was back in command.

Although Thacker was totally confident he had made his escape from the Double-D unseen, it was not entirely true.

Seated on a tree stump on a wooded ridge north of the Double-D, a military-type telescope extended to its full thirty-inch length in his hand, an interested observer remarked to the Palouse gelding grazing behind him. "One of the rats got away."

In his quest to seek out Perley Gates, Kane had decided to scout the Double-D after talking to Chester Rivenbark at the stable. He was at a distinct disadvantage, having never seen the man and preferred not to simply ride in and ask if he was there. Since it was late in the day when Kane had made his decision to go to the ranch, he'd made another decision when he was almost there. *It would be better,* he thought, *to ride in at breakfast time.*

That way, he might be invited to eat with the crew, and consequently, find out which one was Perley Gates. It would give him a chance to take the measure of the man in a casual atmosphere. Chester, back at the stable in town might wonder why he'd never returned, since he had paid him for the night and also kept a key. But the livery owner had no reason to complain. Kane would return the key, and probably keep his horse there until the business with Perley Gates was completed. He'd made a camp for the night on top of the ridge north of the ranch. He'd been awakened in the wee hours of the night by the sounds of gunfire coming from the ranch, and it seemed that he had almost ridden into a raging range war.

It was fully sunup before the fighting stopped, and he was not really sure who the winners were, since even when looking through his field glass, he didn't know who anybody was—until movement from the barn happened to catch his attention. He aimed his glass in that direction in time to capture the image of Duke Thacker galloping out the back door, leading another horse behind him. Thacker, he recognized easily, and that one picture told him the story that had unfolded. Thacker and his men must have tried to take over the Double-D, and they were obviously unsuccessful. The story was very amusing to Kane, and he was delighted to have witnessed Thacker's retreat. He didn't like the man.

Kane's plans for riding into the ranch for breakfast were changed. He was still going to pay them a visit, for he had to make contact with Perley Gates, or whoever he really was. But the gunfighter would bide his time, for he could see it was not a good time for a friendly visit. The ranch hands were busy hauling bodies away from the house and outbuildings. He focused his glass on a couple of horses approaching the house carrying three women. Then he shifted his focus to a couple of men digging what looked to be the start of a grave. He speculated that the grave might be for a member of the family. *Too much going on right now,* he thought. *I'd better give them a little more time.*

He put his telescope away, put out his fire, saddled his horse, and rode back to town. There was no hurry. As far as he was concerned, he would come back tomorrow.

Chapter 13

"Somebody's comin'!" Mutt Thomas exclaimed and picked up his rifle as he ran to the window. After a quick check of the path leading up to the house, he said, "I'll be . . . it's Duke." He turned his head and called, "Hey, Ned, it's Duke! And he brought an extra horse."

Ned Bates came running from the kitchen where he had been in the process of trying to explain to Cora Cross why he and Mutt had come back. She had been promised that the house would be hers when Duke and the gang took over the Double-D and she was not at all happy when the two of them showed up again.

"Wonder if any of the other boys got outta that damn trap," Ned exclaimed when he saw the familiar figure approaching the house.

"Ain't nobody with him." Mutt stated the obvious.

Both men went out on the porch to meet him.

"Glad to see you found you a horse and got on outta that mess," Mutt sang out. "Me and Ned just got out by a hair. We was lucky to find that horse wanderin' back to the barn all by himself."

"We was startin' to worry about you when you didn't

come along right after us," Ned said. "We pulled up right after we crossed the creek to wait for ya. Didn't we, Mutt? We started to go back to look for ya, but there was too many of 'em by then. So we just hoped you found you a good hidin' spot some place, and it looks like you musta."

Thacker didn't respond at once. Taking his time, he got down off the buckskin and walked up the steps to the porch before he spoke. "Glad to see you boys made it safely back here," he said, his tone thick with sarcasm. "It musta been a long, hard ride with both of you havin' to ride the same horse." He paused to watch them squirm. He was angry and they knew he was angry. "You say you stopped and waited for me? Too bad you didn't come back to give me a hand. You'da got a chance to see the rest of the boys gettin' shot to hell. Lem didn't get shot. They hung him, him and two of the other boys that were in the house. I couldn't tell for sure which two it was, but I could tell it was Lem."

"I don't blame you for bein' sore, Duke, but I don't know what me and Mutt coulda done to help you. Like I said, when we stopped and thought about goin' back to help you find a horse, there was a bunch of 'em headed for the barn. We knew your only chance was to find you a hole and stay in it till you got a chance to run. And that's what we was hopin' would happen."

It was total fiction Ned created on the spot, but Thacker looked as if he halfway believed it, so it partially calmed him down. Ned didn't take a chance on meeting Mutt's gaze for fear Thacker might detect the lie between them. In fact, when they'd seen Thacker running toward the barn, they figured that would be the last they ever saw of him. It was every man for himself at that stage of the game.

"What are we gonna do now, Duke?" Mutt asked. He and Ned had already been talking about where they should run, now that the gang was destroyed. "We need to head for parts unknown. We're done here."

"The hell we are," Thacker immediately came back with. "I'm not done here, not by a long shot." When they looked at him as if he had lost his mind, he went on. "You were both outside of that house. Did anybody see you that could identify you?"

They paused to think about that, then shook their heads.

"So, as far as anybody knows, you weren't there. It ain't as easy for me. Those two women can identify me. I wish to hell I had killed both of 'em as soon as we went in that house. But I didn't, so you two are gonna have to be my eyes and ears. You can go into town and find out if they try to bring the U.S. marshals in here to find me. There's a good chance those women will figure the whole thing's over, especially if you tell folks in town that I never showed up. Donovan's people won't know if I'm dead or on the run."

Ned hesitated then said, "I don't know if that'll work or not, Duke. Everybody in town knows me and Mutt are in your gang. Who's gonna believe we weren't out at the Double-D with you and the rest of the gang?"

"That ain't no problem," Thacker said. "Marshal Jonah Creech will swear he saw you two in town last night and told you to go home or you were gonna spend the night in his jail. You can tell people that I kicked you outta the gang. Tell 'em you wouldn't steal cattle. They oughta like that."

"You think Creech will really go along with that?" Mutt asked.

"If he doesn't, I'll kill him," Thacker replied, "and he knows that for a fact. And you can assure him that I'll keep him drownin' in whiskey. That old likker-head would kill his own mother for the promise of a drink of whiskey to celebrate it." He saw them looking unsure and said, "Come to think of it, this might be a good opportunity for both of you. Word gets around town that the two of you quit the Duke Thacker gang because you didn't believe in stealin' and murder, people might start treatin' you with a little respect. That wouldn't be bad, would it?"

"I don't know." Mutt hesitated.

"What are you gonna be doin' while me and Mutt are runnin' for mayor of Texarkana?" Ned asked. "I don't see how this is gonna bring us any money."

"I've got unfinished business to take care of with Mr. Perley Gates," Thacker declared, his anger erupting again. "That man is the only reason Price Shelton got up the nerve to come back to attack that place last night. And I take care of anybody who crosses me. I think you boys know that." On a more positive note, he said, "We'll be back. We always have. When I settle with Perley Gates for all the trouble he's caused me, we'll head for a better part of the country and we'll be back in the cattle business again. I want the two of you to get into town today and let everybody see you ain't got no reason to hide."

"This soon after it happened?" Mutt questioned.

"The sooner, the better," Thacker insisted. "Just make sure you both tell the same story. You tell 'em you quit the gang and you're stayin' in a house by yourself. You ain't seen me or any of the other boys since."

Neither Ned nor Mutt had the brains to think for themselves, and they still had a basic fear of Duke Thacker. For lack of the courage to tell him they wouldn't do as he said, they rode into town that afternoon.

"Afternoon, boys," Shag Felton greeted the two men when they walked in the Last Chance Saloon. "I didn't expect to see you back in here this soon. When you left here yesterday, it looked like Duke suddenly got bit by a snake, the way he hustled you outta here." He reached under the counter, pulled a bottle of whiskey up, and placed it on the bar. "I reckon you want a drink. I've got all the bottles he took off the tables and told me to put under the counter." He set a couple of glasses on the bar beside the one bottle. "The rest of the boys comin' behind you?"

Ned shifted his gaze to meet Mutt's eyes with a silent question. Mutt's answer was a slight shrug of his shoulders.

Ned answered Shag. "I couldn't rightly say when they'll be back 'cause I don't know where they went."

As he could have suspected, his answer served to puzzle Shag. He looked from one of them to the other.

"Go ahead and tell him, Ned," Mutt said when he saw Shag's confusion.

"Me and Mutt don't ride with Duke no more," Ned stated, his speech somewhat hesitant as he tried to think how best to put it. "We're afraid Duke ain't got no respect for honest people's rights, and we don't want no part in doin' anything that's against the law. So we quit. Right, Mutt?"

"That's a fact," Mutt answered. "We're law-abidin' people."

"And he let you do that? I mean just up and quit the gang?" Shag responded, thinking it would have been more in Thacker's character to shoot them down. Something occurred to him. "Maybe I ain't supposed to pour your whiskey outta his bottle."

"Oh, no, that's all right," Mutt quickly replied. "We all chipped in on the whiskey before we quit the gang. And there ain't no hard feelin's about it. We just don't know where him and the boys went last night, or when they'll be back."

Shag couldn't get his head around a picture of a kind and forgiving Duke Thacker when a couple of his ruthless gang quit on him. He was about to say something when they were interrupted by the sudden entrance of the town marshal.

With unshaven face and bloodshot eyes, Marshal Jonah Creech walked directly to the bar for support. "Have you seen Duke Thacker this mornin'?" he asked Shag.

"No, Marshal. I ain't seen him this mornin', or this afternoon, either."

"Fellow came in my office just now. Said he rode by the Double-D on his way to town this mornin', and they'd had a big attack on the house and barn last night. Said they was haulin' dead bodies around like cordwood."

"Forever more," Shag responded. "Who did it? Did he say?"

The marshal paused for a moment; he had forgotten to ask. "He didn't know who it was, just some rustlers, I reckon." Thinking he recognized Ned and Mutt, Creech asked, "Where's Duke?"

"I don't know where he is," Ned answered him. "Me and Mutt don't ride with Duke no more. But you know he'll take care of you. Shag, gimme an unopened bottle of that whiskey from under the bar." When the bartender hesitated, Ned said, "Don't worry. It'll be all right."

Shag gave him the bottle and Ned turned around and put it in Creech's hand. "Here, you take this on back to the office with you. Maybe Duke will be back soon. You don't need to worry about anything that's goin' on out at the Double-D, anyway. Your jurisdiction is in the town."

"That's right," Creech said, "ain't my problem." He pulled himself up into a more dignified posture and said to Shag, "Tell Duke I'd like a word with him when he comes in." He took a firm grip on the full whiskey bottle and headed for the door.

"I'll do that, Marshal," Shag called out after him. "Soon as he comes in." He looked back at Ned. "And you don't know when that might be?"

"I wouldn't have no idea," Ned answered.

"So, what are you boys gonna do, since you ain't ridin' with Duke anymore?"

"Don't know," Mutt answered him. "Me and Ned have been talkin' about that, thinkin' we might could find us some honest work somewhere."

"If what Creech said about some big trouble out at the Double-D is true, maybe you could hire on out there," Shag said. "They might need some new help."

"You know, that might be somethin' for us to look into," Ned responded and gave Mutt a wink of his eye.

"Reckon we'll have to wait to find out what happened out there before we make any decisions."

As far as what was happening at the Double-D, it was a day of mourning and recovery.

Perley had correctly guessed the intended purpose for the small square of ground that had been bordered with small rocks. A small ceremony had been held that morning beside the grave Perley and Possum had dug and interred the body of Donald Donovan. After Annie Hagen and the rest of the crew filed by to pay their respects, Matilda Donovan and her daughter, Frances, stayed to pray together and say their final farewells.

Clyde Humphrey, who did most of the minor repair jobs around the ranch, volunteered to build a fence around the plot as soon as he had the lumber for it. It would wait until the front door and all the bullet holes had been repaired in the walls. Bloodstains had to be cleaned up on stairs and floors, and a broken door needed to be repaired in the master bedroom. Matilda quietly added a job to Clyde Humphrey's list—to permanently nail down the trapdoor beside the pump in the washroom. "If you have to fix the pump, you can crawl under the house to do it," she said.

Outside, in the yard and around the buildings much remained to be cleaned up. The first priority was to remove the casualties Thacker's gang had suffered and dispose of them in a mass grave a full half-mile away from the ranch headquarters.

Based on the estimated number of horses missing, no more than a few of the outlaws had managed to escape

Shelton's counterattack. One horse dearly lamented was Billy Dean's buckskin. Billy could not understand how it had happened since he had not ridden Spunky back to the ranch to attack Thacker's men. Spunky had come back with a small bunch of other horses when the attack was all but over. For Billy, the horse would be hard to replace.

By the end of the day, life at the Double-D Ranch was almost back to normal, with one difference. No longer was a cloud of violence threatening the livelihood of the ranch. Even though Duke Thacker had escaped death or capture, his band of outlaws had been destroyed. The ranch could get back to peacefully raising cattle.

Price Shelton had been managing the operation for quite some time, so nothing was to change. Matilda Donovan felt it necessary the crew should receive some official notice he was making all the decisions, in effect, taking Donald Donovan's place. Thinking she should announce her decision directly to the men herself, she walked down to the cook shack at suppertime and announced it. The men accepted the new order respectfully.

After she returned to the house, Billy couldn't resist asking Shelton a question. "Say, Boss, does that mean you're gonna be bunkin' in the master bedroom now?"

"Watch your mouth, Billy, or I'll put that other arm in a splint, too," Shelton answered him. When the chuckling died down, he said, "I promised Miz Matilda one thing, and that was that I'd make sure Clyde nailed that trapdoor in the washroom shut. I hope it won't inconvenience you and Frances too much."

That was followed by a chorus of catcalls and guffaws.

"How 'bout it, Billy?" George Stone called out. "You gonna have to use the front door now."

Billy knew they had him dead to rights, but he was never going to admit it. "Boy, you jaspers have sure got some dirty imaginations. You ought not talk trash like that about a fine lady like Frances Donovan."

"Billy's right," Shelton said. "We got no business talkin' about Miss Frances like that."

That served to put a stop to it, at least in his presence.

The routine on the ranch was pretty much back on an even keel the next day when a stranger riding a Palouse gelding rode through the front gate and walked the horse up to the barn. The unusual horse caught Hank Martin's eye when it came through the gate, and he watched the rider until he got almost to the barn. Then he walked out to meet him.

A slender fellow, the stranger was dressed in black, with the exception of his shirt. It was white under a black vest. Hank remembered later that the shirt looked like it was fresh and clean, and he thought, *he must not have ridden very far*. The most striking thing about him was the pearl-handled pistol he wore up high on his left side, the pearl handle facing forward.

"Howdy," Hank offered.

"Howdy," the stranger returned. "Wonder if I could water my horse in that trough by the corral?"

"Why, sure," Hank replied. "Help yourself. If you druther, you can water him in the creek. It's right behind the barn." He turned and pointed to it, even though it was pretty obvious. "That's a fine-lookin' horse. He might like the creek better. It's deep and nice and cool. We don't see horses like him very often."

"Mind if I step down?" the man asked politely.

"Don't mind a-tall." Hank stepped back to give him room to dismount.

Stepping down, the man extended his hand. "My name's Kane."

"Hank Martin." He shook Kane's hand. Then he walked over to the creek with him and stood watching the horse drink.

Well, that's one I can cross off my list, Kane thought. "I've been ridin' around this part of the country just to get a good look at it. I'd never been to Texarkana before and I notice there aren't really many big cattle ranches around here. I was beginnin' to think there weren't any, and then I came across this one. Double-D, it says on the gate."

"That's a fact," Hank replied. "This is the Double-D, and you're right, there ain't many this size in this part of the country. The land ain't exactly right for it. You need to get a good ways over into Texas before you see good cattle land."

"That's one of them Nez Perce horses, ain't it?" Papa McCoy called out as he walked up to join them. "If he's tryin' to sell him, I wanna bid on it," he japed.

"You ain't got enough money to bid on this horse," Hank said. To Kane, he said, "This is Papa McCoy. He's poor in his pocket and in his head, too."

Kane smiled for the comment. He had already struck Papa from his list of Perley Gates possibles, just on general appearance. Hank was about to make another comment but was stopped when Poison stepped out of the cook shack and started banging on his triangle.

"Dinnertime," Papa declared. "Was you on your way to the house?"

"No," Kane replied. "I've got no reason to be here. I was just passin' through and thought I'd stop in. I guess it is dinnertime. I won't keep you from your dinner and just be on my way. I let the time get away from me." He felt pretty sure he could count on Papa's next comment, but Hank beat Papa to it.

"You're a long way from town," Hank said. "You might as well eat with us, if you think you can tolerate cowhand cookin'."

"That's mighty neighborly of you, but it wouldn't be fair to surprise your cook with an extra mouth to feed," Kane said, then waited for their insistence.

"Ain't no problem," Papa insisted. "Poison always cooks more 'n enough for everybody."

"Don't let the name scare ya," Hank quickly explained. "We just call him Poison. He won't tell anybody his real name."

"If you're sure," Kane said, playing the part.

"We're sure," Hank replied. "Come on, you can tie your horse up over by the bunkhouse." They walked over to the cook shack and soon had every curious eye turned in their direction.

While Kane led his horse over next to the bunkhouse to tie him there, Shelton walked over to them. "Who the hell's that?"

"Ain't he somethin'?" Papa answered him. "Looks like a gambler or a gunfighter with the way he wears that Colt settin' backward in the holster. His name's Kane."

"He just wandered in," Hank said. "Said he was goin' to Texarkana, and he's just curious about a ranch this size. I invited him to eat dinner as long as he's here. Is that all right?"

"What the hell? Yeah, I'm sure Poison's got plenty. If he ain't, we'll give him yours." Shelton turned as Kane walked up to join them. "Welcome, Mr. Kane. I'm Price Shelton, the foreman here. Hope you find the food edible."

"Thank you, Mr. Shelton, I'm sure I will." Another name was mentally crossed off Kane's list.

Inside the cook shack, the table was already over half occupied, and the loud conversation across the table stopped when Kane walked in behind Shelton and waited for him to explain. "Boys, say howdy to Mr. Kane. He's gonna try out some of Poison's cookin'."

Kane nodded to the table in general and found an empty space on one of the benches on either side amid a chorus of good-natured cracks hoping he had a strong stomach. He tried to smile, but found it difficult since it was not something he did as a rule. Life and death were serious conditions to him. He found nothing humorous in either one.

The room soon became quiet as the men sensed something strange about their dinner guest.

Shelton tried to play the host when Papa and Hank turned their attention to their plates. "Hank said you were just ridin' around this part of Arkansas. Are you lookin' for anything in particular?"

"Just tryin' to get the lay of the land," Kane replied. "New Orleans is getting overcrowded and I'm interested in any new areas that might be worth investing in."

"Is that so?" Shelton responded. "I'd be surprised if you found much potential around these parts. I know there's some in Texarkana who think that little town is gonna boom, since it got a railroad connection, but so far, ain't nothin' really happened there."

"You're absolutely right, Mr. Shelton," Kane quickly agreed. "That's why I was just killin' time this mornin', but I lucked up on a fine bowl of stew. I wanna thank you again for your hospitality. Maybe I oughta be payin' you something for the food."

"No, not at all," Shelton quickly replied. "Glad you stopped by."

The usual dinner conversation came to life again when it seemed the visitor wasn't going to contribute anything of interest to the dinner hour.

Trying to decide the best way to learn everyone's name without asking each man at the table, Kane studied them all, one at a time, to see if he could visually narrow his search—nothing in the way any one of them handled the knife and fork to give him any real candidates. He preferred to be subtle in his search for Perley Gates but was beginning to believe he was going to have to be blunt.

All of a sudden, Poison asked Shelton, "What about Perley and them boys down there at the swamp? Don't look like they're gonna make it back in time to eat. Want me to send a bucket of this stew down there? 'Cause it's goin' to the hogs if I don't."

"Who's down there with Perley?" Shelton asked.

"His other two Triple-G partners, Possum and Sonny," George Stone answered. "I was there, but they didn't need me, so I came on back to eat."

"As much as those three have helped us with our problems, we sure as hell oughta feed 'em," Shelton said. "Yeah, Poison, send Nubby down there with a bucket of stew." He looked down at the end of the table. "You know where they are, Nubby?"

"Yessir," answered Papa McCoy's fourteen-year-old nephew. "They're gettin' cows outta the swamp."

"You mind if I ride along with him?" Kane asked, surprising everyone.

"What for?" Shelton asked before he thought to soften it. "I mean, there's just some of the men gettin' some cows out of a mess they got into and can't get out of by themselves."

"I'd be interested in seein' some of the jobs a cowhand has to do besides drivin' herds to the railroad," Kane said. When Shelton seemed to hesitate, Kane continued. "Then I'll get out of your way and start back to town."

"Well, sure. Take a ride with Nubby," Shelton responded, "and I hope you satisfy your curiosity."

"I thank you again for your hospitality and a good meal," Kane said. "You've helped me more than you know." He left Shelton to puzzle over that and went to get his horse while Poison filled up a bucket with beef stew and added a cake of cornbread on top.

After fixing the bucket so Nubby could hold it on his horse, Poison stood back and said, "Go no farther 'n you have to go. That stew oughta still be warm when you get there. If it ain't, tell 'em to build a little fire under it."

Nubby started out past the barn, heading south. Kane, riding the big Palouse, was behind him. Several curious souls stood outside the cook shack watching them.

"Damned if he ain't one strange city-slicker," Billy Dean commented.

"I don't know what his game is," Shelton replied. "He said somethin' about New Orleans. Maybe he's one of them Creoles."

"I don't know about New Orleans," Papa commented. "My guess would be the moon."

Chapter 14

"All right!" Perley yelled. "He's all yours!" At the edge of the swampy marsh, Possum gave his horse a tap of his heels and the big gray gelding he called Dancer immediately took the slack out of the long rope Perley had managed to tie around the steer's neck. Already in a state of panic from all his struggling to escape the quicksandlike muddy bottom had resulted only in entrapping him further, the steer was not happy with the rope thrust around his neck. Consequently, he struggled even harder to climb straight up, spraying mud and water all over Perley's face and shoulders. Since he was already standing in water up to his waist, he was now covered head to toe in the smelly water. The steer, on the other hand, had settled down somewhat when Possum and Dancer pulled him toward the bank, and he felt a little more solid earth under his hooves.

"Good work, Perley!" Sonny Rice called to him while laughing almost too hard to get the words out.

Perley tried to make his way out after the steer but found, like the steer, his feet were stuck as well. "Shoot," he grunted and stopped trying to walk, knowing if he kept struggling, he would soon be in the same fix as the steer had been. He waited until Possum pulled the steer all the way out before calling to Sonny, "Tell Possum to back up again and you throw me that rope. He's gonna have to pull me out. My boots are stuck."

"No foolin'?" Sonny asked, cackling with laughter. "All right. Soon as I untie this steer." He looked toward Possum, chortling. "Possum, Perley said you gotta pull him out, too." He had to wait a second for another guffaw, before continuing. "His feet are stuck."

"I swear—" Possum started, then looked back to the swamp, disgusted. "I swear, Perley," I told ya you was plum loco to go in there with that rope. What'd you think you was, a frog?" He backed the gray up to give Sonny enough slack to untie the steer.

When it was free, the steer trotted off to join the other three that had also been pulled out, but not in the same fashion. They had been close enough to the bank to be lassoed and pulled out with the horses. The last steer had managed to get into the middle of the marsh too far to throw a rope. Still grumbling, Possum backed his horse close enough for Sonny to throw the rope to Perley. Perley looped it underneath his arms and signaled Possum to take out the slack.

"Dancer, get!" Possum barked, and the big gray jumped to the task, jerking Perley free of the mud.

The entire extraction was watched in fascination by the two riders who had stopped on a low rise a dozen yards away, one of them holding a bucket of stewed beef. Nubby called out, "Hey, Possum! Looks like you landed a big one!"

The three members of the cattle rescue party had been so busy they hadn't noticed the two riders approaching.

"Hey, Nubby," Sonny answered. "We didn't even use bait on this one."

"I brung you a bucket full of bait," Nubby said. "Maybe you can catch a bigger one." He started to ride on down to them, but Kane stopped him briefly.

"Which one of them is Perley Gates?" Kane asked, not sure they had reached the right people.

"Perley's the one layin' on the bank with the rope around him." Nubby nudged his horse and rode on down to the bank.

Not quite sure how this was going to turn out, Kane followed.

When they pulled up, Possum and Perley were arguing. "You're out, ain't you?" Possum asked, obviously a little testy.

"Yeah, Possum, I'm out," Perley answered impatiently. "But my boots ain't. I wanted you to pull me, but you jerked me right outta my boots. Now they're still out there in the bottom of that swamp and I can't tell what spot they're in. Can you?"

"Oh," Possum replied sheepishly, "I mighta kicked a little hard. Sometimes this fool horse don't know what I want." They stared back at the dark, black water, showing not a ripple of a hint. "Doggone it, Perley, I told you it was crazy to wade out in that mess. You shoulda listened to me, and you would still have your boots."

"And Double-D would be short one more steer," Perley said in reply.

"Who's that ridin' with you, Nubby?" Sonny finally asked, interrupting the squabbling between the two.

"This here's Mr. Kane. He was wantin' to ride out here with me to see what cowpokes do all day. I reckon he knows now."

"Mr. Kane," Possum said politely.

Still lying on the sandy bank and feeling a little mortified, Perley acknowledged Kane with a two-finger salute, and a grin, thinking no explanation would be believable.

"Poison sent you a bucket of chuck, since you didn't make it back for dinner," Nubby announced. "Somebody take it while I get down. Poison said to build you a fire to warm it up if it ain't hot enough."

"I better take care of that bucket," Sonny said. "I'll gather up some wood and we'll have us a fire." He looked over to Perley getting himself out of his rope harness, and said to Possum, "How much you reckon this is worth to him to keep our mouths shut about this boggy fishin' when we get back to the Triple-G?"

"Might be enough for you to retire on." Possum turned toward Perley who was walking toward Buck. "Where you goin'?"

"I'm goin' down to the river to wash myself off," Perley answered. He rummaged around in his saddlebags until he found a bar of soap wrapped in a rag. Then he started walking toward the river. "Save me some of that chuck."

"What line of business are you in, Mr. Kane?" Possum asked. "You don't look like a cowhand."

His eyes and concentration still lingering on the gun belt and holster hanging on the saddle horn of the bay horse Perley had just left, Kane was a moment slow in responding to Possum's question. "What? Ah, I'm in the protection business," he said. It was the first thing that popped into his mind. His thoughts were still on the gun and the style of the holster hanging on the bay.

It wasn't typical for a fast-gun operator. And looking at the man walking gingerly down toward the river in his wet stocking feet, Kane could see no clues that would lead anyone to believe the man capable of living up to the reputation he had heard. That reputation, he reminded himself, may have been wholly created by the local saloon dwellers. A thought occurred to him that he had wasted his time and money coming in search of Spade Devlin, if Devlin had, in fact, been bested by this harmless-looking yokel.

"What do you protect?" Possum asked. "You mean like rich people, like a bodyguard?" He was a little suspicious of a man dressed like a dealer in a gambling house and wearing a quick-draw holster with a pearl-handled pistol.

"No," Kane replied. "I set up protective systems to protect companies that deal with a lot of money." He figured that would sound a great deal more impressive than a highly paid assassin whose killings took place in public under the guise of duels.

"You mean like banks?" Sonny asked.

"That's right, banks, too." Kane answered.

"We coulda used him around here a couple of days ago. Couldn't we, Possum?" Sonny laughed, while he fanned his fire into life. "Perley's gonna be disappointed Poison didn't send any coffee with this grub."

Down at the river's edge, Perley stripped down to his underwear and went to work on his shirt and trousers, trying to get all the black stains out of the fabric. Then he washed his underwear while it was still on him. His socks were a sad case, having snagged them in several places when walking down to the river. He had considered the probability of recovering his boots from the swamp but was convinced they were lost forever. And he wondered if the old boots were worth the search in the first place.

Besides, he already needed new boots and had planned to buy new ones at Ben Henderson's store back home in Paris, Texas. Perley had admired a pair for some time, and they were his size.

Unsure when he and Possum and Sonny would be heading back that way, Perley made a decision. "I'll go into Texarkana and look in Johnson's Feed Store, right across the street from the stables. I'm sure Johnson sells more than feed. I've seen coats and trousers hanging in the window. Probably has boots, too." Satisfied, he grinned and headed back to the others. "I'll do it tomorrow."

"Well, you already smell a whole lot better," Possum greeted him. "You'll be a lot cooler walkin' around in your underwear, too."

"I'm goin' into Texarkana tomorrow and buy myself a new pair of boots." Perley proclaimed to Possum. "That is, unless you or Sonny wanna wade out into that marsh and see if you can find my old pair. If you do, it'll be worth a nickel to me, cash on the barrel head."

It was upon that announcement that Kane made a decision, as well. Sorely disappointed when he finally met the celebrated Perley Gates, he felt cheated. The man was a hometown joke, and would certainly provide no satisfaction in shooting the young scarecrow out on the desolate strip of land with no witnesses but his equally bumpkin friends.

On the other hand, Kane was tempted to put a bullet in him for causing the inconvenience of riding out to the ranch and made an announcement of his own. "Well, gentlemen, I've enjoyed this little slice of life on a cattle ranch today. I thank you for your time and your hospitality. Now, I think I'd best turn my horse toward Texarkana. Maybe I'll see you again sometime soon." He favored Perley with a rare smile as he wheeled the Palouse back the way they had come.

"Protection business, my wide behind," Possum declared after Kane rode away. "Murderin' business is what that man's into. Dressed up like a preacher with a quick-draw holster ridin' high for a reach-across draw. What the hell did he want out here?" Possum looked around at them for an answer.

No one spoke.

Possum answered his own question. "He came out here lookin' for the man who shot Spade Devlin. That's what he was after."

"I don't know, Possum," Perley said. "How could he possibly know about that?"

"He knew," Possum insisted.

"Well, if he did, he didn't do anything about it," Perley pointed out. "There ain't no tellin' what that fellow does to earn a livin'."

"Well, howdy, Mr. Kane," Shag Felton greeted him cheerfully. "Wasn't sure you was still in town."

Kane walked over to stand at the bar. "I thought I'd hang around town here for another day or two." He ordered a drink of whiskey, then turned to survey the room while Shag poured.

It was noticeably quieter for that time of day . . . due to the number of bodies Kane had seen dragged away from the Double-D headquarters after Thacker's disastrous attempt to attack the ranch. The thought of it amused him. The only sign of that band of hoodlums were the two men sitting at a table in the middle of the room. They'd been sitting with Thacker when he'd sent Slick Bostic across the room to challenge the gunman. Kane thought of Slick and the contempt he felt for men like him, would-be gun hands with slothlike reflexes.

Kane turned back toward Shag. "Where's Duke Thacker and his crowd this evenin'?"

"Tell you the truth, I don't know," Shag answered. "I ain't seen hide nor hair of any of 'em a-tall, and that's all day, too. There's rumor goin' around that Thacker mighta tried to raid the Double-D the other night and they got shot all to hell."

"That's two of 'em sittin' at that table over there, ain't it?" Kane asked.

"Yeah," Shag replied. "They were ridin' with Thacker but quit him before that business out at the Double-D. Leastways, that's what they told me. Said they wanted to find honest work, was tired of ridin' on the wrong side of the law."

"And you believed them?"

Shag shrugged apologetically. "Well, I reckon I didn't have no reason not to. They were in here the next day and didn't have no idea where Thacker and the rest of the gang had gone. Said they didn't come back to that house they've been stayin' in."

Kane nodded. "Maybe you're right. Maybe they just up and turned honest." He thought it far more likely he was looking at two who'd escaped the massacre at the Double-D, and the third one was Duke Thacker. Kane felt no desire to share that opinion with Shag.

He had another thought, and asked Shag, "You still have that extra room upstairs for rent?"

"Sure do. And that bed ain't been slept in since the sheets was washed."

"I'll move my things in there, in that case. Is that all right with you?"

"Yes, sir," Shag answered. "Glad to have you." He chuckled then. "You get tired of sleepin' in that stable?"

"No," Kane said. "But since Thacker and his crowd ain't gonna be here to keep me awake half the night, I might as well sleep in a bed. I'll go up and take a look at it. It might be in worst shape than the stable."

Shag opened a drawer under the bar, took out a key, and offered it to Kane.

"Before I take that key, what's that nasty old woman cookin' for supper tonight?"

"I declare, I don't know," Shag claimed. "I reckon I could go ask her for you." He hesitated. When Kane didn't stop him, he said, "Won't take a minute."

Shag walked over to the kitchen door and stuck his head in. "Hey, Bertha, whatcha cookin' for supper tonight?"

Standing at the bar, Kane heard a low growling like that of a mama grizzly but couldn't understand what she said.

Shag came back to the bar. "Boiled chicken and rice."

Kane thought about it, then shrugged. "I'll chance it." He took the key and went upstairs to see if the room was okay. Deciding it was not worse than anticipated, he went back down and and paid Shag for the night. "I'll take my horse to the stable, then come back to risk my life on that woman's boiled chicken and rice."

"I'm gonna take the day off, Boss," Perley told Shelton when he walked into the cook shack for breakfast. "I gotta go into town and get myself shod."

The foreman turned to look at Perley as he stepped carefully inside the cook shack to make sure he didn't stub his toe on the doorsill or snag his clean pair of spare socks. "Ain't you forgettin' somethin'?" Shelton japed. "Wouldn't anybody in the bunkhouse lend you a pair of boots to wear to town?"

Perley had taken the ribbing good-naturedly last night in the bunkhouse, much to the entertainment of the Double-D cowhands.

"Nobody had an extra pair," Perley answered. "At least, that's what they said. Papa said he's got a pair of bedroom slippers he wears in the bunkhouse at night. He offered 'em to me, but I'd just as soon go in my socks. If those streets in town are muddy, I'm afraid I might lose one of his slippers."

Everybody enjoyed a good laugh at his expense, including Perley, himself. It was kind of funny and the kind of "cow pie" he was noted for stepping in. None of the japing was done cruel-heartedly, for in the short time he had been there, Perley had made himself a good friend to all the men who worked on the ranch. It was all in fun, with the exception of one person.

Possum, upon thinking of the incident, was of the singular opinion the ridiculous occurrence at the swamp might have saved his good friend's life. He was convinced the mysterious Mr. Kane had made an appearance at the Double-D for one purpose only, and that was to face Perley Gates in a gunfight. No one had been able to come up with any real reason for Kane's appearance at the ranch. He truly suspected when Kane saw the state Perley was in, the gunman decided he was not worth a challenge, that it wouldn't serve to build his reputation to kill a nobody.

It was damn-sure worth the loss of a pair of old boots, Possum thought. When Perley sat down at the table next to him, Possum said, "I think I'll go into town with you. I ain't got nothin' special I need to work on here."

"Glad to have the company," Perley responded. "I'm gonna take a packhorse with me. There's a few things we need to pick up if we're gonna have anything to eat on the way home."

They were planning to leave the Double-D any day since there was really no need to stay. The cattle had been rounded up and moved to safer parts of the range, and the feared assault on the ranch had been met with the elimination of the Duke Thacker gang.

"I don't expect we'll be back today in time for dinner. So if you ain't willin' to take a chance of eatin' dinner at the saloon, you'd best make sure you've got some jerky in you saddlebags."

"Shoot," Possum declared, "I've et worse grub than what that woman cooks. Besides, you and me both said that stew we et there before weren't all that bad, ain't that right?"

"That's right," Perley agreed. "Although I do recall that stew kindled a little fire in my belly that took a while to go out." He rubbed his stomach with his hand. "I ain't afraid to try it one more time. Maybe it'll keep a warm glow in my belly all the way back to the Triple-G."

Sonny heard them talking about it but chose not to accompany them. He had some chores he had volunteered to do to help Billy Dean, since Billy couldn't use his left arm. So, after breakfast, Perley and Possum saddled their horses and headed for town.

Chapter 15

"Where you wanna go first?" Possum asked as they rode into the quiet little town of Texarkana.

"Over there to the feed store," Perley said, pointing to a building with a sign that proclaimed it to be JOHNSON'S FEED STORE, with smaller letters underneath that said, *GENERAL MERCHANDISE*. "I wanna get some boots first thing, before I wear my socks out."

"Reckon so," Possum said, laughing. "We might as well go ahead and get the supplies we need after you get your boots. We can just leave the supplies there till we're ready to go back to the ranch, and let the horses rest up before we load 'em up." He turned his horse in the direction of the store and Perley followed, his stocking feet inconspicuous in his stirrups.

"Mornin'," Walter Johnson offered when Perley and Possum walked in the door. Strangers to him, he glanced down at Perley's stocking feet. "What can I help you with? Some boots, maybe?" He couldn't suppress a grin when he japed, "You musta had kings and the other fellow had aces."

Perley chuckled in appreciation of his humor. "Nope, it wasn't a card game, although it coulda been. I ain't much of a card player. I lost 'em in the water, and I'm hopin' you've got some boots in my size."

"I'll show you what I've got," Johnson said. "I don't carry a lot of boots like I think you're lookin' for. Most of what I carry is work boots like the farmers want, since they're my biggest customers. Let's take a look." He led them into the rear of the store to a little stall where rows of shoes were lined up on several shelves.

Perley looked over the boots on the shelves. Half a dozen pairs were suitable for what he was looking for. None, however, were in his size.

"Well, I'm sorry I ain't got what you want. The rest of these are farm boots and brogans. I'm sure I've got something in your size in them." Johnson picked up a pair and handed them to Perley.

"I'm gonna need to buy a pair of socks, too," Perley said and pointed out the ones he favored. He took off the old socks that had served as shoes and put on the new ones. Then he tried on the brogans. "Well, they're the right size, all right." He tried to picture the heavy shoe in the stirrup, didn't care for the image, and decided to wait until he got back home to buy the boots he had been considering for some time. A good pair of boots would last a long time, and he didn't care for the thought of wearing clodhoppers for years.

Seeing Perley frowning at the boots and shaking his head, Johnson said, "You know, I've got something else and I think they're the same size as those shoes you just tried on. Just depends on how particular you are. I'll be right back." He went into a small storeroom behind the shoe stall and returned holding a pair of boots.

Encouraged immediately, Perley remarked, "Now, those look more like what I was lookin' for." A genuine cowboy boot, much like the worn-out pair he had just lost, he took one and tried it on. It fit, and the leather felt soft and comfortable. "I swear, they don't even feel like new boots."

Johnson smiled. "That's 'cause they ain't."

"What were you hidin' 'em back there for?" Perley asked, turning the other boot over, inspecting the soles and heels. "There's a lotta wear left in these boots." He pulled it on, stood up, and walked back and forth for a couple of minutes. He looked at Possum and nodded his satisfaction.

"I wasn't hidin' 'em," Johnson answered his question. "I had 'em in there, cleanin' and polishin' 'em, and just hadn't brought 'em out here yet. I almost forgot I had 'em. They're used boots." When Perley shrugged to indicate that didn't matter to him, Johnson explained further. "The reason I asked if you were particular about the boots was because, every once in a while, I'll buy some shoes and clothes from Philip Davis. You know him?" Perley shook his head and Johnson continued. "Philip has the barbershop on the other side of the Last Chance, and he's also the undertaker. Sometimes he buries some folks that don't have any family, or there ain't no funeral and there ain't no sense in buryin' good, useable clothin'. I reckon it bothers some folks to know they're wearin' a dead man's boots."

"Well, it doesn't bother me to wear a dead man's

boots, unless he comes back to get 'em," Perley said. "How much you askin' for 'em?"

"Five bucks," Johnson said.

Perley didn't quibble. It felt so good to have some comfortable boots on his feet. "That's a tall price for a pair of secondhand boots, but I'll take 'em. I'm in a desperate situation." He pulled his money out and paid for the boots right away. "We're gonna need a few more supplies. I wrote a list down on this piece of paper. We're gonna rest our horses a little bit before we head back out to the Double-D, and we're thinkin' about gettin' something to eat, too. I'll pay you for the supplies when we're ready to go. Is that all right with you?"

"Yes, sir, it surely is," Johnson replied. "I appreciate your business."

Perley and Possum turned and started for the door.

Johnson glanced at the list Perley gave him, then called after them. "I'll have your supplies ready for you, Mister . . . I didn't get your name."

"Perley Gates," he called back as they went out the door.

"Perley Gates," Johnson repeated. He recognized the name. He hadn't been a witness to any of the story about Perley Gates, but everybody in town was familiar with it. He thought hard on it—whether or not to tell him when he returned that the boots he was wearing originally belonged to Spade Devlin, the man he'd killed in the Last Chance Saloon.

* * *

"Hot damn," Shag Felton blurted when he saw Perley and Possum come through the door. "I sure am surprised to see you two still here. I thought you'da been on your way back to Texas by now. I reckon you were in the middle of that raid out at the Double-D, right? That was quite a surprise for Duke Thacker, weren't it?"

"We thought we might run into Duke Thacker here," Possum said. "This was his headquarters when he wasn't out tryin' to raid somebody's ranch, weren't it?"

"We ain't seen hide nor hair of Duke Thacker since the day that raid happened," Shag said. "Two of his gang that quit him the day before that raid still come in here. They told me they ain't got any idea what happened to Duke."

"He just sorta disappeared, did he?" Possum asked. "Don't nobody know where ol' Duke is."

Not interested in knowing where Duke Thacker was, Perley changed the subject. "What is that lady's name who does the cookin' here?"

"Bertha." Shag then added, "She'll be tickled to hear somebody called her a lady.

"What has Bertha fixed for dinner today?" Perley asked.

"Steak and potatoes," Shag answered. "I already had some of it. It weren't bad."

"How 'bout lettin' her know that two of her admirers want to try some of it," Perley said. "With some coffee and some biscuits, if she baked any. We'll sit down right over there." He pointed to a table on the kitchen wall and started toward it.

Possum didn't follow at once. "Pour me a shot of that corn whiskey first. I need to let my stomach know to get ready for somethin' hard to handle."

Shag held the bottle over the glass for a few moments, hesitating purposely until Perley was almost at the table, then whispered to Possum, "Did Kane find him? Is that why you two are in town today?"

Possum froze for a moment, realizing the worrisome thoughts that had struck him about the mysterious Mr. Kane must have been accurate. "What are you talkin' about?"

"That gunslinger, Kane. He's been lookin' for Perley ever since he heard Perley shot Spade Devlin. He came to town lookin' for Spade, so now he wants Perley." Judging by the look of desperation, Shag saw that Possum and Perley were totally unaware of the situation. "Kane's back in town," he said and poured Possum's drink. "If Perley ain't lookin' to face him, you boys best get the hell outta here."

"Much obliged, Shag." Possum tossed the whiskey down, left the price on the bar, and went to join Perley at the table. "I just got struck by a painful sick in my gut. Let's not eat dinner right now. I need to get outta here."

Perley was at once concerned. "Damn, Possum, is it that bad? Maybe you shouldn'ta took that drink of likker." He didn't know what to do for him. There was no doctor in the town as far as he knew. "Lemme ask Shag if there's anybody in town that does any doctorin'."

"No, no," Possum responded and held Perley's arm. "I don't need no doctorin'. I just need to get the hell outta here."

But it was too late. For at that moment, Kane appeared at the top of the stairs. Seeing the two of them at the table, he stepped purposefully down the stairs, wearing the look of a cat watching a cornered mouse. "Well, well, the boys from the Double-D. Mind if I join you?" He didn't wait for an invitation but pulled a chair back and sat down to the right of Perley.

"Mr. Kane," Perley acknowledged. "Didn't know you were stayin' here."

"Obviously," Kane replied, which seemed an odd reply to Perley.

"Anyway, we'd be glad to have you join us, but Possum has been struck with some kinda sudden stomach ailment, and he needs to get outside," Perley said.

"That doesn't surprise me," Kane commented, again an odd thing to say, in Perley's opinion. "I'll go outside with you."

"Ain't no need," Possum said. "Whatever it was has already passed. I feel fine now."

"Are you sure?" Perley asked, doubtful that his friend could go from such agony to no pain at all in that short a time.

"Take my word for it," Possum stated. "Ain't nothin' wrong."

It struck Perley that Kane seemed amused by the words between him and Possum and was not surprised when he heard Kane's next comment.

"You look a lot different from the first time I saw you. You looked like a drowned rat when they pulled you outta that slop."

Perley laughed, even though Kane hadn't. "Yeah, I

reckon I did. I know I felt like one. I had to come to town today to buy a new pair of boots. I left my old ones out in the middle of that swamp."

Kane was about to make another remark but was interrupted when Bertha suddenly appeared at the table with two plates, one she placed before Perley, the other before Possum.

"Why, thank you, Bertha," Perley said. "How are you this afternoon?"

"I'm tolerable," the huge woman answered. "Thank you, sir. I'll bring your coffee." She looked at Possum, who was wondering what else was going to happen, and asked, "You want coffee?"

When Possum couldn't seem to find the words, Perley answered for him. "He does." Then he glanced over at Kane. "I don't know if Mr. Kane is eating or not." But she had already gone before he got it out. "I reckon Shag already told her we wanted to eat," Perley offered as excuse for her ignoring Kane.

"Yeah, probably so," Possum grunted, knowing that Shag had not.

Bertha had heard them come in and fixed their plates because of Perley's courtesy to her before. That was probably what happened. It was the way he struck most women. Possum kept trying to catch Perley's eye, to somehow alert him that Kane was a threat, but Perley never paid any attention.

When she returned with the coffee, Perley told her the first couple of bites he took told him he was going to enjoy the dinner. That mellowed her enough to ask Kane if he was going to eat.

While she had Kane's attention, Possum tried again to catch Perley's eye, but Perley was focusing his attention on what Bertha and Kane were saying. Kane said he would eat a little later, that he had something he was thinking about doing first and didn't like to feel slowed down by a full belly.

No one cared enough to ask what that chore was except Possum, and he felt he already knew. He made up his mind right then if there was a showdown between Perley and Kane today, Kane was a dead man, whether he beat Perley or not.

"You know," Perley said softly to Kane, "the food really is better than it looks. You sure you don't want to join us?"

Kane actually chuckled, surprising himself. "No, I'll just satisfy myself watching you eat. You go right ahead. Don't mind me." Content to sit there awhile to watch Perley go after his dinner, he didn't notice that Possum was just picking at his. "You're wearin' a Colt Single Action Army six-shooter. How's it workin' for you?"

"It's a fine weapon," Perley answered. "Seems just the thing for snakes and such. Ain't as handsome as that pearl-handled model you're totin'. If it was me, I'd be afraid I'd scratch that up."

"Are you fast with it?" Kane asked.

Perley finally became aware of where the questions were leading and what might become an awkward situation. He glanced up at Possum, and Possum nodded slowly, the lines of frustration evident in his weathered face after having tried so hard to capture Perley's attention before.

"I couldn't tell you, Mr. Kane," Perley answered the question. "I've never timed myself and never had any reason to. I expect I'm about like most cowhands, somewhere in the middle, if there would ever be a contest. Like I said, the gun is used for snakes and other varmints."

"I think you're bein' a little modest, aren't you, Perley?" Kane pressed. "I'm told you're the gun that took Spade Devlin out. That couldn't have been a fluke. I hear that Devlin was fast, but they say you turned and took him out after he had already reached for his weapon."

"I don't know who you've been talkin' to," Perley said. "Possum will tell you Devlin was slow. He just talked fast. I think he got his gun barrel caught in his holster or something. I didn't even know where I was shootin'. Devlin was just unlucky that my shot hit him. It coulda hit something else in here. You can't put much stock in the stories people tell about something like that. They just wanna make more out of it than it actually was. So if you were lookin' for a story about a gunslinger, I'm sorry, there just ain't one."

"Well, I'll tell you what, Perley Gates. I don't know why you've bothered to make up a phony story like that unless you know my reputation. I earned my reputation facing men who were fast. So I'm tellin' you I'm the fastest there is. I've proved it time after time, and once in a while I have to push a local hero a little harder to stand up to face me, just to keep him from shootin' me in the back, so he can say he's the man who shot Kane."

"Well, if that's what you're worried about, you can relax and go ahead and eat some dinner 'cause I ain't gonna shoot you in the back. You have my word on that."

"The word of a gunslinger ain't worth spit," Kane responded bluntly.

Perley's casual attitude bothered Kane, and he decided he would definitely go ahead and kill him. He wondered if Perley's carefree bearing was a trick he often used to catch an opponent off guard. Maybe that was what had caused Devlin to get careless.

Kane looked at Perley. "There's only one sure way to find out the truth about a man, and that's to face him twenty paces apart. So, I'm callin' you out to settle this business between us."

"I feel honored to think you'd invite me to a shootout with you," Perley said. "But I didn't know there was any business between us, so I think I'll pass." He took a bite out of the big biscuit Bertha had put on his plate.

"You'll pass?" Kane erupted. "This ain't no card game. There ain't no passes, and you dealt yourself in when you gunned down Spade Devlin. I'm callin' your hand. Now, let's stop wastin' time. Are you too yellow to face me man-to-man, and live the rest of your life a coward?"

Perley took his time to cut off another bite of steak before answering. "No," he said, "I reckon I'm too smart to face you man-to-man." He shrugged, then explained. "You already told me you're faster than me, so I'd be a real idiot to go up against you, wouldn't I? I'da whole lot rather live a long life as a man with common sense, than a real short one as an idiot. Don't that make sense to you?" When Kane looked as if about to explode, Perley said, "So, why don't you ask Bertha to bring you a good, hot cup of coffee and a plate of this food?

You don't wanna waste your bullets on somebody ain't nobody ever heard of."

"It ain't gonna do you no good, tryin' to play those mind games with me," Kane stated. "I'm callin' you a lowdown dirty coward and I'll shoot you down right where you're sittin', if you don't choose to face me like a man."

"It's a whole lotta trouble to get up and walk out to the middle of the street, and stand there, both of us waitin' to see who was gonna make the first move." Perley shook his head as if weary of it all. He looked at Kane and grinned. "Too bad we can't just sit here and do it without goin' to all that trouble. But that wouldn't be fair 'cause I wear my gun on my hip like everybody else. I'd have my gun down in the chair, hard to draw outta the holster. And you wear your gun way up high, with the butt out." He shrugged. "So all you'd have to do is reach across and pull yours."

Before Kane even saw Perley's hand move, he suddenly found himself looking at the muzzle of a six-shooter pointed straight at his face. His automatic reaction was to reach for his own, but his hand fell on an empty holster. His gun was gone! Suddenly feeling a sickening in his gut, he realized Perley had reached over and pulled his gun so fast he didn't even know what happened. The muzzle of the gun seemed bigger than usual as it held a steady aim at his face.

"Gun has a nice feel. What is that, about a four-and-three-quarter-inch barrel? Just right for a fast-draw holster. I don't care much for the pearl handle, myself. How would you feel about gettin' shot with your own gun?

Not too good, right? 'Course you could reach for that pocket pistol you got in your boot. How fast are you at that? Think you could pull it outta your boot and shoot me before I squeeze this trigger? Possum would help you spread the word that you're the fastest gun out here." Perley paused to let the gunman sweat a little more.

"Well, I'll tell you what, Kane, I don't want a reputation. So, I'm gonna give you back your fancy gun, and you can take it and your reputation back the way you came." Perley emptied the cartridges out of the weapon and laid them on the table but kept the pistol. "Possum, kindly keep your eye on Mr. Kane, here, while I pay Bertha for our dinner."

He got to his feet and went to the kitchen door to find the somber woman standing just inside, obviously listening to the confrontation outside her kitchen. As before, he paid her for the dinner, plus a little extra to show appreciation for the quality.

She smiled at him as she accepted the money. "You take care of yourself, young feller."

Their business finished, Perley laid the pearl-handled pistol on the bar as he walked past, then he and Possum walked out of the saloon. Wide-eyed and gaping mouth, Shag could think of nothing to say.

Outside, Perley and Possum climbed onto their horses and wasted no time heading down the street to Johnson's store. In an act of precaution, they pulled around behind the store, in case Kane decided to take his revenge out with his rifle.

"You shoulda shot that gunslinger when you had his gun on him," Possum complained. When Perley argued that, if he had, it would have been an outright case of murder, Possum asked, "What the hell do you think he was gonna do to you if you didn't face up to him?"

Perley made no reply.

Possum continued. "And we ain't through with him yet. He's got more reason to want you dead than he did before. You pretty much rubbed his nose in it."

"Let's just load up our supplies and get on outta town," Perley said. "I doubt he'll show up at the Double-D now that everybody knows who he really is. Tomorrow, we'll head on back to Texas and leave Kane and what's left of Duke Thacker's gang here."

"We can't go soon enough to suit me," Possum said as they went in through the back door.

"Gotcha all ready to go," Walter Johnson greeted them. "Everything you had on your list. And I didn't charge you anything for grindin' your coffee. That was a little discount because you bought the boots."

"'Preciate it," Perley said, and settled up with him while Possum started loading their supplies on the pack-horse.

Johnson walked outside with Perley, carrying a couple of boxes of .44 cartridges he had just bought. Perley put one box in his saddlebags and tossed the other one to Possum.

"'Preciate the business," Johnson said when they were all packed up. "Come back to see me."

"We'll be headin' back to Texas tomorrow," Perley replied. "But if we're back this way again, we'll surely stop in, won't we, Possum?"

"That we will," Possum replied, anxious to get out of town.

They started back around to the front of the building, leading their horses when Johnson called out, "You boys be careful. Can I help you?"

The question seemed odd to Possum and he turned to see Johnson looking toward the front corner of his building and a man walking toward the store. Realizing the question was meant for the man approaching the store, he continued after Perley.

Then it struck him! "Perley!" he yelled as soon as he recognized Kane, his six-gun in hand.

Perley spun around, recognizing the urgency in Possum's tone.

Kane took a step. "Reach for that gun, damn you," he dared him, then stopped abruptly to take a couple of steps backward, staring in disbelief at the bullet hole in his black vest. Stunned, he looked at Possum, whose gun was still riding in his holster. He dropped to his knees and continued to stare at Perley as if he didn't believe it had happened.

After a few minutes passed and Kane was still on his knees, although obviously dead, Possum dropped his reins to the ground and walked over to poke Kane with his finger. The body fell over onto its side.

"Reckon we'd best go tell Marshal Creech about the shootin'?" Possum asked Johnson. "He might need to know Perley shot in self-defense. Kane already had his pistol out before Perley even knew he was there."

"I'll tell him how it happened," Johnson said, "although I ain't sure I believe what I saw. I expect he's still under the closest bed he could find when he heard the shot."

His comment caused Possum to ask a question that had baffled him ever since he and Perley came to the little town. "How in the world does that drunk keep his job as marshal?"

"That's easy," Johnson answered. "Henry Powell owns the Last Chance Saloon. He's also the mayor. Marshal Creech is his brother-in-law."

Chapter 16

The unexpected demise of the one-name gunslinger brought some positive news to the little town for a change. It had been some time since anything good had come to the town, dating back to when Duke Thacker decided to locate his gang near Texarkana. He was responsible for all the rowdy behavior in town and the importing of gunslingers Spade Devlin and Kane, and to a lesser extent, Slick Bostic. With Thacker gone, the Last Chance Saloon saw an increase in local business. Other individuals also profited briefly from Perley's visit to the town. Chester Rivenbark enjoyed a huge gain when he retained possession of the fine horse bred by the Nez Perce Indians on the Palouse River. And Walter Johnson profited by the acquisition of a pearl-handled Colt Army six-shooter, plus some fancy boots to sell.

The news of the most recent happening in town was not good news to Duke Thacker. When Ned and Mutt returned to the house after the confrontation they had witnessed between Kane and Perley Gates, they were anxious to report the event to Thacker. By happenstance, they had stayed in town long enough to learn the conclusion to the little show Perley had put on in the saloon earlier.

"That's the fastest man alive, Duke," Ned insisted. He looked at Mutt. "Tell me if I'm lyin'. To Thacker, he said, "They was settin' at a table—Perley, Kane, and that one called Possum. From where me and Mutt was settin', we could hear what was goin' on."

"Kane was settin' at a table with Perley Gates?" Thacker interrupted. "I thought he didn't even know what Perley Gates looked like."

"He found out, I reckon." Ned continued. "Kane moved into the room upstairs. Perley and Possum was settin' at the table eatin' dinner, and Kane came walkin' down the stairs and saw 'em. So he sat down at the table and joined 'em." He told the part where Kane called Perley out. "This is the part you ain't gonna believe. Perley reached across and pulled Kane's gun outta his holster. He was holdin' Kane's own gun on him." Ned looked at Mutt for verification.

"That's a fact," Mutt said. "It was so fast Kane didn't even know it was gone till he reached for it and his holster was empty. And there was Perley Gates. Had Kane skunked, holdin' his own gun on him."

"So Kane's dead?" Thacker asked.

"Yeah, Kane's dead," Ned answered him, "but it didn't happen right then. Perley got up and walked out, left Kane settin' there. Kane didn't have enough sense to just shoot Perley in the back, I reckon. He followed him down to the feed store and jumped him when he came outta there. Walter Johnson came in the saloon, tellin' everybody how

Kane tried to beat him to the draw and Perley cut him down."

Thacker continued to sit there, seemingly in a daze, for several minutes, causing Ned and Mutt to exchange puzzled glances. In his mind, Thacker tried to create a picture of Perley reaching across and pulling Kane's gun out of his holster. He found he couldn't create a workable vision of such a feat. It only served to frustrate him more. He had decided that Kane and Perley Gates were the two fastest gun hands he would ever see in his lifetime, and a meeting between the two would be close. But he'd thought the obviously more professional, cruel-hearted Kane would prevail.

To learn that the harmless-looking cowhand with the ridiculous name had taken Kane's measure and cut him down was almost more than Thacker could take. He traced all of the destruction of his once-powerful gang of outlaws to this one innocent-appearing outsider. He was convinced that, aside from the killings of Spade and Kane, the fatal counterattack by the crew of the Double-D would have never happened without Perley Gates, and he, Thacker meant himself, would be encamped as the ruler of a cattle empire, instead of sitting in the rundown farmhouse with the two pathetic remains of his once-feared gang.

Thacker had no religion of any kind. He figured it just the poor man's hope for a reward in the next world, since he was too weak to take one for himself in this world. That was why Thacker was determined to take his reward in this world *and* in the next one. He had no idea why Hell had sent the killing machine—the one with the Heavenly name—to keep him from claiming the reward he sought. But somehow Thacker knew no matter what he tried, Perley Gates would stand in his way. It was plain to see the next step had to be to eliminate Perley Gates. Thacker could then rebuild everything the man had taken down.

Realizing the room had gone silent, Thacker withdrew from his deep thoughts to discover Mutt and Ned staring at him. "What? What the hell are you starin' at?"

"You. You looked like you'd gone off someplace. Me and Mutt was talkin' to you and you acted like you didn't hear a word we was sayin'."

"I was thinkin'," Thacker said.

"You didn't even hear Cora ask if you wanted her to make some more coffee," Mutt commented. "We told her you sure did."

"I told you, I was thinkin'," Thacker came back, a little irritated. "I'm plannin' to be back on top again, and Perley Gates has got to be put under the sod first thing. 'Cause it's plain to see he was sent here just to stop me."

"Who do you think sent him?" Ned asked.

"It don't matter," Thacker replied. "What matters is that our job right now is to get rid of him. Everything will be right back on track again, just like it was before he showed up here."

"Maybe we won't even have to worry about him anymore," Ned suggested. "Walter Johnson said Perley bought supplies for their ride back home tomorrow. So he'll be gone."

"You might think so, but I know better," Thacker snapped. "He'll be back just as soon as we start buildin' the gang back up like it used to be. The only way to be sure he won't be back is to kill him. And I ain't talkin' about callin' him out to have it face-to-face. I'm talkin' about a rifle shot between his shoulder blades. Where is that ranch he's supposed to call home?"

"Triple-G?" Ned asked. "That's in Lamar County, Texas."

"Lamar County," Thacker repeated. "That's one of them counties on the Red River, maybe a hundred miles or so from here. That's a pretty good ride. Oughta be a lot of opportunities to get a good shot at him between here and there."

"You think if we start rustlin' cattle again after we pick up some more men, Perley Gates will come back to Texarkana to put a stop to it?" Ned asked. When Thacker didn't answer, Ned pointed out, "Perley Gates ain't no lawman. Why would he come back here?" With still no answer from Thacker, Ned continued. "The only reason he came out here in the first place was to drive a herd of horses he sold to the Double-D. Ain't that right, Mutt?"

"That's a fact," Mutt said. "Him and two other boys drove 'em out here."

"There's things goin' on here you boys don't under-stand," Thacker said, "and I ain't got the time to try to explain it to ya. Just take my word for it, Perley Gates has got to be stopped and that'll take care of all our problems here." He was starting to get a little testy, so they wisely decided to stop the questions for now.

Cora came in with the coffeepot at that point and the subject was easily dropped.

After supper, Ned lifted the coffeepot. "This is the last of it," he said to Thacker, who was cleaning his rifle and handgun at the end of the kitchen table. "You wanna split this with me?"

Thacker declined, so Ned poured the rest into his cup and joined Mutt out on the front porch to enjoy the cool evening breeze. Mutt was sitting on the front edge of the porch floor with his feet on the steps. Ned sat down beside him. "If we was gonna stay here for any time at all, I might see about buildin' us some porch chairs."

"Shoot," Mutt replied. "If you listen to what Duke was talkin' about before supper, it don't sound like we're gonna be here much longer." He took a quick look behind him at the front door, then asked. "Was he drinkin' a lot this afternoon? That mighta been just whiskey talkin'."

"I don't know," Ned answered. "I wasn't payin' no attention. 'Course we didn't get back from town till just before supper. Hard to say what he was doin' all day." He took a quick look back at the door before he continued. "I don't know how long you've known Duke, but I rode with him for about a year a while back. Listenin' to him rantin' and ravin' now, does it seem to you that maybe a few of the strings in his head have come untied?"

"You mean all that talk about Perley Gates comin' back to get us?" Mutt replied. "Yeah, I was thinkin' somethin' like that. I don't know about you, but I've got no reason to go after that man. I think if you fool around with nature's freaks, you're gonna get yourself messed up good. I say let him go and good riddance. I think if we go after him, all of us ain't comin' back."

"I agree with that," Ned replied. "Perley's a hard one to figure out. Dan Short, Tiny Wilson, and I tried to steal that herd of horses from him and the other two, and both Dan and Tiny got shot. I came after them and got ambushed by Perley. He let me go after I promised to make tracks away from there. I don't expect he's willin' to give me another chance, since I showed up in Texarkana, anyway."

"We've got about everybody in town thinkin' we quit Duke. Maybe we oughta go ahead and make it a fact," Mutt suggested. "Whaddaya reckon he'd do if we quit?"

"I don't know," Ned answered. "He's been actin' awful crazy ever since that night at the Double-D." He lowered his voice to just above a whisper. "And just between you and me, that was a crazy idea to try to take over a ranch and think you're gonna get away with it. Even if the Double-D hadn't come to take it back, they woulda most likely had the army send soldiers after us." He shook his head in disbelief. "I went right along with it because he had always done pretty much what he wanted to and got away with it. This time, I ain't so sure."

"We'd have to find us someplace to shack up," Mutt said. "Somewhere Duke don't know about."

"Hell, why hang around here? There ain't nothin' here we can do. We might as well cut out for Injun Territory, or maybe go on up into Kansas. We can go anywhere we wanna go."

"That might be the best thing to do," Mutt agreed. "When we gonna do it? We can't wait long 'cause he's talkin' about goin' after Perley Gates. And we don't even know when Perley Gates is gonna start back."

"I thought Walter Johnson said he picked up supplies because he was goin' home tomorrow," Ned reminded Mutt. "Ain't that what he said?"

"Maybe them voices inside Duke's head told him different," Mutt japed and laughed at his wit.

"What's so funny?" Thacker wanted to know as he

came out the door to join them. "Tell me, 'cause I ain't seen nothin' funny in a couple of days."

"It weren't nothin'," Mutt said, trying to quickly think of something to explain it. "It was just Ned. He was tryin' to make a sound like a cricket."

"A cricket? Why was he tryin' to do that?"

Mutt couldn't think of any reasonable answer for it, so he said, "He was tryin' to fool a cricket that lit on the step."

"Is that right?" Thacker asked. "Let's hear it, Ned. Let's see how good you are."

At that moment, Ned couldn't recall what a cricket sounded like, but thanks to Mutt, he had to come up with some kind of effort. So he stuck his fingers in his mouth and tried to make a few short chirps.

"That don't sound nothin' like a cricket," Thacker remarked.

"I know," Mutt declared. "That's what I was laughin' at."

"You'd best get to thinkin' in a killin' mood," Thacker scolded, "instead of actin' like a four-year-old tryin' to sound like a cricket. We got work to do. I'm goin' into town with you boys tomorrow. I'm needin' some cartridges and supplies to go after Perley Gates."

"Didn't Johnson say he was leaving tomorrow?" Ned knew that was what they had told Thacker at supper.

"Don't matter what Johnson said," Thacker declared. "Gates ain't headin' back till day after tomorrow."

Ned and Mutt exchanged glances of astonishment.

"You sure you oughta go into town?" Mutt asked. "I mean, since we've been tellin' everybody we don't know where you are. And too many people know you were at the Double-D that night."

"Who the hell's gonna do anything about it if I go into town? I go where I damn well please. If somebody don't like it, they can send for the marshal. When he don't come, they can send for Perley Gates!" He glared at them with defiant eyes as if daring them to challenge him. "I own that town and it's time I reminded everybody about that."

"You're right, Duke. Ain't nobody arguin' with that," Ned attempted to reason. "We was just worryin' about your safety. I mean, somebody might decide to take a shot at you from a window or door, since they know the gang was wiped out."

Thacker's eyes narrowed, pulling his heavy eyebrows down into a deep frown. "This gang ain't wiped out as long as I'm standin'." He swore. "I've been too easy on that town. I ain't gonna be so easy on 'em from now on. We'll go into town in the mornin'. Let 'em know who's still runnin' things and pick up anything we need to go after Perley Gates. I wanna catch him as soon as he leaves the Double-D day after tomorrow."

"Right, Duke. You're the boss." Mutt glanced briefly at Ned, who met his glance with a knowing nod of his head.

They sat in silence for a while after that, until Thacker announced that the beans Cora had cooked for supper were raising hell inside his bowels. When he got up from the porch and headed to the outhouse to take relief, his two lieutenants barely waited until he disappeared around the corner of the house before their rebellious discussion resumed.

It went a step further than before. "He worries the hell outta me," Mutt said, still in a whisper. "This business with Perley Gates has crumbled his crackers for sure, and I'm afraid he's gonna get us killed if we stick with him."

"You know, it's the humane thing to do when you put a dog or a horse down when they're sufferin'," Ned commented. He thought back when he had made just such a decision regarding Dan Short's life. "I ain't sayin' that's what we oughta do for Duke. I'm just sayin' we might have to keep that in the back of our minds if he gets any worse."

"I reckon you're right," Mutt allowed. "I gotta admit it's struck my mind more 'n once after we damn near all got killed out at that ranch." He shook his head, thinking about the disaster that was. "Let's see how he's actin' tomorrow when he goes into town and finds out Perley Gates is done gone. Maybe that'll settle him down some."

They left it at that, and were further encouraged when Thacker went to bed early that night, and they all got a good night's sleep.

The two men who, along with Duke Thacker, were the sole surviving members of the once powerful gang might not have enjoyed that good night's sleep had they known when dawn broke the next morning, Perley Gates did not leave the Double-D. A request from Price Shelton caused Perley and his partners to agree to postpone their departure for a day. Shelton said he needed their help to move the cattle to a new spot for better grass. Since Perley, Possum, nor Sonny were in a big hurry to get back to the Triple-G, they readily agreed to help. This was in light of the fact that the Double-D crew should really be able to move the cattle without their help.

"They've just got too used to havin' us around," Possum speculated.

They found, however, the real reason they were asked to stay had nothing to do with the cattle when Shelton explained his request to Perley at breakfast that morning.

"I hope you ain't gonna be sore about postponin' your trip for a day. Miz Matilda called me up to the house yesterday to talk to me about you and Possum and Sonny. She could never repay you for what you three men did for the Double-D but hoped she could do something to show her appreciation for riskin' your lives alongside the Double-D crew to save this ranch. Well, the women, Matilda, Frances, and Annie, wanna cook up a big supper for you boys and serve it in the dinin' room in the main house, just as a way to say thanks. I was hopin' you boys wouldn't mind stayin' a day longer."

Perley was really surprised. Frankly, having already assumed the Widow Donovan appreciated their help, and he expected no formal show of it, he thought it ought to tickle Possum and Sonny. "We sure ain't gonna pass up an invitation to a big feed like that. It's mighty kind of the lady to wanna do that. You tell her we'd be honored to have supper with her."

"Good, good," Shelton responded. He would have surely hated to disappoint her. He started to tell Perley something else but hesitated, thinking it might not be the right thing to do. Then he decided to tell him anyway. "I ought not say anything about this, but she was kinda hopin' you'd take a shine to Frances." Seeing a flash of genuine surprise in Perley's face, he went on to say, "I reckon I'm gonna have to tell her she's gonna have to settle for Billy Dean."

Perley recovered enough to say, "I kinda think Frances mighta had a lot to say about that." He thought to himself, *Becky Morris might have a little bit to say about it, too.* That thought caused him to think about her, and it seemed it had been months since he had last seen her.

He admitted to himself he was flattered to have Miz Matilda think of him in that way but knew for sure Frances didn't. But it didn't surprise him. Perley figured her mother was interested because he was part owner of the Triple-G and would therefore provide for her daughter.

"Possum and Sonny will be plum tickled when I tell 'em they're gonna dine in style today," he said to Shelton. "All three of us better go polish up our manners so we don't embarrass ourselves."

"Well, you didn't do bad the first time you ate with Mr. Donovan and the missus," Shelton reminded him.

With a whole day to kill until suppertime, Perley thought about how he could spend it. As far as his horses and the supplies he needed, that was all taken care of. Maybe he could find a way to lend a hand to some of the crew. Maybe help Clyde Humphrey build a fence around the little patch of ground where Donald Donovan was buried.

Perley's day was planned for him soon after breakfast, however, when Billy Dean asked if he'd like to ride into town with him to pick up some supplies for Annie.

"It ain't that much she's needin'," Billy said. "Clyde just drove the wagon in a week ago. I think some of this she's wantin' today is for that supper she's gonna cook for you this evenin'. More flour and sugar, I noticed. It ain't enough for me to hitch up the wagon, so I'm just gonna take a packhorse. That's a lot easier for me than messin' with a wagon, since I ain't got but one hand to work with."

"Sure, I'll ride into town with you." Perley couldn't really think of any reason not to, though he was a little surprised Billy asked him instead of any of the other men. Then he thought back to the reason Billy's left arm was bound up in a splint, the result of his trying to ride Buck.

Billy had insisted on riding Buck. He'd learned from Sonny no one could ride the big bay horse but Perley and wanted to prove otherwise. Unsure what he thought about that, but without anything else to do that day, Perley had said he'd go along.

"Are you fixin' to go pretty soon?" Perley asked, 'cause I don't wanna be late for supper tonight."

Billy chuckled when he answered. "Just as soon as we can get saddled up."

Perley couldn't resist the opportunity to jape with him. "You wanna swap horses? I'll ride that roan you're gettin' ready to saddle, and you can ride Buck."

"Hell, no," Billy exclaimed. "I don't want my other arm in a splint."

"Just checkin'. I'd best tell Possum I'm goin', so he won't be pullin' his hair out if he's lookin' for me later on." He found Possum in the bunkhouse.

As he expected, Possum's reaction was, "What for?"

"No particular reason. Just to keep him company," Perley answered.

"What's he need company for?" Possum wanted to know.

Perley couldn't help but chuckle. Possum was getting to be more and more like a parent every day. "Young fellow like Billy most likely needs advice from an older man like me . . . on things about courtin' women like Frances. Things like that."

Possum snorted. "Shoot, you ain't no older than Billy. And you sure as hell don't know the first thing about courtin' women. You be careful. You never know if some of that Thacker gang might be lookin' to ambush Double-D riders."

Perley assured him he would, although he didn't think there was much danger of that. More likely they might have lain in wait for them when they set out on a trail to the west, heading for Texas.

Chapter 17

"Oh, My Lord . . ." Chester Rivenbark muttered slowly, his coffee cup suspended halfway between the table and his mouth.

When Chester gasped under his breath. "Duke Thacker!" Scarcely able to believe the fearsome outlaw leader had returned, he whispered, "What is he doin' back here? Everybody knows he led the raid on the Double-D. He's got some gall, comin' back here after what he tried to do."

The shock of seeing the big, cruel-looking man was so menacing they failed to notice Ned and Mutt walking in right behind him until Mutt spoke to Shag.

"Bertha make any biscuits this mornin'?"

Shag didn't make a sound, but answered Mutt's question with a nod, his eyes never leaving Thacker, as if expecting him to explode into a fit of violence any minute.

"Tell her to fix us up some biscuits and gravy and bring us some coffee. We ain't had no breakfast and we're hungry."

Thacker went directly to his favorite table in the back

corner while Mutt was still placing their order. Biscuits and gravy was one of the few selections safe to eat from Bertha's kitchen. That was the only reason Chester and Philip were eating there that morning. Both were already wondering if they would regret the decision.

While Shag left the bar to take Mutt's order to the kitchen, Mutt walked after Ned to the table where Thacker was sitting. He was in a sinister mood, even more so than his usual gruff bearing. They had had no breakfast before coming to town because Cora was missing. Ned, who was always the first one up, had walked into the kitchen and quickly realized no one was there. The stove was cold and there was no sign anyone had been there. Cora had taken her leave during the night, obviously deciding things were going to get worse and worse.

It had sent Thacker into a rage, swearing to track the gray-haired old woman down and cut her throat. "I even gave her this house," he'd railed, forgetting that he took it back right away.

Ned had told Mutt he was afraid if the biscuits weren't baked the way Thacker liked them, he might take out his vengeance on Bertha.

With only a scrap of a sense of humor left, Mutt had commented that it would be a helluva fight if they went at it hand-to-hand. "Hard to say who would win, since Bertha's the only person in town bigger than Duke."

Thinking he had better give them some attention, Shag walked over to the table and asked if they wanted any whiskey, or if they were just drinking coffee.

"Bring a bottle and put it on the table," Thacker said.

"I might want a drink after I finish the biscuits. Is there anybody in my room?"

"No, sir, Duke," Shag replied immediately. "That's your room. We don't put nobody in that room but you."

"I heard Kane was stayin' upstairs," Thacker said. "Till he went and got his fool-self shot."

"Yeah, he was," Shag responded, "but not in your room, Duke. That room's yours till you say it ain't."

His reply seemed to satisfy Thacker, who gave his attention to the plate of biscuits arriving at the table.

In an effort to lighten the mood, Mutt said, "Man, those look like they're fresh outta the oven. Oughta thank Bertha for bringin' us a whole plate full of 'em. She must know we're hungry."

The stoic woman paused to look at him for a couple of seconds before commenting. "I brought the whole plate full to keep from walkin' my tail off, comin' back and forth every time one of you yaps want for a biscuit."

It struck Thacker as funny and he roared with laughter. She turned around and returned to the kitchen, wondering what was so funny about that.

About half an hour later, Walter Johnson came in, attracted by the same simple item on the menu. He was already inside and walking past the bar when he realized Duke Thacker and his two men were sitting at the back corner table. By then, it was too late to turn around and leave without being noticed, so he just sidled over to the bar. "What the hell is he doin' back here?" he asked Shag. "I thought he had left this town for good."

"So did I," Shag said. "But clabber always rises to the top."

"Anybody tell Marshal Creech?"

"What for?" Shag asked. "So he can come over here and have a drink with him?"

"Johnson," Thacker called out, having just noticed him talking to Shag. "Anybody tendin' your store? Or is everybody takin' the day off? I'm needin' some cartridges."

"Yes, sir," Johnson said. "My son's tendin' the store, and I'll be goin' back right away."

"How 'bout that blacksmith beside your store? Is he there?"

"Yep," Johnson answered. "Lonnie's there. I saw him when I opened up this mornin'."

"If you're goin' right back, take my horse back with you and tell Lonnie to shoe him. Save me a little time," Thacker said.

"Sure thing, Duke," Johnson replied. "No trouble a-tall. Tied out front, is he?"

"Yeah, he's out front. The buckskin. I'll be down to do some business with you directly. 'Preciate it." He returned his attention to the coffee and biscuits on the table.

"You gonna stay long enough to eat some biscuits and drink a little coffee?" Shag asked.

"No, damn it. I was," Johnson said, "but I just lost my appetite. Duke Thacker is the last person I wanted to see when I walked in here this mornin'. What the hell is he doin' here? Are we gonna have to wire the U.S. marshal in Fort Smith to come get this murderer out of our town?"

"He's actin' like he's fixin' to go somewhere," Shag said. "Talkin' about needin' to buy some cartridges and supplies from ya. Now, he wants his horse shod. Maybe the three of 'em are gettin' ready to move on to another town somewhere. That 'ud be all right, wouldn't it?"

Johnson nodded his head deliberately. "We can always hope for the best."

It was a pleasant day for a ride into town and Billy and Perley made it a leisurely trip with casual conversation. Billy wanted to ask questions about Perley's quickness with a gun, but Perley was reluctant to discuss a subject that was as much a mystery to him as it was to anyone who knew him. He steered Billy away from that subject and talked about the future of the Double-D now that Donald Donovan was deceased. Billy thought everyone was satisfied with Price Shelton in charge. Billy came back with questions about how young Perley was when he first realized how fast he was. Perley countered with, "How are you and Frances sneakin' out to see each other since Clyde nailed up that trapdoor in the washroom?"

As they approached Johnson's Feed Store, Billy came back with "That's right. I have you to thank for that, don't I?" That prompted another question. "Do you think I have any chance—" He stopped in midsentence and pulled the roan to a stop.

"What is it?" Perley asked, pulling up beside him.

"That's my horse!" Billy exclaimed. "That's Spunky! And that's my saddle!"

Perley saw him then. Walter Johnson was leading a buckskin horse past his store and into the blacksmith's shop next door. "Are you sure?" Perley asked.

"Damn right, I'm sure," Billy exclaimed. "That's my horse. One of that Thacker gang ran off with him." He didn't wait for Perley to respond and wheeled the roan and galloped after Johnson.

Perley wheeled Buck and started after him. When they got to the blacksmith shop, Johnson was talking to Lonnie Pope about shoeing the buckskin. Both were startled when Billy suddenly appeared, pulling the roan to a sliding stop almost at their feet.

With his broken arm straight up in the air, he came off the horse with one hand on the saddle horn. "That's my horse! Where'd you get him?" Billy walked up to the buckskin and took hold of the bridle. No doubt the horse knew him. It immediately whinnied and rubbed its nose on Billy's chest. "Where'd you get him?" Billy repeated.

Walter and Lonnie were at a loss to respond to Billy's questions, combined with the surprise of seeing Perley with him.

Finally, Johnson asked, "Are you sure, Billy? A lot of these buckskins look alike."

"A man knows a horse he's raised from a colt," Perley said. "And it's plain to see the horse knows Billy."

"If you don't believe the horse, maybe you'll believe the saddle." Billy looked at Lonnie and said, "If you'll lift that saddle skirt on that side, you might see the owner's name."

They waited while Lonnie looked under the skirt.

Impatient, Billy asked, "What's it say?"

"Billy Dean," Lonnie answered, exchanging worried glances with Johnson.

Seeing the discomfort between the two men, Perley sought to get it out in the open. "Whoever's ridin' this horse is clearly a horse thief. More than that, he stole it after he attacked the people in the house. And I'm wonderin' why both of you are reluctant to say who the thief·is." Looking at Johnson then, he asked, "Did one of you buy this horse from the thief?"

Johnson gave in. "It ain't nothin' like that. It ain't my horse. I just led it down here from the saloon." He paused again, reluctant. "The man ridin' this horse is Duke Thacker." It had the effect he thought it would have and was obvious why he had hesitated to say it.

Perley and Billy registered the shock in their faces, and both were speechless for a few moments.

Perley found his voice first. "That answers the question of what happened to Duke Thacker." He looked over at Billy. "He got away after the fight and stole your horse to make his escape on." Turning back to Johnson and Lonnie, Perley continued. "And lo and behold, he comes right back home to Texarkana. Where is he? Is he in the jail?"

"He's at the Last Chance Saloon," Johnson said sheepishly.

"Everything's back to normal, right?" Perley asked. "The town's celebratin' his safe return at the local saloon. It's too bad you boys out at the Double-D didn't get a notice about the celebration, Billy. I expect there's a lot of your people that woulda liked to come. Maybe the Widow Donovan mighta come." Finished with his sarcastic display of his disgust for the town's reaction to Thacker's return, he got serious. "That man not only tried to take over the ranch, he broke in the house and murdered Donald Donovan and held two women prisoners.

He oughta be in the jail, not in the saloon, while he's waitin' for his stolen horse to be shod."

"Doggone it, Perley," Johnson pleaded. "There ain't nobody in this town who wanted to see Duke Thacker show up here again. He's been gone a couple of days and everybody was startin' to get back to the way it was before he first set foot in town. Then he shows up this mornin' with those two who claimed they had quit him. There ain't nothin' we can do about him. I hate to say it, Billy, but there were some of us who were glad when Thacker decided to raid the Double-D, after we heard how the Double-D crew wiped out Thacker's gang. The only thing good about this mornin' is the fact that Thacker told me to take his horse—I mean your horse, Billy—to Lonnie and he was comin' down to my store to buy supplies. I think he's gettin' ready to go somewhere and I hope it's for good."

It was a pathetic excuse for taking no action against a wanton killer, but Perley could understand the town's lack of backbone. Under different circumstances, the town could look to their sheriff to maintain law and order. But this little town had no such recourse. One thing was certain, Billy was going to take possession of his horse. They could pick up the items Annie had sent Billy in to buy then they could take Spunky and go home, leaving the town to take care of the problem that would cause.

But Perley couldn't do that. The words *cow pie* came to his mind and he slowly shook his head. "Billy, I'm fixin' to stir up some trouble you ain't obligated to participate in. So if you want to, you can pick up that stuff Annie wants and take it and your buckskin back to the Double-D. Just don't tell Possum what I'm doin'."

"Hell, no," Billy replied. "Deal me in."

"All right." Perley grinned. "I thought you'd say that." He turned to Lonnie. "That jail over there across the street, has it got an honest to God cell in it that will hold a prisoner?"

"It does," Lonnie answered. "I built that cell, myself. It'll hold a prisoner, but you ain't gonna get Marshal Creech to arrest anybody, especially if his name is Duke Thacker."

"What about that young fellow who acts like Creech's deputy?" Perley asked.

"Clint Cross?"

"Yeah, Clint Cross," Perley said. "Is he as big a drunk as the marshal?"

"No," Johnson answered his question. "Clint's a good man. He's just stuck in a bad place. And I ain't ever seen Clint drunk. What are you plannin' to do?"

"Well, the quickest way to solve your town's problem would be to wait for Thacker to set foot outta the saloon and shoot him down. But if I can, I'd rather arrest him, lock him up, and let your town decide what to do with him. Try him, wire the U.S. marshal to send a deputy down here to get him, hang him, whatever you and the other citizens wanna do. That ain't none of my business."

"That's a mighty ambitious plan," Walter Johnson commented. "The problem you're gonna run into right at the start is that Marshal Jonah Creech ain't gonna go along with any plan to arrest Duke Thacker. I'd be surprised if you found him sober in the first place."

"He might not be drunk this early in the mornin'," Lonnie offered, "but he'll be so hung over from last night that he might as well be drunk."

"Will Clint be there?" Perley asked. When they said that he would, Perley nodded. "Then that's all I need." He glanced at Billy. "You still wanna be in on this?"

"Just tell me what to do."

"I'll most likely need your gun hand," Perley told him. "You'll probably know when without me tellin' you. It depends on those two with him."

"What do you want us to do, me and Lonnie?" Johnson asked, although not with the enthusiasm that Billy had shown.

"Nothin', really. Just do what you woulda done if Billy and I hadn't showed up here this mornin'," Perley said, much to Johnson's relief. "All right. I guess that about takes care of it. Lonnie, you can go ahead and shoe that buckskin. Is that all right with you, Billy?"

"Yeah, if he needs new shoes, he needs 'em whether I'm ridin' him or Thacker's big butt is in the saddle." He went over and rubbed the buckskin's neck. "Don't worry, boy, I'll be back for you."

Then he and Perley led their horses across the street and walked about a dozen yards to the jail where they tied them at the hitching rail. They paused a couple of seconds to regard the rundown appearance of the small frame building then stepped up on the porch. Perley tried the door, found it unlocked, and stepped inside the tiny office.

"Clint Cross, right?" Perley asked the young man at

the desk, stepping to the side to give Billy room to stand beside him.

"Yes, sir," Clint answered. "What can I do for you?" As soon as he said it he recognized Perley as the man who shot Spade Devlin. "If you're lookin' for the marshal, he ain't in the office right now."

"I see he ain't. Wouldn't hardly be room for all of us if he was. You're the man we came to see, anyway." Perley pointed to the door behind the young man. "Is that the cell room behind you there?"

"Yes, sir," Clint answered, not comfortable with where this might be leading. "But there ain't no prisoners in there right now."

"If I was to guess, I'd say the marshal is in there now, sleepin' one off. Am I right?"

Clint didn't answer the question. He asked one instead. "Is there something I can do for you fellows?"

"Clint, are you familiar with the raid Duke Thacker and his gang made on the Double-D ranch? That they kicked in the door to the house and murdered Donald Donovan? That they held two women as prisoners? You know about that, don't you, Clint?"

"Yes, sir. I heard all about it."

"Well, Clint, that murderer, Duke Thacker, showed up here in town this mornin'. What do you reckon Marshal Creech would do about that . . . if he was in his office when he found out about it?"

"But he's not in his office—" Clint started.

"Would he arrest Thacker and lock him up in jail?" Perley asked.

Clint didn't answer. He knew Perley wouldn't care for the answer.

"That's what a marshal should do, ain't it, Clint?"

Clint nodded slowly.

"Good, 'cause with the marshal out of the office, that's what the deputy will do. And we've come to help you do that."

Clint looked totally confused and uncertain. Before he could protest, Perley continued.

"Billy and I have talked to some members of the town council and they've authorized us to help you arrest Duke Thacker and anybody else who tries to help him avoid arrest. The town council said they could count on you to do the right thing, and Billy and I will be right there to back you up." Perley didn't actually know if there was a town council or not but had an idea Clint didn't know either since he showed no sign of doubting Perley's word. "I'll tell you the truth, Clint. This arrest will go a long way to lettin' the town know they've got a responsible man in the marshal's office. They'll see that you can handle the job when Marshal Creech ain't here."

Perley paused to see if his motivational talk had any effect on the young man. It was hard to say, but it was obvious wheels were spinning inside his head. Perley knew he was probably trying to make up his mind. "Billy and I are gonna be right there with you when you tell him he's under arrest for the murder of Donald Donovan. If he makes one false move, we'll cut him down." He waited for Clint to commit to the arrest while Billy stood by the window, watching for any sign of Thacker.

Finally, Clint said, "Marshal Creech is asleep in the cell room. It's gonna be hard to wake him up."

"Let's take a look at that cell," Perley suggested.

Without a word, Clint got up from the desk and opened the cell room door. He led Perley into the room, which was almost entirely walled off with bars, leaving a space just adequate to accommodate a straight-back chair between the office door and the cell itself. Marshal Jonah Creech was sprawled facedown on one of the two beds inside, a steady snoring like the sound of a chair being dragged across a wooden floor emanating from his mouth. Perley went to the bars and tested them. They seemed solid enough.

"He's kinda hard to wake up," Clint said apologetically.

It was plain to see he was very much embarrassed for the marshal to be caught out. On the floor next to the bed was a half-full bottle of whiskey. Clint was sure Perley saw it, even though the light was very dim in the cell room.

"He's gonna want it as soon as he wakes up."

"I think it'd be a good idea to leave the marshal right where he is," Perley said. "We'll put Thacker in there with him. There's an empty bed, and from what I've heard, he and the marshal get along pretty well. Ought not be a problem. Maybe they'll have a drink together when the marshal wakes up."

They went back into the office.

"No sign of Thacker yet," Billy reported, still at the window. "I reckon he's givin' Lonnie time to shoe my horse. That's another thing you're arrestin' him for," he said to Clint. "He stole my horse."

Clint did not reply, just as he had with almost everything that had been said. Billy really had doubts he would make the arrest, but Perley still had faith in Clint's principles. Thinking about that, he decided maybe it would be a good idea to go ahead and make the arrest in the saloon, instead of waiting for Thacker to walk down the street to the feed store. That way, if any of the town's citizens were there, they could see Clint was on the job. It might mean more support for the marshal's office. Perley had not said the arrest was going to be in the street when Thacker came outside, so it shouldn't make any difference to Clint as far as his will to do the job.

"Are you ready to take the responsibility for arresting this outlaw who's been terrorizin' your town for so long?" Perley asked.

"I reckon I am," Clint replied, much to Perley's relief, even though it was lacking in determination.

"Good man," Perley said. "Here's the way it's gonna happen." He went on to explain how Clint was to make the arrest and where he and Billy would be in support.

Clint seemed determined to do what was right for the town, and Perley saw the definite possibility of changing Clint's image from that of the marshal's caretaker and servant. "Have you got a badge somewhere?" Perley asked.

Clint said, "There's a deputy's badge in the desk drawer."

"Might as well pin it on to make it look official."

Clint got the badge and pinned it on his shirt pocket. He put his hat on and started for the door.

Perley said, "It'd be a good idea to strap your gun on, too. Make it look even more official."

"I forgot it," Clint said, flushed with embarrassment. He pulled his gun belt out of another drawer and strapped it on.

"Is it loaded?" Perley asked. "I don't think you're gonna need it, with Billy and me backin' you, but you never know. It's always a good idea to keep it loaded." He watched as Clint checked the .44 six-gun and returned it to his holster. He was impressed when he saw no signs of nervousness from the young deputy, especially when Clint had never exhibited an aggressive side before. Perley decided there might be a lot more to the character of Clint Cross than he had shown to the outside world.

When all seemed ready, Perley walked over and opened the door. "Well, I reckon it's time to get to work." They went outside and started toward the Last Chance. Before reaching it, Perley and Billy broke off and headed for the back of the saloon, while Clint continued toward the front door.

Chapter 18

The atmosphere was still a little tense in the Last Chance Saloon where Duke Thacker was still enjoying his commanding presence and the fear he instilled in those around him. A few times one of the regular townsmen had dropped in to get Bertha's biscuits, having already seen the lack of a threat with only Mutt and Ned inside. Seeing the return of Thacker, however, customers' visits to the saloon were shortened considerably.

It was an unexpected surprise when Clint Cross walked in the front door. The most noticeable difference in his appearance was his wearing of a badge and gun.

"Well, lookee here," Thacker remarked. "Here comes ol' Marshal Creech's nursemaid, and he ain't got the marshal with him. He musta run outta medicine since I was outta town for a couple of days. I reckon I'll send him a bottle to keep him outta our way."

"I thought we was leavin' town tomorrow," Ned commented. "Why waste a bottle of whiskey on that ol' drunk? He ain't done us any good for a long time."

"We ain't had no trouble from the law ever since that old fool was hired as the marshal. Look out. Here he comes," Thacker japed loudly when Clint saw them and started walking toward their table. "Don't nobody run." He chuckled for his wit.

Clint walked right up to their table and stopped to stand squarely in front of Thacker.

The amused outlaw said, "Howdy, sonny boy. Did your daddy send you for some more medicine?"

"Duke Thacker, you're under arrest for the murder of Donald Donovan, the kidnappin' of the Widow Donovan and her cook. You're also under arrest for the theft of a buckskin horse that belongs to Billy Dean."

It was no longer funny to Thacker. "Why, you snot-nosed young pup, have you been drinkin' the marshal's likker? I think I'll have to teach you some respect."

"I warn you, you'd best come peacefully," Clint said, bravely maintaining his calm.

"Or you'll do what? I'm gonna show you some peace," Thacker roared, hardly able to believe what he was hearing.

"I'd do what he says if I was you," Perley said.

All three at the table jerked to attention and looked around to discover him standing to one side behind them, his Colt .44 in hand. Hearing the cocking of another hammer, they looked toward the other side to see Billy, his weapon in hand as well.

"Now," Perley continued, "Deputy Cross wants to see three pairs of hands, palms down, flat on the table."

Having witnessed the speed with which Perley Gates handled a handgun, there was no hesitation on the part of the surprised outlaws.

Perley quickly slipped behind them and relieved each holster of its weapon. "Ned, you and the other fellow just sit right where you are. The deputy ain't got any reason to arrest you today."

He turned his attention to Thacker then. "Stand up, Thacker."

"You go to hell," Thacker replied.

"I was hopin' you wouldn't be a lotta trouble," Perley said, "but I figured you might be. Billy, you and the deputy keep your guns on this big buffalo here while I get him ready to move." To Thacker, he said again, "Stand up, Thacker," and received the same response he got the first time. So he dropped his Colt back into his holster and drew his skinning knife. One hard jab in Thacker's behind brought the cantankerous outlaw howling to his feet and reaching for his wounded butt.

He was immediately set upon with a coil of rope Perley had brought in with him. He trapped Thacker's groping hand with a small noose in the end of the rope and drew it tight then looped the free end around and around the big man's body until he was bound up with his arms trapped to his sides.

"I reckon we're ready to go, Deputy Cross," Perley announced, which served as a signal for Thacker to plop back down in the chair, but not without a little yelp for the puncture wound in his behind.

"You just signed your death warrant," Thacker threatened. "You'd better shoot me while you've got the chance. 'Cause if you don't, I'll hunt you down and you'll never see me comin'."

"I gotta hand it to ya, Thacker. You've got a way of lookin' at the bright side of things that ain't got no bright side. You need to learn to pay attention. Are you tellin' me you ain't noticed that you're the one tied up tighter 'n a tick's belly button? Now, all you gotta do to get outta all the rope is walk on over to the jailhouse and we'll take it offa ya."

"I ain't movin'," Thacker said.

"Let's just shoot the damn horse thief," Billy suggested.

"That would be the solution most of the folks in town would approve of," Perley replied. "But Deputy Cross wants to do this by the book, and give ol' Thacker here a fair trial. So we'll take him to the jail. You and Clint keep an eye on him while I go get a transporter." He left them to watch the prisoner while he walked out the front door.

"What's a transporter?" Clint asked Billy.

"I ain't got no idea," Billy responded "I thought maybe you knew."

"That fool don't know what he's cuttin' hisself in for," Thacker said to Clint. "You know Jonah Creech ain't gonna hold me in no damn jail cell. You cut me loose now and I won't hold no grudges about this nonsense here. You just go on back to that jail like this never happened and that's the way it'll be with me."

"What about me?" Billy asked. "You want me to give my horse back to you? Would that square things up between us?"

Thacker just stared at him with a grin of contempt on his dark face. "Oh, I'll remember you, Billy Dean, and I'll be seein' you. There ain't no jail that can hold me. You just remember that."

"All right. I brought the transporter," Perley announced as he came striding back in the door. "I borrowed a coil of rope offa that roan you're ridin'," he said to Billy.

"Where's the transporter?" Billy asked, seeing nothing but the end of a rope in Perley's hand.

"It's on the other end of this rope," Perley answered and went directly to the big man sitting tightly bound. In the midst of vile and lethal curses, he tied the loose end of the rope to Thacker's body, pushing it through both armpits before tying it off. He ended up with a strong connection under Thacker's shoulders, and said, "That feels pretty solid. Last chance, Thacker. Sure you hadn't rather walk on over to the jail?"

"Go to hell." The outlaw repeated his first reply to the invitation.

"I wanted to be fair and humane about it, but I'm kinda glad you refused the offer. I wanted to see how my knots hold up under a strain. I think Buck likes the game, too. He'll be tickled when he hears you refused the easy way. See, he's a horse, and he don't understand that all humans ain't got common sense." Perley stood back and pulled the table out of the way.

"Okay, Deputy Cross, we're ready to go." He walked toward the front door clearing other chairs and tables out of the way. "We need a clear path, so we can make it as comfortable for your prisoner as possible."

"Hey, what about our six-guns?" Mutt Thomas yelled after him.

"You can pick 'em up at the deputy's office after we get Thacker in jail," Perley yelled back as he walked across the porch and stepped down to the street where his horse waited patiently.

Inside, Thacker made an appeal to Clint Cross. "Clint,

that man's a crazy man. An officer of the law can't treat a prisoner like this."

"He's not an officer of the law," Clint replied. "It woulda been a whole lot easier, if you had just walked across the street to the jail."

Thacker got to his feet in an attempt to threaten Clint, then was suddenly jerked off his feet and flying through the air for a good ten feet before he was slammed to the floor, bumping and scraping toward the door. Everyone in the saloon ran to the front door, including Bertha, who had been watching from the kitchen door.

A wide, out-of-place grin spread across her homely face as she watched Thacker's body bound up like a mummy as it bounced along the rough street, up past the depot and back again. She grinned wider, thinking she had a part in the setup. She'd let Perley and Billy into the back door to her kitchen, and it was something she would not have let anyone else do. The area back of the kitchen was her private area. But she had taken a shine to Perley Gates and had no use for Duke Thacker at all.

Perley pulled Buck up in front of the jail and dismounted. He walked back to Thacker, who was bruised and bleeding from a hundred scratches. "How we doin' back here? You 'bout ready to walk on into that cell and lay down on the bed? Or you want another ride around town?"

Gasping for air after having it knocked out of his lungs, his face covered with dust, Thacker was hurting too badly to maintain his defiant stance. "You win this round," he gasped. "I'll go in peacefully."

"Well, that's a whole lot more sensible," Perley said.

"I'm glad you decided to quit resistin'. Gimme a hand and help me get him on his feet," he said to Clint and Billy as they ran up.

It took all three of them to get the big man on his feet. They removed his gun belt and dumped a couple of pounds of dirt the heavy bullet belt had scraped from the street. Perley and Clint helped support him as they walked him into the office and into the jail cell. Marshal Creech was still unconscious on one bed.

"Who the hell is that?" Thacker grunted.

"Ain't nobody that'll bother you," Perley said. "You got your own nice bed over on that side of the cell. You just lay down and rest up. You'll be good as new in a little while."

"Where's Marshal Creech?" Thacker demanded from the other bed. "I wanna talk to Marshal Creech."

Clint looked as if he wasn't sure what to say, so Perley answered Thacker. "He's out at the moment, but he's real close to things goin' on in the jail right now. He oughta be back soon to talk to ya."

Seeing the whiskey bottle beside Creech's cot, Clint picked it up and said to Thacker, "I'll make arrangements with Bertha to fix your meals."

That pleased Perley. He hadn't thought about that. It made him think maybe he had been wrong about Jonah Creech. Maybe he had actually arrested someone before.

"I need to refill the water bucket, too," Clint said as he locked the cell door.

He, Perley, and Billy returned to the office and Clint locked the door leading to the cells. He held out the whiskey bottle and said, "I thought it best to take this outta the cell. I'll keep it in here. The marshal's gonna want it as soon as he wakes up."

"Billy and I'll stick around while you're doin' those chores and keep an eye on your prisoner for you," Perley said. "You look to me like you know what you're doin'. You got any worries about how you're gonna handle Creech when he wakes up? He might wanna let Thacker go and that wouldn't be too good for you, would it?"

"No, sir, it wouldn't," Clint answered frankly. "I decided you and Billy are right. Somebody has to stand up to Duke Thacker. I'm tryin' to do what's right, even if I lose my job."

"You figure Jonah Creech will fire you and let Thacker out right away?" Billy asked.

"Jonah Creech couldn't fire me," Clint answered. "He didn't hire me. Henry Powell hired me to look after Marshal Creech. The marshal's his brother-in-law, and Mr. Powell ain't just the owner of the Last Chance, he's the mayor, too."

"Is there a town council?" Perley asked.

"Not really," Clint answered. "I know you haven't really talked to any council members. There's a few of the business owners, like Walter Johnson and Philip Davis, who talk to Mr. Powell about different problems, but Mr. Powell does things pretty much the way he wants to."

"How'd he get elected mayor?" Perley asked.

"I don't know. I think it was because he and Walter Johnson were the first two businessmen to build in town. And Mr. Powell's saloon was doin' a lot more business than the feed store right off, so he just sorta assumed the job as mayor."

"Sounds to me like you folks need to get together and have a real election," Perley commented. "Elect a mayor and vote on a town council. Then you could decide whether or not to keep Jonah Creech in the marshal's office."

By the expression on Clint's face, Perley could see what he was proposing might be out of the question, at least in Clint's mind. "I think you can handle the town marshal's job. What do you think?"

"I'd like to try," Clint answered frankly. "I know I could do better than Marshal Creech."

"Well, I think the town deserves somebody who's willin' to do the right job," Perley declared. "So you need to go talk to some of the business owners right now while you've got Thacker in jail. Talk to Johnson, over at the store, and Lonnie Pope, Chester Rivenbark, Philip Davis. I'd bet they're sick enough of the way things have been goin' in this town they're ready to organize a council. And they oughta be impressed that you arrested Thacker instead of just shootin' him down."

"I'll do it," Clint decided. "You wanna come with me and talk to them?"

"I don't think that would be a good idea," Perley said. "Number one, it ain't none of my business. And number two, some of these folks think I'm another gunslinger like the ones you just got rid of. Besides, you want the idea to come from you."

"Yeah," Clint replied, "I see what you mean. I'll give it a try"—he was convinced it was his chance to make a big move in his heretofore uneventful existence—"even though I might wind up out at the Double-D, lookin' for a job punchin' cows."

The three men stepped outside and Clint locked the office door. Still wearing his deputy's badge and his gun belt, he said, "Wish me luck."

"I think you're on the right path," Perley said. "Don't you, Billy?"

Billy agreed wholeheartedly, saying the town was waiting for somebody to take charge.

"We'll be over at the blacksmith," Perley said, "waitin' for Billy's horse."

They parted then, all three feeling as if they were responsible for something important.

Gradually, he began to be aware of his existence and the groggy feeling he knew so well. He slowly opened his eyes and tried to focus on the striped canvas mattress cover for a long few moments before he realized he was lying facedown. Somehow while he was asleep, his heart had moved up into his head, and he could feel it pounding away in its effort to escape the confined space. He needed a drink badly and reached down beside the cot to find the bottle.

Feeling nothing, he groped around carefully, in case he might have left the cork out after his last drink. He didn't want to knock it over. Although it was late morning and a clear, sunny day, the light in the cell was dim, since the only source was a small slit of a window near the ceiling on the outside wall. Feeling a wave of nausea swelling deep down inside his intestines, he rolled off the cot and crawled to the slop bucket that was always kept in the corner. But, like his bottle, it had been moved.

Confused, he looked around until he saw the bucket halfway between the two beds in the cell. It was too late. His gut attempted to empty its contents right there on the spot, the spot being the wooden floor. He was helpless to stop the painful retching that produced nothing more than liquid, for he had not eaten any solid food in twenty-four hours.

Finally feeling he could function again, he yelled, "Clint! Where's my bottle? What did you move the slop bucket for?" He started toward it, holding onto the bars of the cell for support. "What the—?" He stopped, startled. "Who the—? Clint!" he yelled again. When there was no response to his yelling but an aroused grumble from the huge body on the other cot, he staggered to the cell door. Finding it locked, he thought he must be having a nightmare, so he stood. Grasping the bars of the cell door, he shook it violently and called for Clint until he heard the gruff command behind him.

"Shut up, you drunken fool, or I'm gonna break your back, so you'll have somethin' else to yell about."

"You watch your tongue," Creech blurted. "You're talkin' to the marshal."

"I'm talkin' to a damn fool. A lousy, no-account drunk. That's who I'm talkin' to." Duke was sitting up on the cot by then."

"Duke?" Creech exclaimed when his bloodshot eyes finally could focus on the dirt-covered face. "What are you doin' here?" Creech asked, totally confused and hoping he was having a nightmare.

"I'm under arrest," Thacker answered in disgust. "Your deputy arrested me."

"Clint?" Creech responded in surprise. "Clint Cross arrested you and put you in here?" The marshal was having a hard time believing that.

"Yes, damn it," Thacker replied angrily. "He had a little help gettin' me in this cell. He couldn'ta done it by hisself."

Creech was still finding it hard to picture. "Who helped him?" He couldn't think of anyone with enough brass to take on the job.

"Who else?" Thacker roared. "Perley Gates. He's the one who's caused nothin' but trouble since the first day he rode into town. Him and one of the hands from the Double-D sneaked up behind me when that sissy boy you call your deputy came marchin' up to me in the saloon to tell me I was under arrest."

"Why didn't you tell him to come get me?" Creech asked. "I'da set 'em straight." He paused to ask, "What happened to you? You look like you lost a fight with a grizzly." He knelt briefly to take a quick look under Thacker's cot and gasped. "Man! I need a drink!"

"You was layin' on that bed, sleepin' off a drunk," Thacker railed. "That's the reason nobody thought about sendin' for you. And I look like this on account I was dragged behind a horse, up and down the street before they put me in here. And the whole time I was bouncing my butt offa them ruts I was wonderin' what the hell I keep you supplied with likker for. If somebody can come into your town and ambush me like this, then you ain't worth keepin' alive."

"Now, hold on there, Duke," the marshal responded fearfully. "It weren't drinkin' likker to blame. I've been a little under the weather for a day or two, most likely somethin' I et at the saloon. You know, sometimes that ol' woman will let some meat set too long before she cooks it. That'll give you the belly cramps. Don't you worry about this little mix-up. I'll straighten Clint out as soon as he gets back from wherever he went. That was a mistake puttin' you in here."

"He's gotta pay for it," Thacker declared. "He's gonna know he made a big mistake, and you're gonna need to find you another deputy. Maybe him and Perley Gates can ride the same train to Hell, because that is one man I personally aim to kill. I ain't hirin' it done. I'm claimin' this one for myself. You don't drag Duke Thacker through the street like he done, and live."

"You're right, Duke. You're absolutely right," Creech said.

"As soon as he gets back here to let you outta this cell, you go straight over to the Last Chance and find Mutt Thomas and Ned Bates. They'll most likely be there to get somethin' to eat, since we ain't got no cook out at the house no more. You tell them my plans for tomorrow ain't changed. We was plannin' to take a little ride over toward Texas tomorrow and I'm still goin'. But first thing they've got to do is come break me outta this jail. After you tell 'em, if you don't wanna get in the way of a stray bullet, you'd best take a little ride outta town."

"What if Perley Gates and that other fellow with him are still in town?" Creech asked. "He might give your boys some trouble."

That thought was enough to make Thacker pause. He wasn't confident Ned and Mutt could handle Perley Gates. He wanted that kill for himself, anyway. He was sure Perley was going back to Texas tomorrow. He just somehow knew it. He had been right, so far. Perley was still here today. "All right. You tell my boys this. Tell 'em to break me out of this jail about suppertime this evenin'. Perley and Billy Dean will go back to the Double-D for supper and all we'll have to worry about is Clint Cross."

Creech was quick to agree. "I'll tell 'em, Duke. Then later this afternoon, I'll just make myself scarce and leave Clint to watch the office." That seemed to pacify the angry outlaw for the moment, but the marshal had other thoughts in mind as well. He wasn't sure he could continue to drown his fears in alcohol for much longer. He had given it thought before, but just maybe he could summon enough fortitude to get on his horse and ride as far away from Texarkana as he could get.

Chapter 19

"Never mind what's happenin' here in town," Billy told Perley. "If we hang around this town much longer, we ain't gonna get back to the ranch in time with that stuff Annie Hagen sent us for. And you're gonna see something when you rile Annie up. You think Duke Thacker's a handful? Annie's an armload if you mess up her cookin'."

"We ain't gonna be hangin' around much longer," Perley said. "We got the stuff she sent us for, and Lonnie's about done shoein' your buckskin so you can head on back right away. If I can, I'll try to make it back for that supper she's plannin' for us. Walter Johnson asked me to stay and help Clint when he goes to let the marshal out of that jail cell, and I can understand why. Clint's gonna have his hands full. We started this whole arrest thing. I can't just drop it in Clint's lap and ride away." He shook his head, perplexed. "Tell Possum to make sure he and Sonny are there for that supper."

Perley and Billy had been in the feed store when Clint walked in to talk to Walter Johnson. They tried to distance themselves from Clint and the store owner to give the deputy an opportunity to persuade Johnson that a town council was the answer to questions of this nature in the future. But it was a natural reaction for Johnson to call Perley in on the discussion, since Cross had not previously impressed anyone in town that he was capable of taking on the job of town marshal.

Perley gave his opinion that Clint was more than ready, and he was willing. "Don't you think it's time for you and the other merchants to stand together to take over the management of your own town?" Perley asked.

"If he doesn't, I do," Chester Rivenbark announced, having heard Perley's question as he came in the back door. "I was at the post office talkin' to Broadus Fisher when Clint there came in to talk to us about a town council. Broadus and I both agree. We sure as hell need one, and we need to elect us a new mayor. What about it, Walter? Are you in?"

"I'm in," Lonnie Pope called out, as he came in the front door. Seeing Billy standing by, he said, "Your horse is shod, Billy." Back to Johnson then, he said, "I think we oughta have a meetin' tonight of the new town council. I think we oughta have it in the Last Chance Saloon, so Henry Powell will be there. He can be a member of the new council, but we'll *vote* on who's gonna be mayor."

"I reckon I'm in, too," Walter Johnson spoke up then. "And I believe we need to give Clint Cross a chance to run the marshal's office. We've sure got to fire Jonah Creech. Because of him, Duke Thacker was able to do anything he wanted and nobody dared to say a word about it. If you did, you'd find yourself in a coffin, and Jonah Creech ain't arrested the first member of that gang of scum. It took the Double-D Ranch and Perley Gates to whittle that gang down to Thacker, himself, and two we ain't really sure about."

"We talked some about what to do with Thacker, now that we've got our rat in the trap." Chester Rivenbark spoke up. "There was a suggestion we should wire the U.S. marshal's office in Fort Smith to send a deputy down here to take him back for trial. Hell, it'd take a deputy eight or nine days to get down here if he brought a jail-wagon. If he goes on trial up there, they're gonna find him guilty of murder and horse stealin', not to mention tryin' to take a whole cattle ranch hostage. And they're gonna hang him. And we'd have to feed him while we're waitin' for the jail-wagon. I say we have a trial right here and hang him. Save everybody the time and money."

"What should we do about Jonah Creech?" Lonnie asked. "He's locked up in the jail with Thacker."

"Too bad worthlessness ain't a hangin' offense," Chester remarked. "I reckon we just let him go and he'll drown himself in a likker barrel."

"Maybe Henry will give him a job in the saloon," Lonnie said.

"I expect you oughta go ahead and let him out of that cell. I feel sorry for the man in a way, and there ain't no use in makin' him stay locked up with that monster." Walter looked at Perley for a long moment before suggesting, "Perley, it might be a good thing if you could go with Clint while he lets Creech outta that cell. You know, an extra pair of eyes on Thacker and some insurance that he ain't talked Creech into tryin' something to help him escape."

"Yeah, Perley," Chester said. "Just to be sure nothin' goes wrong. The town would appreciate it."

Perley thought that was a good suggestion, considering the special circumstances. "I would help Marshal Cross with the release of Jonah Creech, but only if he wants the help. He might be afraid I'd be in the way."

"I'd appreciate the help," Clint said at once. "We can do it right away, if you want to."

"All right." Perley turned toward Billy and said, "You'd best get goin' and take those things to Annie. Looks like I'll be here a little bit longer, but I'll get back to the ranch as soon as I can." That prompted him to think of something else he had intended to do. "I almost forgot, I need to send a wire to my brothers to let 'em know we're all right and I'll be a couple of days late gettin' back." He looked back at Clint. "We'll go let the marshal out of jail first."

Happy to be reunited with his buckskin, Billy climbed on Spunky, and with the roan and the packhorse on a lead line, he headed for the Double-D. Perley and Clint went to the jail.

"Listen!" Jonah Creech exclaimed. "It's Clint! I hear the key in the office door. He's back!"

"Yeah, and you'd better get us out of here right away," Thacker ordered. "I've got some huntin' to do after I teach your prissy little deputy a lesson on who runs this town."

In a moment, they heard the rattle of the key in the cell room door. The door opened and Clint walked in, holding a large key on a ring.

"Where the hell have you been?" Thacker demanded.

"Locked up in here with this drunk fool," he complained.

"Where's the bottle of whiskey that was by my bed?" Jonah Creech asked. "Why'd you lock me in here?"

Very calmly, Clint answered, "So you wouldn't get out. I'm gonna let you out now. You ain't done anything I can charge you with besides disorderly conduct and drunkenness. And it looks like you've sobered up enough to go home, so I'm gonna let you go."

"Damn right," Thacker said. "Unlock that door and let us outta here."

"You're stayin' here, Thacker. You're under arrest for murder, assault, and horse stealin'. You'll be given a trial and a chance to speak for yourself at that time."

"What?" Thacker blurted. "A trial? Creech, you better tell this young pup to let me outta here right now! I ain't got time to play games! I'll tear this whole place down."

"You make a lot of noise, Thacker," Perley said when he stepped into the cell room behind Clint. He had purposefully held back to see how Clint would handle the confrontation. He'd decided it was a tough situation to handle alone, no matter who you were, so he stepped in. "Here's the way Marshal Cross wants it."

"Marshal Cross?" Creech interrupted, his headache returning as a result of his sudden outburst. "Whadda you talkin' about? I'm the marshal."

"Not anymore," Perley said. "You've been replaced. Thacker, you sit down on your bed over there and behave yourself, then Marshal Cross is gonna unlock the door and, Creech, you'll walk out. Then the marshal will lock the door again and Thacker will have the whole room to himself. In case, you've got a different idea on how this is gonna work, I picked up this twelve gauge shotgun out of the rack in the office to help persuade you that Marshal Cross' way is the safest way."

Thacker was boiling mad as he once again faced the man who had become the curse of his life. Helpless in the face of a double-barrel shotgun, he nevertheless spent insane seconds deciding what his odds were of withstanding the shotgun blast and getting to the shooter— sacrificing his life just to get his hands around Perley's neck. Only the knowledge that Perley was so fast his .44 probably would stop Thacker if the shotgun failed. He cautioned himself to be patient. His ego would not permit him to believe he would not escape this flimsy excuse for a jail.

He turned around and went back to the cot and sat down, sneering contemptuously at Perley while Clint unlocked the cell, Creech hurried out, and Clint relocked the cell.

Creech looked back through the bars and said, "Just remember this ain't been none of my doin', Duke." For, like him, he didn't believe the jail could hold Thacker very long, either. And he knew the violent man's vengeance list would be long.

They went into the tiny office and Clint closed the cell room door.

Creech tried to play on Clint's sympathy one last time. "Clint, you've been listenin' to this gunslinger fillin' your head with a bunch of crazy talk. You know you ain't near ready to take on the job of marshal of this town. You're gonna need me to show you the way."

"You may be right, Jonah," Clint replied. "I might not be quite ready, but I know for sure you're not. You've had plenty of time to show the folks in this town what kinda man you are, and they've decided you ain't right for the job. I don't blame you none for your drinkin'. I figure it's just because you ain't comfortable in the marshal's job. Maybe you'll find something to do that's more to your likin'. You might even wanna try farmin' that patch of land Mr. Powell built his house on. You said you used to do some farmin' when you were about my age."

The look of melancholy didn't leave Creech's face, but he nodded slowly. "Maybe I will. Henry ain't usin' it for anything."

Clint helped him clear his personal items out of the desk and the cabinet in the corner. When he had everything, Creech nodded to both of them and walked out the door.

Watching the parting with some interest, Perley had to comment. "That looked like it was a little harder than I expected it to be. It seemed to suggest a parting like that of a father and son."

"I reckon," Clint said. "I don't wish the old man any harm. He can't help it if that devil in the whiskey bottle jumped out and grabbed him."

"Just don't let this job drive you to jump in the bottle after him," Perley advised. "If you feel like you're gettin' that way, move on before it gets a hold on you."

"I'll most likely get shot in the back before I have time to go to the bottle," Clint said.

"There you go," Perley replied with a grin. "That's a better way to look at it. If you feel like you've got a handle on it now, I'll go on over to the depot and send a telegram to Paris, Texas. Then I'm gonna have to raise some dust between here and the Double-D, or I'm gonna be in big trouble there."

Clint walked outside the front door with Perley, pinning the marshal's badge on his shirt while Perley climbed aboard Buck. "I wanna thank you for all the help you gave me and the town with this business with Duke Thacker. And for talkin' them into givin' me this job."

"Glad I could help. I just hope you don't hate me for it later." Perley wheeled the big bay and headed off toward the depot.

That took more time than I figured, he thought as he left town and loped along the trail to the ranch. "I'm gonna make you work a little bit, boy," he said to the bay gelding, holding him to a spirited pace. "We ain't goin' but twelve miles, then you can have the rest of the night off."

Buck seemed willing enough, so he dropped into a comfortable mile-eating pace and maintained it all the way to the ranch.

Perley pulled Buck up smartly before Possum and Sonny, who were talking to Billy and Hank Martin outside the bunkhouse, then dismounted. "Hey, it's about time to get some supper, ain't it?"

"It's a good thing you did show up," Possum railed, "or we'da come lookin' for you with a rope."

Billy and Hank laughed at that.

"I knew he'd make it," Billy said. "I think I scared him when I told him how mad Annie gets if you don't show up on time for her cookin'." Changing the subject abruptly, he asked, "How'd ol' Jonah Creech take it when you told him he lost his job as town marshal?"

"He looked pretty disappointed," Perley said. "But I didn't tell him. Clint told him he was fired. He figured it was his job to tell him, so I didn't have much to do with it." He waited a moment when he saw Price Shelton come out of the barn and head toward them.

"You might be interested in this, Boss," Perley said. "I reckon Billy's told you about Clint Cross talkin' to all the merchants about organizin' the town council. Well, they're havin' a meetin' tonight after supper to set it up and vote on a new mayor. And I doubt very seriously if they'll vote Henry Powell in as mayor again."

"With Henry Powell out as mayor, I don't reckon Jonah Creech will get back in the marshal's office again," Shelton said. "That's good for the town and Double-D, too." He looked around the circle of Double-D hands and nodded to punctuate his statement. "Now, I reckon those of us who have been invited, best move on up to the house for supper. You ready, Perley?"

"Sure am," he answered. "Just as soon as I take my saddle off Buck and turn him out to water and graze." Billy and Hank volunteered to do those chores for him, so he handed the reins to Billy. "Better just lead him over to the barn," he couldn't resist japing.

"Too bad you can't go eat with 'em," Hank said to Billy. "I reckon Frances didn't make up the official guest list."

"I swear," Billy complained. "Ain't there nobody on the whole ranch who don't know about me and Frances?"

"Only Miz Matilda," Shelton remarked. "And if she finds out, I expect she'll have us geld you."

The dinner was as fine as Price Shelton had promised it would be, featuring roast beef, scalloped potatoes, and sourdough bread. The Widow Donovan brought out a bottle of her late husband's scotch whisky and she proposed a toast in appreciation of Perley, Possum, and Sonny's help in the Double-D's time of need.

Unknown to the widow, whose eyesight was not as sharp as in bygone years, even Frances drank the toast, although her scotch was sipped from a coffee cup, with a wink from Price Shelton and a frown from Annie Hagen. On this occasion, however, Annie decided not to inform Matilda of Frances' imbibing of the fiery liquid.

When asked if they were going to stay on a while longer, Perley responded that he had planned to leave the next morning, but after consulting with Possum and Sonny, and finding they were in no particular hurry, he decided he would very much like to see how it went with the town council meeting. So he planned to ride into Texarkana in the morning, then maybe start back home from there. At any rate, this would be their final night at the Double-D.

In the little settlement of Texarkana, two diners were consuming a much less tantalizing supper at the Last Chance Saloon. It was a dark stew. When asked what it was, Bertha had said it was Cosmopolitan Stew, a mixture of several different meats, including rabbit, goat, beef, and some pork, flavored with molasses.

Ned Bates and Mutt Thomas had learned long before not to show any doubts or dislikes for the food they paid her for. Their complaints were held to a murmur as they downed it with great hunks of bread. They couldn't resist a grin at each other when the indifferent woman gave Jim

Gordon a dinner pail of the mysterious stew to take over to the jail for Duke Thacker's supper. "Ain't ol' Duke gonna love this slop?" Ned whispered.

His comment brought up a discussion that had gone on between the two outlaws ever since Thacker was dragged to jail by Perley Gates. "I don't know what we oughta do now," Mutt declared.

Already having decided Thacker's mind was tilting toward loco, they had talked about taking off on their own, somewhere away from there. And that was before he was arrested. Now, they feared his wrath even more/ They knew no jail would hold him, especially when Clint Cross was the jailer. And when Thacker broke out of that jail, he was going to be a flaming terror, intent on destroying everyone who had crossed him. Perley Gates would be number one on his list, but anyone who ran out on him would not be far behind Perley.

Mutt sighed. "You know he's settin' in that little jailhouse wonderin' when we're gonna come break him out."

"Well, if we're gonna do it, we better do it pretty quick 'cause those vigilantes back there in the corner are talkin' about a hanging."

When they had come into the saloon to eat supper, Mutt and Ned had noticed several of the smaller tables had been set up together to form one big one in the back corner where Duke's favorite table was. When asked why, Shag had told them the tables were set up for a meeting to officially form the town council because there hadn't been one and it was needed to protect the town from outlaws.

"You know, from people like you two and Duke." He chuckled, thinking it was funny.

While the two of them sat at a table in the front part of the saloon, eating Bertha's concoction, they noticed most every one of the town's merchants came into the meeting. And as it progressed, it became louder and louder until they were able to hear all the discussion. Much to their distress, what Shag had said was true. They were organizing the town to fight gangs like Duke Thacker's. Before the Double-D disaster, when the gang was at full strength, they would have simply cleaned the meeting out, and that would have been the end of any council notions in the future.

Now, the two of them would be easily overcome by the number of organizers.

Mutt and Ned quietly ate their supper, regretting the sudden disappearance of Cora Black, their cook back at the farmhouse. They had been dependent upon Duke Thacker for protection for so long, they found themselves thinking they should break him out of jail. And then Clint Cross walked into the meeting.

They looked at each other, both thinking the same thing.

They got up from their table when they saw Clint sit down at the meeting.

"We need to check one thing first," Ned insisted, so Mutt followed him to the bar.

"You boys wantin' seconds?" Shag asked, knowing well the answer to that. No one asked for second helpings of Bertha's suppers.

"Nah, we gotta head for the house," Ned answered. "Have you seen Perley Gates tonight?"

"Not so far, I ain't," Shag replied. "Why?"

"No reason. I just thought with all that noise in the

back about formin' a town council, he'd most likely be here."

"Nah. I think he had to do somethin' out at the Double-D."

"Well, I reckon we oughta ride on back to the house," Ned remarked. "Be seein' ya, Shag."

They went out to the street and climbed on their horses and rode off toward the northern end of it.

Chapter 20

When they reached the north end of the street, Mutt and Ned rode their horses around behind the railroad depot, and went back the way they had just come, then rode behind the stores until they reached the jail. They knew the jail consisted of one cell only, so the little slit of a window had to be where Thacker was being held.

Ned pulled his horse up under the window and called out almost in a whisper. "Duke." When there was no answer right away, he called again.

"I hear ya," Thacker answered. "Where the hell you been?"

"We had to wait till Clint Cross left the office, so we could talk to ya and figure out the best way to try to get you out," Ned answered.

Completely out of patience at that point, Thacker said, "The best way to get me outta here is to walk into the office and shoot Clint Cross down. That ain't too complicated for ya, is it?"

"It ain't really that easy, Duke," Ned replied. "You ain't got no horse. That buckskin you took from the Double-D belonged to Billy Dean and he took it back.

So we gotta steal you another horse. And another thing. There's a big bunch of the business owners and other men havin' a meetin' in the saloon right now to form a town council . . . so they'll be a lot more ready to fight any outlaws who come here." He turned and gave Mutt a helpless look while he waited for Thacker to respond.

"You say most of the businessmen are at that meetin'?" Thacker asked, after he thought about the problem for a moment. "How 'bout Chester Rivenbark? Is he there?"

"Oh, yeah. He was one of the main ones doin' all the talkin'," Ned answered.

"Well, that's the best place to get me a horse and saddle, ain't it?" Thacker came back. "Ought not be no trouble a-tall, with nobody there to watch the stable. And if that meetin' is goin' on as strong as you say it is, it sounds like Marshal Clint Cross won't be back here before we're gone."

He was making it sound simple enough, but Ned and Mutt weren't so sure. Again, they exchanged questioning doubts. "How we gonna get you outta there when we come back with a horse? The jail's locked up."

"Take a look at that office door," Thacker said. "When you come back, if Cross is here, kill him. If he's still gone, just kick the door in, find the keys to the cell door and cell and let me out. That oughta be simple enough, even for you two. So, get goin'. We're just wastin' time here talkin'."

"Right," Ned replied. "We're goin' to get you a horse. We'll be back as soon as we can."

They pulled away from the back of the jail and went directly to the stable.

"Better pick him out a good one, you know how he is about ridin' a strong horse."

They tied their horses behind the corral, having decided to find a good saddle first. When they picked out one of the three saddles in the tack room, they took it and the bridle with it out to the corral.

"I'm lookin' at that black Morgan over against the far rail," Ned suggested. "He looks just like the kind Duke would pick out for himself."

"Yeah, he oughta like that one," Mutt concurred, then stalled. "You still think we're doin' the smart thing, breakin' him outta that jail?"

"Hell, no," Ned answered at once. "I expect it's a dumb move, but we ain't got nothin' else to count on. At least, we know he'll be back on top, and we might ride along with him. He'll break outta that dang jail, whether we help him or not. And if we don't help him, he'll be after our behinds before he starts after Perley Gates."

Strictly because of fear of one violent man, they went into the corral and cut the dark Morgan out of the bunch of horses and were in the process of saddling it when they heard the voice behind them.

"What are you fellers fixin' to do with Mr. Powell's horse?" Jim Gordon asked.

"Whup!" Ned blurted in surprise. "Where'd you come from?"

"I was back in the barn gettin' some new hay for Devil's stall and I saw you come outta the tack room with that saddle. I told Mr. Rivenbark I'd keep an eye on the stable for him while he went to the meetin'. He didn't say nothin' about Mr. Powell maybe needed his horse tonight."

"That's right. He did say you was gonna watch the stable," Ned said. "I clear forgot that. Well, anyway, Mr. Powell wants his horse and we said we weren't doin' nothin', so we'd pick his horse up for him. We'll tell him you were right on the job."

"Maybe I better go ask him if it's all right," Jim said. "He's awful particular about that horse. And even though you fellers don't ride with Duke Thacker no more, I need to let Mr. Powell know you took Devil."

"That sounds like the very thing you oughta do," Mutt said to him. "And when you see him, give him this." He pulled his .44 and pumped a bullet into Jim's gut, doubling the surprised man over to sit down hard on the hard ground, his face a mask of severe pain.

Surprised as well, Ned let out a little yelp, then blurted, "What did you do that for?"

Mutt gave him a look of disbelief. "'Cause he knows who we are, and he'd tell 'em we stole Powell's horse. And maybe we could have our names on every wanted poster in Arkansas and Texas as horse thieves."

Ned looked down at Jim, gut-shot and doubled up in pain, and remarked, "I hope to hell nobody heard that shot." He looked back toward the street to see any sign that someone had, but no one was close to the stable. "Even if they did, they most likely wouldn't pay it no mind. We need to make sure he don't do no talkin'."

When Jim heard him, he looked up in distress, but Mutt yanked his head back and cut his throat. "He won't now," Mutt declared.

"I reckon there ain't no more deciding to do now,"

Ned remarked. "Looks like we're back in business with Duke Thacker."

After they dragged Jim Gordon's body back inside the barn, they finished saddling Henry Powell's Morgan gelding, and led the horse back to the jail. With no sign indicating Clint Cross had returned to the office, they tested Thacker's assessment of the outside office door. They had to agree, while the lock was solid, the door and its frame were as flimsy as the rest of the building. Still, it took several tries from each man before the door tore loose on one side and they pushed it open with the lock still in place.

"Did you get me a horse?" Thacker asked when they opened the door to the cell room after Mutt managed to pick the lock with a whittled down dinner knife.

"Sure did," Ned answered. "One you mighta picked out, yourself. A black Morgan and his name is Devil."

"We had to shoot a feller at the stable," Mutt said. "He saw us takin' the horse and he knows us, so we had to shut him up. It was that Jim Gordon feller that works at the Last Chance."

Thacker knew who he was talking about, but it was of no concern to him. "Get busy and find the key to this cell."

They wasted no more time and started searching the desk drawers and cabinets, the shelves and any box or bag that looked like it would be a good place to hide a key. Some keys were found in the desk drawer, but none big enough to fit the lock of the heavy cell door. In the gun cabinet on the wall, they found Thacker's gun belt and announced it to the increasingly impatient prisoner.

"I swear, Duke, he musta took it with him," Mutt

reported. "We've turned this place upside down and inside out. Ain't no sign of a key for that cell."

Unable to witness their efforts, since he couldn't see beyond the wall between the cell room and the office, he could only communicate with them by yelling back and forth through the open cell room door.

"He wouldn't hardly carry the cell key in his pocket," Thacker insisted. "Big key like that, most likely on a ring too big to fit in a pocket. It'd be hangin' on a nail somewhere."

"Like that one hangin' beside the door to the cell room," Mutt said as he turned to come eyeball-level with the big, heavy ring with one big key on it. "Ain't no problem, Duke. I found it." He hurried to the door with the newly found key and unlocked the cell.

Thacker walked out of the cell, into the office and stopped in the middle of the room to look all around him at the evidence of Ned and Mutt's frantic search for a key that almost hit you in the face, as you walked through the cell room door. He decided it a waste of time to comment on their stupidity, so he simply said, "Let's get outta here."

In an effort not to attract attention, they slow walked their horses up the middle of the dark street and past the Last Chance Saloon where the meeting appeared to still be in full progress. Thacker murmured a low comment of contempt for the merchants' efforts as they continued out the north end of town. Feeling secure in the belief no one in town had the foggiest idea where it was, he intended to ride back to the farmhouse he had referred to as his ranch. They had certainly had no visitors. They should be safe there for as long as he planned to stay, which was for only that night. He planned to get on Perley Gates' trail the next day.

Behind them, Philip Davis had walked outside the saloon to stand on the porch and take a few breaths of fresh air. He noticed the three riders plodding slowly past the saloon. It was too dark to make out who they were, even if he had wanted to know. Everyone who was anyone in the town was inside the saloon, making history for the railroad settlement.

It was another hour before Clint Cross announced he had left the jail unguarded for too long, and was going to call it a night. All of the merchants pledged their cooperation to the new town council. When nominations were called for mayor, the popular vote went to the postmaster, Broadus Fisher.

The meeting was not yet over when Clint Cross returned with the dreadful news that Duke Thacker had broken out of the jail, almost destroying the building in the process. It would be later, still, when Chester Rivenbark found Jim Gordon's body in his barn and Henry Powell's Morgan missing. Philip Davis remembered the three dark figures riding past the saloon, but he decided not to mention it.

It was a troubled and disheartened town Perley, Possum, and Sonny rode into the next morning.

The first stop Perley had planned to make was the marshal's office to see how the new marshal had fared the night. At once concerned at seeing the battered door to the office, he hurriedly dismounted, went inside, and realized why the door looked odd. It had been knocked loose from the hinges and simply pulled shut again. Immediately alert for what he might walk in on, he pushed the door away from the frame and called out, "Clint!" He could see right away no one was in the office, so he pushed the door far enough to gain entry. The trashed condition of the office caused him to look immediately toward the cell room door.

He feared the new marshal's body would be inside the cell, the result of getting too close to the prisoner. No one was in the cell, which could be good or bad. The jail break could have happened while Clint was away from the office, or Thacker could have managed to take him as a hostage. Perley couldn't buy the second option. Thacker would not have wanted the bother of taking Clint hostage. He would have simply killed him.

"Lord, help us," Possum exclaimed, coming in behind Perley. "Clint?" Possum questioned at once.

Perley shook his head.

Looking around him at the destruction left by Mutt and Ned's search for the key, Possum mentioned, "Thacker said no jail could hold him."

"Looks like he had help breakin' out," Perley said. "Judgin' by the way that front door was broken in. Clint wasn't here when Thacker broke out." The thought that the padlock was still locked on the outside of the door should have told him that right away.

"Ain't a very good way for the new marshal to start off, is it?" Sonny asked, stepping into the mess.

"No, it ain't," Perley agreed, "and I need to find him."

He couldn't help feeling responsible for Clint taking the job. Afraid he had pushed the young man into taking it when he was really not ready to take that responsibility.

Perley looked at Possum and said, "I'm afraid we're gonna be in town a little longer than I figured." Possum gave him a nod of understanding, so Perley continued. "I don't want the horses to stand around with their saddles and packs on, no tellin' how long. Let's take 'em over to the stable and unload 'em and put 'em in Chester's corral."

Chester Rivenbark walked out to meet them when they approached his corral. "Mornin'," he called out. "You just ride in?"

"Yep," Perley answered. "We saw the jail. I was lookin' for Clint."

"Clint led a posse outta here early this mornin', headin' north. I didn't go with 'em 'cause I didn't have anybody to watch the stable for me. Did you hear about Jim Gordon? He was watchin' it for me durin' the meeting last night, and they killed him. Shot him once in the stomach and cut his throat."

"That's bad news, all right." Perley didn't really know Jim, just that he did odd jobs for Henry Powell, but thought he should show some sympathy.

"Not only that. They stole Henry Powell's horse and saddle. For Thacker to ride, I reckon." Chester shook his head and spat a stream of tobacco juice toward the corner post of the corral. "He had help, and they couldn'ta picked a better time to bust outta that jail. Dang near the whole town was at the meetin'."

"I don't reckon those two model citizens were at

the meetin'," Perley asked. "You know, Ned Bates and Mutt Thomas?"

"No, they didn't stay for the meetin'," Chester answered. "That was mentioned after we found out what had happened. Shag Felton said they was there earlier to eat supper, but they left after the meetin' got started."

"And they ain't been seen since, right?" Possum asked.

When Chester said that was the case, Possum said, "So the posse's chasin' three of 'em; Thacker and those two lyin' skunks that claimed they weren't in on the raid at the Double-D."

Marshal Clint Cross and his posse of six men were stopped beside the Red River at a point about nine miles north of Texarkana. The question before them was which way to proceed—across the Red and on up into Arkansas, or to follow the Red west where it formed the boundary between Texas and Oklahoma Indian Territory? The tracks they picked up north of town had led them to this point and then disappeared. So now, it was a guessing game.

Lonnie Pope crossed the river and searched east and west for about a mile in each direction but found no tracks at all. Thinking therefore Thacker must have followed the river west, they started out that way until they had to stop to rest the horses.

Clint sensed a definite lack of enthusiasm to continue the search, especially from Philip Davis. "I don't know how much longer we oughta be ridin' along this river," he complained. "We're just foolin' ourselves now, just not wantin' to say they gave us the slip."

"You know, we ain't even sure those tracks we followed outta town were their tracks," Jack Sessions, owner of the saddle shop, suggested. "Hell, they mighta rode out the other end of town."

"No, they rode out the north, all right," Davis insisted. He didn't care to tell them why he was sure of that, but it could have been no one else he saw pass by the Last Chance while he was on the porch. "They just out-smarted us. That's all there is to it. They could have gone in any direction, and we ain't got the first clue which way to go. They got way too much head start on us in the first place. The main thing is Duke Thacker is gone from our town and I don't think we'll ever see him again."

Clint looked at Lonnie for his opinion.

Lonnie shook his head. "I expect Philip's right. We'd just be lookin' and hopin'. We might as well turn around and go home."

"All right," Clint announced to the posse. "Looks like we're wastin' our time out here. I wanna thank all of you for ridin' in the posse. I reckon I shouldn'ta been at the meetin'. I shoulda been guardin' my prisoner. We'll rest up the horses, then go on back to town."

"Don't go gettin' down on yourself," Lonnie told him. "Your prisoner escaped because that shack we've been usin' for a jail couldn't keep chickens from gettin' out. That's something we're gonna need to build."

It was just as well that the posse turned around and returned to town, for the three outlaws they chased were not heading farther north in Arkansas or riding northwest into Oklahoma. They had passed the night back in their hideout, the old farmhouse near the Red River. And when morning came, they'd ridden back toward the south to circle around Texarkana on the Texas side to intercept the common wagon track leading into Texas. It was where they expected to ambush Perley Gates on his trip back to the Triple-G.

Chapter 21

John Gates walked into the dining room of the Paris Hotel, unbuckled his gun belt, and left it on the table beside the door. He seated himself at one of the small tables beside the window.

Lucy Tate saw him come in, put the stack of clean plates she was carrying on the sideboard, and walked over to greet him. "Well, if this isn't a special day," she teased, always the flirt, even with men like John, who enjoyed a solid marriage. "We haven't seen you in so long, I thought you were avoiding me."

John laughed and responded in kind. "You know better than that. My wife just won't let me outta the house much anymore. She knows I'd head straight for town to see you. She said to tell you she's thinkin' about settin' me free. Said you'd be about seventy-five then."

Lucy laughed good-naturedly. "Tell her I'll be waiting. You want some coffee?"

"I do," John answered, "and whatever the special is today."

"You got it," she said and headed back to the kitchen.

In a few seconds, Becky Morris came from the kitchen

with his cup of coffee. "Hello, Mr. Gates," she greeted him cheerfully. "Lucy said you were out here. She's fixing you a plate. She'll be right out with it."

"Howdy, Becky. I was gonna ask if you were here. When are you gonna stop callin' me Mr. Gates? My name's John, and unless I've got the wrong idea about what you and Perley are plannin' to do, I'm gonna be your brother-in-law."

Becky flushed visibly.

"And now I've gone and embarrassed you. Well, Perley's probably told you I'm the crude one of we three brothers."

"No such a thing," Becky quickly replied. "The way Perley talks about you and your brother, Rubin, I think he almost worships you."

"I doubt that," John said with a chuckle. "Anyway, I thought I'd let you know I just came from the telegraph office. Grover Jones got a wire from Perley this mornin'."

"Oh," Becky reacted, "is he all right?"

"I reckon. All the wire said was that the town near the ranch where he took those horses ran into some trouble and they want him to stay a day or two longer." He paused as Lucy placed a plate of food down before him. "That's all it said," he continued, "so that's all I can tell you. What in the world Perley's got to do with that town's business, I can't even imagine. He was just drivin' a herd of horses to a ranch near there. But you oughta know him well enough by now to know that it ain't surprisin', Perley being Perley."

John was thinking about a connection between Perley and cow pies but refrained from making the remark to the young lady. "They've already been gone longer than they figured they would be. I thought you might be wonderin' what's keepin' him. I don't know what the trouble is, but at least he and Possum and Sonny must be all right."

"Thank you so much for telling me, John. I was getting a little worried, I have to admit."

"Good mornin', Bertha," Possum greeted the surly woman when she approached their table. "We're gonna be headin' back to Texas today, so we thought we'd have us one last chance to enjoy your coffee and biscuits."

Her dour expression never varied as she responded with a question. "Is Perley comin' in to eat?"

"Yes, ma'am, he sure is," Possum answered. "Said he couldn't leave town without comin' to see you. Ain't that right, Sonny?"

"Yes, ma'am," Sonny replied. "That's what he said."

Both men thought it possible they were overplaying their intent to stay on the huge woman's good side. They had heard about some of the vile things she had done to the food of customers she didn't like. It was worth the risk, though. The one thing she outshined all others on were her baked biscuits. Possum was certain the only reason Bertha kept her job was her one gift, baking the best biscuits in the West.

"Perley had to go talk to Walter Johnson about the town council meetin'," Possum said. "He oughta be here any minute now."

She grunted and placed three coffee cups on the table

before turning around to go back to the kitchen to get biscuits and the coffeepot.

Down the street at the feed store, Perley was in conversation with Walter Johnson and Broadus Fisher. They were bringing Perley up to date on the accomplishments of the meeting and the status of the fugitive, Duke Thacker, which was still uncertain, since the posse hadn't returned yet.

"Congratulations on bein' voted the new mayor," Perley said to Broadus Fisher. He couldn't resist japing him. "I hope you'll be as effective as the outgoin' mayor."

"If he ain't, we're gonna string him up," Walter said.

"They only picked me because they thought I could read, since I run the post office," Broadus came back. "If we had a key to the city, I think we'd give it to you."

"Really?" Perley replied, truly surprised. "What for?"

"For getting rid of Duke Thacker for starters," Walter chimed in, "and talkin' Clint Cross into takin' on the marshal's job."

"If I hadn't, I'm sure one of you folks would have," Perley said. "Clint's a good man. He'll get better when he gets used to the job, I'll bet." He was starting to feel extremely uneasy, a feeling that was quite common for him when someone complimented him, so accustomed was he to the reverse. "Well, I've gotta go. Possum and Sonny are waitin' for me. Good luck with the new council." Perley turned abruptly and hurried away toward the saloon.

"Unusual young man," Broadus Fisher remarked as they watched his departure. "Too bad he doesn't want to settle around here."

"If he did," Walter said, "every gunslinger in the country

would be comin' to town to try their luck against him. It would be worst than Spade Devlin and Kane."

"Maybe you're right," Broadus said. "I reckon I wasn't thinking."

"And we made you the mayor," Walter japed.

At the Last Chance Saloon, Perley found Possum and Sonny already eating from a large plate of biscuits. As soon as he sat down, Bertha arrived with the coffeepot and filled his cup.

"Good mornin', Bertha," he greeted her.

The corners of the brutelike woman's mouth started to lift up toward a smile, but when Perley reached for a biscuit, she barked, "No!" and jerked the plate away from him. Stunned, he watched as she took the plate off the table. And on her way back to the kitchen, she dumped the biscuits off onto a plate on a table of some other hungry biscuit eaters.

"Dang," Possum asked. "What the hell did you do? I'da liked to have a couple more of those biscuits."

"So would I," Sonny remarked. "You musta done somethin', looked at her crosswise, or something."

"I swear, I didn't do a thing," Perley pleaded. "I'm sorry if I did. I'll apologize when she comes out of the kitchen again."

It was a couple of minutes before she emerged from the kitchen. He didn't have to signal her, for she came straight to their table.

Before he could apologize, she placed another plate on the table, stacked with hot biscuits, fresh from the oven. "These are better," she said. As he looked up at her,

her lips began to move, not at once, but slowly. And the corners of her mouth began to widen gradually, like the unfolding of a blooming flower bud, until her lips parted to show a row of uneven teeth. She maintained it for only a few seconds before her face shrank back to its usual stoic mask.

"Thank you, Bertha," Perley said almost reverently, "for the fresh biscuits, but most of all for the smile."

Again, she turned abruptly and retreated to her kitchen.

Possum and Sonny were still in a state of shock. After a long moment, Possum declared, "That was the dangdest thing I've ever seen. Like the first time I ever saw a calf bein' born."

"I ain't sure I wanna see it again," Sonny remarked. "That was downright spooky." He picked up one of the hot biscuits and looked it over. "Reckon what she mixes up in these biscuits?"

"I don't wanna know," Possum said. "Just hand me another one."

They took their time over the coffee and biscuits, but eventually decided to pick up their horses and start for Texas. As he did each time before, Perley went to the kitchen door to give Bertha the money for their coffee and biscuits. He found her standing just inside the door. "I'll pay you for our food and I wanna leave you a little extra to show you how much we appreciated those fresh biscuits. They were extra special."

"Possum said you was leavin' today to go back to Texas," she said. "I was waitin' to see if you would stop to see me when you was ready to go."

"I wouldn't miss it," Perley said and handed her the money.

She took it and said, "I got somethin' to give you." She placed a round object in his hand.

It felt like a coin. He started to refuse it, thinking it was money, but decided that might hurt her feelings. So he thanked her.

"It's a lucky piece," she said. "My mama sewed it in my mitten when I was a young'un. I'm fifty-seven years old, and I ain't never been sick a day in my life. I think you need it to bring you some luck."

He wasn't really sure what to say in response. He looked at the silver disc, about the size of a quarter, and realized it was a button. "It's mighty pretty," he said, "and I 'preciate it more than I could ever say. But I don't wanna take your lucky piece away from you if it's been takin' care of you all your life."

"I've had all the luck I need," she insisted. "I'm pretty much settled right where I'm gonna end up, and that's all right with me. But I've been thinkin' about you, son. For some reason, the Good Lord gave you the fastest move with a firearm in the whole country. But I've been studyin' you ever since you first came in here, and it looks to me like you ain't all that anxious to show it off. Like it or not, you're gonna be tried everywhere you go, so you need all the luck you can get."

It was a pretty sober assessment of the trials he had already experienced in his young years. Coming from her, it caught him totally by surprise, however. He didn't have much faith in lucky charms of any kind, but he appreciated her thoughtfulness and concern for him. He closed his fist tightly around the silver button and said,

"I don't know what to say, Bertha. Thank you for this gift. I promise I'll always keep it with me. And thank you for the smile. I won't ever forget that, either."

"Your friends are waitin' for you. You'd best get along. Stop in to see me if you're out this way again." She turned and walked back into her kitchen.

"You bet I will," he called after her. "I wouldn't miss it."

He walked over to the bar where Possum and Sonny were standing, waiting for him.

"What was that all about?" Possum asked.

"What was what all about?" Perley answered.

"All that chit-chat between you and that mama grizzly," Possum said. "Am I gonna have to go tell Becky Morris you found you a more mature kinda woman?"

"You oughta have more respect for Bertha," Perley told him. He dropped his good luck button in his pocket without a mention of it, thinking not to give Possum something more to jape him about. "She does pretty good to handle the rough crowd that comes in here to drink." Winking at Sonny, he said, "To tell you the truth, she was askin' me about your marital status and I told her you were lookin' for a good solid woman, who could cook for you in your old age. She got interested when I told her you were half owner of a hotel in Bison Gap."

"Ha," Sonny responded. "You ain't gonna find no more solid a woman than Bertha. I bet she can lick any man in town."

"You better be japin' me now," Possum said to Perley. "Let's get outta here."

They said their good-byes to Chester Rivenbark while

they saddled their horses and loaded the packs onto the packhorse.

"Kinda got used to havin' you fellows around," Chester remarked. "Ya think you'll be back this way any-time soon?"

"No time soon, I reckon," Possum answered him, "unless Perley decides to make a trip out here to visit Bertha."

Perley and Sonny chuckled, but Chester wasn't in on the joke, so he just responded with a puzzled look. "How long you figure it'll take you to ride back to your ranch?"

"About two and a half or three days," Perley answered. "We ain't got any reason to wear these horses out to get back any sooner. We're startin' so late today we most likely won't ride but fifteen miles or so, dependin' on where we find the best campin' spot."

"I know Clint will be disappointed he didn't get back here before you left," Chester said. "I think he still can't believe you talked him into arrestin' Duke Thacker."

"He's gonna make you a good sheriff, or marshal. Whatever you wanna call him. Tell him to rely on Lonnie Pope when he needs help. You folks might wanna think about makin' Lonnie a deputy."

Chester nodded his head thoughtfully.

Perley could tell that idea appealed to him for future consideration. Something he might introduce at one of the council meetings.

Packed up and ready to ride, they shook hands all around and climbed into their saddles. Sonny led the way out of town to intercept a common wagon road that paralleled the Red River. It was the trail they pushed the herd of horses over on their way out to the Double-D. The Red was too snakelike in its course to the west, but the wagon track they followed was not that far from the river's winding path, so they were never far from water and good camping sites. In no hurry, they let the horses decide how far they wanted to ride on this first afternoon.

Perley made sure to get out in front of Possum to let Buck set the pace, leisurely or not. If left up to Possum's gray gelding with the inappropriate name of Dancer, they were in danger of dropping back to a dreary pace that would add days to the journey. As it turned out, the decision on that day's march was made by the riders when crossing a narrow creek.

"Whaddaya think?" Perley asked. "Wanna check this creek out?" He was looking toward the river, which wasn't very far away, and pointed to the large cottonwoods only a couple hundred yards away that grew along the banks of the river.

"That might be just what we're lookin' for," Possum said. "Might even catch a fish for supper."

They followed the creek to its confluence with the river and decided they had made a good choice. With plenty of grass for the horses, they relieved them of their saddles and turned them loose to go to the water. Sonny started gathering wood for a fire while Possum got some line and sinkers out of his saddlebags and a cork he used for a float.

"I swear," Mutt whispered to Ned. "It's him, all right. It's Perley Gates!" They looked at each other, astonished. "How did Thacker know they would camp here?"

"Same way he knew they weren't goin' back to the Triple-G until today," Ned answered. "I don't know about you, but this business with the messages to his brain is spookin' me out somethin' awful. Look at him up there. He's hearin' them voices in his head again."

Thacker had ordered them to stay with the horses while he advanced closer to the camp. Kneeling down behind the bank on the other side, he was checking his Henry rifle to make sure it was ready to fire. They could see his lips moving constantly, so they knew he was railing on about something. He had ordered them to stay back because he didn't want any interference with his shot. Perley Gates had to die by his hand.

"Well, there ain't much chance of missin' from that distance," Mutt decided. "After he shoots Perley, we're supposed to get the other two. Maybe after that, he'll quit hearing them voices. "What are we gonna do if his voices tell him to wipe us out?"

"Don't think I ain't thought about that," Ned replied. "He's liable to do anythin'." He shook his head solemnly. "I wish to hell we had took off when we first talked about it."

"You and me both. Uh-oh, here we go! Boss is gettin' ready to cut him down. Got him right where he wants him, standin' up in front of that big cottonwood. Don't shoot till he cuts Perley down, then we cut them other two down."

With no thoughts at all about the possibility of riding into an ambush, Perley stood watching Sonny kindle his fire and wishing he'd hurry up. A little over thirteen miles from Texarkana, he was looking forward to a fresh cup of coffee. It wouldn't be as strong as Bertha's coffee, which suited him just fine. Thinking of the huge woman, Perley reached in his pocket and felt around until he pulled out the flat button. He thought he'd take a closer look at it, while Possum and Sonny had their attentions elsewhere. It was really a plain button, nothing that would lead you to believe it was anything special. He flipped it up in the air but missed it when he tried to catch it. He bent over at once to trap it before it hit the ground and felt the breeze caused by the .44 slug as it slammed into the tree trunk behind him with a sharp splat and the report of the Henry rifle immediately following.

There was no need to think. All three men showered the riverbank with return fire. Perley dropped to the ground, automatically rolling over and over until he found cover behind another tree and returned fire with Possum and Sonny who saw the rifle's muzzle flash, which pinpointed the shooter.

With his missed shot, Thacker was furious. Seeing the riverbank torn away around him by the return rifle fire, he knew he couldn't stay there. "Run!" he shouted. "Get to the horses and get outta here!"

The three Triple-G men continued to throw shots after the retreating outlaws for as long as they had a glimpse of them. They couldn't get a clear enough look at their bushwhackers, but could tell there were three of them, which naturally led them to believe it was Thacker and the two men who broke him out of jail.

"They doubled back on the posse," Possum said. "And it's pretty clear what's on Thacker's mind. He ain't gonna quit till it's settled between you and him."

Sonny had another mystery on his mind, sure of what

he had seen with his own eyes. He asked Perley, "How did you see that bullet comin' at you before you ducked?"

"I didn't see it," Perley said. "You can't see a bullet flyin' through the air. I dropped my lucky piece and tried to catch it before it hit the ground."

"What lucky piece?" Possum wanted to know.

Perley flipped the silver button to him. Possum caught it and examined it closely. "This ain't nothin' but a button. I ain't ever seen that before. You never said anything about a lucky piece."

"I never had one before," Perley said. "Bertha gave it to me this mornin'. I'll tell you all about it, but first, we'd best see how far those bushwhackers ran. They might be gettin' ready to come back for another try."

It was not difficult to follow the trail left by their would-be executioners. They'd left a wide swath of broken limbs and bushes in their haste to get out of rifle range. Once they cleared the trees lining the river, the Triple-G men got one fleeting glimpse of the three riders as they disappeared over the brow of a hill.

"They won't be back anytime soon," Perley speculated. "I reckon that'll give us enough time to move our camp 'cause they will be back."

"Shoot," Sonny complained, "I just got this blame fire goin' good."

"Well, we could just stay here, and when they come back, we could invite 'em to come on in for supper," Possum japed. "You never know. Duke Thacker might be one of the nicest fellows you ever met."

"Yeah, that's really funny, Possum," Sonny said. "That man's crazy, and he's out to get Perley. That's for sure." He looked at Perley. "I'm thinkin' you'd best hang onto that lucky piece Bertha gave you 'cause I don't care what you say, that thing saved your life."

"I reckon I can't argue with that. Lucky charm or not, if I hadn't dropped it, that rifle slug woulda caught me right in the chest. I ain't gonna argue with anything Bertha says, anyway." What had started out as a casual ride back to the Triple-G had just taken a perilous turn.

"Whaddaya think, Possum? You think we oughta go after them? Or do you think we oughta wait for them to come after us?"

"I reckon I'd rather be the hunter, instead of the hunted," Possum answered.

"What about you, Sonny?" Perley asked next. He wanted them both to know he didn't consider himself the boss, just because he was one of the Gates brothers.

"What Possum said, I reckon," was Sonny's answer. "Whatever you two decide you wanna do is all right by me."

They pushed their horses hard for about three miles before stopping at a U-shaped bend in the river to see if anyone was trailing them. Still burning from the missed shot he had taken when he was right on target to shoot Perley in the chest, Thacker ordered Ned and Mutt to stay with the horses while he looked over their back trail. *Perley should be dead*, Thacker fumed. He couldn't help wondering if the universe had decided to interfere with his plans.

He was not the only one harboring such thoughts. Ned and Mutt decided Thacker was talking to the devil.

"Who else could he be talkin' to?" Mutt wanted to

know. "Every time he's off by hisself, he's talkin' away, just like there was somebody talkin' to him. Doggone it, he had his chance and he missed. So, what's he gonna do now? Keep after that gunslinger till he kills all of us? I'm tellin' ya, Ned, I've had all of Perley Gates I want. And Duke is bound and determined to get us all killed. As crazy as he's actin', he might get one of his messages from the devil to kill us."

"I hear what you're sayin', and I think the same thing," Ned responded. "But what are you thinkin' to do? We've been talkin' about cuttin' out for other parts of the country, but we ain't ever had the gumption to do it."

"There ain't but one way to get away from Duke Thacker, and that's to kill him," Mutt said. When he saw a look of panic in Ned's face, he sought to persuade him. "You know, as crazy as he is, he'd hunt us down if we just took off and left him. Don't you know that?"

"Maybe you're right. I don't know. As crazy as he's gotten, he probably would come after us. But tryin' to kill him would be like tryin' to kill a buffalo."

"Not if we're both shootin' at the same time," Mutt said. "And right now would be a good time, when he's tryin' to save his butt from Perley Gates."

"Yeah, well, we gotta try to save our butts from Perley Gates, too, thanks to Duke," Ned replied. Of all in the old Duke Thacker gang, he had the most history with the innocent-looking young man with the ridiculous name.

Starting back when he, Dan Short, and Tiny Wilson had attempted to steal the small herd of thirty-five horses from Perley. Recalling that disaster brought another thought to Ned's mind—the regret he had for not being able to tell his younger sister, Mavis, her husband,

Tiny, was killed. Ned felt bad about that. If he wound up getting killed, Mavis would never know why Tiny never came home. Ned looked up and realized Mutt had been staring at him while his mind was on his sister. "What?"

"Are you in this with me?" Mutt asked. "Yes or no? We send him back to Hell where he came from, then maybe we can get the hell outta this part of the country."

"Count me in," Ned replied.

Chapter 22

"The way they took off, it looked like they were headed back to that wagon trail we were on before we followed this creek down here to the river. Whaddaya think, Perley?"

"That's what it looked like to me," Perley answered Possum. "Trouble is, it won't be long before dark, so I'm thinkin' we'd best find us a better campsite. Whaddaya say we follow this old Indian trail right beside the river, instead of goin' back to the road. Maybe we can get ahead of 'em and catch 'em in an ambush."

"I reckon it's better than tryin' to follow that trail they left out of here on and runnin' into another one of their ambushes," Possum said. "It's gonna be touch and go for us and them up and down this river. Let's get packed up again and get movin'."

Back in the saddle, they set out on an old trail that followed the river before settlers and freighters beat out a kinder road for their wagons, one on more level ground. With an overgrowth of weeds and bushes, it was obvious the trail had not been used very often, but it was not a problem on horseback. They were able to make good time while there was still enough daylight to see any holes or obstacles that might break a horse's leg in the dark. Before the sun's last fading rays disappeared, however, they started looking for a good place to make their camp. They agreed on one of the river's many bends where a high bluff formed when the river flowed around the butt of a long ridge, leading off to the north.

"Don't think we're gonna find much better," Possum said. "We can build us a fire up under this bluff where it'd be hard to see, and the bluff will make it difficult for anybody to get a shot at us. They'd have to cross the river to come in behind us. It ain't perfect, but I don't think perfect's out here."

"We'd best take turns standing watch until mornin'," Perley suggested. "Just in case they do find our camp tonight."

"Shoot," Sonny responded. "We'll all be keepin' watch. Who can sleep with that bunch of killers huntin' for ya? I ain't even gonna close one eye."

"I expect you're right," Possum agreed with a little chuckle. "I suppose it is worth it to lose a night's sleep to keep from losin' the rest of your life. Ain't it, Perley?"

"I can't argue with that. I reckon we'd better build us a big pot of coffee."

They got to work setting up camp to prepare for visitors they hoped would fail to show. They turned the horses loose to get water and nibble on the small amount of grass between the bluff and the river. Luckily, they had thought to buy a sack of grain at Walter Johnson's feed store, so they could feed the horses a little extra supplement to go with the grass and the shoots growing in the water's edge. By the time the twilight faded away, they were already heavy into the coffee and chewing on thick strips of bacon.

Duke Thacker and his two men had ridden straight away from their failed attack on Perley's camp until they struck the wagon track again. Then they rode back down the road to set up in ambush at the spot where the road crossed the creek.

Thacker figured if the three he stalked decided to move to a new campsite, they would follow the creek back out to the road, thinking to ride a little farther on the wagon track until finding a place to cut back to the river again. "If they don't show up pretty soon, it'll mean they've decided to stay right where they were and don't think I'll try it a second time. But they don't know me, do they?"

"Nah, they don't know you, Duke," Mutt said, giving Ned a sideways glance.

They continued to wait until Ned had to ask, "It's already pretty doggoned dark, Duke. You reckon they moved their camp without coming back here to this road?" The thought had entered his mind that maybe Perley Gates and his two friends were stalking them. He was about to express that thought, but Mutt beat him to it.

"What if they've circled around and now they're tryin' to come up behind us?"

"They ain't doin' no such a thing," Thacker answered gruffly. "They're hunkered down in the same place they were, so we're goin' back there the same way. We'll follow the creek to the river. But this time, we'll be comin' at 'em from the opposite direction. They ain't gonna be expectin' that. I'll get another shot at that devil, and we'll see if he can bend over and dodge another slug." He climbed onto the black Morgan gelding. "Come on, let's go," he ordered, and they scrambled to their horses.

When Thacker started down the creek, Mutt and Ned stayed well behind him.

"We could shoot him right now, but if Perley Gates and his friends are sneakin' around lookin' for us, it's best to wait till we don't need his gun to help us," Mutt said. "And if they are waiting down at that river for us to show up again, it's best to have him right out front. Give 'em a nice big target. Then we'll cut and run and won't slow down till we hit Kansas."

They continued down the creek until they reached the Red River. Although they were seeing it from the opposite side, they recognized the spot where Perley and the other two had made their camp. It was deserted.

Hard to tell who was the more disappointed. Thacker was even more enraged and felt he had been cheated out of something he deserved to have. Ned and Mutt were disappointed when Thacker was not shot down in front of them. What to do next was a difficult decision for Mutt and Ned. They simply wanted to be away and free themselves from Duke Thacker but knew Thacker would keep searching until he could kill the one individual who had destroyed his master plan.

He dismounted and walked to the ashes of Sonny's

fire. "I'll track that snake to the ends of the earth," he swore when he kicked the ashes into the air.

"Now, Ned. Do it now!" Mutt said excitedly when he saw Thacker was in a fit of a rage. Without looking to see if Ned was following suit, he pulled his pistol.

Thacker stopped abruptly when he saw the gun in Mutt's hand and heard him say something. "What?" he exclaimed, confused, thinking Mutt saw Perley, then realizing Mutt had brought his .44 to bear on him.

No longer confused, Thacker turned to shield himself with his shoulder just as Mutt fired, catching the bullet behind his left shoulder. Turning back, he held his six-gun in his hand, and fired a shot into Mutt's stomach. Mutt bent double in pain. Thacker cocked his pistol and turned at once toward Ned, who was frozen in a state of shock, his weapon never having been drawn from his holster.

Seeing no threat from Ned, Thacker walked forward and put another bullet into Mutt's skull. "There ain't nothin' more lowdown than a sneaky assassin unless it's one that didn't have spit before he came to ride with me. What did he try to kill me for? Who's payin' him for that? Did he talk to you at all?"

Ned did his best to come out of his shock. "He never said nothin' about this, or I'da done told you. He's been actin' kinda funny lately, so we ain't talked about anything on his mind. I don't know what in the world would make him do somethin' like that. He musta went crazy." Anxious to change the subject, he said, "You've been shot. We better take a look and see how bad that is."

"He put a bullet in my shoulder," Thacker said. "I've

been shot a lot worse than that. We'll need to get away from here to do it, though. Somebody's bound to have heard those shots. Perley Gates couldn't have gotten far enough by now not to hear 'em."

"I've got some clean rags in my saddlebags," Ned offered. "Lemme give you one of those and you can stuff it inside your shirt and maybe that'll keep it from bleedin' too much while we go somewhere to fix it."

"Get everything offa Mutt's body you think we can use. I doubt if he's got any money, but you can look in his pockets to be sure."

Ned did as Thacker directed. He pulled his gun belt from under him and hung it on Mutt's saddle horn. As Thacker had predicted, Mutt didn't have any money. All Ned came up with was a pocketknife and a plug of chewing tobacco. His boots were too worn and too small to be of interest. It was not much of an estate to settle.

"You want me to do anything with his body?" Ned asked, not really expecting anything.

To show he had a sense of humor over the attempt on his life, Thacker answered. "What did you have in mind? Do some tap dancin' or somethin'? Mutt don't look too lively right now. He wouldn't be much of a partner." When Ned looked lost, Thacker said, "Never mind. I like him just like he is right there, so let's go."

Ned did as he was told. Climbed up on his horse and followed Thacker back up the creek to the road again, more confused than ever. He didn't know why he froze like he did. Maybe it was because Mutt acted so suddenly without giving him some warning. All he was sure of was if he had had his gun in hand, Thacker would have shot him before giving him a chance to speak.

There seemed to be a change in Thacker's manner after he got shot. If anything, his seething anger appeared to be calming down a little. Maybe the killing of Mutt restored some of his confidence in his ability to always come out on top when facing those who would try to dominate him. As for Ned Bates, he wondered how he would be feeling if he had drawn his weapon when Mutt gave him the signal, and both would have fired at Thacker. That didn't happen. He'd missed his chance. He was not proud of collapsing when Mutt made the sacrifice, but he had just not been able to respond as he had promised Mutt he would.

Ned was convinced more than ever that he would soon be dead, just like Mutt, unless he separated himself from Duke Thacker.

Perley sat up straight to listen when he heard two pistol shots. He looked over at Possum on the other side of the fire and saw that he had heard them, too. Sonny, down at the river's edge to refill the coffeepot, appeared not to have noticed.

"They came from downriver," Possum said. "And if I had to guess, I'd estimate the distance just about exactly how far it is from here back to our first camp."

"That sounds about right to me," Perley said. "Now, I wonder what in the world would our friends back there be shootin' at this time of night. Maybe a possum? No offense."

"None taken," Possum said. "It sure makes me curious, though. Why would they be back at our old camp?"

"Maybe they've been lookin' for us and since they

haven't found us, they mighta decided we never left that camp," Perley speculated. "So they went back to be sure. But there ain't no tellin' what the shootin' was about."

"The question now is what are they gonna do next?" Possum asked. "Are they gonna make camp for the night? Or are they gonna stay on the move and hope they find our camp while it's still dark?" He looked over at Perley and shrugged, truly undecided about what they should do.

Perley studied his old friend for several long seconds, realizing it was one of the few times he could recall when Possum was not ready to suggest what action needed to be taken next.

Perley was the first to admit it, though. "I don't know about you, partner, but I don't know what's the best thing for us to do right now. I can't help but think Thacker's in the same fix we are. He doesn't know where we are and if we're runnin' or campin' for the night. I have an idea he doesn't know this territory any better than we do, so it's like the blind chasin' the blind. Since we've already made camp here, whaddaya say we just stay right here till mornin'. We can keep a sharp eye out in case he shows up in the middle of the night, and deal with it if that happens. Whaddaya think?"

"I like it better 'n us wanderin' around in these woods, hopin' we stumble over him before he sees us," Possum admitted. "When daylight hits us in the mornin', we might as well get back on the road and head for home. I reckon we'll find out then if he's in front of us, or behind us."

* * *

Riding up the creek, Thacker and Ned were concerned the sound of the gunshots might lead Perley and his partners to pay them a visit.

"We'll follow this creek back to the wagon road again and find a place to camp up the trail a ways," Thacker said.

The arrival of a full moon contributed to the comfort of the riders following the bank of the creek that emptied into the river. Ned was the first to notice all of the tracks from Perley's original camping site did not turn to follow the road but continued to follow the creek across the road to the south side of the wagon trace. Finding that strange, he took a closer look and discovered the tracks he found following the creek on the south side of the road were not a continuation of tracks striking the road from the north side of the creek. Rather, they were a separate set of tracks that turned from the middle of the road to follow the creek on the other side of the road. He called it to Thacker's attention.

But Thacker took a look for himself and saw that Ned was accurate. "Who the hell . . . ?" he wondered aloud.

"Looks to me like a couple of riders," Ned decided, after he struck a match to examine the tracks a little more closely. "There's another party of campers mixed up in here. Two riders, each one of 'em leadin' a packhorse. I'll bet they ain't even paid no attention to all the tracks comin' up the creek. They just got to the creek and turned up it.

"They most likely got 'em a little pea patch or some bean vines on up this creek, tryin' to homestead a little shack. Most likely nobody we have to worry about. They was probably comin' back from Texarkana with some supplies. Musta been earlier this afternoon. We just didn't notice their tracks." He was talking as fast as he could, hoping to distract Thacker from any notions of further complicating their search for Perley Gates.

"We can take a little time to find out what these two riders are up to," Thacker decided after studying the tracks leaving the road. I don't want no surprises, so it's best to know who else is hangin' around when goin' after a fish like Perley Gates." He turned the black Morgan down toward the narrow path following along beside the creek. Enough moonlight filtered through the tree branches to lessen the risk of the horses making a misstep.

Thacker and Ned had not gone far down the trail before the thick foliage thinned out considerably. A few yards farther and they heard a horse whinny.

Thinking he'd better respond, Thacker called out, "Hello, the camp! Just wanted to find out who you are. We're what's left of a marshal's posse, lookin' to arrest some fellers who escaped from the Texarkana jail. If you've got any information could help us with these arrests, we'd be beholden to ya. We're lookin' for Perley Gates, Possum Smith, and Sonny Rice. When we catch 'em, we'll be takin' 'em back to stand trial."

They could see reaction among the thicker patches behind the larger trees, but no one stepped forward to offer assistance. Obviously surprised to find they had visitors.

"Could you give us a little help?" Thacker called out. "I'm Marshal Thacker. Who am I talkin' to?"

Taking a lengthy pause to decide to comply or not a young man looked at the young lady with him. They always camped at this spot on their way back from Texarkana. Realizing he had no choice, he finally responded. "My name's Art Denson. And we ain't seen hide nor hair of those three you're talkin' about. We've been in Texarkana all day. Just got back tonight and you're the only folks we've seen."

"Fine," Thacker replied. "That's all we need to know. Who else is with you?"

Again, Art hesitated, but finally answered, "Just the two of us, me and Penny."

"Art and Penny Denson, right?" Thacker pronounced. "What are you doin', ridin' up this creek in the middle of the night?"

"Well, we was tryin' to get a few hours' sleep until you fellers started shootin'. We've got a homestead on the south fork of the Sulphur River and we just started back too late to make it home tonight. This is a spot we usually camp in when we see we ain't gonna make it home till tomorrow."

Thinking this a fortunate coincidence, Thacker said, "Maybe you could give me a little help. Those shots you heard came from the other side of the road where I tried to make an arrest. I had to kill one of those outlaws after he put a bullet in my shoulder. My deputy is all thumbs when it comes to delicate work like pickin' this .44 slug outta my shoulder. I'd appreciate it if your lady could try her hand at it."

There was a bit of a delay in the Densons' response while they obviously had a quick discussion.

Thacker said, "I don't blame you for bein' cautious. Runnin' into a manhunt in the middle of the woods ain't exactly what you'd expect, is it?"

Finally, Art said, "I reckon it wouldn't be too neighborly if we refused to help a wounded lawman. Penny said she'd take a look at the wound. It wouldn't be her first one."

"Good," Thacker replied, as he and Ned dismounted. "Let's everybody come outta the bushes now and we'll see what we've got. I hope you'll understand why I've gotta get a look at everybody. In my business, we have to make sure there ain't nobody hidin' back there, holdin' a gun. Deputy Bates, throw some wood on that fire, then maybe we can see a little better."

When the fire returned to life, Art and Penny Denson stepped clear of the tree branches to reveal two very young and slim figures. Art was carrying a double-barrel shotgun in one arm and both were dressed in denim riding pants. They were obviously leery of the two rough-looking men, especially the big heavyset one who said he was the marshal. The situation was not helped by the fact that Art and Penny had just come from Texarkana where everyone in town was talking about the jailbreak. They were not sure of the new marshal's name, but they knew it wasn't Thacker. It was a shorter name that started with a *C*. They knew they were dealing with a couple of wanted men, but decided to play along in hopes the two outlaws would leave them unharmed.

Although reluctant to leave Art's side, Penny summoned the courage to take some action. She started toward her packs, but Thacker stepped in front of her. She stopped.

Giving him an impatient look, she said, "I need to

get a pan, so I can heat some water to clean up your shoulder."

He stepped aside and chuckled. "You're a feisty little slip of a woman, ain'tcha? I ain't gonna get in your way." He watched her intently as she heated water from the creek, and he took his shirt off when she told him to.

After she had cleaned the dried blood away and took a good look at the wound, she said, "That bullet drove straight into your shoulder muscle. I don't think you could stand it if I was to probe as deep as I'd have to, just to get to the bullet. Then I'd have to work at it pretty hard to pry it loose from the muscle. You'd be better off just leavin' it in there. I can't get it out without half killin' ya."

"And I'm sayin' you can do your worst, but I can stand all the pain you make. So don't tell me I can't stand the pain, sweetheart." Thacker fixed her with a foolish grin for being considerate. He had an insane obsession with pain.

"Mister," she finally informed him, "I don't care whether you can stand the pain or not, I'll do what I can for your wound. Let's just get on with it." She put the pan aside. "Have you got any whiskey?"

"Now, you're talkin'," he responded with a loud chuckle. "Let's have a drink. Ned, get that bottle outta my saddlebag."

Ned retrieved the bottle, Penny took it outta his hand and splashed a generous amount on Thacker's wound. Not expecting it, Thacker released a little yelp of pain.

"I'm sorry. Did I hurt you?" Penny couldn't resist japing the obnoxious brute.

She caught Art's eye as he tried to warn her to watch her step. He was afraid she was waving the red flag in front of this bull to her peril. She probed as best she could, but the shot had been fired at such a close distance, it had buried so deeply in the massive shoulder, and she had to finally give up. As he had predicted, Thacker uttered not a sound, his concentration centered on the young body of his nurse.

"I'm sorry, but you're just gonna have to carry that bullet in your shoulder," Penny told him. "A doctor most likely would tell you you're just as well off leavin' it in there."

Thacker was ready to accept the prognosis. Too much time had already been spent working on his shoulder.

The early rays of the sun began their daily chores of sliding back the shades of night. And Perley Gates was out there somewhere, running or stalking, Thacker wasn't sure which. Since his first attempt on Perley's life had been unsuccessful, he had to allow for the possibility that Perley was hoping to ambush him.

Ordinarily on a trip to Texarkana to get supplies, morning was met with an enthusiasm for a hot breakfast before riding the final leg of their journey. On this morning, however, Art and Penny stood by dejectedly. Having abandoned the pretense as a marshal and deputy, Thatcher and Ned rifled through the Densons' packs to supplement their own supplies.

There wasn't much Art could have done to resist the two violent criminals, and Penny was relieved when he didn't try. Although they knew what had descended upon their camp right from the start, had they known what was coming their way, they would have hidden their supplies. There was no sense in crying over it now.

The hardest part was yet to come, when they had to tell Grandpa Cletus that Ned Bates had taken his bottle of rheumatism pills.

Chapter 23

"Looks like you were right," Perley said to Possum. "They went back to where we first made camp."

"At least they ain't too far ahead of us," Possum said. "I think we need to make sure we're all three thinkin' the same way here. We ain't workin' for the law. We're out to kill a couple of wolves."

Perley knew Possum was saying it for his benefit.

"They've even started killin' off each other," Possum continued. "So I'm sayin' we need to move up close enough to the two of 'em to take 'em out with two rifle shots. Agreed?"

"I agree," Perley said, expecting the two outlaws to lead their horses up onto the road.

But instead of turning onto the road, they continued following the creek across it.

"Where the hell are they goin'?" Possum whispered.

"Let's don't lose 'em," Perley warned and quickly picked up his step.

With Perley in the lead, they followed the creek across the road and down along the bank, not sure where they were being led. When the trees thinned out to reveal a clearing by the creek, they realized it was another camp. Standing near the remains of a campfire, was a young couple, obviously under duress.

"Damn, that ain't good," Possum complained. "Now they've got hostages. We're gonna have to be careful when we shoot into that camp."

During what appeared to be an argument between Thacker and Ned Bates, the young man took hold of his wife's hand and led her slowly away from the two arguing outlaws. Perley suddenly caught Possum's arm when the young man pushed the girl down the bank and she quickly disappeared into the bushes ringing the creek.

"She's makin' a run for it!" Perley whispered. "Maybe we can help her. Sonny, go back and get your horse, and circle around upstream of that creek. If we're lucky, you might be able to pick her up before they find out which way she ran. If you can, take her back to that camping spot on the other side of the road. Can you do that?"

"I sure as hell can," Sonny answered and took off.

"We're wastin' time here," Ned said. "These folks ain't got nothin' else we can use. Let's make some tracks while we've still got a little lead on Perley and them."

"All right. We're goin'," Duke said, "and I'm takin' the woman with me." He was completely overcome by the vision of a perfect young woman, little more than a girl, really. And he'd decided he would have her for his own.

At once alarmed, Ned Bates was sure it was another certain sign Thacker had lost his mind. "Duke, you ain't thinkin' straight! We ain't got time to fool with that woman now. We came out here to ambush Perley Gates. We'd best get our minds back on our business 'cause Perley Gates ain't gonna forget. With all them tracks on that road back there, I wouldn't be surprised if they ain't already caught up to us. They mighta already found this camp."

"Quit your bellyaching and get ready to ride. Come here, pretty Penny," he called out as he climbed up into the saddle. "You're gonna ride with me." He looked around the little camp but did not see her. Suddenly overcome with anger, he reached out, grabbed Art's shirt by the collar, and demanded, "Where is she?"

"I don't know!" Art pleaded. "She was standin' right here a minute ago. She gets nervous real easy and she mighta had to pee." Actually, he'd pushed Penny down the creek bank when no one was looking and told her to run as far as she could and not to look back. Unable to abide the thought of what Thacker might have in mind for her under his captivity. Art wished there had been more time, so he could have run with her. He knew it was too late for him.

"Call her back!" Thacker ordered.

Fearing for his life, Art started yelling her name while Ned and Thacker rode their horses back and forth, searching the bushes by the creek.

"Let's get the hell outta here," Ned roared. No longer willing to wait for the madman to come to his senses, he kicked his heels and galloped along the creek bank.

Having been sent to help the girl when Perley and Possum sprang the trap on Thacker and Ned, Sonny Rice was well hidden near the bank of the creek. He could hear the thunderous hoofbeats of a horse as it approached.

Raising his rifle, he laid the front sight where he anticipated the shot to come, but didn't take the shot for fear it would cause the girl to panic. The horse galloped on through the target window and continued on. Behind it, a young woman rose up from the bushes and walked toward where he was hidden. She was the most beautiful girl he had ever seen.

Sonny's job was to carry her away from the two maniacs who would capture her. How to do it without scaring her to death was his next problem. He gradually removed most of the leaves and branches he had used for cover.

She was almost upon him, when he called out softly, "Miss, my name's Sonny. I've come to take you somewhere you'll be safe."

Startled, she stopped abruptly when she saw the red roan gelding emerge from the clump of oak trees to meet her, but showed no sign of being alarmed. "Sonny?"

"Yes, ma'am. Sonny Rice. My job is to take you somewhere you'll be safe. I expect we'd best hurry. I saw Ned Bates pass by here a minute ago, so Duke Thacker can't be far behind, and I wanna have you away before he gets here." He held out his hand. As she came forward to grasp it, he asked, "What is your name?"

"Penny," she answered.

He told himself that was perfect, a perfect name for a goddess.

Before she took his hand, she asked, "Do you know what they've done with Art?"

Of course, she wants to know about her husband, he thought at once. "I can't really tell you for sure, but I ain't heard no gunshots from back that way. My two partners will most likely get the jump on Thacker and then we'll see if Art's all right. Hurry now, please." He held out his hand again and she grasped it tightly.

Light as a feather, he raised her effortlessly to slide onto his horse behind him. Trusting him completely, she wrapped her arms around his waist and pulled herself firmly against his back. As they loped along the bank of the creek, he could feel her face against his back, and it was like a sensation he had never felt before. He wanted to take care of her for the rest of her life. He was also aware that her husband might have objections to that.

He was further reminded he was caught in a fantasy when she asked, "If your friends rescue Art, will they bring him to the same place you're taking me?"

"Yes, ma'am. We're all supposed to meet back at the same place."

"Are you and your friends lawmen?" Penny asked.

"No, ma'am. We ride for the Triple-G Ranch in Lamar County, Texas. Those two men who held you captive are the last two outlaws in the Duke Thacker gang."

"Why are you chasing them, if you're not lawmen?" she asked.

"Actually," Sonny replied, "we wasn't chasin' them. They was chasin' us, hopin' to get a chance to ambush Perley Gates." When she asked why, Sonny told her that Perley had been one of the major reasons Thacker's gang had been cleared out of Texarkana. "But today, all we're tryin' to do is go back to the Triple-G and get back to work."

When they emerged from the trees to enter the little clearing where the Triple-G camp was, Sonny pulled the red roan to a stop. Then he took her wrist again and assisted her gently to the ground. He dismounted then and released the red roan to drink water. "I'll get this fire goin' again and make you a cup of coffee."

"What if they follow us here?" Penny asked.

"Perley and Possum won't let 'em get that far," Sonny assured her. "Even if they did, they'd have to get by me before they got to you. And I ain't gonna let that happen."

She fixed a warm smile upon him as he vowed to protect her. "With all the fighting for your lives, you took the time to carry me away to safety. You and your friends are special, indeed." She walked up before him. "Would you mind if I gave you a hug?"

Taken completely by surprise, Sonny stumbled over his response. "Why, no, ma'am," he finally managed. "You can take a stick and beat me to the ground with it, if you want."

She laughed delightedly. "Well, I appreciate that, but I think I had rather just give you a hug." She took another step forward, and he automatically took her gently in his arms, so not to break her. She squeezed him tightly, gave him a light kiss on his cheek before stepping back and smiling warmly. "You're my hero, Sonny, and I want to thank you for taking care of me."

Things had turned chaotic at Art and Penny's camp. Thacker, still in a rage over the sudden disappearance of Penny Denson, leaned down and grabbed Art by his collar and picked the slim young man off his feet. "Where is she?" he demanded. When Art pleaded that he didn't know where she went, Thacker wrapped one large hand around his throat and clamped down. "Now, I'm gonna ask you again, where is she? She got a hidin' place she ran to?" His massive hand squeezed tighter and tighter.

Barely able to talk, Art tried to tell him she just ran, and he didn't know where. "I can't tell you what I don't know," he choked out.

"Maybe you oughta ask me where she is, Thacker."

Recognizing the voice right away, Thacker drew his pistol and held it next to Art's head, while still holding him prisoner with one hand around his throat. "You make one false move and I'll put another airhole in his head. This trigger is mighty touchy. Now, you step outta them shadows where I can see you. You know, I'm glad you got away after that first shot I took at you. Now we can settle it the way men like you are so famous for. That 'ud suit you just fine, wouldn't it?

"Only, this time we'll make it fair. We're gonna use our left hands only. That's fair, ain't it? When I turn loose of ol' Art here, that's the signal to go for your gun. Stick it in your belt on your left side. When you see Art drop, you go for it. All right?"

Perley had to hand it to him. Thacker was going to a lot of trouble to make it look like a fast-draw competition, although it was nothing of the kind. He was obviously of the impression Perley would actually reach for his weapon with his left hand, cock it, and fire it left-handed.

"All right," he agreed. "Just make sure you drop that young man outta the way, so he doesn't get shot by a stray."

"Anything you say, Perley." Thacker chuckled and released Art.

The slender young man had not yet landed on the ground when a portion of Thacker's skull covered with brain matter flew out the side of his head in concert with the solid report of Possum's Winchester rifle.

Perley stopped the black Morgan when it started to bolt and calmed it down. "Are you all right, Art?" he asked the young man getting to his feet.

"Yes, sir, I'm all right. I'm just gonna have a sore throat for a week."

"I wouldn't be surprised," Perley said.

Possum came walking out of the woods.

Perley frowned. "I was beginnin' to wonder if you were gonna shoot or not."

"I knew I had plenty of time and wanted to get to a good position where I could switch him off right quick," Possum said. "I expect we're gonna have to find out where Ned Bates got to now."

"And Penny," Art said.

"Right," Perley said. "I expect she's all right. Since we didn't hear any gunshots from up the creek, I think Sonny picked her up. If he had shot Bates, there's a good chance Penny would have run off in a different direction. We might have to search for her, but let's check to see if she and Sonny are at our camp first. Here, Art, you can use this horse." He took hold of Thacker's boot and shoved it up out of the stirrup. The huge body keeled over sideways and crashed to the ground.

Art climbed aboard. Possum brought up Dancer and Buck, and they followed the obvious trail left by Ned Bates.

Reaching a point where they saw hoofprints coming out of a grove of trees and heading in the direction of the agreed-upon meeting place, it was decided the prints could have been left by Sonny's red roan. Perley decided it best to make sure Penny was safe.

They found Sonny gazing dreamily at the princesslike young woman over a cup of coffee.

Penny jumped up and ran to meet them. "Thank you, thank you," she uttered over and over. Art dismounted, and she gave him a big hug. "I was so worried about you."

"I was worried about you. I wasn't sure you got away." He looked at Sonny, who walked slowly up to the reunion. "I reckon I owe you an awful lot for what you did."

"It wasn't much of anything," Sonny replied.

"It was a lot more than that," Penny insisted. "He's my hero. He came riding out of the trees, reached down and lifted me up onto his red roan and carried me away from those monsters." She walked up to stand beside him, put her arm around his waist and gave him another light peck on his cheek.

A little surprised by her behavior, all three Triple-G riders looked to see Art's reaction.

He reacted with a grin, as if it was a natural way to react. When he finally commented, it was just a casual remark. "I reckon we ain't gonna forget this trip to town for a spell, right Sis?

Everyone was surprised, but Sonny's chin dropped down to land on his chest.

Possum was the first to comment. "We thought you two was husband and wife. I swear, brother and sister. Ain't that somethin', Sonny?"

Sonny didn't answer. He couldn't. He couldn't take his eyes off Penny, who was very much aware of it. Whenever their gazes met, she smiled warmly.

Before they all got carried away with the possible attraction between the two young people, Perley reminded Possum there was still the problem of Ned Bates somewhere along the Red River. With no way anyone could predict Ned's mind, Perley was of the opinion Ned was not likely to avenge Thacker's death, that he'd long ago had enough of Thacker's violent world. But Perley had trusted him to withdraw before and he had failed him.

This time, however, there was no one to draw him back. Minus the history of Ned Bates that Perley and Possum shared, young Art Denson had some concerns about the possibility of another visit from the violent outlaw. He and Penny had watched while Ned and Thacker had rifled through their possessions, laying waste to anything they had no use for themselves. To Art's way of thinking, their supplies were the quickest source for sorely needed food supplies for Ned Bates.

"I don't think you've got a worry in the world. Do you really think he'll be back after the way he ran off?" Perley insisted. "He left a trail outta here like a man with only one thought in mind—to put distance between us. You said you and your sister and your grandpa are homesteadin' a place on the Sulphur River, right? About how long a ride is that from right here?"

"About five hours," Art said.

"So, you'll be home for supper." Perley turned toward Sonny. "If it'd make you feel any better, Art, we could ask Sonny if he wouldn't mind ridin' with you and Penny. He's a smart tracker and a crack shot." Perley shot a mischievous grin toward Possum as Penny's face blossomed into a smile. "Whaddaya think, Sonny? Think you could do that?"

"I reckon I could," Sonny responded. "We wanna keep the lady safe."

"Good," Perley said. "Then Possum and I will get on Ned Bates' trail and make sure he's leaving this part of Texas."

Everyone brought great enthusiasm to the preparation of the packhorses, with Sonny showing Penny how to tighten down the packs and Penny oohing and aahing over each new knot. No one enjoyed it more than Perley and Possum. Art agreed to return the black Morgan gelding to Powell on his next trip to Texarkana. Perley insisted Art should keep Thacker's packhorses as some payment for their part in the ordeal.

Finally, the Art and Penny Denson party was in the saddle and filing out through the trees beside the creek with Sonny Rice leading the way.

Possum said, "We might not ever see ol' Sonny again after this."

"It'll be a test of true love if there ain't nobody but Art, Penny, and Grandpa to run things like it sounds. Hell, Sonny'll be the boss. From what they've described, there ain't nobody back home but Grandpa. The three of 'em are homesteadin'. Sonny, a farmer? Yep, a test of true love, all right."

As Perley and Possum had already discovered, they had no problem picking up the disillusioned outlaw's trail. The more Perley thought about the chaotic turns in Ned's life, like trying to survive the last days of Duke

Thacker's insane attempt to kill him, he wondered how Ned had held on to his sanity as long as he had.

The longer they followed the trail, the more it appeared Ned was planning to stop at Marvin Davis' trading post, the place where they had first crossed paths.

"Looks like he's fixin' to make camp on this creek," Possum said as they followed along the narrow creek path. "He's got company, though." He stopped then and waited for Perley to catch up.

"Let's ride on in a little closer and see what's going on."

Within about thirty yards of the camp, they could hear conversation. Dismounting, they moved quietly through the dark creek bottom until close enough to hear what was being said. They hadn't counted on two drifters who had tied on to Ned's trail.

"Where the hell's your packhorse?" one of the drifters asked. "You ain't even got anythin' to cook."

"I told you fellers I had to run for it, or get caught in an ambush," Ned said. "I didn't have no time to get my packhorse. All I've got to eat is a few strips of jerky."

"Who's chasin' you?" the second drifter asked.

"I hope nobody's chasin' me anymore," Ned said. "I just wanna get to Injun Territory. I've got some friends that'll help me there."

"That's a long walk from here into Injun Territory," the first drifter commented. "Ain't that right, Lige?"

Lige agreed.

"I've got a good horse," Ned replied. "Won't be no trouble for him a-tall."

"Well, that's where your problem is. See, me and

Lige ain't goin' to Injun Territory and your horse is goin' with us."

Both drifters' guns were drawn, followed by two quick shots . . . both from Perley's .44. The would-be assailants crumpled to the ground.

With a fair idea who the shooter was, Ned made no attempt for his gun. He remained seated by his little fire, saying nothing. "Perley, Possum," he acknowledged as they walked up. "I reckon I knew I couldn't get very far. Is Duke dead?"

"Yep, he's dead," Perley answered. "Where were you headed in Injun Territory?"

"Tishomingo."

"You got kin there?"

Ned nodded in response. "Same as."

"Well, thanks to your two guests, it looks like you've got three extra horses and whatever guns, ammunition, and supplies you find on 'em," Perley said. "Oughta be enough to get you back where you belong."

Ned didn't respond right away. He wasn't sure he had heard what he thought he had. He glanced quickly from Perley to Possum, but he could read no deception in either face. "You ain't gonna kill me?" he asked plaintively.

"What good would that do?" Perley answered him. "With Duke Thacker gone, you might have a chance to turn out to be a good man. Good luck with that. Come on, Possum, we've still got a piece to ride tonight."

Able only then to get to his feet, Ned Bates got up and watched in amazement as Perley and Possum climbed up into the saddle and disappeared into the night.

* * *

It was a nice sunny day at the Triple-G. Perley and Possum pulled the saddles off Buck and Dancer and turned the horses loose. Walking toward the barn to get rid of their saddles, they were met by John Gates. "See you got back," John commented. "Have any trouble delivering the horses?"

"Nope," Perley answered, "no problem. Lost one man."

"Lost one man," John repeated, "Who'd you lose?"

"Sonny Rice," Perley answered, and he and Possum both laughed, picturing Sonny behind a plow. "I expect he'll show up here any day now."

Keep reading for more Johnstone!

SLAUGHTER OF THE MOUNTAIN MAN

**In this action-packed western from national
bestselling authors William W. Johnstone and
J.A. Johnstone, mountain man Smoke Jensen sets
his sharpshooting sights on an unhinged outlaw
who's carved out his own kingdom in the West—
and declared war on the United States . . .**

He calls himself the King. Once a respected professor,
he was ruined by scandal. Now, he rules his own
"country"—an area of Western territory where an army
of outlaws enforce his laws. Any town he claims as his
own must pay "taxes," collected from bank,
stagecoach, and train robberies. When he learns that
President Rutherford B. Hayes and General William
Tecumseh Sherman are venturing into the far West on a
tour of the nation, the King devises a plan to kidnap
America's leaders and expand his empire.

But the King didn't reckon that Smoke Jensen had
already staked his claim on the frontier. Traveling with
the president's entourage, the mountain man is not
about to let this bloodthirsty, evil tyrant endanger his
commander-in-chief and threaten American liberty . . .

Look for
SLAUGHTER OF THE MOUNTAIN MAN,
on sale now!

Chapter 1

In the pre-dawn darkness, Smoke Jensen stared through the window at the moonlit Kansas prairie passing outside. Smoke and Sally, occupying a private roomette, were two days into their return trip from Chicago where Smoke had been investigating the commodities market, not just the price of cattle, but, specifically, the going price for registered bulls and dams. Over the last few years Smoke had gotten into raising registered cattle to be used for breeding, rather than to provide beef.

As Smoke sat there, watching the sun rise, Sally stirred in the bed.

"You awake?" Smoke asked.

"No."

"What do you mean, you aren't awake? You just answered me."

"I'm talking in my sleep."

Smoke laughed. "How about breakfast?"

Sally yawned, stretched, and rolled over. "You go without me," she mumbled.

Smoke went into the dining car where he was met by the waiter, a relatively small man, swarthy complexioned with what had once been very dark hair, though a considerable amount of gray had gathered at the temples.

"What's for breakfast?" Smoke asked.

"Why, Mr. Jensen, I'm sure you are aware that we have a most extensive menu," Peabody replied.

"What do you suggest? No, tell me what the engineer and fireman chose for breakfast."

"They have not eaten, sir. They'll do without until the next stop," the waiter replied.

"Really? That doesn't sound very good. All right, put together some biscuit-and-bacon sandwiches and drop them in a bag, would you?"

"Yes, sir," Peabody replied. "You wish to take breakfast back to Mrs. Jensen, do you?"

"No, I think I'll have breakfast with the engine crew."

"Mr. Jensen, how do you plan to do that? Why, there is no way to reach the engine crew from here."

"Leave that up to me," Smoke replied. "Please, just put the biscuits and bacon in a bag."

"Yes, sir." Peabody smiled. "I expect that Mr. Barnes and Mr. Prouty are going to be quite surprised. Pleased, but surprised."

A few minutes later Smoke, carrying the sack, climbed over the top of the express car then crawled across the tender and dropped down onto the platform of the locomotive.

"Here!" the fireman asked, startled by Smoke's sudden appearance. "Who are you, and what are you doing here?"

Smoke smiled, and held out the sack. "I'm Smoke Jensen, and I've come to have breakfast with you," he said.

The fireman opened the bag and looked down inside.

"Hey, Clyde, what do you think? You just said you was hungry. This feller has brought us some biscuits 'n bacon."

"They aren't all for you, one of them is mine. I plan to eat with you," Smoke said. "I just heard the engineer's name. What's yours?"

"Austin Prouty. The engineer is Clyde Barnes."

"It's good to meet the two of you," Smoke said, taking a bite of his biscuit. As Smoke looked at the two men, he could see scars, like little pits on their faces and necks. He was puzzled at first, then he realized that they were actually scars made by the red-hot sparks that over the many years and miles of railroading, had found their skin.

It was hot in the engine cab, and Smoke saw how Clyde was dealing with it. The engineer's arm was laid along the base of the window, the sleeve open to catch the breeze created by the twenty-five-mile-per-hour forward speed of the engine. That had the effect of causing the air to pass through the sleeve to the inside of his shirt, then circle all around his body.

"Pretty good idea," Smoke said, pointing to the shirt-sleeve.

Clyde smiled. "The feller I apprenticed under taught me this little trick," he said. "I don't know who taught it to him."

As Smoke watched the two men the difference in their jobs could not be more obvious. Clyde was standing at the throttle cooled by the breeze, casually eating his breakfast, the small raft of chin whiskers that stuck forward waving up and down as he chewed.

By contrast the fireman was sweating profusely, not only from the heat of the locomotive cab, but also from the effort of his labors. He tossed a few shovels full of coal into the boiler furnace, closed the door, then checked the steam pressure gauge.

"What's it reading, Austin?" Clyde asked.

"A hunnert forty 'n holdin'," Austin replied.

"Good, good," Clyde said with an approving nod of his head.

Austin sat on his bench and wiped the sweat from his face. The fire was roaring, the steam was hissing, and the rolling wheels were pounding out a thunder of steel on steel.

"What brought you up here, Mr. Jensen?" Austin asked. "I know you said it was to have breakfast with us, but what really brought you up here?"

"Curiosity, I suppose," Smoke answered. "Also, I have an appreciation for work, and for men who know what they are doing. I'm always honored to spend some time with such men."

"You're the feller that owns Sugarloaf Ranch, ain't you?" Clyde asked.

"How did you know that?"

"We're always told when we got someone important travelin' with us," Clyde replied. "We was told about you." Clyde chuckled. "Sure didn't expect you to come crawlin' down over the tender, though."

Smoke laughed. "I had no idea I was considered important enough to be reported to the cab crew. But the concept is interesting. Who is the most important person you ever had on your train?"

"I've had two Presidents ride on my train, only there warn't neither one of 'em President then. I drove a train durin' the war 'n President Grant rode on it, only he was a general then. 'N President Hayes rode on my train when he was the governor of Ohio. But I reckon the most important one would be General Custer. Fact is, the last train he ever rode on was one I was drivin'."

"You've had an interesting career," Smoke said.

"Yes, sir, I reckon I have."

Back in the roomette, Sally was awake now and dressed, waiting for Smoke to return. When he didn't return, she thought perhaps he was in the parlor car, but he wasn't there either, so she went to the diner, thinking perhaps he had lingered in conversation. When he wasn't there, she decided she would have her breakfast without him.

"Mr. Peabody, have you seen my husband this morning?" Sally asked the waiter when he approached her table.

"Yes, ma'am, Mr. Jensen was here, earlier this morning," Peabody replied.

"Really? That's odd, I haven't been able to find him."

"He's in the engine cab," Peabody said.

"I beg your pardon?"

"Mr. Jensen ordered a sack of biscuits and bacon to take up to the engine. If you can believe it, he stated that it was his intention to have breakfast with the engine crew."

Sally laughed. "Yes, I can quite easily believe that. Such a thing would be just like him."

At that moment, Bob Dempster came into the dining car. Dempster, who was an officer at the Bank of Big Rock, had made the trip to Chicago with them, as Smoke's personal banker.

"Mr. Dempster, won't you join me for breakfast?" Sally invited.

"Where is Smoke?"

"He's driving the train," Sally said with a little laugh.

"I beg your pardon?"

"Mr. Peabody said he took some biscuits and bacon up to the engineer and fireman."

"My word, why would he do something like that?"

"You can ask him yourself," Sally said. "Here he comes now." Smoke had just stepped in through the door of the car.

"I thought you weren't going to eat," Smoke said as he joined them.

"And I thought you had already eaten," Sally replied. "Mr. Peabody said you had decided to take your breakfast up in the engine cab."

"Yes, I did. I just came back for some coffee. Hello, Bob. Did you sleep well?"

"Not particularly well," Dempster replied. "I did nothing but run numbers through my head last night. Smoke, are you sure you want to reduce your herd? You would be giving up quite a large source of revenue."

"We've been all through this, Bob. If I take five hundred head to market, I'll do well to clear four dollars a head. That's two thousand dollars. You may recall that I made two thousand five hundred dollars for Prince

Dandy. He was sired by HRH Charles, and three of HRH Charles's issue have given me six more bulls, all who can trace their lineage back to HRH Charles."

"But you are forgetting one thing," Dempster said. "Five hundred head spreads out your risk. If you lose one cow, you will lose, at most, thirty-five dollars. If you lose one registered bull, you can lose twenty-five hundred dollars, or more."

"There are always trade-offs," Smoke replied. "You should know that, Bob. You're in a business that deals with money."

"I know, I know," Dempster replied. "I just feel that it is my job to point out every contingency to you."

"And I appreciate that," Smoke replied. "That's why I asked you to go to Chicago with Sally and me."

"Tell me, Smoke, did you show the nice men how to drive the train?" Sally asked with a smile.

"I did indeed," Smoke replied. "I pointed to those two long strips of iron, rails I think they are called, and I said, 'Boys, keep this train on those rails, and it'll take us exactly where we want to go.'"

Both Sally and Dempster laughed.

Chapter 2

Smoke and Sally were met at the Big Rock depot by Pearlie Fontaine and Cal Wood. More than employees, the two men who had shared many dangers with both Smoke and Sally were practically members of the family.

"How was your trip?" Cal asked as he put their luggage into the back of the buckboard.

"It was a good trip," Smoke replied. "The market for registered bulls is quite good right now. Did you get the flyers printed?"

Pearlie laughed. "What'd I tell you, Cal? I told you that the first thing Smoke would say soon as he got back would be 'Did you get the flyers printed yet?'"

"Yeah? Well that wasn't the first thing he said. First thing he said was, 'It was a good trip.'"

"He wasn't saying, he was answering."

"Which is what I would like now," Smoke said, laughing at the argument between the two. "An answer, I mean. Did you get the flyers printed or not?"

"Here it is," Pearlie said, unfolding the paper that he had kept in his pocket.

REGISTERED BULLS FOR SALE
Mr. Kirby Jensen, owner of
SUGARLOAF RANCH
Big Rock, Colorado
Has five registered bulls for sale;
HRH Charles III, Prince Oscar, Sir McGinnis,
Count Edward, and Sir Victorious
Papers available price negotiable
Inquire of Kirby Jensen Big Rock Colorado

"Good job," Smoke said, examining the flyer. "I'll get these sent out to every major rancher in Colorado, Wyoming, Nevada, and Texas."

"I hope nobody wants Sir McGinnis," Cal said.

"You mean you don't want Smoke to make money?" Pearlie asked.

"He has to keep some back, doesn't he? I think he should keep Sir McGinnis back."

Washington University, St. Louis, Missouri

As Smoke, Sally, Pearlie, and Cal headed toward Sugarloaf Ranch from Big Rock, nine hundred and fifty miles east in St. Louis, Missouri, Clemente Pecorino, Doctor of Philosophy, and a professor at Washington University, was responding to the invitation of William Elliot, the chancellor. It was an invitation he had been expecting, because he was certain that he was about to be offered a "chair" at the university.

"You sent for me, sir?" Pecorino asked, sporting a confident smile.

Elliot opened the drawer of his desk, and took out the copy of a book that the university press had printed.

"Empiricism and Human Experience," Elliot said, reading the title. "I believe this is your book, Dr. Pecorino?"

"Yes, sir, it is," Pecorino replied, the smile of confidence changing to one of pride.

"And in this book you address the practical problems of implementing Empiricism into society? You say, and I am reading here, 'Under the motto of love, order, and progress, organized religion will eventually be replaced by Humanism.'"

Pecorino raised his hand. "Chancellor Elliot, I realize that you, being an ordained minister, probably don't appreciate that position, but I think my thesis is well-documented in the body of the text."

"No, I don't appreciate it," Chancellor Elliot said. Reaching into his desk, he pulled out another book. "I also didn't appreciate it when I read it in Auguste Comte's book *A General View of Positivism.* But what I most don't appreciate, Dr. Pecorino, is having our university publish a volume replete with plagiarism."

The smile froze on Pecorino's face.

"I . . . uh, admit that I was influenced by Comte's work, but I wouldn't go so far as to say I plagiarized his work."

"Oh? It was one of your students who pointed it out to me, Dr. Pecorino. I then read the work in comparison with Comte's own book, and I had two others read both books and give me a report. Yes, you change some of the language here and there, but more than eighty-five percent of your book, *Empiricism and Human Experience*, is a direct English translation of the French in Comte's work *A General View of Positivism.* What do you have to say for yourself, Doctor?"

"I don't agree with that. I will admit only to being influenced by Comte, to publish my own thoughts on the philosophy."

"Yes, well, whether you agree or not, we are pulling back all the books we have published under your name, and we are apologizing to all the other universities and colleges who are using your book as text. We are also terminating your position with us. Please vacate your office as quickly as possible."

"I have a class at ten," Pecorino said.

"No, you don't. Professor Walker has assumed all of your classes."

Pecorino reached for the copy of his book. "If you don't mind, I would like to keep this book as a souvenir," he said.

"By all means," Chancellor Elliot said. "I want no copies left here, at the school, and I've no doubt but that this will soon be the last such book in existence."

Pecorino returned to his office where he saw a maintenance man already scraping his name off the frosted glass of the door. Without exchanging greetings, he went inside and began removing his belongings. When he had everything packed that he intended to take, he sat down to contemplate what had just happened to him. After the publication of his book, which had become a text in colleges all over the country, he had received several invitations to lecture, which would have provided a lucrative second income for him. There was talk of establishing a chair in his name. Now his academic career was ruined.

Comte's book had been published almost forty years ago, in France.

It had a very limited circulation in the United States and had never been translated into English. What were the chances, he wondered, of anyone making the connection between Comte's book and his?

Pecorino picked up the book he had received from the chancellor and opened it. That was when he saw something written on the title page.

This book has been plagiarized from Auguste Comte's book A General View of Positivism. I think Dr. Pecorino should be held to account for it. Jason Kennedy

Jason Kennedy, Pecorino thought. Yes, it would be him. Kennedy was one of his students, intelligent, but a real problem who showed him none of the respect due a man of his position. Kennedy constantly questioned his authority and challenged the information he imparted in his lectures. Those were insults and could only be regarded as insults by design.

But this was the ultimate insult, for this challenge as to the legitimate authorship of the book had cost Pecorino his career in academia.

Half an hour later, Pecorino was standing in front of the university building on Washington Avenue, holding a satchel that contained the personal belongings he had removed from what had been his office. He was waiting for one of the horse-cars to take him to his apartment on Olive.

"Going somewhere, Professor?" a young man asked, his voice clearly meant to be taunting.

"Shouldn't you be in class, Mr. Kennedy?" Pecorino replied.

"Oh, you mean the philosophy course? I've still got fifteen minutes, plenty of time to make it. What about you? Aren't you in danger of being late, as well? After all, you have to teach the class and . . .oh, wait, you can't teach it, can you? You have been . . . what is the word they used? Terminated, yes, that's it. You have no class, because you have been terminated."

"Tell me, Mr. Kennedy, do you consider destroying a man's career to be an accomplishment?"

"If that career is built upon deception, I believe destroying that career to be not only an accomplishment, but a necessity, to prevent students from being influenced by someone who operates under false colors. The book you are so proud of, the one you were using as the text for the class, was not your work. It was the work of the French philosopher, Comte."

"Did you read Comte, Mr. Kennedy?"

"Yes, I read it."

"Then, I have opened your eyes to the subject, haven't I? You'll have to excuse me now. I see the horse-car is arriving."

"You're a fraud, Professor Pecorino. No, wait, you aren't a professor anymore, are you?" Kennedy added with a little laugh. "You're a fraud, Dr. Pecorino. Wait, you probably lied and cheated to get your Ph.D., so you don't deserve to be called Dr. Pecorino either. No doubt you will be relieved of that title, as well."

The horse-car arrived, and with his satchel in hand,

Pecorino mounted the steps, paid his fare, then moved to the back, choosing a seat by the window.

"You're a fraud, Pecorino," Kennedy called through the open window. "You're a fraud, and never again will you be in a position to fill vulnerable students' minds with your lies and deceit."

The car started down the tracks, the team of horses pulling it at a brisk pace.

"You're a fraud, Pecorino!" Kennedy shouted again, though mercifully, his shout was dimmed by distance as the car moved quickly down the track.

Leroy, Wyoming

The small town of Leroy was in the extreme western part of the territory. It had not even existed until the spur line was built that connected Granger, Wyoming, with Echo, Utah. Like any boomtown, it was suffering from the effects of growing too fast. Saloons, brothels, and gambling halls were being built faster than stores, schools, and churches, so that many of the town's newly arrived residents were less-than-desirable citizens.

A recent article in the *Leroy Times* bemoaned that fact when the editor, Dean McClain, wrote:

> From all outside appearances, the town of Leroy is making a rapid growth. But I ask the good citizens of this town, is this really the kind of growth we want? Instead of boardinghouses, we have bordellos, saloons rather than family businesses, dance halls where there should be churches.

> We are a town that attracts, not families
> upon which there can be real growth, but the
> very dregs of humanity. Our streets are filled
> with drunken and debased men and women
> who have no regard for decency, nor respect
> for the rights of others.

When five men, Franklin, Logan, Moss, Mason, and Jenner, came riding into the town of Leroy, no one paid any particular attention to them. If they had, some of the more informed might have noticed that they were all wanted men.

Although saloons and brothels would normally be an attraction for such men, these men were here for a different reason. They were here to rob the bank.

"There it is," Franklin said. "Logan, Mason, you stay out front with the horses. Moss, Jenner, you come in with me."

As soon as the three men stepped into the bank, they drew their pistols.

"This is a holdup!" Franklin shouted.

There were two customers in the bank, and they looked around, shocked at the sudden intrusion.

"You two, get up against the wall!" Franklin shouted.

There was only one teller in the bank, and taking advantage of the temporary distraction, he grabbed a gun.

"The son of a bitch has a gun!" Moss shouted, shooting, even as he gave the warning. The bank teller went down.

"Now what are we going to do?" Jenner asked. "How are we goin' to get the safe door open?"

They heard shots from outside.

"Franklin! Get out here, fast!" Logan shouted.

"Let's go," Franklin said.

"We ain't got no money, yet," Jenner complained.

"You want to wait around?"

The shooting outside grew more intense, and as the three failed robbers started toward the door, one of the two men who had been in the bank as a customer drew his own pistol. Franklin, sensing the movement, shot the would-be hero.

"Hurry, hurry!" Logan was shouting as the three rushed outside. Leaping into the saddle, the five men galloped out of town, shooting anyone who got in their way. By the time they rode out of town they had killed four, but had come away from the bank with not one dollar.